The Progressionists, And Angela

by

Conrad Von Bolanden

Double 9
BOOKS

The progressionists, and angela
by Conrad Von Bolanden

ISBN: 978-93-65783-47-6

Published by

DOUBLE 9 BOOKS

2/13-B, Ansari Road
Daryaganj, New Delhi – 110002
info@double9books.com
www.double9books.com
Tel. 011-40042856

ABOUT THE AUTHOR

CONRAD VON BOLANDEN born on August 9, 1828, and died on May 30, 1920, Conrad von Bolanden was a German bishop and author in the Roman Catholic Diocese of Speyer. He wrote A Wedding Trip, Queen Bertha, and Historical Tales of Frederick II. He was a German author and the son of a wealthy trader. He was born on August 9, 1828, in Niedergailbach, a village in the Palatinate, which was then part of Bavaria. Niedergailbach is now part of the Saarland, but the main part of the Palatinate area is now part of the neighboring state Rheinland-Pfalz. Bolanden went to the Latin school at Blieskastel and the seminary at Speyer. In 1849, he started studying religion at the University of Munich. He was made a priest in Speyer in 1852 and then given the job of assistant pastor at the cathedral (Speyer Cathedral). After two years, he was made priest at Kirchheimbolanden. The next year, he was sent to Borrstadt, and three years after that, to Berghausen. He wrote his first four books during this time: "A Wedding Trip" (about Martin Luther), "Queen Bertha" (about Bertha of Savoy), "Historical Tales of Frederick II." (about Frederick II of Prussia), and "Gustav Adolf" (about Gustavus Adolphus of Sweden). "Conrad von Bolanden" was the name of his pen name. Bolanden is a castle and village between Kirchheim-Bolanden and Borrstadt.

CONTENTS

THE PROGRESSIONISTS

CHAPTER I
THE WAGER

The balcony of the *palais* Greifmann contains three persons who together represent four million florins. It is not often that one sees a group of this kind. The youthful landholder, Seraphin Gerlach, is possessor of two millions. His is a quiet disposition; very calm, and habitually thoughtful; innocence looks from his clear eye upon the world; physically, he is a man of twenty-three; morally, he is a child in purity; a profusion of rich brown hair clusters about his head; his cheeks are ruddy, and an attractive sweetness plays round his mouth.

The third million belongs to Carl Greifmann, the oldest member of the group, head *pro tem.* of the banking-house of the same name. This gentlemen is tall, slender, animated; his cheeks wear no bloom; they are pale. His carriage is easy and smooth. Some levity is visible in his features, which are delicate, but his keen, glancing eye is disagreeable beside Seraphin's pure soul-mirror. Greifmann's sister Louise, not an ordinary beauty, owns the fourth million. She is seated between the young gentlemen; the folds of her costly dress lie heaped around her; her hands are engaged with a fan, and her eyes are sending electric glances into Gerlach's quick depths. But these flashing beams fail to kindle; they expire before they penetrate far into those depths. His eyes are bright, but they refuse to gleam with intenser fire. Strange, too, for a twofold reason; first, because glances from the eyes of beautiful women seldom suffer young men to remain cool; secondly, because a paternal scheme designs that Louise shall be engaged and married to the fire-proof hero.

Millions of money are rare; and should millions strive to form an alliance, it is in conformity with the genius of every solid banking establishment to view this as quite a natural tendency.

For eight days Mr. Seraphin has been on a visit at the *palais* Greifmann, but as yet he has yielded no positive evidence of intending to join his own couple of millions with the million of Miss Louise.

Whilst Seraphin converses with the beautiful young lady, Carl Greifmann cursorily examines a newspaper which a servant has just brought him on a silver salver.

"Every age has its folly," suddenly exclaims the banker. "In the seventeenth century people were busy during thirty years cutting one another's throats for religion's sake--or rather, in deference to the pious hero of the faith from Sweden and his fugleman Oxenstiern. In the eighteenth century, they decorated their heads with periwigs and pigtails, making it a matter of conjecture whether both ladies and gentlemen were not in the act of developing themselves from monkeydom into manhood.

"Elections are the folly of our century. See here, my good fellow, look what is written here: In three days the municipal elections will come off throughout the country--in eighteen days the election of delegates. For eighteen days the whole country is to labor in election throes. Every man twenty-one years of age, having a wife and a homestead, is to be employed in rooting from out the soil of party councilmen, mayors, and deputies.

"And during the period these rooters not unfrequently get at loggerheads. Some are in favor of Streichein the miller, because Streichein has lavishly greased their palms; others insist upon re-electing Leimer the manufacturer, because Leimer threatens a reduction of wages if they refuse to keep him in the honorable position. In the heat of dispute, quite a storm of oaths and ugly epithets, yes, and of blows too, rages, and many is the voter who retires from the scene of action with a bloody head. The beer-shops are the chief battle-fields for this sort of skirmishing. Here, zealous voters swill down hogsheads of beer: brewers drive a brisk trade during elections. But you must not think, Seraphin, that these absurd election scenes are confined to cities. In rural districts the game is conducted with no less interest and fury. There is a village not far away, where a corpulent ploughman set his mind on becoming mayor. What does he, to get the reins of village government into his great fat fist? Two days previous to the election he butchers three fatted hogs, has several hundred ringlets of sausage made, gets ready his pots, and pans for cooking and roasting, and then advertises: eating and drinking *ad libitum* and *gratis* for every voter willing to aid him to ascend the mayor's throne. He obtained his object.

"Now, I put the question to you, Seraphin, is not this sort of election jugglery far more ridiculous and disgusting than the most preposterous periwigs of the last century?"

"Ignorance and passion may occasion the abuse of the best institutions," answered the double millionaire. "However, if beer and pork determine the choice of councilmen and mayors, voters have no right to complain of misrule. It would be most disastrous to the state, I should think, were such

corrupt means to decide also the election of the deputies of our legislative assembly."

The banker smiled.

"The self-same manœuvring, only on a larger scale," replied he. Of course, in this instance, petty jealousies disappear. Streichein the miller and Leimer the manufacturer make concessions in the interest of the common party. All stand shoulder to shoulder in the cause of *progress* against Ultramontanes and democrats, who in these days have begun to be troublesome.

"Whilst at municipal elections office-seekers employed money and position for furthering their personal aims, at deputy elections *progress* men cast their means into a common cauldron, from which the mob are fed and made to drink in order to stimulate them with the spirit of *progress* for the coming election. At bottom it amounts to the same--the stupefaction of the multitude, the rule of a minority, in which, however, all consider themselves as having part, the folly of the nineteenth century."

"This is an unhealthy condition of things, which gives reason to fear the corruption of the whole body politic," remarked the landholder with seriousness. "The seats of the legislative chamber should be filled not through bribery and deception of the masses, nor through party passion, but through a right appreciation of the qualifications that fit a man for the office of deputy."

"I ask your pardon, my dear friend," interposed the banker with a laugh. "Being reared by a mother having a rigorous faith has prompted you to speak thus, not acquaintance with the spirit of the age. Right appreciation! Heavens, what *naïveté*! Are you not aware that *progress*, the autocrat of our times, follows a fixed, unchanging programme? It matters not whether Tom or Dick occupies the cushions of the legislative hall; the main point is to wear the color of *progress*, and for this no special qualifications are needed. I will give you an illustration of the way in which these things work. Let us suppose that every member is provided with a trumpet which he takes with him to the assembly. To blow this trumpet neither skill, nor quick perception, nor experience, nor knowledge--neither of these qualifications is necessary. Now, we will suppose these gentlemen assembled in the great hall where the destinies of the country are decided; should abuses need correction, should legislation for church or state be required, they have only to blow the trumpet of *progress*. The trumpet's tone invariably accords with the spirit of progress, for it has been attuned to it. Should it happen that at a final vote upon a measure the trumpets bray loudly enough to drown the opposition of democrats and Ultramontanes, the matter is settled, the law is passed, the question is decided."

"Evidently you exaggerate!" said Seraphin with a shake of the head. "Your illustration beats the enchanted horn of the fable. Do not you think so. Miss Louise?"

"Brother's trumpet story is rather odd, 'tis true, yet I believe that at bottom such is really the state of things."

"The instrument in question is objectionable in your opinion, my friend, only because you still bear about you the narrow conscience of an age long since buried. As you never spend more than two short winter months in the city, where alone the life-pulse of our century can be felt beating, you remain unacquainted with the present and its spirit. The rest of the year you pass in riding about on your lands, suffering yourself to be impressed by the stern rigor of nature's laws, and concluding that human society harmonizes in the same manner with the behests of fixed principles. I shall have to brush you up a little. I shall have to let you into the mysteries of progress, so that you may cease groping like a blind man in the noonday of enlightenment. Above all, let us have no narrow-mindedness, no scrupulosity, I beg of you. Whosoever nowadays walks the grass-grown paths of rigorism is a doomed man."

Whilst he was saying this, a smile was on the banker's countenance. Seraphin mused in silence on the meaning and purpose of his extraordinary language.

"Look down the street, if you please," continued Carl Greifmann. "Do you observe yon dark mass just passing under the gas-lamp?"

"I notice a pretty corpulent gentleman," answered Seraphin.

"The corpulent gentleman is Mr. Hans Shund, formerly treasurer of this city," explained Greifmann. "Many years ago, Mr. Shund put his hand into the public treasury, was detected, removed for dishonesty, and imprisoned for five years. When set at liberty, the ex-treasurer made the loaning of money on interest a source of revenue. He conducted this business with shrewdness, ruined many a family that needed money and in its necessity applied to him, and became rich. Shund the usurer is known to all the town, despised and hated by everybody. Even the dogs cannot endure the odor of usury that hangs about him; just see--all the dogs bark at him. Shund is moreover an extravagant admirer of the gentler sex. All the town is aware that this Jack Falstaff contributes largely to the scandal that is afloat. The pious go so far as to declare that the gallant Shund will be burned and roasted in hell for all eternity for not respecting the sixth commandment. Considered in the light of the time honored morality of Old Franconia, Shund, the thief, the usurer and adulterer, is a low, good-for-nothing scoundrel, no question about it. But in the light of the indulgent spirit of the times, no more can be said than that he has his foibles. He is about to pass by on the other side, and, as a well-bred man, will salute us."

Seraphin had attentively observed the man thus characterized, but with the feelings with which one views an ugly blotch, a dirty page in the record of humanity.

Mr. Shund lowered his hat, his neck and back, with oriental ceremoniousness in presence of the millions on the balcony. Carl acknowledged the salute, and even Louise returned it with a friendly inclination of the head.

The landholder, on the contrary, was cold, and felt hurt at Greifmann's bowing to a fellow whom he had just described as a scoundrel. That Louise, too, should condescend to smile to a thief, swindler, usurer, and immoral wretch! In his opinion, Louise should have followed the dictates of a noble womanhood, and have looked with honest pity on the scapegrace. She, on the contrary, greeted the bad man as though he were respectable, and this conduct wounded the young man's feelings.

"Apropos of Hans Shund, I will take occasion to convince you of the correctness of my statements," said Carl Greifmann. "Three days hence, the municipal election is to come off. Mr. Shund is to be elected mayor. And when the election of deputies takes place, this same Shund will command enough of the confidence and esteem of his fellow-citizens to be elected to the legislative assembly, thief and usurer though he be. You will then, I trust, learn to understand that the might of progress is far removed from the bigotry that would subject a man's qualifications to a microscopic examination. The enlarged and liberal principles prevailing in secular concerns are opposed to the intolerance that would insist on knowing something of an able man's antecedents before consenting to make use of him. All that Shund will have to do will be to fall in under the glorious banner of the spirit of the age; his voting trumpet will be given him; and forthwith he will turn out a finished mayor and deputy. Do you not admire the power and stretch of *liberalism*?"

"I certainly do admire your faculty for making up plausible stories," answered Seraphin.

"Plausible stories? Not at all! Downright earnest, every word of it. Hans Shund, take my word for it, will be elected mayor and member of the assembly."

"In that event," replied the landholder, "Shund's disreputable antecedents and disgusting conduct at present must be altogether a secret to his constituents."

"Again you are mistaken, my dear friend. This remark proceeds from your want of acquaintance with the genius of our times. This city has thirty thousand inhabitants. Every adult among them has heard of Hans Shund the thief, usurer, and companion of harlots. And I assure you that not a voter, not a progressive member of our community, thinks himself doing what is at all reprehensible by conferring dignity and trust on Hans Shund. You have no idea how comprehensive is the soul of liberalism."

"Let us quit a subject that appears to me impossible, nay, even unnatural," said Gerlach.

"No, no; for this very reason you need to be convinced," insisted the banker with earnestness. "My prospective--but hold--I was almost guilty of a want of delicacy. No matter, my *actual* friend, landholder and millionaire, must be made see with his eyes and touch with his fingers what marvels *progress* can effect. Let us make a bet: Eighteen days from now Hans Shund will be mayor and member for this city. I shall stake ten thousand florins. You may put in the pair of bays that won the best prizes at the last races."

Seraphin hesitated.

"Come on!" urged the banker. "Since you refuse to believe my assertions, let us make a bet. May be you consider my stakes too small against yours? Very well, I will say twenty thousand florins."

"You will be the loser, Greifmann! Your statements are too unreasonable."

"Never mind; if I lose, you will be the winner. Do you take me up?"

"Pshaw, Carl! you are too sure," said Louise reproachfully.

"My feeling so sure is what makes me eager to win the finest pair of horses I ever saw. Is it possible that you are a coward?"

The landholder's face reddened. He put his right hand in the banker's. "My dear fellow," exclaimed he jubilantly, "I have just driven a splendid bargain. To convince you of the entire fairness of the transaction, you are to be present at the manipulation that is to decide. Even though you lose the horses, your gain is incalculable, for it consists in nothing less than being convinced of the wonderful nature and of the omnipotence of progress. I repeat, then, that, wherever progress reigns, the elections are the supreme folly of the nineteenth century; for in reality there is no electing; but what progress decrees, that is fulfilled."

CHAPTER II
THE LEADERS

The banker was seated at his office table working for his chance in the wager with the industry of a thorough business man. Whilst he was engaged in writing notes, a smile indicative of certainty of success lit up his countenance; for he was thoroughly familiar with the figures that entered into his calculations, and, withal, Hans Shund invested with offices and dignity could not but strike him as a comical anomaly. "Happy thought! My father travels half of the globe; many wonderful things come under his observation, no doubt, but the greatest of all prodigies is to be witnessed right here: Hans Shund, the thief, swindler, usurer, wanton--mayor and law-maker! And it is the venerable sire *Progress* that alone could have begotten the prodigy of a Hans Shund invested with honors. My Lord Progress is therefore himself a prodigy--a very extraordinary offspring of the human mind, the culminating point of enlightenment. Admitting humanity to be ten thousand million years old, or even more, as the most learned of scientific men have accurately calculated it, during this rather long series of years nature never produced a marvel that might presume to claim rank with progress. Progress is the acme of human culture--about this there can be no question. Yes, indeed, *the acme.*" And he finished the last word in the last note. "Humanity will therefore have to face about and begin again at the beginning; for after progress nothing else is possible." He rang his bell.

"Take these three notes to their respective addresses immediately," said he to the servant who had answered the ring. Greifmann stepped into the front office, and gave an order to the cashier. Returning to his own cabinet, he locked the door that opened into the front office. He then examined several iron safes, the modest and smooth polish of which suggested neither the hardness of their iron nature nor the splendor of their treasures.

"Gold or paper?" said the banker to himself. After some indecision, he opened the second of the safes. This he effected by touching several concealed springs, using various keys, and finally shoving back a huge bolt by means of a very small blade. He drew out twenty packages of paper, and laid them in two rows on the table. He undid the tape encircling the packages, and then it appeared that every leaf of both rows was a five-hundred florin banknote. The banker had exposed a considerable sum on the table. A sudden thought caused him to smile, and he shoved the banknotes where they came more prominently into view.

The blooming double millionaire entered.

"Sit down a moment, friend Seraphin, and listen to a short account of my scheme. I have said before that our city is prospering and growing under the benign sceptre of progress. The powers and honors of the sceptre are portioned among three leaders. Everything is directed and conducted by them--of course, in harmony with the spirit of the times. I have summoned the aforesaid magnates to appear. That the business may be despatched with a comfortable degree of expedition, the time when the visit is expected has been designated in each note; and those gentlemen are punctual in all matters connected with money and the bank. You can enter this little apartment, next to us, and by leaving the door open hear the conversation. The mightiest of the corypheuses is Schwefel, the straw-hat manufacturer. This potentate resides at a three-minutes walk from here, and can put in an appearance at any time."

"I am on tiptoe!" said Gerlach. "You promise what is so utterly incredible, that the things you are preparing to reveal appear to me like adventures belonging to another world."

"To another world!--quite right, my dear fellow! I am indeed about to display to your astounded eyes some wonders of the world of progress that hitherto have been entirely unknown to you. Within eighteen days you shall, under my tutorship, receive useful and thorough instruction. This promise I can make you, as we are just in face of the elections, a time when minds put aside their disguises, when they not unfrequently shock one another, and when many secrets come to light!"

"You put me under many obligations!"

"Only doing my duty, my most esteemed! We are both aware that, according to the wishes of parents and the desired inclinations of parties known, our respective millions are to approach each other in closer relationship. To do a relative of mine *in spe* a favor, gives me unspeakable satisfaction. I shall proceed with my course of instruction. See here! Every one of these twenty packages contains twenty five-hundred florin banknotes. Consequently, both rows contain just two hundred thousand florins--an imposing sum assuredly, and, for the purpose of being imposing, the two hundred thousand have been laid upon this table. Explanation: the mightiest of the spirits of progress is--Money.

"All forces, all sympathies, revolve about money as the heavenly bodies revolve about the sun. For this reason the mere proximity of a considerable sum of money acts upon every man of progress like a current of electricity: it carries him away, it intoxicates his senses. The leaders whom I have invited will at once notice the collection of five-hundred florin notes: in the rapidity of calculating, they will overestimate the amount, and obtain impressions in proportion, somewhat like the Jews that prostrated themselves in the dust in adoration of the golden calf. As for me, my dear fellow, I shall carry on my operations in the auspicious presence of this power of two hundred thousands. Such a display of power will produce in the leaders a frame of mind made up of veneration, worship, and unconditional submissiveness. Every word of mine will proceed authoritatively from the golden mouth of the two hundred thousands, and my proposals it will be impossible for them to reject. But listen! The door of the ante-room is being opened. The mightiest is approaching. Go in quick." He pressed the spring of a concealed door, and Seraphin disappeared.

When the straw-hat manufacturer entered, the banker was sitting before the banknotes apparently absorbed in intricate calculations.

"Ah Mr. Schwefel! pardon the liberty I have taken of sending for you. The pressure of business," motioning significantly towards the banknotes, "has made it impossible for me to call upon you."

"No trouble, Mr. Greifmann, no trouble whatever!" rejoined the manufacturer with profound bows.

"Have the goodness to take a seat!" And he drew an arm-chair quite near to where the money lay displayed. Schwefel perceived they were five-hundreds, estimated the amount of the pile in a few rapid glances, and felt secret shudderings of awe passing through his person.

"The cause of my asking you in is a business matter of some magnitude," began the banker. "There is a house in Vienna with which we stand in friendly relations, and which has very extensive connections in Hungary. The gentlemen of this house have contracts for furnishing large orders of straw hats destined mostly for Hungary, and they wish to know whether they can obtain favorable terms of purchase at the manufactories of this country. It is a business matter involving a great deal of money. Their confidence in the friendly interest of our firm, and in our thorough acquaintance with local circumstances, has encouraged them to apply to us for an accurate report upon this subject. They intimate, moreover, that they desire to enter into negotiations with none but solid establishments, and for this reason are supposed to be guided by our judgment. As you are aware, this country has a goodly number of straw-hat manufactories. I would feel inclined, however, as far as it may be in my power, to give your establishment the advantage of our recommendation, and would therefore like to get from you a written list of fixed prices of all the various sorts."

"I am, indeed, under many obligations to you, Mr. Greifmann, for your kind consideration," said the manufacturer, nodding repeatedly. "Your own experience can testify to the durability of my work, and I shall give the most favorable rates possible."

"No doubt," rejoined the banker with haughty reserve. "You must not forget that the straw-hat business is out of our line. It is incumbent on us, however, to oblige a friendly house. I shall therefore make a similar proposal to two other large manufactories, and, after consulting with men of experience in this branch, shall give the house in Vienna the advice we consider most to its interest, that is, shall recommend the establishment most worthy of recommendation."

Mr. Schwefel's excited countenance became somewhat lengthy.

"You should not fail of an acceptable acknowledgment from me, were you to do me the favor of recommending my goods," explained the manufacturer.

The banker's coldness was not in the slightest degree altered by the implied bribe. He appeared not even to have noticed it. "It is also my desire to be able to recommend you," said he curtly, carelessly taking up a package of the banknotes and playing with ten thousand florins as if they were so many valueless scraps of paper. "Well, we are on the eve of the election," remarked he ingenuously. "Have you fixed upon a magistrate and mayor?"

"All in order, thank you, Mr. Greifmann!"

"And are you quite sure of the order?"

"Yes; for we are well organized, Mr. Greifmann. If it interests you, I will consider it as an honor to be allowed to send you a list of the candidates."

"I hope you have not passed over ex-treasurer Shund?"

This question took Mr. Schwefel by surprise, and a peculiar smile played on his features.

"The world is and ever will be ungrateful," continued the banker, as though he did not notice the astonishment of the manufacturer. "I could hardly think of an abler and more sterling character for the office of mayor of the city than Mr. Shund. Our corporation is considerably in debt. Mr. Shund is known to be an accurate financier, and an economical householder.

We just now need for the administration of our city household a mayor that understands reckoning closely, and that will curtail unnecessary expenses, so as to do away with the yearly increasing deficit in the budget. Moreover, Mr. Shund is a noble character; for he is always ready to aid those who are in want of money--on interest, of course. Then, again, he knows law, and we very much want a lawyer at the head of our city government. In short, the interests of this corporation require that Mr. Shund be chosen chief magistrate. It is a subject of wonder to me that progress, usually so clear-sighted, has heretofore passed Mr. Shund by, despite his numerous qualifications. Abilities should be called into requisition for the public weal. To be candid, Mr. Schwefel, nothing disgusts me so much as the slighting of great ability," concluded the banker contemptuously.

"Are you acquainted with Shund's past career?" asked the leader diffidently.

"Why, yes! Mr. Shund once put his hand in the wrong drawer, but that was a long time ago. Whosoever amongst you is innocent, let him cast the first stone at him. Besides, Shund has made good his fault by restoring what he filched. He has even atoned for the momentary weakness by five years of imprisonment."

"'Tis true; but Shund's theft and imprisonment are still very fresh in people's memory," said Schwefel. "Shund is notorious, moreover, as a hard-hearted usurer. He has gotten rich through shrewd money speculations, but he has also brought several families to utter ruin. The indignation of the whole city is excited against the usurer; and, finally, Shund indulges a certain filthy passion with such effrontery and barefacedness that every respectable female cannot but blush at being near him. These characteristics were unknown to you, Mr. Greifmann; for you too will not hesitate an instant to admit that a man-of such low practices must never fill a public office."

"I do not understand you, and I am surprised!" said the millionaire. "You call Shund a usurer, and you say that the indignation of the whole town is upon him. Might I request from you the definition of a usurer?"

"They are commonly called usurers who put out money at exorbitant, illegal interest."

"You forget, my dear Mr. Schwefel, that speculation is no longer confined to the five per cent. rate. A correct insight into the circumstances of the times has induced our legislature to leave the rate of interest altogether free. Consequently, a usurer has gotten to be an impossibility. Were Shund to ask fifty per cent, and more, he would be entitled to it."

"That is so; for the moment I had overlooked the existence of the law," said the manufacturer, somewhat humiliated. "Yet I have not told you all concerning the usurer. Beasts of prey and vampires inspire an involuntary disgust or fear. Nobody could find pleasure in meeting a hungry wolf, or in having his blood sucked by a vampire. The usurer is both vampire and wolf. He hankers to suck the very marrow from the bones of those who in financial straits have recourse to him. When an embarrassed person borrows from him, that person is obliged to mortgage twice the amount that he actually receives. The usurer is a heartless strangler, an insatiable glutton. He is perpetually goaded on by covetousness to work the material ruin of others, only so that the ruin of his neighbor may benefit himself. In short, the usurer is a monster so frightful, a brute so devoid of conscience, that the very sight of him excites horror and disgust. Just such a monster is Shund in the eyes of all who know him--and the whole city knows him. Hence the man is the object of general aversion."

"Why, this is still worse, still more astonishing!" rejoined the millionaire with animation. "I thought our city enlightened. I should have expected from the intelligence and judgment of our citizens that they would have deferred neither to the sickly sentimentalism of a bigoted morality nor to the absurdity of obsolete dogmas. If your description of the usurer, which might at least be styled poetico-religious, is an expression of the prevailing spirit of this city, I shall certainly have to lower my estimate of its intelligence and culture."

The leader hastened to correct the misunderstanding.

"I beg your pardon, Mr. Greifmann! You may rest assured that we can boast all the various conquests made by modern advancement. Religious enthusiasm and foolish credulity are poisonous plants that superannuated devotees are perhaps still continuing to cultivate here and there in pots, but which the soil will no longer produce in the open air. The sort of education prevailing hereabout is that which has freed itself from hereditary religious prejudices. Our town is blessed with all the benefits of progress, with liberty of thought, and freedom from the thraldom of a dark, designing priesthood."

"How comes it, then, that a man is an object of contempt for acting in accordance with the principles of this much lauded progress?" asked the millionaire, with unexpected sarcasm. "We are indebted to progress for the abolition of a legal rate of interest. Shund takes advantage of this conquest, and for doing so citizens who boast of being progressive look upon him with aversion. A further triumph secured by progress is freedom from the tyranny of dogmas and the tortures of a conscience created by a contracted morality. This beautiful fruit of the tree of enlightened knowledge Shund partakes of and enjoys; and for this he has the distinction of passing for a vampire. And because he displays the spirit of an energetic business man, because his capacity for speculating occasionally overwhelms blockheads and dunces, he is decried as a ravenous wolf. It is sad! If your statements are correct, Mr. Schwefel, our city ought not to boast of being progressive. Its citizens are still groping in the midnight darkness of religious superstition, scarcely even united with modern intellectual advancement. And to me the consciousness is most uncomfortable of breathing an atmosphere poisoned by the decaying remnants of an age long since buried."

"My own personal views accord with yours," protested Schwefel candidly. "The subversion of the antiquated, absurd articles of faith and moral precept necessarily entails the abrogation of the consequences that flow from them for public life. For centuries the cross was a symbol of dignity, and the doctrine of the Crucified resulted in holiness. Paganism, on the contrary, looked upon the gospel as foolishness, as a hallucination, and upon the cross as a sign of shame. I belong to the classic ranks, and so do millions like myself--among them Mr. Shund. Viewed in the light of progress, Shund is neither a vampire nor a wolf; at the worst, he is merely an ill used business man. They who suffer themselves to be humbugged and fleeced by him have their own stupidity to thank for it. This exposition will convince you that I stand on a level with yourself in the matter of advanced enlightenment. Nevertheless, you overlook, Mr. Greifmann, that, so far as the masses of the people are concerned, reverence for the cross and the holiness of its doctrines continue to prevail. The acquisitions of progress are not yet generally diffused. The mines of modern intellectual culture are being provisionally worked by a select number of independent, bold natures. The multitude, on the other hand, still continue folding about them the winding-sheet of Christianity. The views, customs, principles, and judgments of men are as yet widely controlled by Christian elements. Our city does homage to progress, pretty nearly, however, in the manner of a blind man that discourses of colors."

"I do not catch the drift of your simile of the blind man and colors," interrupted Greifmann.

"I wanted to intimate that thousands swear allegiance to progress without comprehending its nature. Very many imagine progress to be a struggle in behalf of Germany against the enfeebling system of innumerable small states, or a battling against religious rigorism and priest-rule in secular concerns. In unpretending guises like these, the spirit of the age circulates among the crowd travestied in the fashionable epithet *progressive*. Were you, however, to remove the shell from around the kernel of progress, were you to exhibit it to the multitude undisguised as the nullification of religion, as the denial of the God of Christians, as the rejection of immortality, and of an essential difference between man and the beast--were you to venture thus far, you would see the millions flying in consternation before the monster Progress. Now, just because the multitude, although progressive-minded, everywhere judges men by Christian standards, very often, too, unconsciously, therefore Shund has to pass, not for an able speculator, but for a miserable usurer and an unconscionable scoundrel."

"For this very cause, the liberal leaders of this city should stand up for Shund," opposed the banker. "Just appreciation and respect should not be denied a deserving man. To speak candidly, Mr. Schwefel, what first accidentally arrested my attention, now excites my most lively interest. I wish to see justice done Mr. Shund, to see his uncommon abilities recognized. You must set his light upon a candlestick. You must have him elected mayor and member of the legislature; in both capacities he will fill his position with distinction. I repeat, our deeply indebted city stands in want of a mayor that will reckon closely and economize. And in the legislative assembly Shund's fluency will talk down all opposition, his readiness of speech will do wonders. Were it only to spite the stupid mob, you must put Shund in nomination."

"It will not do, Mr. Greifmann! it is impracticable! We have to proceed cautiously and by degrees. Our policy lies in conducting the unsophisticated masses from darkness into light, quite gradually, inch by inch, and with the utmost caution. A sudden unveiling of the inmost significance of the spirit of the age would scare the people, and drive them back heels over head into the clerical camp."

"I do not at all share your apprehensions," contended the millionaire. "Our people are further advanced than you think. Make the trial. Your vast influence will easily manage to have Shund returned mayor and delegate."

"Undoubtedly, but my standing would be jeopardized," rejoined Schwefel.

"That is a mistake, sir! You employ four hundred families."

"Four hundred and seventy now," said the manufacturer, correcting him blandly.

"Four hundred and seventy families, therefore, are getting a living through you, consequently you have four hundred and seventy voters at your command. Add to these a considerable force of mechanics who earn wages in your employ. You have, moreover, a number of warm friends who also command a host of laborers and mechanics. Hence you risk neither standing nor influence, that is," added he with a smile, "unless perhaps you dread the anathemas of Ultramontanes and impostors."

"The pious wrath of believers has no terrors deserving notice," observed the leader with indifference.

"And yet all this time Shund's remarkable abilities have not been able to win the slightest notice on the part of progressive men--it is revolting!" cried the banker. "Mr. Schwefel, I will speak plainly, trusting to your being discreet; I will recommend your factory at Vienna, but only on condition that you have Hans Shund elected mayor and member of the legislature."

"This is asking a great deal--quite flattering for Shund and very tempting to me," said the leader with a bright face and a thrice repeated nod to the banker. "Since, however, what you ask is neither incompatible with the spirit of the times nor dishonorable to the sense of a liberal man, I accept your offer, for it is no small advantage for me from a business point of view."

"Capital, Mr. Schwefel! Capital, because very sensible!" spoke Carl Greifmann approvingly. A short groan, resembling the violent bursting forth of suppressed indignation, resounded from the adjoining apartment. The banker shuffled on the floor and drowned the groan by loudly rasping his throat.

"One condition, however, I must insist upon," continued the manufacturer of straw hats. "My arm might prove unequal to a task that will create no ordinary sensation. But if you succeeded in winning over Erdblatt and Sand to the scheme, it would prosper without fail and without much noise."

"I shall do so with pleasure, Mr. Schwefel! Both those gentlemen will, in all probability, call on me today in relation to matters of business. It will be for me a pleasing consciousness to have aided in obtaining merited recognition for Hans Shund."

"Our agreement is, however, to be kept strictly secret from the public."

"Of course, of course!"

"You will not forget, at the same time, Mr. Greifmann, that our very extraordinary undertaking will necessitate greater than ordinary outlay. It is a custom among laborers not to work on the day before election, and the same on election day itself. Yet, in order to keep them in good humor, they must get wages the same as if they had worked. This is for the manufacturer no insignificant disadvantage. Moreover, workingmen and doubtful voters, require to be stimulated with beer gratis--another tax on our purses."

"How high do these expenses run?" asked the millionaire.

"For Sand, Erdblatt, and myself, they never fall short of twelve hundred florins."

"That would make each one's share of the costs four hundred florins."

Taking a five-hundred florin banknote between his thumb and forefinger, the banker reached it carelessly to the somewhat puzzled leader.

"My contribution to the promotion of the interests of progress! I shall give as much to Messrs. Sand and Erdblatt."

"Many thanks, Mr. Greifmann!" said Schwefel, pocketing the money with satisfaction.

The millionaire drew himself up. "I have no doubt," said he, in his former cold and haughty tone, "that my recommendation will secure your establishment the custom already alluded to."

"I entertain a similar confidence in your influence, and will take the liberty of commending myself most respectfully to your favor." Bowing frequently, Schwefel retreated backwards towards the door, and disappeared. Greifmann stepped to the open entrance of the side apartment. There sat the youthful landholder, his head resting heavily on his hand. He looked up, and Carl's smiling face was met by a pair of stern, almost fierce eyes.

"Have you heard, friend Seraphin?" asked he triumphantly.

"Yes--and what I have heard surpasses everything. You have bargained with a member of that vile class who recognize no difference between honor and disgrace, between good and evil, between self-respect and infamy, who know only one god--which is money."

"Do not show yourself so implacable against these *vile* beings, my dearest! There is much that is useful in them, at any rate they are helping me to the finest horses belonging to the aristocracy."

A stealthy step was heard at the door of the cabinet.

"Do you hear that timid rap?" asked the banker. "The rapper's heart is at this moment in his knuckles. It is curious how men betray in trifles what at the time has possession of their feelings. The mere rapping gives a keen observer an insight into the heart of a person whom he does not as yet see. Listen--" Rapping again, still more stealthily and imploringly. "I must go and relieve the poor devil, whom nobody would suspect for a mighty leader. Now, Mr. Seraphin, Act the Second. Come in!"

The man who entered, attired in a dress coat and kids, was Erdblatt, a tobacco merchant, spare in person, and with restless, spering eyes. The millionaire greeted him coldly, then pointed him to the chair that had been occupied by Schwefel. The impression produced by the two hundred thousands on the man of tobacco was far more decided than in the case of the manufacturer of straw hats. Erdblatt was restless in his chair, and as the needle is attracted by the pole, so did Erdblatt's whole being turn towards the money. His eyes glanced constantly over the paper treasures, and a spasmodic jerking seized upon his fingers. But he soon sat motionless and stiff, as if thunderstruck at Greifmann's terrible words.

"Your substantial firm," began the mighty man of money, after some few formalities, "has awaked in me a degree of attention which the ordinary course of business does not require. I have to-day received notice from an English banking-house that in a few days several bills first of exchange, amounting to sixty thousand florins, will be presented to be paid by you."

Erdblatt was dumfounded and turned pale.

"The amount is not precisely what can be called insignificant," continued Greifmann coolly, "and I did not wish to omit notifying you concerning the bills, because, as you are aware, the banking business is regulated by rigorous and indiscriminating forms."

Erdblatt took the hint, turned still more pale, and uttered not a word.

"This accumulation of bills of exchange is something abnormal," proceeded Greifmann with indifference. "As they are all made payable on sight, you are no doubt ready to meet this sudden rush with proud composure," concluded the banker, with a smile of cold politeness.

But the dumfounded Erdblatt was far from enjoying proud composure. His manner rather indicated inability to pay and panic terror. "Not only is the accumulation of bills of exchange to the amount of sixty thousand florins something abnormal, but it also argues carelessness," said he tersely. "Were it attributable to accident, I should not complain; but it has been occasioned by jealous rivalry. Besides, they are bills first of exchange--it is something never heard of before--it is revolting--there is a plot to ruin me! And I have no plea to allege for putting off these bills, and I am, moreover, unable to pay them."

The banker shrugged his shoulders coldly, and his countenance became grave.

"Might I not beg you to aid me, Mr. Greifmann?" said he anxiously. "Of course, I shall allow you a high rate of interest."

"That is not practicable with bills of exchange," rejoined the banker relentlessly.

"When will the bills be presented?" asked the leader, with increasing anxiety.

"Perhaps as early as to-morrow," answered Greifmann, still more relentless.

The manufacturer of tobacco was near fainting.

"I cannot conceive of your being embarrassed," said the banker coldly. "Your popularity and influence will get you assistance from friends, in case your exchequer happens not to be in a favorable condition."

"The amount is too great; I should have to borrow in several quarters. This would give rise to reports, and endanger the credit of my firm."

"You are not wrong in your view," answered the banker coldly. "Accidents may shake the credit of the most solid firm, and other accidents may often change trifling difficulties into fatal catastrophes. How often does it not occur that houses of the best standing, which take in money at different places, are brought to the verge of bankruptcy through public distrust?"

The words of the money prince were nowise calculated to reassure Mr. Erdblatt.

"Be kind enough to accept the bills, and grant me time," pleaded he piteously.

"That, sir, would be contrary to all precedents in business," rejoined Greifmann, with an icy smile. "Our house never deviates from the paths of hereditary custom."

"I could pay in ten thousand florins at once," said Erdblatt once more. "Within eight weeks I could place fifty thousand more in your hands."

"I am very sorry, but, as I said, this plan is impracticable," opposed Greifmann. "Yet I have half a mind to accept those bills, but only on a certain condition."

"I am willing to indemnify you in any way possible," assured the tobacco merchant, with a feeling of relief!

"Hear the condition stated in a few words. As you know, I live exclusively for business, never meddle in city or state affairs. Moreover, labor devoted by me to political matters would be superfluous, in view of the undisputed sway of liberalism. Nevertheless, I am forced to learn, to my astonishment, that progress itself neglects to take talent and ability into account, and exhibits the most aristocratic nepotism. The remarkable abilities of Mr. Shund are lost, both to the city and state, merely because Mr. Shund's fellow-citizens will not elect him to offices of trust. This is unjust; to speak plainly, it is revolting, when one considers that there is many a brainless fellow in the City Council who has no better recommendation than to have descended from an old family, and whose sole ability lies in chinking ducats which he inherited but never earned. Shund is a genius compared with such boobies; but genius does not pass current here, whilst incapacity does. Now, if you will use your influence to have Shund nominated for mayor of this city, and for delegate to the legislature, and guarantee his election, you may consider the bills of exchange as covered."

Not even the critical financial trouble by which he was beset could prevent an expression of overwhelming surprise in the tobacco man's face.

"I certainly cannot have misunderstood you. You surely mean to speak of Ex-Treasurer Shund, of this place?"

"The same--the very same."

"But, Mr. Greifmann, perhaps you are not aware--"

"I am aware of everything," interrupted the banker. "I know that many years ago Mr. Shund awkwardly put his hand into the city treasury, that he was sent to the penitentiary, that people imagine they still see him in the penitentiary garb, and, finally, that in the stern judgment of the same people he is a low usurer. But usury has been abrogated by law. The theft Shund has not only made good by restoring what he stole, but also atoned for by years of imprisonment. Now, why is a man to be despised who has indeed done wrong, but not worse than others whose sins have long since been forgotten? Why condemn to obscurity a man that possesses the most brilliant kind of talent for public offices? The contempt felt for Shund on the part of a population who boast of their progress is unaccountable--may be it would not be far from the truth to believe that some influential persons are jealous of the gifted man," concluded the banker reproachfully.

"Pardon me, please! The *thief* and *usurer* it might perhaps be possible to elect," conceded Erdblatt. "But Shund's disgusting and shameless amours could not possibly find grace with the moral sense of the public."

"Yes, and the origin of this *moral sense* is the sixth commandment of the Jew Moses," said the millionaire scornfully. "I cannot understand' how you, a man of advanced views; can talk in this manner."

"You misinterpret my words," rejoined the leader deprecatingly. "To me, personally, Shund exists neither as a usurer nor as a debauchee. Christian modes of judging are, of course, relegated among absurdities that we have triumphed over. In this instance, however, there is no question of my own personal conviction, but of the conviction of the great multitude. And in the estimation of the multitude unbridled liberty is just as disgraceful as the free enjoyment of what, *morally*, is forbidden."

"You are altogether in the same rut as Schwefel."

"Have you spoken with Schwefel on this subject?" asked Erdblatt eagerly.

"Only a moment ago. Mr. Schwefel puts greater trust in his power than you do in yours, for he agreed to have Shund elected mayor and delegate. Mr. Schwefel only wishes you and Sand would lend your aid."

"With pleasure! If Schwefel and Sand are won over, then all is right."

"From a hint of Schwefel's," said Greifmann, taking up a five-hundred-florin banknote from the table, "I infer that the election canvass is accompanied with some expense. Accept this small contribution. As for the bills of exchange, the matter is to rest by our agreement."

Erdblatt also backed out of the cabinet, bowing repeatedly as he retreated.

Seraphin rushed from his hiding-place in great excitement.

"Why, Greifmann, this is terrible! Do you call that advanced education? Do you call that progress? Those are demoralized, infernal beings. I spit upon them! And are these the rabble that are trying to arrogate to themselves the leadership of the German people?--rabble who ignore the Deity, the human soul, and morality generally! But what completely unsettles me is your connivance--at least, your connection with these infernal spirits."

"But be easy, my good fellow, be easy! *I* connected with tobacco and straw?"

"At all events, you have been ridiculing the ten commandments and Christian morals and faith."

"Was I not obliged to do so in order to show how well the thief, usurer, and filthy dog Shund harmonizes with the spirit of progress? Can he who wishes to make use of the devil confer with the devil in the costume of light? Not at all; he must clothe himself in the mantle of darkness. And you must not object to my using the demon Progress for the purpose of winning your span of horses and saving my stakes. Let us not have a disgraceful altercation. Consider me as a stage actor, whilst you are a spectator that is being initiated into the latest style of popular education. Ah, do you hear? The last one is drawing near. Be pleased to vanish."

The third leader, house-builder Sand, appeared. The greater portion of his face is hidden by a heavy black beard; in one hand he carries a stout bamboo cane; and it is only after having fully entered, that he deliberately removes his hat.

"I wish you a pleasant morning, Mr. Greifmann. You have sent for me: what do you want?"

The banker slowly raised his eyes from the latest exchange list to the rough features of the builder, and remembering that the man had risen up from the mortarboard to his present position, and had gained wealth and influence through personal energy, he returned the short greeting with a friendly inclination of the head.

"Will you have the goodness to be seated, Mr. Sand?"

The man of the black beard took a seat, and, having noticed the handsome collection of banknotes, his coarse face settled itself into a not very attractive grin.

"I want to impart to you my intention of erecting a villa on the Sauerberg, near the middle of our estate at Wilheim," continued the millionaire.

"Ah, that is a capital idea!" And the man of the beard became very deeply interested. "The site is charming, no view equal to it; healthy location, vineyards round about, your own vineyards moreover. I could put you up a gem there."

"That is what I think, Mr. Sand! My father, who has been abroad for the last three months, is quite satisfied with the plan; in fact, he is the original projector of it."

"I know, I know! your father has a taste for what is grand. We shall try and give him satisfaction, which, by the bye, is not so very easy. But you have the money, and fine fortunes can command fine houses."

"What I want principally is to get you to draw a plan, consulting your own taste and experience in doing so. You will show it to me when ready, and I will tell you whether I like it or not."

"Very well, Mr. Greifmann, very well! But I must know beforehand what amount of money you are willing to spend upon the house; for all depends upon the cost."

"Well," said the millionaire, after some deliberation, "I am willing to spend eighty thousand florins on it, and something over, perhaps."

"Ah, well, for that amount of money something can be put up--something small but elegant. Are you in a hurry with the building?"

"To be sure! As soon as the matter is determined upon, there is to be no delay in carrying it out."

"I am altogether of your opinion, Mr. Greifmann--I agree with you entirely!" assented the builder, with an increase of animation. "I shall draw up a plan for a magnificent house. If it pleases you, all hands shall at once be set at work, and by next autumn you shall behold the villa under roof."

"Of course you are yourself to furnish all the materials," added the banker shrewdly. "When once the plan will have been settled upon, you can reach me an estimate of the costs, and I will pay over the money."

"To be sure, Mr. Greifmann--that is the way in which it should be done, Mr. Greifmann!" responded the man of the black beard with a satisfied air. "You are not to have the slightest bother. I shall take all the bother upon myself."

"That, then is agreed upon! Well, now, have you learned yet who is to be the next mayor?"

"Why, yes, the old one is to be reelected!"

"Not at all! We must have an economical and intelligent man for next mayor. Of this I am convinced, because the annual deficit in the treasury is constantly on the increase."

"Alas, 'tis true! And who is the man of economy and intelligence to be?"

"Mr. Hans Shund."

"Who--what? Hans Shund? The thief, the usurer, the convict, the debauchee? Who has been making a fool of you?"

"Pardon me, sir! I never suffer people to make a fool of me!" rejoined the banker with much dignity.

"Yes, yes--somebody has dished up a canard for you. What, that good-for-nothing scoundrel to be elected mayor! Never in his life! Hans Shund mayor--really that is good now--ha, ha!"

"Mr. Sand, you lead me to suspect that you belong to the party of Ultramontanes."

"Who--*I* an Ultramontane? That is ridiculous! Sir, I am at the head of the men of progress--I am the most liberal of the liberals--that, sir, is placarded on every wall."

"How come you, then, to call Mr. Sand a good-for-nothing scoundrel?"

"Simply for this reason, because, he is a usurer and a dissipated wretch."

"Then I am in the right, after all! Mr. Sand belongs to the ranks of the *pious*," jeered the banker.

"Mr. Greifmann, you are insulting!"

"Nothing is further from my intention than to wound your feelings, my dear Mr. Sand! Be cool and reasonable. Reflect, if you please. Shund, you say, puts out money at thirty per cent. and higher, and therefore he is a usurer. Is it not thus that you reason?"

"Why, yes! The scoundrel has brought many a poor devil to ruin by means of his Jewish speculations!"

"Your pious indignation," commended the millionaire, "is praiseworthy, because it is directed against what you mistake for a piece of scoundrelism. Meanwhile, please to calm down your feelings, and let your reason resume her seat of honor so that you may reflect upon my words. You know that in consequence of recent legislation every capitalist is free to put out money at what rate soever he pleases. Were Shund to ask *fifty* per cent., he would not be stepping outside of the law. He would then be, as he now is, an honest man. Would he not?"

"It is as you say, so far as the law is concerned!"

"Furthermore, if after prudently weighing, after wisely calculating, the *pros* and *cons*, Shund concludes to draw in his money, and in consequence many a poor devil is ruined, as you say, surely no reasonable man will on that account condemn legally authorized speculation!"

"Don't talk to me of legally authorized speculation. The law must not legalize scoundrelism; but whosoever by cunning usury brings such to ruin is and ever will be a scoundrel."

"Why a scoundrel, Mr. Sand? Why, pray?"

"Surely it is clear enough--because he has ruined men!"

"Ruined! How? Evidently through means legally permitted. Therefore, according to your notion the law *does* legalize scoundrelism; at least it allows free scope to scoundrels. Mr. Sand, no offence intended: I am forced, however, once more to suspect that you do, perhaps without knowing it, belong to the *pious*. For they think and feel just as you do, that is, in accordance with so-called laws of morality, religious views and principles. That, judged by such standards, Shund is a scoundrel who hereafter will be burned eternally in hell, I do not pretend to dispute."

"At bottom, I believe you are in the right, after all--yes, it is as you say," conceded the leader reluctantly. "Ahem--and yet I am surprised at your being in the right. I would rather, however that you were in the right, because I really do not wish to blame anybody or judge him by the standard of the Ultramontanes."

"That tone sounds genuinely progressive, and it does honor to your judgment!" lauded the banker. "Again, you called Shund a good-for-nothing scoundrel because he loves the company of women. Mr. Sand, do you mean to vindicate the sacred nature of the sixth commandment in an age that has emancipated itself from the thrall of symbols and has liberated natural inclinations from the servitude of a bigoted priesthood?--you, who profess to stand at the head and front of the party of progress?"

"It is really odd--you are in the right again! Viewed from the standpoint of the times, contemplated in the light of modern intellectual culture, Shund must not really be called good-for-nothing for being a usurer and an admirer of women.

"Shund's qualifications consequently fit him admirably for the office of mayor. He will be economical, he will make the expenditures balance with the revenue. Even in the legislature, Shund's principles and experience will be of considerable service to the country and to the cause of progress. I am so much in favor of the man that I shall award you the building of my villa only on condition that you will use all your influence for the election of Shund to the office of mayor and to the legislature."

"Mayor--assemblyman, too--ahem! that will be hard to do."

"By no means! Messrs. Schwefel and Erdblatt will do their best for the same end."

"Is that so, really? In that case there is no difficulty! Mr. Greifmann, consider me the man that will build your villa."

"The canvass will cost you some money--here, take this, my contribution to the noble cause," and he gave him a five-hundred-florin banknote.

"That will suffice, Mr. Greifmann, that will suffice. The plan you cannot have until after the election, for Shund will give us enough to do."

"Everything is possible to you, Mr. Sand! Whatever Cæsar, Lepidus, and Antony wish at Rome, that same must be."

"Very true, very true." And the last of the leaders disappeared.

"I would never have imagined the like to be possible," spoke the landholder, entering. "They all regard Shund as a low, abandoned wretch, and yet material interest determines every one of them to espouse the cause of the unworthy, contemptible fellow. It is extraordinary! It is monstrous!"

"You cannot deny that progress is eminently liberal," replied the banker, laughing.

"Nor will I deny that it possesses neither uprightness nor conscience, nor, especially, morals," rejoined the young man with seriousness.

Carl saw with astonishment Seraphin's crimsoned cheeks and flaming eyes.

"My dear fellow, times and men must be taken as they are, not as they should be," said the banker. "Interest controls both men and things. At bottom, it has ever been thus. In the believing times of the middle ages, men's interest lay in heaven. All their acts were done for heaven; they considered no sacrifice as too costly. Thousands quit their homes and families to have their skulls cloven by the Turks, or to be broiled by the glowing heats of Palestine. For the interests of heaven, thousands abandoned the world, fed on roots in deserts, gave up all the pleasures of life. At present, the interest lies in this world, in material possessions, in money. Do not therefore get angry at progress if it refuses to starve itself or to be cut down by Moorish scimitars, but, on the other hand, has strength of mind and self-renunciation enough to promote Hans Shund to honors and offices."

Seraphin contemplated Greifmann, who smiled, and hardly knew how to take him.

"An inborn longing for happiness has possession of all men," said he with reserve. "The days of faith were ruled by moral influences; the spirit of this age is ruled by base matter. Between the moral struggles of the past strong in faith, and the base matter of the present, there is, say what you will, a notable difference."

"Doubtless!" conceded Greifmann. "The middle ages were incontestably the grandest epoch of history. I am actuated by the honest intention of acquainting you with the active principles of the present."

"Yes, and you have been not immaterially aided by luck. But for the order from Vienna for straw hats, the bills of exchange, and that villa, you would hardly have attained your aim."

Greifmann smiled.

"The straw-hat story is merely a mystification, my dear friend. When the end will have been reached, when Hans Shund will have been elected mayor and assemblyman, a few lines will be sufficient to inform Mr. Schwefel that the house in Vienna has countermanded its order. Nor is any villa to be constructed. I shall pay Sand for his drawings, and this will be the end of the project. The matter of the bills of exchange is not a hoax, and I am still free to proceed against Erdblatt in the manner required by the interests of my business."

Seraphin stood before the ingenuous banker, and looked at him aghast.

"It is true," said Greifmann gaily, "I have laid out fifteen hundred florins, but I have done so against one hundred per cent.; for they are to secure me victory in our wager."

"Your professional routine is truly admirable," said Gerlach.

"Not exactly that, but practical, and not at all sentimental, my friend."

"I shall take a walk through the garden to get over my astonishment," concluded Gerlach; and he walked away from the astute man of money.

CHAPTER III
SERAPHIN AND LOUISE

Sombre spirits flitted about the head of the young man with the blooming cheeks and light eyes. He was unable to rid himself of a feeling of depression; for he had taken a step into the domain of progress, and had there witnessed things which, like slimy reptiles, drew a cold trail over his warm heart. Trained up on Christian principles, schooled by enlightened professors of the faith, and watched over with affectionate vigilance by a pious mother, Seraphin had had no conception of the state of modern society. For this reason, both Greifmann *Senior* and Gerlach *Senior* committed a blunder in wishing to unite by marriage three millions of florins, the owners of which not merely differed, but were the direct opposites of each other in disposition and education.

Louise belonged to the class of emancipated females who have in vain attempted to enhance the worth of noble womanhood by impressing on their own sex the sterner type of the masculine gender. In Louise's opinion, the beauty of woman does not consist in graceful gentleness, amiable concession and purity, but in proudly overstepping the bounds set for woman by the innate modesty of her sex. The beautiful young lady had no idea of the repulsiveness of a woman who strives to make a man of herself, but she was sure that the cause and origin of woman's degradation is religion. For it was to Eve that God had said: "Thou shalt be under thy husband's power, and he shall have dominion over thee." Louise considered this decree as revolting, and she detested the book whose authority among men gives effect to its meaning. On the other hand, she failed to observe that woman's sway is powerful and acknowledged wherever it exerts itself over weak man through affection and grace. Quite as little did Miss Louise observe that men assume the stature of giants so soon as women presume to appear in relation to them strong and manlike. Least of all did she discover anything gigantic in the kind-hearted Seraphin. In the consciousness of her fancied superiority of education, she smiled at the simplicity of his faith, and, as the handsome young gentleman appeared by no means an ineligible *parti*, she believed it to be her special task to train her prospective husband according to her own notions. She imagined this course of training would prove an easy undertaking for a lady whose charms had been uniformly triumphant over the hearts of gentlemen. But one circumstance appeared to her unaccountable--that was Seraphin's cold-bloodedness and unshaken independence. For eight days she had plied her arts in vain, the most exquisite coquetry had been wasted to no purpose, even the irresistible fire of her most lovely eyes had produced no perceptible impression on the impregnable citadel of the landholder's heart.

"He is a mere child as yet, the most spotless innocence," she would muse hopefully. "He has been sheltered under a mother's wings like a pullet, and for this I am beholden to Madame Gerlach, for she has trained up an obedient husband for me."

Seraphin sauntered through the walks of the garden, absorbed in gloomy reflections on the leaders of progress. Their utter disregard of honor and unparalleled baseness were disgusting to him as an honorable man, whilst their corruption and readiness for deeds of meanness were offensive to him as a Christian. Regarding Greifmann, also, he entertained misgivings. Upon closer examination, however, the unsuspecting youth thought he discovered in the banker's manner of treating the leaders and their principles a strong infusion of ridicule and irony. Hence, imposed upon by his own good nature, he concluded that Greifmann ought not in justice to be ranked among the hideous monstrosities of progress.

With head sunk and rapt in thought, Gerlach strayed indefinitely amid the flowers and shrubbery. All at once he stood before Louise. The young lady was seated under a vine-covered arbor; in one hand she held a book, but she had allowed both hand and book to sink with graceful carelessness upon her lap. For some time back she had been observing the thoughtful young man. She had been struck by his manly carriage and vigorous step, and had come to the conclusion that his profusion of curling auburn hair was the most becoming set-off to his handsome countenance. She now welcomed the surprised youth with a smile so winning, and with a play of eyes and features so exquisite, that Seraphin, dazzled by the beauty of the apparition, felt constrained to lower his eyes like a bashful girl. What probably contributed much to this effect was the circumstance of his being at the time in a rather vacant and cheerless state of mind, so that, coming suddenly into the presence of this brilliant being, he experienced the power of the contrast. She appeared to him indescribably beautiful, and he wondered that this discovery had not forced itself upon him before. Unfortunately, the young gentleman possessed but little of the philosophy which will not suffer itself to be deceived by seductive appearances, and refuses to recognize the beautiful anywhere but in its agreement with the true and good.

Louise perceived in an instant that now was at hand the long-looked-for fulfilment of her wishes. The certainty which she felt that the conquest was achieved diffused a bewitching loveliness over her person. Seraphin, on the other hand, stood leaning against the arbor, and became conscious with fear and surprise of a turmoil in his soul that he had never before experienced.

"I have been keeping myself quiet in this shady retreat," said she sweetly, "not wishing to disturb your meditations. Carl's wager is a strange one, but it is a peculiarity of my brother's occasionally to manifest a relish for what is strange."

"You are right--strange, very strange!" replied Seraphin, evidently in allusion to his actual state of mind. The beautiful young lady, perceiving the allusion, became still more dazzling.

"I should regret very much that the wager were lost by a guest of ours, and still more that you were deprived of your splendid race-horses. I will prevail on Carl not to take advantage of his victory."

"Many thanks, miss; but I would much rather you would not do so. If I lose the wager, honor and duty compel me to give up the stakes to the winner. Moreover, in the event of my losing, there would be another loss far more severe for me than the loss of my racers."

"What would that be?" inquired she with some amazement.

"The loss of my good opinion of men," answered he sadly. "What I have heard, miss, is base and vile beyond description." And he recounted for her in detail what had taken place.

"Such things are new to you, Mr. Seraphin; hence your astonishment and indignation."

The youth felt his soul pierced because she uttered not a word of disapproval against the villainy.

"Carl's object was good," continued she, "in so far as his manœuvre has procured you an insight into the principles by which the world is just now ruled."

"I would be satisfied to lose the wager a thousand times, and even more, did I know that the world is not under such rule."

"It is wrong to risk one's property for the sake of a delusion," said she reprovingly. "And it would be a gross delusion not to estimate men according to their real worth. A proprietor of fields and woodland, who, faithful to his calling, leads an existence pure and in accord with nature's laws, must not permit himself to be so far misled by the harmlessness of his own career as to idealize the human species. For were you at some future day to become more intimately acquainted with city life and society, you would then find yourself forced to smile at the views which you once held concerning the present."

"Smile at, my dear miss? Hardly. I should rather have to mourn the destruction of my belief. Moreover, it is questionable whether I could breathe in an atmosphere which is unhealthy and destructive of all the genuine enjoyments of life!"

"And what do you look upon as the genuine enjoyments of life?" asked she with evident curiosity.

He hesitated, and his childlike embarrassment appeared to her most lovely.

"I beg your pardon, Mr. Seraphin! I have been indiscreet, for such a question is allowable to those only who are on terms of intimacy." And the beauty exhibited a masterly semblance of modesty and amiability. The artifice proved successful, the young man's diffidence fled, and his heart opened.

"You possess my utmost confidence, most esteemed Miss Greifmann! Intercourse with good, or at least honorable, persons appears to me to be the first condition for enjoying life. How could any one's existence be cheerful in the society of people whose character is naught and whose moral sense expired with the rejection of every religious principle?"

"Yet perhaps it might, Mr. Seraphin!" rejoined she, with a smile of imagined superiority. "Refinement, the polished manners of society, may be substituted for the rigor of religious conviction."

"Polished manners without moral earnestness are mere hypocrisy," answered he decidedly. "A wolf, though enveloped in a thousand lambskins, still retains his nature."

"How stern you are!" exclaimed she, laughing. "And what is the second condition for the true enjoyment of life, Mr. Seraphin?"

"It is evidently the accord of moral consciousness with the behests of a supreme authority; or to use the ordinary expression, a good conscience," answered the millionaire earnestly.

A sneering expression spontaneously glided over her countenance. She felt the hateful handwriting of her soul in her features, turned crimson, and cast down her eyes in confusion. The young man had not observed the expression of mockery, and could not account for her confusion. He thought he had perhaps awkwardly wounded her sensitiveness.

"I merely meant to express my private conviction," said Mr. Seraphin apologetically.

"Which is grand and admirable," lauded she.

Her approbation pleased him, for his simplicity failed to detect the concealed ridicule. After a walk outside of the city which Gerlach took towards evening, in the company of the brother and sister, Carl Greifmann made his appearance in Louise's apartment.

"You have at last succeeded in capturing him," began he with a chuckle of satisfaction. "I was almost beginning to lose confidence in your well-tried powers. This time you seemed unable to keep the field, to the astonishment of all your acquaintances. They never knew you to be baffled where the heart of a weak male was to be won."

"What are you talking about?"

"About the fat codfish of two million weight whom you have been successful in angling."

"I do not understand you, most mysterious brother!"

"You do not understand me, and yet you blush like the skies before a rainstorm! What means the vermilion of those cheeks, if you do not understand?"

"I blush, first, on account of my limited understanding, which cannot grasp your philosophy; and, secondly, because I am amazed at the monstrous figures of your language."

"Then I shall have to speak without figures and similes upon a subject which loses a great deal in the light of bare reality, which, I might indeed say, loses all, dissolves into vapor, like will-o'-the-wisps and cloud phantoms before the rising sun. I hardly know how to mention the subject without figures, I can hardly handle it except with poetic figures," exclaimed he gaily, seating himself in Louise's rocking--chair, rocking himself. "Speaking in the commonest prose, my remarks refer to the last victim immolated to your highness--to the last brand kindled by the fire of your eyes. To talk quite broadly, I mean the millionaire and landholder Seraphin Gerlach, who is head and ears in love with you. Considered from a business and solid point of view, it is exceedingly flattering for the banker's brother to see his sister adored by so considerable a sum of money."

"Madman, you profane the noblest feelings of the heart," she chidingly said, with a smile.

"I am a man of business, my dear child, and am acquainted with no sanctuary but the exchange. Relations of a tender nature, noble feelings of the heart, lying as they do without the domain of speculation, are to me something incomprehensible and not at all desirable. On the other hand, I entertain for two millions of money a most prodigious sympathy, and a love that casts the flames of all your heroes and heroines of romance into the shade. Meanwhile, my sweet little sister, there are two aspects to everything. An alliance between our house and two millions of florins claims admiration, 'tis true; yet it is accompanied with difficulties which require serious reflection." The banker actually ceased rocking and grew serious.

"Might I ask a solution of your enigma?"

"All jesting aside, Louise, this alliance is not altogether free from risks," answered he. "Just consider the contrast between yourself and Seraphin Gerlach's good nature is touching, and his credulous simplicity is calculated to excite apprehension. Guided, imposed upon, entirely bewitched by religious phantasms, he gropes about in the darkness of superstition. You, on the contrary, sneer at what Seraphin cherishes as holy, and despise such religious nonsense. Reflect now upon the enormous contrast between yourself and the gentleman whom fate and your father's shrewdness have selected for your husband. Honestly, I am in dread. I am already beginning to dream of divorce and every possible tale of scandal, which would not be precisely propitious for our firm."

"What contradictions!" exclaimed the beauty with self-reliance. "You just a moment ago announced my triumph over Seraphin, and now you proclaim my defeat."

"Your defeat! Not at all! But I apprehend wrangling and discord in your married life."

"Wrangling and discord because Seraphin loves me?"

"No--not exactly--but because he is a believer and you are an unbeliever; in short, because he does not share your aims and views."

"How short-sighted you are! As you conceive of it, love is not a passion; at most, only, a cool mood which cannot be modified by the lovers themselves. Your apprehension would be well grounded concerning that kind of love. But suppose love were something quite different? Suppose it were a passion, a glowing, dazzling, omnipotent passion, and that Seraphin really loved me, do you think that I would not skilfully and prudently take advantage of this passion? Cannot a woman exert a decisive and directing influence over the husband who loves her tenderly? I have no fears because I do not view love with the eyes of a trader. I hope and trust with the adjurations of love to expel from Seraphin all superstitious spirits."

"How sly! Surely nothing can surpass a daughter of Eve in the matter of seductive arts!" exclaimed he, laughing. "Hem--yes, indeed, after what I have seen to-day, it is plain that the Adam Seraphin will taste of the forbidden fruit of ripened knowledge, persuaded by this tenderly beloved Eve. Look at him: there he wanders in the shade of the garden, sighing to the rose-bushes, dreaming, of your majesty, and little suspecting that he is threatened with conversion and redemption from the kingdom of darkness."

CHAPTER IV
HANS SHUND

Hans Shund returned home from business in high feather. Something unusual must have happened him, for his behavior was exceptional. Standing before his desk, he mechanically drew various papers from his pockets, and laid them in different drawers and pigeon-holes. The mechanical manner of his behavior was what was exceptional, for usually Hans Shund bestowed particular attention upon certain papers; his soul's life was in those papers. Moreover, on the present occasion, he kept shaking his head as if astonishment would not suffer him to remain quiet. Yet habitually Hans Shund never shook his head, for that proceeding betrays interior emotion, and Shund's neck was as hardened and stiff as his usurer's soul. The other exceptional feature of his behavior was a continuous growing, which at length waxed into a genuine soliloquy. But Hans Shund was never known to talk to himself, for talking to one's self indicates a kindly disposition, whilst Shund had no disposition whatever, as they maintain who knew him; or, if he had ever had one, it had smouldered into a hard, impenetrable crust of slag.

"Strange--remarkably strange!" said he. "Hem! what can it mean? How am I to account for it? Has the usurer undergone a transformation during the night?" And a hideous grin distorted his face. "Am I metamorphosed, am I enchanted, or am I myself an enchanter? Unaccountable, marvellous, unheard of!"

The papers had been locked up in the desk. A secret power urged him up and down the room, and finally into the adjoining sitting-room, where Mrs. Shund, a pale, careworn lady, sat near a sewing-stand, intent on her lonely occupation.

"Wife, queer things have befallen me. Only think, all the city notables have raised their hats to your humble servant, and have saluted me in a friendly, almost an obsequious manner. And this has happened to me to-day--to me, the hated and despised usurer! Isn't that quite amazing? Even the city regent, Schwefel's son, took off his hat, and bowed as if I were some live grandee. How do you explain that prodigy?"

The careworn woman kept on sewing without raising her head.

"Why don't you answer me, wife? Don't you find that most astonishing?"

"I am incapable of being astonished, since grief and care have so filled my heart that no room is left in it for feelings of any other kind."

"Well, well! what is up again?" asked he, with curiosity.

She drew a letter written in a female hand from one of the drawers of the sewing-stand.

"Read this, villain!"

Hastily snatching the letter, he began to read.

"Hem," growled he indifferently. "The drab complains of being neglected, of not getting any money from me. That should not be a cause of rage for you, I should think. The drab is brazen enough to write to you to reveal my weaknesses, all with the amicable intention of getting up a thundergust in our matrimonial heaven. Do learn sense, wife, and stop noticing my secret enjoyments."

"Fie, villain. Fie upon you, shameless wretch!" cried she, trembling in every limb.

"Listen to me, wife! Above all things, let us not have a scene, an unnecessary row," interrupted he. "You know how fruitless are your censures. Don't pester me with your stale lectures on morals."

"Nearly every month I get a letter of that sort written in the most disreputable purlieus of the town, and addressed to my husband. It is revolting! Am I to keep silent, shameless man--*I* your wedded wife? Am I to be silent in presence of such infamous deeds?"

"Rather too pathetic, wife! Save your breath. Don't grieve at the liberties which I take. Try and accustom yourself to pay as little attention to my conduct as I bestow upon yours. When years ago I entered the contract with you vulgarly denominated marriage, I did it with the understanding that I was uniting myself to a subject that was willing to share with me a life free from restraints; I mean, a life free from the odor of so-called hereditary moral considerations and of religious restrictions. Accustom yourself to this view of the matter, rise to my level, enjoy an emancipated existence."

He spoke and left the room. In his office he read the letter over.

"This creature is insatiable!" murmured he to himself. "I shall have to turn her off and enter into less expensive connections. I am talking with myself to-day--queer, very queer!"

A heavy knock was heard at the door.

"Come in!"

A man and woman scantily clad entered the room. The sight of the wretched couple brought a fierce passion into the usurer's countenance. He seemed suddenly transformed into a tiger, bloodthirstily crouching to seize his prey.

"What is the matter. Holt?"

"Mr. Shund," began the man in a dejected tone, "the officer of the law has served the writ upon us: it is to take effect in ten days."

"That is, unless you make payment," interrupted Shund.

"We are not able to pay just now, Mr. Shund, it is impossible. I wished therefore to entreat you very earnestly to have patience with us poor people."

The woman seconded her husband's petition by weeping bitterly, wringing her hands piteously. The usurer shook his head relentlessly.

"Patience, patience, you say. For eight years I have been using patience with you; my patience is exhausted now. There must be limits to everything. There is a limit to patience also. I insist upon your paying."

"Consider, Mr. Shund, I am the father of eight children. If you insist on payment now and permit the law to take its course, you will ruin a family of ten persons. Surely your conscience will not permit you to do this?"

"Conscience! What do you mean? Do not trouble me with your nonsense. For me, conscience means to have; for you, it means you must. Therefore, pay."

"Mr. Shund, you know it is yourself that have reduced us to this wretched condition!"

"You don't say I did! How so?"

"May I remind you, Mr. Shund, may I remind you of all the circumstances by which this was brought about? How it happened that from a man of means I have been brought to poverty?"

"Go on, dearest Holt--go on; it will be interesting to me!" The usurer settled himself comfortably to hear the summary of his successful villanies from the mouth of the unfortunate man with the same satisfaction with which a tiger regales itself on the tortures of its victim.

"Nine years ago, Mr. Shund, I was not in debt, as you know. I labored and supported my family honestly, without any extraordinary exertion. A field was for sale next to my field at the Rothenbush. You came at the time-- it is now upwards of eight years, and said in a friendly way, 'Holt, my good man, buy that field. It lies next to yours, and you ought not to let the chance slip.' I wanted the field, but had no money. This I told you. You encouraged me, saying, 'Holt, my good man, I will let you have the money--on interest, of course; for I am a man doing business, and I make my living off my money. I will never push you for the amount. You may pay it whenever and in what way you wish. Suit yourself.' You gave me this encouragement at the time. You loaned me nine hundred and fifty florins--in the note, however, you wrote one thousand and fifty, and, besides, at five per cent. For three years I paid interest on one thousand and fifty, although you had loaned me only nine hundred and fifty. All of a sudden--I was just in trouble at the time, for one of my draught-cattle had been crippled, and the harvest had turned out poorly, you came and demanded your money. I had none. 'I am sorry,' said you, 'I need my money, and could put it out at much higher interest.' I begged and begged. You threatened to sue me. Finally, after much begging, you proposed that I should sell you the field, for which three years previous I had paid nine hundred and fifty florins, for seven hundred florins, alleging that land was no longer as valuable as it had been. You were willing to rent me the field at a high rate. And to enable me to get along, you offered to lend me another thousand, but drew up a note for eleven hundred florins at ten per cent., because, as you pretended, money was now bringing ten per cent. since the law regulating interest had been abrogated. For a long while I objected to the proposal, but found myself forced at last to yield because you threatened to attach my effects. From this time I began to go downhill, I could no longer meet expenses, my family was large, and I had to work for you to pay up the interest and rent. But for some time back I had been unable to do as I wished. I could not even sell any of my own property; for you were holding me fast, and I was obliged to mortgage everything to you for a merely nominal price. My cottage, my barn, my garden, and the field in front of my house--worth at least two thousand florins--I had to give you a mortgage upon for one thousand. The rest of my immovable property, fields and meadows, you took. Nothing was left to me but the little hut and what adjoined it. With respects, Mr. Shund, you had long since sucked the very marrow from my bones, next you put the rope about my neck, and now you are about to hang me."

"Hang you? Ha--ha! That's good, Holt! You are in fine humor," cried the usurer, after hearing with a relish the simple account of his atrocious deeds. "I have no hankering for your neck. Pay up, Holt, pay up, that is all I want. Pay me over the trifle of a thousand florins and the interest, and the house with everything pertaining to it shall be yours. But if you cannot pay up, it will have to be sold at auction, so that I may get my money."

"For heaven's sake, Mr. Shund, be merciful," entreated the wife. "We have saved up the interest with much trouble; every farthing of it you are to receive. For God's sake, do not drive us from our home, Mr. Shund, we will gladly toil for you day and night. Take pity, Mr. Shund, do take pity on my poor children!"

"Stop your whining. Pay up, money alone has any value in my estimation--pay, all the rest is fudge. Pay up!"

"God knows, Mr. Shund," sobbed the woman, wringing her hands, "I would give my heart's blood to keep my poor children out of misery--with my life I would be willing to pay you. Oh! do have some commiseration, do be merciful! Almighty God will requite you for it."

"Almighty God, nonsense! Don't mention such stuff to me. Stupid palaver like that might go down with some bigoted fool, but it will not affect a man of enlightenment. Pay up, and there's an end of it!"

"Is it your determination then, Mr. Shund, to cast us out mercilessly under the open sky?" inquired the countryman with deep earnestness.

"I only want what belongs to me. Pay over the thousand florins with the interest, and we shall be quits. That's my position, you may go."

In feeling words the woman once more appealed to Hans Shund. He remained indifferent to her pleading, and smiled scornfully whenever she adduced religious considerations to support her petition. Suddenly Holt took her by the arm and drew her towards the door.

"Say no more, wife, say no more, but come away. You could more easily soften stones than a man who has no conscience and does not believe in God."

"There you have spoken the truth," sneered Shund.

"You sneer, Mr. Shund," and the man's eyes glared. "Do you know to whom you owe it that your head is not broken?"

"What sort of language is that?"

"It is the language of a father driven to despair. I tell you"--and the countryman raised his clenched fists--"it is to the good God that you are indebted for your life; for, if I believed as little in an almighty and just God as you, with this pair of strong hands I would wring your neck. Yes, stare at me! With these hands I would strangle Shund, who has brought want upon my children and misery upon me. Come away, wife, come away. He is resolved to reduce us to beggary as he has done to so many others. Do your worst, Mr. Shund, but there above we shall have a reckoning with each other."

He dragged his wife out of the room, and went away without saluting, but casting a terrible scowl back upon Hans Shund.

For a long while the usurer sat thoughtfully, impressed by the ominous scowl and threat, which were not empty ones, for rage and despair swept like a rack over the man's countenance. Mr. Shund felt distinctly that but for the God of Christians he would have been murdered by the infuriated man. He discovered, moreover, that religious belief is to be recommended as a safeguard against the fury of the mob. On the other hand, he found this belief repugnant to a usurer's conscience and a hindrance to the free enjoyment of life. Hans Shund thus sat making reflections on religion, and endeavoring to drown the echo which Holt's summons before the supreme tribunal had awakened in a secret recess of his soul, when hasty steps resounded from the front yard and the door was suddenly burst open. Hans' agent rushed in breathless, sank upon the nearest chair, and, opening his mouth widely, gasped for breath.

"What is the matter, Braun?" inquired Shund in surprise. "What has happened?"

Braun flung his arms about, rolled his eyes wildly, and labored to get breath, like a person that is being smothered.

"Get your breath, you fool!" growled the usurer. "What business had you running like a maniac? Something very extraordinary must be the matter, is it not?"

Braun assented with violent nodding.

"Anything terrible?" asked he further.

More nodding from Braun. The usurer began to feel uneasy. Many a nefarious deed stuck to his hands, but not one that had not been committed with all possible caution and secured against any afterclaps of the law. Yet might he not for once have been off his guard? "What has been detected? Speak!" urged the conscience-stricken villain anxiously.

"Mr. Shund, you are to be--in this place--"

"Arrested?" suggested the other, appalled, as the agent's breath failed him again.

"No--mayor!"

Shund straightened himself, and raised his hands to feel his ears.

"I am surely in possession of my hearing! Are you gone mad, fellow?"

"Mr. Shund, you are to be mayor and member of the legislature. It is a settled fact!"

"Indeed, 'tis quite a settled fact that you have lost your wits. It is a pity, poor devil! You once were useful, now you are insane; quite a loss for me! Where am I to get another bloodhound as good as you? Your scent was keen, you drove many a nice bit of game into my nets. Hem--so many instances of insanity in these enlightened times of ours are really something peculiar. Braun, dearest Braun, have you really lost your mind entirely? Completely deranged?"

"I am not insane, Mr. Shund. I have been assured from various sources that you are to be elected mayor and delegate to the legislative assembly."

"Well, then, various persons have been running a rig upon you."

"Running a rig upon me, Mr. Shund? Bamboozle me--me who understand and have practised bamboozling others for so long?"

"Still, I maintain that people have been playing off a hoax on you--and what an outrageous hoax it is, too!

"I believe a hoax? Just listen to me. I have never been more clearheaded than I am to-day. Acquaintances and strangers in different quarters of the town have assured me that it is a fixed fact that you are to be mayor of this city and member of the legislative assembly. Now, were it a hoax, would you not have to presuppose that both acquaintances and strangers conspired to make a fool of me? Yet such a supposition is most improbable."

"Your reasoning is correct, Braun. Still, such a conspiracy must really have been gotten up. *I* mayor of this city? *I*? Reflect for an instant, Braun. You know what an enviable reputation I bear throughout the city. Many persons would go a hundred paces out of their direction to avoid me, specially they who owe or have owed me anything. Moreover, who appoints the mayor? The men who give the keynote, the leaders of the town. Now, these men would consider themselves defiled by the slightest contact with the outlawed usurer--which, of course, is very unjust and inconsistent on the part of those gentlemen--for my views are the same as theirs."

"Spite of all that, I put faith in the report, Mr. Shund. Schwefel's bookkeeper also, when I met him, smiled significantly, and even raised his hat."

"Hold on, Braun, hold! The deuce--it just now occurs to me--you might not be so much mistaken after all. Strange things have happened to me also. Gentlemen who are intimate with our city magnates have saluted me and nodded to me quite confidentially; I was unable to solve this riddle, now it's clear. Braun, you are right, your information is perfectly true." And Mr. Shund rubbed his hands.

"Don't forget, Mr. Shund, that I first brought you the astounding intelligence, the joyful tidings, the information on which the very best sort of speculations may be based."

"You shall be recompensed, Braun! Go over to the sign of the Bear, and drink a bottle of the best, and I will pay for it."

"At a thaler a bottle?"

"That quality isn't good for the health, my dear fellow! You may drink a bottle at forty-eight kreutzers on my credit. But no--I don't wish to occasion you an injury, nor do I wish to see you disgraced. You shall not acquire the name of a toper in my employ. You may therefore call for a pint glass at twelve kreutzers a glass. Go, now, and leave me to myself."

When the agent was gone, Hans Shund rushed about the room as if out of his mind.

"Don't tell me that miracles no longer occur!" cried he. "*I*, the discharged treasurer--*I*, the thief, usurer, and profligate, at the mere sight of whom every young miss and respectable lady turn up their noses a thousand paces off--I am chosen to be mayor and assemblyman! How has this come to pass? Where lie the secret springs of this astonishing event?" And he laid his finger against his nose in a brown study. "Here it is--yes, here! The thinkers of progress have at length discovered that a man who from small beginnings has risen to an independent fortune, whose shrewdness and energy have amassed enormous sums, ought to be placed at the head of the city administration in order to convert the tide of public debt into a tide of prosperity. Yes, herein lies the secret. Nor are the gentlemen entirely mistaken. There are ways and means of making plus out of minus, of converting stones into money. But the gentlemen have taken the liberty of disposing of me without my previous knowledge and consent. I have not even been asked. Quite natural, of course. Who asks a dog for permission to stroke him? This is, I own, an unpleasant aftertaste. Hem, suppose I were too proud to accept, suppose I wanted to bestow my abilities and energies on my own personal interests. Come, now, old Hans, don't be sensitive! Pride, self-respect, character, sense of honor, and such things are valuable only when they bring emolument. Now, the mayor of a great city has it in his power to direct many a measure eminently to his own interest."

Another knock was heard at the door, and the usurer, taken by surprise, saw before him the leader Erdblatt.

"Have you been informed of a fact that is very flattering to you?" began the tobacco manufacturer.

"Not the slightest intimation of a fact of that nature has reached me," answered Shund with reserve.

"Then I am very happy to be the first to give you the news," assured Erdblatt. "It has been decided to promote you at the next election to the office of mayor and of delegate to the legislative assembly."

A malignant smile flitted athwart Shund's face. He shook his sandy head in feigned astonishment, and fixed upon the other a look that was the next thing to a sneer.

"There are almost as many marvels in your announcement as words. You speak of a decision and of a fact which, however, without my humble co-operation, are hardly practicable. I thought all along that the disposition of my person belonged to myself. How could anything be resolved upon or become a fact in which I myself happen to have the casting vote?"

"Your cordial correspondence with the flattering intention of your fellow-citizens was presumed upon; moreover, you were to be agreeably surprised," explained the progressionist leader.

"That, sir, was a very violent presumption! I am a free citizen, and am at liberty to dispose of my time and faculties as I please. In the capacity of mayor, I should find myself trammelled and no longer independent on account of the office. Moreover, a weighty responsibility would then rest upon my shoulders, especially in the present deplorable circumstances of the administration. Could I prevail on my myself to accept the proffered situation, it would become my duty to attempt a thorough reform in the thoughtless and extravagant management of city affairs. You certainly cannot fail to perceive that a reformer in this department would be the aim of dangerous machinations. And lastly, sir, why is it that I individually have been selected for appointments which are universally regarded as honorable distinctions in public life? I repeat, why are they to be conferred, upon me in particular who cannot flatter myself with enjoying very high favor among the people of this city?" And there glistened something like revengeful triumph in Shund's feline, eyes. "When you will have given a satisfactory solution to these reflections and questions, it may become possible for me to think of assenting to your proposal."

Erdblatt had not anticipated a reception of this nature, and for a moment he sat nonplussed.

"I ask your pardon, Mr. Shund, you have taken the words fact and decision in too positive a sense. What is a decided fact is that the leaders of progress assign the honorable positions mentioned to you. Of course it rests with you to accept or decline them. The motive of our decision was, if you will pardon my candor, your distinguished talent for economizing. It is plain to us that a man of your abilities and thorough knowledge of local circumstances could by prudent management and, by eliminating unnecessary expenditure, do much towards relieving the deplorable condition of the city budget. We thought, moreover, that your well-known philanthropy would not refuse the sacrifices of personal exertion and unremitting activity for the public good. Finally, as regards the disrespect to which you have alluded, I assure you I knew nothing of it. The stupid and mad rabble may perhaps have cast stones at you, but can or will you hold respectable men responsible for their deeds? Progress has ever proudly counted you in its ranks. We have always found you living according to the principles of progress, despising the impotent yelping of a religiously besotted mob. Be pleased to consider the tendered honors as amends for the insults of intolerant fanatics in this city."

"Your explanation, sir, is satisfactory. I shall accept. I am particularly pleased to know that my conduct and principles are in perfect accord with the spirit of progress. I am touched by the flattering recognition of my greatly misconstrued position."

The leader bowed graciously.

"There now remains for me the pleasant duty," said he, "of requesting you to honor with your presence a meeting of influential men who are to assemble this evening in Mr. Schwefel's drawing-room. Particulars are to be discussed there. The ultramontanes and democrats are turbulent beyond all anticipation. We shall have to proceed with the greatest caution about the delegate elections."

"I shall be there without fail, sir! Now that I have made up my mind to devote my experience to the interests of city and state, I cheerfully enter into every measure which it lies in my power to further."

"As you are out for the first time as candidate for the assembly," said Erdblatt, "a declaration of your political creed addressed to a meeting of the constituents would not fail of a good effect."

"Agreed, sir! I shall take pleasure in making known my views in a public speech."

Erdblatt rose, and Mr. Hans Shund was condescending enough to reach the mighty chieftain his hand as the latter took his leave.

CHAPTER V
ELECTIONEERING

The four millions of the balcony are at present standing before two suits of male apparel of the kind worn by the working class, contemplating them with an interest one would scarcely expect from millionaires in materials of so ordinary a quality. Spread out on the elegant and costly table cover are two blouses of striped gray at fifteen kreutzers a yard. There are, besides, two pairs of trowsers of a texture well adapted to the temperature of the month of July. There are also two neckties, sold at fairs for six kreutzers apiece. And, lastly, two cheap caps with long broad peaks. These suits were intended to serve as disguises for Seraphin and Carl on this evening, for the banker did not consider it becoming gentlemen to visit electioneering meetings, dressed in a costume in which they might be recognized. As Greifmann's face was familiar to every street-boy, he had provided himself with a false beard of sandy hue to complete his *incognito*. For Seraphin this last adjunct was unnecessary, for he was a stranger, was thus left free to exhibit his innocent countenance unmasked for the gratification of curious starers.

"This will be a pleasant change from the monotony of a banking house existence," said the banker gleefully. "I enjoy this masquerade: it enables me to mingle without constraint among the unconstrained. You are going to see marvellous things to-night, friend Seraphin. If your organs of hearing are not very sound, I advise you to provide yourself with some cotton, so that the drums of your ears may not be endangered from the noise of the election skirmish."

"Your caution is far from inspiring confidence," said Louise with some humor. "I charge it upon your soul that you bring back Mr. Gerlach safe and sound, for I too am responsible for our guest."

"And I, it seems, am less near to you than the guest, for you feel no anxiety about me," said the brother archly.

"Eight o'clock--it is our time."

He pulled the bell. A servant carried off the suits to the gentlemen's rooms.

"May I beseech the men in blouses for the honor of a visit before they go?"

"You shall have an opportunity to admire us," said Carl. The transformation of the young men was more rapidly effected than the self-satisfied mustering of Louise before the large mirror which reflected her elegant form entire. She laughingly welcomed her brother in his sandy beard, and fixed a look of surprise upon Seraphin, whose innocent person appeared to great advantage in the simple costume.

"Impossible to recognize you," decided the young lady. "You, brother Redbeard, look for all the world like a cattle dealer."

"The gracious lady has hit it exactly," said the banker with an assumed voice. "I am a horse jockey, bent on euchreing this young gentleman out of a splendid pair of horses."

"Friend Seraphin is most lovely," said she in an undertone. "How well the country costume becomes him!" And her sparkling eyes darted expressive glances at the subject of her compliments.

For the first time she had called him friend, and the word friend made him more happy than titles and honors that a prince might have bestowed. He felt his soul kindle at the sight of the lovely being whose delicate and bewitching coquetry the inexperienced youth failed to detect, but the influence of which he was surely undergoing. His cheeks glowed still more highly, and he became uneasy and embarrassed.

"Your indulgent criticism is encouraging, Miss Louise," replied he.

"I have merely told the truth," replied she.

"But our hands--what are we to do with our hands?" interposed Carl. "Soft white hands like these do not belong to drovers. First of all, away with diamonds and rubies. Gold rings and precious stones are not in keeping with blouses. Nor will it do, in hot weather like this, to bring gloves to our aid--that's too bad! What *are* we to do?"

"Nobody will notice our hands," thought Seraphin.

"My good fellow, you do not understand the situation. We are on the eve of the election. Everybody is out electioneering. Whoever to-day visits a public place must expect to be hailed by a thousand eyes, stared at, criticised, estimated, appraised, and weighed. The deuce take these hands! Good advice would really be worth something in this instance."

"To a powerful imagination like your own," added Louise playfully. She disappeared for a moment and then returned with a washbowl. Pouring the contents of her inkstand into the water, she laughingly pointed them to the dark mass.

"Dip your precious hands in here, and you will make them correspond with your blouses in color and appearance."

"How ingenious she is!" cried Carl, following her direction.

"Most assuredly nothing comes up to the ingenuity of women. We are beautifully tattooed, our hands are horrible! We must give the stuff time to dry. Had I only thought of it sooner, Louise, you should have accompanied us disguised as a drover's daughter, and have drunk a bumper of wine with us. The adventure might have proved useful to you, and served as an addition to the sum of your experiences in life."

"I will content myself with looking on from a distance," answered she gaily. "The extraordinary progressionist movement that is going on to-day might make it a difficult task even for a drover's daughter to keep her footing."

The two millionaires sallied forth, Carl making tremendous strides. Seraphin followed mechanically, the potent charm of her parting glances hovering around him.

"We shall first steer for the sign of the 'Green Hat,'" said Greifmann. "There you will hear a full orchestra of progressionist music, especially trumpets and drums, playing flourishes on Hans Shund. 'The Green Hat' is the largest beer cellar in the town, and the proprietor ranks among the leaders next after housebuilder Sand. All the representatives of the city *régime* gather to-day at the establishment of Mr. Belladonna--that's the name of the gentleman of the 'Green Hat.' Besides the leaders, there will be upward of a thousand citizens, big and small, to hold a preliminary celebration of election day. There will also be 'wild men' on hand," proceeded Carl, explaining. "These are citizens who in a manner float about like atoms in the bright atmosphere of the times without being incorporated in any brilliant body of progress. The main object of the leaders this evening is to secure these so-called 'wild men' in favor of their ticket for the city council. Glib-tongued agents will be employed to spread their nets to catch the floating atoms--to tame these savages by means of smart witticisms. When, at length, a prize is captured and the tide of favorable votes runs high, it is towed into the safe haven of agreement with the majority. Resistance would turn out a serious matter for a mechanic, trader, shopkeeper, or any man whose position condemns him to obtain his livelihood from others. Opposition to progress dooms every man that is in a dependent condition to certain ruin. For these reasons I have no misgivings about being able to convince you that elections are a folly wherever the banner of progress waves triumphant."

"The conviction with which you threaten me would be anything but gratifying, for I abhor every form of terrorism," rejoined Seraphin.

"Very well, my good fellow! But we must accustom ourselves to take things as they are and not as they ought to be. Therefore, my youthful Telemachus, you are under everlasting obligations to me, your experienced Mentor, for procuring you an opportunity of becoming acquainted with the world, and constraining you to think less well of men than your generous heart would incline you to do."

They had reached the outskirts of the city. A distant roaring, resembling the sound of shallow waters falling, struck upon the ears of the maskers. The noise grew more distinct as they advanced, and finally swelled into the brawling and hum of many voices. Passing through a wide gate-way, the millionaires entered a square ornamented with maple-trees. Under the trees, stretching away into the distance, were long rows of tables lit up by gaslights, and densely crowded with men drinking beer and talking noisily. The middle of the square was occupied by a rotunda elevated on columns, with a zinc roof, and bestuck in the barbarous taste of the age with a profusion of tin figures and plaster-of-paris ornaments. Beneath the rotunda, around a circular table, sat the leaders and chieftains of progress, conspicuous to all, and with a flood of light from numerous large gas-burners streaming upon them. Between Sand and Schwefel was throned Hans Shund, extravagantly dressed, and proving by his manner that he was quite at his ease. Nothing in his deportment indicated that he had so suddenly risen from general contempt to universal homage. Mr. Shund frequently monopolized the conversation, and, when this was the case, the company listened to his sententious words with breathless attention and many marks of approbation.

Mentor Greifmann conducted his ward to a retired corner, into which the rays of light, intercepted by low branches, penetrated but faintly, and from which a good view of the whole scene could be enjoyed.

"Do you observe Hans there under the baldachin surrounded by his vassals?" rouned Carl into his companion's ear. "Even you will be made to feel that progress can lay claim to a touching spirit of magnanimity and forgiveness. It is disposed to raise the degraded from the dust. The man who only yesterday was engaged in shoving a car, sweeping streets, or even worse, to-day may preside over the great council, provided only he has the luck to secure the good graces of the princes of progress. Hans Shund, thief, usurer, and nightwalker, is a most striking illustration of my assertion."

"What particularly disgusts and incenses me," replied the double millionaire gravely, "is that, under the *régime* of progress, they who are degraded, immoral, and criminal, may rise to power without any reformation of conduct and principles."

"What you say is so much philosophy, my dear fellow, and philosophy is an antique, obsolete kind of thing that has no weight in times when continents are being cut asunder and threads of iron laid around the globe. Moreover, such has ever been the state of things. In the dark ages, also, criminals attained to power. Just think of those bloody monarchs who trifled with human heads, and whose ministers, for the sake of a patch of territory, stirred up horrible wars. Compared with such monsters, Hans Shund is spotless innocence."

"Quite right, sir," rejoined the landholder, with a smile. "Those bloody kings and their satanic ministers were monsters--but only--and I beg you to mark this well--only when judged by principles which modern progress sneers at as stupid morality and senseless dogma. I even find that those princely monsters and their conscienceless ministers shared the species of enlightenment that prides itself on repudiating all positive religion and moral obligations."

"Thunder and lightning, Seraphin! were not you sitting bodily before me, I should believe I was actually listening to a Jesuit. But be quiet! It will not do to attract notice. Ah! splendid. There you see some of the 'wild men,'" continued he, pointing to a table opposite. "The fellow with the bald head and fox's face is an agent, a salaried bellwether, a polished electioneer. He has the 'wild men' already half-tamed. Watch how cleverly he will decoy them into the progressionist camp. Let us listen to what he has to say; it will amuse you, and add to your knowledge of the developments of progress."

"We want men for the city council," spoke he of the bald head, "that are accurately and thoroughly informed upon the condition and circumstances of the city. Of what use would blockheads be but to fuss and grope about blindly? What need have we of fellows whose stupidity would compromise the public welfare? The men we want in our city council must understand what measures the social, commercial, and industrial interests of a city of thirty thousand inhabitants require in order that the greatest good of the largest portion of the community may be secured. Nor is this enough," proceeded he with increasing enthusiasm. "Besides knowledge, experience, and judgment, they must also be gifted with the necessary amount of energy to carry out whatever orders the council has thought fit to pass. They must be resolute enough to break down every obstacle that stands in the way of the public good. Now, who are the men to render these services? None but independent men who by their position need have no regard to others placed above them--free-spirited and sensible men, who have a heart for the people. Now, gentlemen, have you any objections to urge against my views?"

"None, Mr. Spitzkopf! Your views are perfectly sound," lauded a semi-barbarian. "We have read exactly what you have been telling us in the evening paper."

"Of course, of course!" cried Mr. Spitzkopf. "My views are so evidently correct that a thinking man cannot help stumbling upon them. None but the slaves of priests, the wily brood of Jesuits, refuse to accept these views," thundered the orator with the bald head. "And why do they refuse to accept them? Because they are hostile to enlightenment, opposed to the common good, opposed to the prosperity of mankind, in a word, because they are the bitter enemies of progress. But take my word for it, gentlemen, our city contains but a small number of these creatures of darkness, and those few are spotted," emphasized he threateningly. "Therefore, gentlemen," proceeded he insinuatingly, "I am convinced, and every man of intelligence shares my conviction, that Mr. Shund is eminently fitted for the city council--eminently! He would be a splendid acquisition in behalf of the public interests! He understands our local concerns thoroughly, possesses the experience of many years, is conversant with business, knows what industrial pursuits and social life require, and, what is better still, he maintains an independent standing to which he unites a rare degree of activity. Were it possible to prevail on Mr. Shund to take upon himself the cares of the mayoralty, the deficit of the city treasury would soon be wiped out. We would all have reason to consider ourselves fortunate in seeing the interests of our city confided to such a man."

The "wild men" looked perplexed.

"Right enough, Mr. Spitzkopf," explained a timid coppersmith. "Shund is a clever, well-informed man. Nobody denies this. But do you know that it is a question whether, besides his clever head, he also possesses a conscience in behalf of the commonwealth?"

"The most enlarged sort of a conscience, gentlemen--the warmest kind of a heart!" exclaimed the bald man in a convincing tone. "Don't listen to stories that circulate concerning Shund. There is not a word of truth in them. They are sheer misconstructions--inventions of the priests and of their helots."

"I beg your pardon, Mr. Spitzkopf, they are not all inventions," opposed the coppersmith. "In the street where I live, Shund keeps up a certain connection that would not be proper for any decent person, not to say for a married man."

"And does that scandalize you?" exclaimed the bald-headed agent merrily. "Mr. Shund is a jovial fellow, he enjoys life, and is rich. Mr. Shund will not permit religious rigorism to put restraints upon his enjoyments. His liberal and independent spirit scorns to lead a miserable existence under the rod of priestly bigotry. And, mark ye, gentlemen, this is just what recommends him to all who are not priest-ridden or leagued with the hirelings of Rome," concluded the electioneer, casting a sharp look upon the coppersmith.

"But I am a Lutheran, Mr. Spitzkopf," protested the coppersmith.

"There are hypocrites among the Lutherans who are even worse than the Romish Jesuits," retorted the man with the bald head. "Consider, gentlemen, that the leading men of our city have, in consideration of his abilities, concluded to place Mr. Shund in the position which he ought to occupy. Are you going, on to-morrow, to vote against the decision of the leading men? Are you actually going to make yourselves guilty of such an absurdity? You may, of course, if you wish, for every citizen is free to do as he pleases. But the men of influence are also at liberty to do as they please. I will explain my meaning more fully. You, gentlemen, are, all of you, mechanics--shoemakers, tailors, blacksmiths, carpenters, etc. From whom do you get your living? Do you get it from the handful of hypocrites and men of darkness? No; you get your living from the liberals, for they are the moneyed men, the men of power and authority. It is they who scatter money among the people. You obtain employment, you get bread and meat, from the liberals. And now to whom, do you think, will the liberals give employment? They will give it to such as hold their views, and not--mark my word--to such as are opposed to them. The man, therefore, that is prepared recklessly to ruin his business has only to vote against Mr. Shund."

"That will do the business, that will fetch them," said Greifmann. "Just look how dumfounded the poor savages appear!"

"It is brutal terrorism!" protested Seraphin indignantly.

"But don't misunderstand me. Mr. Spitzkopf! I am neither a hypocritical devotee nor a Jesuit!" exclaimed the coppersmith deprecatingly. "If Shund is good enough for them," pointing to the leaders under the rotunda, "he is good enough for me."

"For me, too!" exclaimed a tailor.

"There isn't a worthier man than Shund," declared a shopkeeper.

"And not a cleverer," said a carpenter.

"And none more demoralized," lauded a joiner, unconscious of the import of his encomium.

"That's so, and therefore I am satisfied with him," assured a shoemaker.

"So am I--so am I," chorussed the others eagerly.

"That is sensible, gentlemen," approved the bald man. "Just keep in harmony with liberalism and progress, and you will never be the worse for it, gentlemen. Above all, beware of reaction--do not fall back into the immoral morasses of the middle ages. Let us guard the light and liberty of our beautiful age. Vote for these men," and he produced a package of printed tickets, "and you will enjoy the delightful consciousness of having disposed of your vote in the interests of the common good."

Spitzkopf distributed the tickets on which were the names of the councilmen elect. At the head of the list appeared in large characters the name of Mr. Hans Shund.

"The curtain falls, the farce is ended," said Greifmann. "What you have here heard and seen has been repeated at every table where 'wild men' chanced to make their appearance. Everywhere the same arguments, the same grounds of conviction."

Seraphin had become quite grave, and cast his eyes to the ground in silence.

"By Jove, the rogue is going to try his hand on us!" said Carl, nudging the thoughtful young man. "The bald-headed fellow has spied us, and is getting ready to bag a couple of what he takes to be 'wild men.' Come, let us be off."

They left the beer cellar and took the direction of the city.

"Now let us descend a little lower, to what I might call the amphibia of society," said Greifmann. "We are going to visit a place where masons, sawyers, cobblers, laborers, and other small fry are in the habit of slaking their thirst. You will there find going on the same sort of electioneering, or, as you call it, the same sort of terrorism, only in a rougher style. There beer-jugs occasionally go flying about, and bloody heads and rough-and-tumble, fights may be witnessed."

"I have no stomach for fisticuffs and whizzing beer-mugs," said Gerlach.

"Never mind, come along. I have undertaken to initiate you into the mysteries of elections, and you are to get a correct idea of the life action of a cultivated state."

They entered an obscure alley where a fetid, sultry atmosphere assailed them. Greifmann stopped before a lofty house, and pointed to a transparency on which a brimming beer-tankard was represented. A wild tumult was audible through the windows, through which the cry of "Shund!" rose at times like the swell of a great wave from the midst of corrupted waters. As they were passing the doorway a dense fog of tobacco smoke mingled with divers filthy odors assailed their nostrils. Seraphin, who was accustomed to inhaling the pure atmosphere of the country, showed an inclination to retreat, and had already half-way faced about when his companion seized and held him. "Courage, my friend! wade into the slough boldly," cried he into the struggling youth's ear. "Hereafter, when you will be riding through woodland and meadows, the recollection of this subterranean den will enable you to appreciate the pure atmosphere of the country twice as well. Look at those sodden faces and swollen heads. Those fellows are literally wallowing and seething in beer, and they feel as comfortable as ten thousand cannibals. It is really a joy to be among men who are natural."

The millionaires, having with no little difficulty succeeded in finding seats, were accosted by a female waiter.

"Do the gentlemen wish to have election beer?"

"No," replied Gerlach.

His abrupt tone in declining excited the surprise of the fellows who sat next to them. Several of them stared at the landholder.

"So you don't want any election beer?" cried a fellow who was pretty well fired.

"Why not? May be it isn't good enough for you?"

"Oh, yes! oh, yes!" replied the banker hastily. "You see, Mr. Shund"--

"That's good! You call me Shund," interrupted the fellow with a coarse laugh. "My name isn't Shund--my name is Koenig--yes, Koenig--with all due respect to you."

"Well, Mr. Koenig--you see, Mr. Koenig, we decline drinking election beer because we are not entitled to it--we do not belong to this place."

"Ah, yes--well, that's honest!" lauded Koenig. "Being that you are a couple of honest fellows, you must partake of some of the good things of our feast. I say, Kate," cried he to the female waiter, "bring these gentlemen some of the election sausages."

Greifmann, perceiving that Seraphin was about putting in a protest, nudged him.

"What feast are you celebrating to-day?" inquired the banker.

"That I will explain to you. We are to have an election here to-morrow; these men on the ticket, you see, are to be elected." And he drew forth one of Spitzkopf's tickets. "Every one of us has received a ticket like this, and we are all going to vote according to the ticket--of course, you know, we don't do it for nothing. To-day and to-morrow, what we eat and drink is free of charge. And if Satan's own grandmother were on the ticket, I would vote for her."

"The first one on the list is Mr. Hans Shund. What sort of a man is he?" asked Seraphin. "No doubt he is the most honorable and most respectable man in the place!"

"Ha! ha! that's funny! The most honorable man in the place! Really you make me laugh. Never mind, however, I don't mean to be impolite. You are a stranger hereabout, and cannot, of course, be expected to know anything of it. Shund, you see, was formerly--that, is a couple of days ago--Shund was a man of whom nobody knew any good. For my part, I wouldn't just like to be sticking in Shund's hide. Well, that's the way things are: you know it won't do to babble it all just as it is. But you understand me. To make a long story short, since day before yesterday Shund is the honestest man in the world. Our men of money have made him that, you know," giving a sly wink. "What the men of money do, is well done, of course, for the proverb says, 'Whose bread I eat, his song I sing.'"

"Shut your mouth, Koenig! What stuff is that you are talking there?" said another fellow roughly. "Hans Shund is a free-spirited, clever, first-class, distinguished man. Taken altogether, he is a liberal man. For this reason he will be elected councilman to-morrow, then mayor of the city, and finally member of the assembly."

"That's so, that's so, my partner is right," confirmed Koenig. "But listen, Flachsen, you will agree that formerly--you know, formerly--he was an arrant scoundrel."

"Why was he? Why?" inquired Flachsen.

"Why? Ha, ha! I say, Flachsen, go to Shund's wife, she can tell you best. Go to those whom he has reduced to beggary, for instance, to Holt over there. They all can tell you what Shund is, or rather what he has been. But don't get mad, brother Flachsen! Spite of all that, I shall vote for Shund. That's settled." And he poured the contents of his beer-pot down his throat.

"As you gentlemen are strangers, I will undertake to explain this business for you," said Flachsen, who evidently was an agent for the lower classes, and who did his best to put on an appearance of learning by affecting high-sounding words of foreign origin.

"Shund is quite a rational man, learned and full of intelligence. But the priests have calumniated him horribly because he will not howl with them. For this reason we intend to elect him, not for the sake of the free beer. When Shund will have been elected, a system of economy will be inaugurated, taxes will be removed, and the encyclical letter with which the Pope has tried to stultify the people, together with the syllabus, will be sent to the dogs. And in the legislative assembly the liberal-minded Shund will manage to have the priests excluded from the schools, and we will have none but secular schools. In short, the dismal rule of the priesthood that would like to keep the people in leading-strings will be put an end to, and liberal views will control our affairs. As for Shund's doings outside of legitimate wedlock, that is one of the boons of liberty--it is a right of humanity; and when Koenig lets loose against Shund's money speculations, he is only talking so much bigoted nonsense."

Flachsen's apologetic discourse was interrupted by a row that took place at the next table. There sat a victim of Shund's usury, the land-cultivator Holt. He drank no beer, but wine, to dispel gloomy thoughts and the temptations of desperation. It had cost him no ordinary struggle to listen quietly to eulogies passed on Shund. He had maintained silence, and had at times smiled a very peculiar smile. His bruised heart must have suffered a fearful contraction as he heard men sounding the praises of a wretch whom he knew to be wicked and devoid of conscience. For a long time he succeeded in restraining himself. But the wine he had drunk at last fanned his smouldering passion into a hot flame of rage, and, clenching his fist, he struck the table violently.

"The fellow whom you extol is a scoundrel!" cried he.

"Who is a scoundrel?" roared several voices.

"Your man, your councilman, your mayor, is a scoundrel! Shund is a scoundrel!" cried the ruined countryman passionately.

"And you, Holt, are a fool!"

"You are drunk, Holt!"

"Holt is an ass," maintained Flachsen. "He cannot read, otherwise he would have seen in the *Evening Gazette* that Shund is a man of honor, a friend of the people, a progressive man, a liberal man, a brilliant genius, a despiser of religion, a death-dealer to superstition, a--a--I don't remember what all besides. Had you read all that in the evening paper, you fool, you wouldn't presume to open your foul mouth against a man of honor like

Hans Shund. Yes, stare; if you had read the evening paper, you would have seen the enumeration of the great qualities and deeds of Hans Shund in black and white."

"The evening paper, indeed!" cried Holt contemptuously. "Does the evening paper also mention how Shund brought about the ruin of the father of a family of eight children?"

"What's that you say, you dog?" yelled a furious fellow. "That's a lie against Shund!"

"Easy, Graeulich, easy," replied Holt to the last speaker, who was about to set upon him. "It is not a lie, for I am the man whom Shund has strangled with his usurer's clutches. He has reduced me to beggary--me and my wife and my children."

Graeulich lowered his fists, for Holt spoke so convincingly, and the anguish in his face appealed so touchingly, that the man's fury was in an instant changed to sympathy. Holt had stood up. He related at length the wily and unscrupulous proceedings through which he had been brought to ruin. The company listened to his story, many nodded in token of sympathy, for everybody was acquainted with the ways of the hero of the day.

"That's the way Shund has made a beggar of me," concluded Holt. "And I am not the only one, you know it well. If, then, I call Shund a usurer, a scoundrel, a villain, you cannot help agreeing with me."

Flachsen noticed with alarm that the feeling of the company was becoming hostile to his cause. He approached the table, where he was met by perplexed looks from his aids.

"Don't you perceive," cried he, "that Holt is a hireling of the priests? Will you permit yourselves to be imposed upon by this salaried slave? Hear me, you scapegrace, you rascal, you ass, listen to what I have to tell you! Hans Shund is the lion of the day--the greatest man of this century! Hans Shund is greater than Bismarck, sharper than Napoleon. Out of nothing God made the universe: from nothing Hans Shund has got to be a rich man. Shund has a mouthpiece that moves like a mill-wheel on which entire streams fall. In the assembly Shund will talk down all opposition. He will talk even better than that fellow Voelk, over in Bavaria, who is merely a lawyer, but talks upon everything, even things he knows nothing about. And do you, lousy beggar, presume to malign a man of this kind? If you open that filthy mouth of yours once more, I will stop it for you with paving-stones."

"Hold, Flachsen, hold! *I* am not the man that is paid; you are the one that is paid," retorted the countryman indignantly. "My mouth has not been honey-fed like yours. Nor do I drink your election beer or eat your election sausages. But with my last breath I will maintain that Shund is a scoundrel, a usurer, a villain."

"Out with the fellow!" cried Flachsen. "He has insulted us all, for we have all been drinking election beer. Out with the helot of the priests!"

The progressionist mob fell upon the unhappy man, throttled him, beat him, and drove him into the street.

"Let us leave this den of cutthroats," said Gerlach, rising.

Outside they found Holt leaning against a wall, wiping the blood from his face. Seraphin approached him. "Are you badly hurt, my good man?" asked he kindly. The wounded man, looking up, saw a noble countenance before him, and, whilst he continued to gaze hard at Seraphin's fine features, tears began to roll from his eyes.

"O God! O God!" sighed he, and then relapsed into silence. But in the tone of his words could be noticed the terrible agony he was suffering.

"Is the wound deep--is it dangerous?" asked the young man.

"No, sir, no! The wound on my forehead is nothing--signifies nothing; but in here," pointing to his breast--"in here are care, anxiety, despair. I am thankful, sir, for your sympathy; it is soothing. But you may go your way; the blows signify nothing."

CHAPTER V

Gerlach whispered something to the banker. Holt pressed his pocket-handkerchief to the wound.

"Please yourself!" said the banker loudly, in a business tone. Seraphin again approached the beaten man.

"Will you please, my good man, to accompany us?"

"What for, sir?"

"Because I would like to do something towards healing up your wound; I mean the wound in there."

Holt stood motionless before the stranger, and looked at him.

"I thank you, sir; there is no remedy for me; I am doomed!"

"Still, I will assist you. Follow me."

"Who are you, sir, if I may ask the question?"

"I am a man whom Providence seems to have chosen to rescue the prey from the jaws of a usurer. Come along with us, and fear nothing."

"Very well, I will go in the name of God! I do not precisely know your object, and you are a stranger to me. But your countenance looks innocent and kind, therefore I will go with you."

They passed through alleys and streets.

"Do you often visit that tavern?" inquired Seraphin.

"Not six times in a year," answered Holt. "Sometimes of a Sunday I drink half a glass of wine, that's all. I am poor, and have to be saving. I would not have gone to the tavern to-day but that I wanted to get rid of my feelings of misery."

"I overheard your story," rejoined Seraphin. "Shund's treatment of you was inhuman. He behaved towards you like a trickish devil."

"That he did! And I am ruined together with my family," replied the poor man dejectedly.

"Take my advice, and never abuse Shund. You know how respectable he has suddenly got to be, how many influential friends he has. You can easily perceive that one cannot say anything unfavorable of such a man without great risk, no matter were it true ten times over."

"I am not given to disputing," replied Holt. "But it stirred the bile within me to hear him extolled, and it broke out. Oh! I have learned to suffer in silence. I haven't time to think of other matters. After God, my business and my family were my only care. I attended to my occupation faithfully and quietly as long as I had any to attend to, but now I haven't any to take care of. O God! it is hard. It will bring me to the grave."

"You are a land cultivator?"

"Yes, sir."

"Shund intends to have you sold out?"

"Yes; immediately after the election he intends to complete my ruin."

"How much money would you need in order with industry to get along?"

"A great deal of money, a great deal--at least a thousand florins. I have given him a mortgage for a thousand florins on my house and what was left to me. A thousand florins would suffice to help me out of trouble. I might save my little cottage, my two cows, and a field. I might then plough and sow for other people. I could get along and subsist honestly. But as I told you, nothing less than a thousand florins would do; and where am I to get so much money? You see there is no hope for me, no help for me. I am doomed!"

"The mortgaged property is considerable," said Gerlach. "A house, even though a small one, moreover, a field, a barn, a garden, all these together are surely worth a much higher price. Could you not borrow a thousand florins on it and pay off the usurer?"

"No, sir. Nobody would be willing to lend me that amount of money upon property mortgaged to a man like Shund. Besides, my little property is out of town, and who wants to go there? I, for my part, of course, like no spot as much, for it is the house my father built, and I was born and brought up there."

The man lapsed into silence, and walked at Seraphin's side like one weighed down by a heavy load. The delicate sympathy of the young man enabled him to guess what was passing in the breast of the man under the load. He knew that Holt was recalling his childhood passed under the paternal roof; that little spot of home was hallowed for him by events connected with his mother, his father, his brothers and sisters, or with other objects more trifling, which, however, remained fresh and bright in memory, like balmy days of spring.

From this consecrated spot he was to be exiled, driven out with wife and children, through the inhumanity and despicable cunning of an usurer. The man heaved a deep sigh, and Gerlach, watching him sidewise, noticed his lips were compressed, and that large tears rolled down his weather-browned cheeks. The tender heart of the young man was deeply affected at this sight, and the millionaire for once rejoiced in the consciousness of possessing the might of money.

They halted before the Palais Greifmann. Holt noticed with surprise how the man in blouse drew from his waistcoat pocket a small instrument resembling a toothpick, and with it opened a door near the carriage gate. Had not every shadow of suspicion been driven from Holt's mind by Seraphin's appearance, he would surely have believed that he had fallen into the company of burglars, who entrapped him to aid in breaking into this palace.

Reluctantly, after repeated encouragement from Gerlach, he crossed the threshold of the stately mansion. He had not quite passed the door when he took off his cap, stared at the costly furniture of the hall through which they were passing, and was reminded of St. Peter's thought as the angel was rescuing him from the clutches of Herod. Holt imagined he saw a vision. The man who had unlocked the door disappeared. Seraphin entered an apartment followed by Shund's victim.

"Do you know where you are?" inquired the millionaire.

"Yes, sir, in the house of Mr. Greifmann the banker."

"And you are somewhat surprised, are you not?"

"I am so much astonished, sir, that I have several times pinched my arms and legs, for it all seems to me like a dream."

Seraphin smiled and laid aside his cap. Holt scanned the noble features of the young man more minutely, his handsome face, his stately bearing, and concluded the man in the blouse must be some distinguished gentleman.

"Take courage," said the noble looking young man in a kindly tone. "You shall be assisted. I am convinced that you are an honest, industrious man, brought to the verge of ruin through no fault of your own. Nor do I blame you for inadvertently falling into the nets of the usurer, for I believe your honest nature never suspected that there could exist so fiendish a monster as the one that lives in the soul of an usurer."

"You may rely upon it, sir. If I had had the slightest suspicion of such a thing, Shund never would have got me into his clutches."

"I am convinced of it. You are partially the victim of your own good nature, and partially the prey of the wild beast Shund. Now listen to me: Suppose somebody were to give you a thousand florins, and to say: 'Holt, take this money, 'tis yours. Be industrious, get along, be a prudent housekeeper, serve God to the end of your days, and in future beware of usurers'--suppose somebody were to address you in this way, what would you do?"

"Supposing the case, sir, although it is not possible, but supposing the case, what would I do? I would do precisely what that person would have told me, and a great deal more. I would work day and night. Every day, at evening prayer, I would get on my knees with my wife and children, and invoke God's protection on that person. I would do that, sir; but, as I said, the case is impossible."

"Nevertheless, suppose it did happen," explained Seraphin in a preliminary way. "Give me your hand that you will fulfil the promise you have just given."

For a moment Seraphin's hand lay in a callous, iron palm, which pressed his soft fingers in an uncomfortable but well-meant grasp.

"Well, now follow me," said Gerlach.

He led the way; Holt followed with an unsteady step like a drunken man. They presented themselves before the banker's counter. The latter was standing behind the trellis of his desk, and on a table lay ten rolls of money.

"You have just now by word and hand confirmed a promise," said Gerlach, turning to the countryman, "which cannot be appreciated in money, for that promise comprises almost all the duties of the father of a family. But to make the fulfilment of the promise possible, a thousand florins are needed. Here lies the money. Accept it from me as a gift, and be happy."

Holt did not stir. He looked from the money at Gerlach, was motionless and rigid, until, at last, the paralyzing surprise began to resolve itself into a spasmodic quivering of the lips, and then into a mighty flood of tears. Seizing Seraphin's hands, he kissed them with an emotion that convulsed his whole being.

"That will do now," said the millionaire, "take the money, and go home."

"My God! I cannot find utterance," said Holt, stammering forth the words with difficulty. "Good heaven! is it possible? Is it true? I am still thinking 'tis only a dream."

"Downright reality, my man!" said the banker. "Stop crying; save your tears for a more fitting occasion. Put the rolls in your pocket, and go home."

Greifmann's coldness was effective in sobering down the man intoxicated with joy.

"May I ask, sir, what your name is, that I may at least know to whom I owe my rescue?"

"Seraphin is my name."

"Your name sounds like an angel's, and you are an angel to me. I am not acquainted with you, but God knows you, and he will requite you according to your deeds."

Gerlach nodded gravely. The banker was impatient and murmured discontentedly. Holt carefully pocketed the rolls of money, made an inclination of gratitude to Gerlach, and went out. He passed slowly through the hall. The porter opened the door. Holt stood still before him.

"I ask your pardon, but do you know Mr. Seraphin?" asked he.

"Why shouldn't I know a gentleman that has been our guest for the last two weeks?"

"You must pardon my presumption, Mr. Porter. Will Mr. Seraphin remain here much longer?"

"He will remain another week for certain."

"I am very much obliged to you," said Holt, passing into the street and hurrying away.

"Your intended has a queer way of applying his money," said the banker to his sister the next morning. And he reported to her the story of Seraphin's munificence. "I do not exactly like this sort of kindness, for it oversteps all bounds, and undoubtedly results from religious enthusiasm."

"That, too, can be cured," replied Louise confidently. "I will make him understand that eternity restores nothing, that consequently it is safer and more prudent to exact interest from the present."

"'Tis true, the situation of that fellow Holt was a pitiable one, and Hans Shund's treatment of him was a masterpiece of speculation. He had stripped the fellow completely. The stupid Holt had for years been laboring for the cunning Shund, who continued drawing his meshes more and more tightly about him. Like a huge spider, he leisurely sucked out the life of the fly he had entrapped."

"Your hostler says there was light in Seraphin's room long after midnight. I wonder what hindered him from sleeping?"

"That is not hard to divine. In all probability he was composing a sentimental ditty to his much adored," answered Carl teasingly. "Midnight is said to be a propitious time for occupations of that sort."

"Do be quiet, you tease! But I too was thinking that he must have been engaged in writing. May be he was making a memorandum of yesterday's experience in his journal."

"May be he was. At all events, the impressions made on him were very strong."

"But I do not like your venture; it may turn out disastrous,"

"How can it, my most learned sister?"

"You know Seraphin's position," explained she. "He has been reared in the rigor of sectarian credulity. The spirit of modern civilization being thus abruptly placed before his one-sided judgment without previous preparation may alarm, nay, may even disgust him. And when once he will have perceived that the brother is a partisan of the horrible monster, is it probable that he will feel favorably disposed towards the sister whose views harmonize with those of her brother?"

"I have done nothing to justify him in setting me down for a partisan. I maintain strict neutrality. My purpose is to accustom the weakling to the atmosphere of enlightenment which is fatal to all religious phantasms. Have no fear of his growing cold towards you," proceeded he in his customary tone of irony. "Your ever victorious power holds him spell-bound in the magic circle of your enchantment. Besides, Louise," continued he frowning, "I do not think I could tolerate a brother-in-law steeped over head and ears in prejudices. You yourself might find it highly uncomfortable to live with a husband of this kind."

"Uncomfortable! No, I would not. I would find it exciting, for it would become my task to train and cultivate an abnormal specimen of the male gender."

"Very praiseworthy, sister! And if I now endeavor by means of living illustrations to familiarize your intended with the nature of modern intellectual enlightenment, I am merely preparing the way for your future labors."

CHAPTER VI
MASTERS AND SLAVES

Under the much despised discipline of religious requirements, the child Seraphin had grown up to boyhood spotless in morals, and then had developed himself into a young man of great firmness of character, whose faith was as unshaken as the correctness of his behavior was constant.

The bloom of his cheeks, the innocent brightness of his eye, the suavity of his disposition, were the natural results of the training which his heart had received. No foul passion had ever disturbed the serenity of his soul. When under the smiling sky of a spring morning he took his ride over the extensive possessions of his father, his interior accorded perfectly with the peace and loveliness of the sights and sounds of blooming nature around him. On earth, however, no spring, be it ever so beautiful, is entirely safe from storms. Evil spirits lie in waiting in the air, dark powers threaten destruction to all blossoms and all incipient life. And the more inevitable is the dread might of those lurking spirits, that in every blossom of living plant lies concealed a germ of ruin, sleeps a treacherous passion--even in the heart of the innocent Seraphin.

The strategic arts of the beautiful young lady received no small degree of additional power from the genuine effort made by her to please the stately double millionaire. In a short time she was to such an extent successful that one day Carl rallied her in the following humorous strain: "Your intended is sitting in the arbor singing a most dismal song! You will have to allow him a little more line, Louise, else you run the risk of unsettling his brain. Moreover, I cannot be expected to instruct a man in the mysteries of progress, if he sees, feels, and thinks nothing but Louise."

The banker had not uttered an exaggeration. It sometimes happens that a first love bursts forth with an impetuosity so uncontrollable, that, for a time, every other domain of the intellectual and moral nature of a young man is, as it were, submerged under a mighty flood. This temporary inundation of passion cannot, of course, maintain its high tide in presence of calm experience, and the sunshine of more ripened knowledge soon dries up its waters. But Seraphin possessed only the scanty experience of a young man, and his knowledge of the world was also very limited.

Hence, in his case, the stream rose alarmingly high, but it did not reach an overflow, for the hand of a pious mother had thrown up in the heart of the child a living dike strong enough to resist the greatest violence of the swell. The height and solidity of the dike increased with the growth of the child; it was a bulwark of defence for the man, who stood secure against humiliating defeats behind the adamantine wall of religious principles--yet only so long as life sought protection behind this bulwark. Faith uttered a serious warning against an unconditional surrender of himself to the object of his attachment. For he could not put to rest some misgivings raised in his mind by the strange and, to him, inexplicable attitude which Louise assumed upon the highest questions of human existence. The uninitiated youth had no suspicion of the existence of that most disgusting product of modern enlightenment, the *emancipated* female. Had he discovered in Louise the emancipated woman in all the ugliness of her real nature, he would have conceived unutterable loathing for such a monstrosity. And yet he could not but feel that between himself and Louise there yawned an abyss, there existed an essential repulsion, which, at times, gave rise within him to considerable uneasiness.

To obtain a solution of the enigma of this antipathy, the young gentleman concluded to trust entirely to the results of his observations, which, however, were far from being definitive; for his reason was imposed upon by his feelings, and, from day to day, the charms of the beautiful woman were steadily progressing in throwing a seductive spell over his judgment. The banker's daughter possessed a high degree of culture; she was a perfect mistress of the tactics employed on the field of coquetry; her tact was exquisite; and she understood thoroughly how to take advantage of a kindly disposition and of the tenderness inspired by passion. How was the eye of Seraphin, strengthened neither by knowledge nor by experience, to detect the true worth of what lay hidden beneath this fascinating delusion?

Here again his religious training came to the rescue of the inexperienced youth, by furnishing him with standards safe and unfalsified, by which to weigh and come to a conclusion.

Louise's indifference to practices of piety annoyed him. She never attended divine service, not even on Sundays. He never saw her with a prayer-book, nor was a single picture illustrative of a moral subject to be found hung up in her apartment. Her conversation, at all times, ran upon commonplaces of everyday concern, such as the toilet, theatre, society. He noticed that whenever he ventured to launch matter of a more serious import upon the current of conversation, it immediately became constrained and soon ceased to flow. Louise appeared to his heart at the same time so fascinating and yet so peculiar, so seductive and yet so repulsive, that the contradictions of her being caused him to feel quite unhappy.

He was again sitting in his room thinking about her. In the interview he had just had with her, the young lady had exerted such admirable powers of womanly charms that the poor young man had had a great deal of trouble to maintain his self-possession. Her ringing, mischievous laugh was still sounding in his ears, and the brightness of her sparkling, eyes was still lighting up his memory. And the unsuspecting youth had no Solomon at his side to repeat to him: "My son, can a man hide fire in his bosom, and his garments not burn? Or can he walk upon hot coals, and his feet not be burnt?... She entangleth him with many words, and she draweth him away with the flattery of her lips. Immediately he followeth her as an ox led to be a victim, and as a lamb playing the wanton, and not knowing that he is drawn like a fool to bonds, till the arrow pierce his liver. As if a bird should make haste to the snare, and knoweth not that his life is in danger. Now, therefore, my son, hear me, and attend to the words of my mouth. Let not thy mind be drawn away in her ways: neither be thou deceived with her paths. For she hath cast down many wounded, and the strongest have been slain by her. Her house is the way to hell, reaching even to the inner chambers of death."[1]

For Seraphin, however, no Solomon was at hand who might give him counsel. Sustained by his virtue and by his faith alone, he struggled against the temptress, not precisely of the kind referred to by Solomon, but still a dangerous one from the ranks of progress.

Greifmann had notified him that the general assembly election was to be held that day, that Mayor Hans Shund would certainly be returned as a delegate, and that he intended to call for Gerlach, and go out to watch the progress of the election.

Seraphin felt rather indifferent respecting the election; but he would have considered himself under weighty obligation to the brother for an explanation of the peculiar behavior of the sister at which he was so greatly perplexed.

Carl himself he had for a while regarded as an enigma. Now, however, he believed that he had reached a correct conclusion concerning the brother. It appeared to him that the principal characteristic of Carl's disposition was to treat every subject, except what strictly pertained to business, in a spirit of levity. To the faults of others Carl was always ready to accord a praiseworthy degree of indulgence, he never uttered harsh words in a tone of bitterness, and when he pronounced censure, his reproof was invariably clothed in some form of pleasantry. In general, he behaved like a man not having time to occupy himself seriously with any subject that did not lie within the particular sphere of his occupation. Even their wager he managed like a matter of business, although the landowner could not but take umbrage at the banker's ready and natural way of dealing with men whose want of principle he himself abominated. Greifmann seemed good-natured, minute, and cautious in business, and in all other things exceedingly liberal and full of levity. Such was the judgment arrived at by Seraphin, inexperienced and little inclined to fault-finding as he was, respecting a gentleman who stood at the summit of modern culture, who had skill in elegantly cloaking great faults and foibles, and whose sole religion consisted in the accumulation of papers and coins of arbitrary value.

Gerlach's servant entered, and disturbed his meditation.

"There is a man here with a family who begs hard to be allowed to speak with you."

"A man with a family!" repeated the millionaire, astonished. "I know nobody round here, and have no desire to form acquaintances."

"The man will not be denied. He says his name is Holt, and that he has something to say to you."

"Ah, yes!" exclaimed Seraphin, with a smile that revealed a pleasant surprise. "Send the man and those who are with him in to me."

Closing a diary, in which he was recording circumstantially the experiences of his present visit, he awaited the visitors. A loud knock from a weighty fist reminded him of a pair of callous hands, then Holt, followed by his wife and children, presented himself before his benefactor. They all made a small courtesy, even the flaxen-headed little children, and the bright, healthy babe in the arms of the mother met his gaze with the smile of an angel. The dark spirits that were hovering around him, torturing and tempting, instantly vanished, and he became serene and unconstrained whilst conversing with these simple people.

"You must excuse us, Mr. Seraphin," began Holt. "This is my wife, and these are seven of my children. There is one more; her name is Mechtild. She had to stay at home and mind the house. She will pay you an extra visit, and present her thanks. We have called that you might become acquainted with the family whom you have rescued, and that we might thank you with all our hearts."

After this speech, the father gave a signal, whereupon the little ones gathered around the amiable young man, made their courtesies, and kissed his hands.

"May God bless you, Mr. Seraphin!" first spoke a half-grown girl.

"We greet you, dear Seraphin!" said another, five years old.

"We pray for you every day, Mr. Seraphin," said the next in succession.

"We are thankful to you from our hearts, Mr. Seraphin," spoke a small lad, in a tone of deep earnestness.

And thus did every child deliver its little address. It was touching to witness the noble dignity of the children, which may, at times, be found beautifully investing their innocence. Gerlach was moved. He looked down upon the little ones around him with an expression of affectionate thankfulness. Holt's lips also quivered, and bright tears of happiness streamed from the eyes of the mother.

"I am obliged to you, my little friends, for your greetings and for your prayers," spoke the millionaire. "You are well brought up. Continue always to be good children, such as you now are; have the fear of God, and honor your parents."

"Mr. Seraphin," said Holt, drawing a paper from his pocket, "here is the note that I have redeemed with the money you gave me. I wanted to show it to you, so that you might know for certain that the money had been applied to the proper purpose."

Gerlach affected to take an interest in the paper, and read over the receipt.

"But there is one thing, Mr. Seraphin," continued Holt, "that grieves me. And that is, that there is not anything better than mere words with which I can testify my gratitude to you. I would like ever so much to do something for you--to do something for you worth speaking of. Do you know, Mr. Seraphin, I would be willing to shed the last drop of my blood for you?"

"Never mind that, Holt! It is ample recompense for me to know that I have helped a worthy man out of trouble. You can now, Mrs. Holt, set to work with renewed courage. But," added he archly, "you will have to watch your husband that he may not again fall into the clutches of beasts of prey like Shund."

"He has had to pay dearly for his experience, Mr. Seraphin. I used often to say to him: 'Michael, don't trust Shund. Shund talks too much, he is too sweet altogether, he has some wicked design upon us--don't trust him.' But, you see, Mr. Seraphin, my husband thinks that all people are as upright as he is himself, and he believed that Shund really meant to deal fairly as he pretended. But Michael's wits are sharpened now, and he will not in future be so ready to believe every man upon his word. Nor will he, hereafter, borrow one single penny, and he will never again undertake to buy anything unless he has the money in hand to pay for it."

"In what street do you live?" inquired Gerlach.

"Near the turnpike road, Mr. Seraphin. Do you see that knoll?" He pointed through the window in a direction unobstructed by the trees of the garden. "Do you see that dense shade-tree, and yon whitewashed wall behind the tree? That is our walnut-tree--my grandfather planted it. And the white wall is the wall of our house."

"I have passed there twice--the road leads to the beech grove," said the millionaire. "I remarked the little cottage, and was much pleased with its air of neatness. It struck me, too, that the barn is larger than the dwelling, which is a creditable sign for a farmer. Near the front entrance there is a carefully cultivated flower garden, in which I particularly admired the roses, and further off from the road lies an apple orchard."

"All that belongs to us. That is what you have rescued and made a present of to us," replied the land cultivator joyfully. "Everybody stops to view the roses; they belong to our daughter Mechtild."

"The soil is good and deep, and must bring splendid crops of wheat. I, too, am a farmer, and understand something about such matters. But it appeared to me as though the soil were of a cold nature. You should use lime upon it pretty freely."

In this manner he spent some time conversing with these good and simple people. Before dismissing them, he made a present to every one of the children of a shining dollar, having previously overcome Holt's protest against this new instance generosity.

Old and young then courtesied once more, and Gerlach was left to himself in a mood differing greatly from that in which the visitors had found him.

He had been conversing with good and happy people, and revelled in the consciousness of having been the originator of their happiness.

Suddenly Greifmann's appearance in the room put to flight the bright spirits that hovered about him, and the sunshine that had been lighting up the apartment was obscured by dark shadows as of a heavy mass of clouds.

"What sort of a horde was that?" asked he.

"They were Holt and his family. The gratitude of these simple people was touching. The innocent little ones gave me an ovation of which a prince might be envious, for the courts of princes are never graced by a naturalness at once so sincere and so beautiful. It is an intense happiness for me to have assured the livelihood of ten human beings with so paltry a gift."

"A mere matter of taste, my most sympathetic friend!" rejoined the banker with indifference. "You are not made of the proper stuff to be a business man. Your feelings would easily tempt you into very unbusinesslike transactions. But you must come with me! The hubbub of the election is astir through all the streets and thoroughfares. I am going out to discharge my duties as a citizen, and I want you to accompany me."

"I have no inclination to see any of this disgusting turmoil," replied Gerlach.

"Inclination or disinclination is out of the question when interest demands it," insisted the banker. "You must profit by the opportunity which you now have of enriching your knowledge of men and things, or rather of correcting it; for heretofore your manner of viewing things has been mere ideal enthusiasm. Come with me, my good fellow!"

Seraphin followed with interior reluctance. Greifmann went on to impart to him the following information:

"During the past night, there have sprung up, as if out of the earth, a most formidable host, ready to do battle against the uniformly victorious army of progress--men thoroughly armed and accoutred, real crusaders. A bloody struggle is imminent. Try and make of your heart a sort of monitor covered with plates of iron, so that you may not be overpowered by the horrifying spectacle of the election affray. I am not joking at all! True as gospel, what I tell you! If you do not want to be stifled by indignation at sight of the fiercest kind of terrorism, of the most revolting tyranny, you will have to lay aside, at least for to-day, every feeling of humanity."

Gerlach perceived a degree of seriousness in the bubbling current of Greifmann's levity.

"Who is the enemy that presumes to stand in the way of progress?" enquired he.

"The ultramontanes! Listen to what I have to tell you. This morning Schwefel came in to get a check cashed. With surprise I observed that the manufacturer's soul was not in business? 'How are things going?' asked I when we had got through.

"'I feel like a man,' exclaimed he, 'that has just seen a horrible monster! Would you believe it, those accursed ultramontanes have been secretly meddling in the election. They have mustered a number of votes, and have even gone so far as to have a yellow ticket printed. Their yellow placards were to be seen this morning stuck up at every street corner--of course they were immediately torn down.'

"'And are you provoked at that, Mr. Schwefel! You certainly are not going to deny the poor ultramontanes the liberty of existing, or, at least, the liberty of voting for whom they please?'

"'Yes, I am, I am! That must not be tolerated,' cried he wildly. 'The black brood are hatching dark schemes, they are conspiring against civilization, and would fain wrest from us the trophies won by progress. It is high time to apply the axe to the root of the upas-tree. Our duty is to disinfect thoroughly, to banish the absurdities of religious dogma from our schools. The black spawn will have to be rendered harmless: we must kill them politically.'

"'Very well,' said I. 'Just make negroes of them. Now that in America the slaves are emancipated, Europe would perhaps do well to take her turn at the slave-trade.' But the fellow would not take my joke. He made threatening gesticulations, his eyes gleamed like hot coals, and he muttered words of a belligerent import.

"'The ultramontane rabble are to hold a meeting at the "Key of Heaven,"' reported he. 'There the stupid victims of credulity are to be harangued by several of their best talkers. The black tide is afterwards to diffuse itself through the various wards where the voting is to take place. But let the priest-ridden slaves come, they will have other memoranda to carry home with them beside their yellow rags of tickets.'

"You perceive, friend Seraphin, that the progress men mean mischief. We may expect to witness scenes of violence."

"That is unjustifiable brutality on the part of the progressionists," declared Gerlach indignantly. "Are not the ultramontanes entitled to vote and to receive votes? Are they not free citizens? Do they not enjoy the same privileges as others? It is a disgrace and an outrage thus to tyrannize over men who are their brothers, sons of Germania, their common mother."

"Granted! Violence is disgraceful. The intention of progress, however, is not quite as bad as you think it. Being convinced of its own infallibility, it cannot help feeling indignant at the unbelief of ultramontanism, which continues deaf to the saving truths of the progressionist gospel. Hence a holy zeal for making converts urges progress so irresistibly that it would fain force wanderers into the path of salvation by violence. This is simply human, and should not be regarded as unpardonable. In the self-same spirit did my namesake Charles the Great butcher the Saxons because the besotted heathens presumed to entertain convictions differing from his own. And those who were not butchered had to see their sacred groves cut down, their altars demolished, their time-honored laws changed, and had to resign themselves to following the ways which he thought fit to have opened through the land of the Saxons. You cannot fail to perceive that Charles the Great was a member of the school progress."

"But your comparison is defective," opposed the millionaire. "Charles subdued a wild and bloodthirsty horde who made it a practice to set upon and butcher peaceful neighbors. Charles was the protector of the realm, and the Saxons were forced to bend under the weight of his powerful arm. If Charles, however, did violence to the consciences of his vanquished enemies, and converted them to Christianity with the sword and mace, then Charles himself is not to be excused, for moral freedom is expressly proclaimed by the spirit of Christianity."

"There is no doubt but that the Saxons were blundering fools for rousing the lion by making inroads into Charles' domain. The ultramontanes, are, however, in a similar situation. They have attacked the giant Progress, and have themselves to blame for the consequences."

"The ultramontanes have attacked nobody," maintained Gerlach. "They are merely asserting their own rights, and are not putting restrictions on the rights of other people. But progress will concede neither rights nor freedom to others. It is a disgusting egotist, an unscrupulous tyrant, that tries to build up his own brutal authority on the ruins of the rights of others."

"Still, it would have been far more prudent on the part of the ultramontanes to keep quiet, seeing that their inferiority of numbers cannot alter the situation. The indisputable rights of the ascendency are in our days with the sceptre and crown of progress."

"A brave man never counts the foe," cried Gerlach. "He stands to his convictions, and behaves manfully in the struggle."

"Well said!" applauded the banker, "And since progress also is forced by the opposition of principles to man itself for the contest, it will naturally beat up all its forces in defence of its conviction. Here we are at the 'Key of Heaven,' where the ultramontanes are holding their meeting. Let us go in, for the proverb says, *Audiatur et altera pars*--the other side should also get a hearing."

They drew near to a lengthy old building. Over the doorway was a pair of crossed keys hewn out of stone, and gilt, informing the stranger that it was the hostelry of the "Key of Heaven," where, since the days of hoar antiquity, hospitality was dispensed to pilgrims and travellers. The principal hall of the house contained a gathering of about three hundred men. They were attentively listening to the words of a speaker who was warmly advocating the principles of his party. The speaker stood behind a desk which was placed upon a platform at the far end of the hall.

Seraphin cast a glance over the assembly. He received the painful impression of a hopeless minority. Barely forty votes would the ultramontanes be able to send to each of the wards. To compensate for numbers, intelligence and faith were represented in the meeting. Elegant gentlemen with intellectual countenances sat or stood in the company of respectable tradesmen, and the long black coats of the clergy were not few in number. On a table lay two packages of yellow tickets to be distributed among the members of the assembly. At the same table sat the chairman, a commissary of police named Parteiling, whose business it was to watch the proceedings, and several other gentlemen.

"Compared with the colossal preponderance of progress, our influence is insignificant, and, compared with the masses of our opponents our numerical strength is still less encouraging," said the speaker. "If in connection with this disheartening fact you take into consideration the pressure which progress has it in its power to exert on the various relations of life through numerous auxiliary means, if you remember that our opponents can dismiss from employment all such as dare uphold views differing from their own, it becomes clear that no ordinary amount of courage is required to entertain and proclaim convictions hostile to progress."

Seraphin thought of Spitzkopf's mode of electioneering, and of the terrible threats made to the "wild men," and concluded the incredible statement was lamentably correct.

"Viewing things in this light," proceeded the orator, "I congratulate the present assembly upon its unusual degree of pluck, for courage is required to go into battle with a clear knowledge of the overwhelming strength of the enemy. We have rallied round the banner of our convictions notwithstanding that the numbers of the enemy make victory hopeless. We are determined to cast our votes in support of religion and morality in defiance of the scorn, blasphemy, and violence which the well-known terrorism of progress will not fail to employ in order to frighten us from the exercise of our privilege as citizens. We must be prepared, gentlemen, to hear a multitude of sarcastic remarks and coarse witticisms, both in the streets and at the polls. I adjure you to maintain the deportment alone worthy of our cause. A gentleman never replies to the aggressions of rudeness, and should you wish to take the conduct of our opponents in gay good-humor, just try, gentlemen, to fancy that you are being treated to some elegant exhibition of the refinement and liberal culture of the times."

Loud bursts of hilarity now and then relieved the seriousness of the meeting. Even Greifmann would clap applause and cry, "Bravo!"

"Let us stand united to a man, prepared against all the wiles of intimidation and corruption, undismayed by the onset of the enemy. The struggle is grave beyond expression. For you are acquainted with the aims and purposes of the liberals. Progress would like to sweep away all the religious heritages that our fathers held sacred. Education is to be violently wrested from under the influence of the church; the church herself is to be enslaved and strangled in the thrall of the liberal state. I am aware that our opponents pretend to respect religion--but the religion of would-be progress is infidelity. Divine revelation, of which the church is the faithful guardian, is rejected with scorn by liberalism. Look at the tone of the press and the style of the literature of the day. You have only to notice the derision and fierceness with which the press daily assails the mysteries and dogmas of religion, the Sovereign Pontiff, the clergy, religious orders, the ultramontanes, and you cannot long remain in the dark concerning the aim and object of progress. Christ or Antichrist is the watchword of the day, gentlemen! Hence the imperative duty for us to be active at the elections; for the legislature has the presumption to wish to dictate in matters belonging exclusively to the jurisdiction of the church. We are threatened with school laws the purpose of which is to unchristianize our children, to estrange them from the spirit of religion. No man having the sentiment of religion can remain indifferent in presence of this danger, for it means nothing less than the defection from Christianity of the masses of the coming generation.

"Gentlemen, there is a reproach being uttered just now by the progressionist press, which, far from repelling, I would feel proud to deserve. A priest should have said, so goes the report, that it is a mortal sin to elect a progressionist to the chamber of deputies. Some of the writers of our press have met this reproach by simply denying that a priest ever expressed himself in those terms. But, gentlemen, let us take for granted that a priest did actually say that it is a mortal sin to elect a progressionist to the chamber of deputies, is there anything opposed to morality in such a declaration?

"By no means, if you remember that it is to be presumed the progressionist will use his vote in the assembly to oppose religion. Mortal sin, gentlemen, is any wilful transgression of God's law in grave matters. Now I put it to you: Does he gravely transgress the law of God who controverts what God has revealed, who would exclude God and all holy subjects from the schools, who would rob the church of her independence, and make of her a mere state machine unfit for the fulfilment of her high mission? There is not one of you but is ready to declare: 'Yes, such an one transgresses grievously the law of God.' This answer at the same time solves the other question, whether it is a mortal sin to put arms in the hands of an enemy of religion that he may use them against faith and morality. Would that all men of Christian sentiment seriously adverted to this connection of things and acted accordingly, the baneful sway of the pernicious spirit that governs the age would soon be at an end; for I have confidence in the sound sense and moral rectitude of the German people. Heathenism is repugnant to the deeply religious nature of our nation; the German people do not wish to dethrone God, nor are they ready to bow the knee before the empty idol of a soulless enlightenment."

Here the speaker was interrupted by a tumult. A band of factorymen, yelling and laughing, rushed into the hall to disturb the meeting. All eyes were immediately turned upon the rioters. In every countenance indignation could be seen kindling at this outrage of the liberals. The commissary of police alone sat motionless as a statue. The progressionist rioters elbowed their way into the crowd, and, when the excitement caused by this strategic movement had subsided, the speaker resumed his discourse.

"For a number of years back our conduct has been misrepresented and calumniated. They call us men of no nationality, and pretend that we get our orders from Rome. This reproach does honor neither to the intelligence nor to the judgment of our opponents. Whence dates the division of Germany into discordant factions? When began the present faint and languishing condition of our fatherland? From the moment when it separated from Rome. So long as Germany continued united in the bond of the same holy faith, and the voice of the head of the church was hearkened to by every member of her population, her sovereigns held the golden apple, the symbol of universal empire. Our nation was then the mightiest, the proudest, the most glorious upon earth. The church who speaks through the Sovereign Pontiff had civilized the fierce sons of Germany, had conjured the hatred and feuds of hostile tribes, had united the interests and energies of our people in one holy faith, and had ennobled and enriched German genius through the spirit of religion. The church had formed out of the chaos of barbarism the Holy Roman Empire of the German nation--that gigantic and wonderful organization the like of which the world will never see again. But the church has long since been deprived of the leadership in German affairs, and what in consequence is now the condition of our fatherland? It is divided into discordant factions, it is an ailing trunk, with many members, but without a head.

"It is rather amusing that the ultramontanes should be charged with receiving orders from Rome, for the voice of the Father of Christianity has not been heard for many years back, in the council of state."

"Hurrah for the Syllabus!" cried Spitzkopf, who was at the head of the rioters. "Hurrah for the Syllabus!" echoed his gang, yelling and stamping wildly.

The ultramontanes were aroused, eyes glared fiercely, and fists were clenched ready to make a summary clearing of the hall. But no scuffle ensued; the ultramontanes maintained a dignified bearing. The speaker calmly remained in his place, and when the tumult had ceased he again went on with his discourse.

"Such only," said he, "take offence at the Syllabus as know nothing about it. There is not a word in the Syllabus opposed to political liberty or the most untrammelled self-government of the German people. But it is opposed to the fiendish terrorism of infidelity. The Syllabus condemns the diabolical principles by which the foundations of the Christian state are sapped and a most disastrous tyranny over conscience is proclaimed."

"Hallo! listen to that," cried one of the liberals, and the yelling was renewed, louder, longer, and more furious than before.

The chairman rang his bell. The revellers relapsed into silence.

"Ours is not a public meeting, but a mere private gathering," explained the chairman. "None but men of Christian principles have been invited. If others have intruded violently, I request them to leave the room, or, at least, to refrain from conduct unbecoming men of good-breeding."

Spitzkopf laughed aloud, his comrades yelled and stamped.

"Let us go!" said Greifmann to Gerlach in an angry tone.

"Let us stay!" rejoined the latter with excitement. "The affair is becoming interesting. I want to see how this will end."

The banker noticed Gerlach's suppressed indignation; he observed it in the fire of his eyes and the expression of unutterable contempt that had spread over his features, and he began to consider the situation as alarming. He had not expected this exhibition of brutal impertinence. In his estimation an infringement of propriety like the one he had just witnessed was a far more heinous transgression than the grossest violations in the sphere of morals. He judged of Gerlach's impressions by this standard of appreciation, and feared the behavior of the progressionist mob would produce an effect in the young man's mind far from favorable to the cause which they represented. He execrated the disturbance of the liberals, and took Seraphin's arm to lead him away.

"Come away, I beg of you! I cannot imagine what interest the rudeness of that uncultivated horde can have for you."

"Do not scorn them, for they are honestly earning their pay," rejoined Gerlach.

"What do you mean?"

"Those fellows are whistling, bawling, stamping, and yelling in the employ of progress. You are trying to give me an insight into the nature of modern civilization: could there be a better opportunity than this?"

"There you make a mistake, my dear fellow! Enlightened progress is never rude."

CHAPTER VII

The tumult continued. As soon as the orator attempted to speak, his voice was drowned by cries and stamping.

"Commissary!" cried the chairman to that officer, "I demand that you extend to our assembly the protection of the law."

"I am here simply to watch the proceedings of your meeting," replied Parteiling with cool indifference. "Everybody is at liberty in meetings to signify his approval or disapproval by signs. No act forbidden by the law has been committed by your opponents, in my opinion."

"Bravo! bravo! Three cheers for the commissary!"

All at once the noise was subdued to a whisper of astonishment. A miracle was taking place under the very eyes of progress. Banker Greifmann, the moneyed prince and liberal, made his appearance upon the platform. The rioters saw with amazement how the mighty man before whom the necks of all such as were in want of money bowed--even the necks of the puissant leaders--stepped before the president of the assembly, how he politely bowed and spoke a few words in an undertone. They observed how the chairman nodded assent, and then how the banker, as if to excite their wonder to the highest pitch, mounted to the speaker's desk.

"Gentlemen," began Carl Greifmann, "although I have not the honor of sharing your political views, I feel myself nevertheless urged to address a few words to you. In the name of true progress, I ask this honorable assembly's pardon for the disturbance occasioned a moment ago by a band of uncultivated rioters, who dare to pretend that they are acting in the cause and with the sanction of progress. I solemnly protest against the assumption that their disgraceful and outrageous conduct is in accordance with the spirit of the party which they dishonor. Progress holds firmly to its principles, and defends them manfully in the struggle with its opposers, but it is far from making itself odious by rudely overstepping the bounds of decency set by humanity and civilization. In political contests, it may be perfectly lawful to employ earnest persuasion and even influences that partake of the rigor of compulsion, but rudeness, impertinence, is never justifiable in an age of civilization. Commissary Parteiling discovers no legally prohibited offence in the expression of vulgarity and lowness--may be. Nevertheless, a high misdemeanor has been perpetrated against decorum and against the deference which man owes to man. Should the slightest disturbance be again attempted, I shall use the whole weight of my influence in prosecuting the guilty parties, and convince them that even in the spirit of progress they are offenders and can be reached by punishment."

He spoke, and retired to the other end of the hall, followed by loud applause from the ultramontanes. Nor were the threats of the mighty man uttered in vain. Spitzkopf hung his head abashed. The other revellers were tamed, they listened demurely to the speakers, ceased their contemptuous hootings, and stood on their good behavior. Greifmann's proceeding had taken Seraphin also by surprise, and the power which the banker possessed over the rioters set him to speculating deeply. He saw plainly that Louise's brother commanded an extraordinary degree of respect in the camp of the enemies of religion, and the only cause that could sufficiently account for the fact was a community of principles of which they were well aware. Hence the opinion he had formed of Greifmann was utterly erroneous, concluded Gerlach, The banker was not a mere secluded business man--he was not indifferent about the great questions of the age. Then there was another circumstance that perplexed the ruddy-cheeked millionaire to no inconsiderable degree--Greifmann's unaccountable way of taking things. The tyrannical mode of electioneering which they had witnessed at the sign of the "Green Hat" had not at all disgusted Greifmann. Spitzkopf's threats had not excited his indignation. He had with a smiling countenance looked on whilst the most brutal species of terrorism was being enacted before him, he had not expressed a word of contempt at the constraint which they who held the power inhumanly placed on the political liberty of their dependents. On the other hand, his indignation was aroused by a mere breach of good behavior, an offence which in Gerlach's estimation was as nothing compared with the other instances of progressionist violence. The banker seemed to him to have strained out a gnat after having swallowed a whole drove of camels. The youth's suspicions being excited, he began to study the strainer of gnats and swallower of camels more closely, and soon the banker turned out in his estimation a hollow stickler for mere outward decency, devoid of all deeper merit. He now recollected also Greifmann's dealings with the leaders of progress, and those transactions only confirmed his present views. What he had considered as an extraordinary degree of shrewdness in the man of business, which enabled him to take advantage of the peculiar convictions and manner of thinking of other men, was now to his mind a real affinity with their principles, and he could not help being shocked at the discovery.

He hung his head in a melancholy mood, and his heart protested earnestly against the inference which was irresistibly forcing itself upon his mind, that the sister shared her brother's sentiments.

"This doubt must be cleared up, cost what it may," thought he. "My God, what if Louise also turned out to be a progressionist, a woman without any faith, an infidel! No, that cannot be! Yet suppose it really were the case--suppose she actually held principles in common with such vile beings as Schwefel, Sand, Erdblatt, and Shund? Suppose her moral nature did not harmonize with the beauty of her person--what then?" He experienced a spasmodic contraction in his heart at the question, he hesitated with the answer, but, his better self finally getting the victory, he said: "Then all is over. The impressions of a dream; however delightful, must not influence a waking man. My father's calculation was wrong, and I have wasted my kindness on an undeserving object."

So completely wrapt up was he in his meditations that he heard not a word of the speeches, not even the concluding remarks of the president. Greifmann's approach roused him, and they left the hall together.

"That was ruffianly conduct, of which progress would have for ever to be ashamed," said the banker indignantly, "They bayed and yelped like a pack of hounds. At their first volley I was as embarrassed and confused as a modest girl would be at the impertinence of some young scapegrace. Fierce rage then hurried me to the platform, and my words have never done better service, for they vindicated civilization."

"I cannot conceive how a trifle could thus exasperate you."

Greifmann stood still and looked at his companion in astonishment.

"A trifle!" echoed he reproachfully. "Do you call a piece of wanton impudence, a ruffianly outrage against several hundreds of men entitled to respect, a trifle?

"I do, compared with other crimes that you have suffered to pass unheeded and uncensured," answered Gerlach. "You had not an indignant word for the unutterable meanness of those three leaders, who were immoral and unprincipled enough to invest a notorious villain with office and honors. Nor did you show any exasperation at the brutal terrorism practised by men of power in this town over their weak and unfortunate dependents."

"Take my advice, and be on your guard against erroneous and narrow-minded judgments. The leaders merely had a view to their own ends, but they in no manner sinned against propriety. The raising a man of Shund's abilities to the office of mayor is an act of prudence--by no means an offence against humanity."

"Yet it was an outrage to moral sentiment," opposed Seraphin.

"See here, Gerlach, moral sentiment is a very elastic sort of thing. Sentiment goes for nothing in practical life, and such is the character of life in our century."

"Well, then, the mere sense of propriety is not worth a whit more."

"I ask your pardon! Propriety belongs to the realm of actualities or of practical experiences, and not to the shadowland of sentiment. Propriety is the rule that regulates the intercourse of men, it is therefore a necessity, nothing else will serve as a substitute for it, and it must continue to be so regarded as long as a difference is recognized between rational man and the irrational brute."

"The same may be said with much more reason of morality, for it also is a rule, it regulates our actions, it determines the ethic worth or worthlessness of a man. Mere outward decorum does not necessarily argue any interior excellence. The most abandoned wretch may be distinguished for easy manners and elegant deportment, yet he is none the less a criminal. A dog may be trained to many little arts, but for all that it continues to be a dog.

"It is delightful to see you breaking through that uniform patience of yours for once and showing a little of the fire of indignation," said the banker pleasantly. "I shall tell Louise of it, I know she will be glad to learn that Seraphin too is susceptible of a human passion. But this by the way. Now watch how I shall meet your arguments. That very moral sentiment of which you speak has caused and is still causing the most enormous crimes against humanity, and the laws of morality are as changeable as the wind. When an Indian who has not been raised from barbarism by civilization dies, the religious custom of the country requires that his wife should permit herself to be burned alive on the funeral pyre of her husband. Moral sentiment teaches the uncivilized woman that it is a horrible crime to refuse to devote herself to this cruel death. The pious Jews used to stone every woman to death who was taken in adultery--in our day, such a deed of blood would be revolting to moral sentiment, and would claim tears from the eyes of cultivated people. I could mention many other horrors that were practised more or less remotely in the past, and were sanctioned by the prevailing moral sentiment. Here is my last instance: according to laws of morality, the usurer was at one time a monster, an arch-villain--at present, he is merely a man of great enterprise. Propriety, on the other hand, enlightenment, and polish are absolute and unalterable. Whilst rudeness and impertinence will ever be looked upon as disgusting, good manners and politeness will be considered as commendable and beautiful."

Seraphin could not but admire the skill with which Greifmann jumbled together subjects of the most heterogeneous nature. But he could not, at the same time, divest himself of some alarm at the banker's declarations, for they betrayed a soul-life of little or absolutely no moral worth. Money, interest, and respectability constituted the only trinity in which the banker believed. Morality, binding the conscience of man, a true and only God, and divine revelation, were in his opinion so many worn-out and useless notions, which the progress of mankind had successfully got beyond.

"When those who hold power take advantage of it at elections, they in no manner offend against propriety," proceeded Carl. "Progress has convictions as well as ultramontanism. If the latter is active, why should not the former be so too? If, on the side of progress, the weak and dependent permit themselves to be cowed and driven, it is merely an advantage for the powerful, and for the others it is a weakness or cowardice. For this reason, the mode of electioneering pursued by Spitzkopf and his comrades amused but nowise shocked me, for they were not acting against propriety."

Seraphin saw it plainly: for Carl Greifmann there existed no distinction between good and evil; he recognized only a cold and empty system of formalities.

The two young men issued from a narrow street upon the market-place. This was occupied by a large public building. In the open space stood a group of men, among whom Flachsen appeared conspicuous. He was telling the others about Greifmann's speech at the meeting of the ultramontanes. They all manifested great astonishment that the influential moneyed prince should have appeared in such company, and, above all, should have made a speech in their behalf.

"He declared it was vulgar, impudent, ruffianly, to disturb a respectable assembly," reported Flachsen. "He said he knew some of us, and that he would have us put where the dogs would not bite us if we attempted to disturb them again. That's what he said; and I actually rubbed my eyes to be quite sure it was banker Greifmann that was speaking, and really it was he, the banker Greifmann himself, bodily, and not a mere apparition."

"I must say the banker was right, for it isn't exactly good manners to howl, stamp, and whistle to annoy one's neighbors," owned another.

"But we were paid for doing it, and we only carried out the orders given by certain gentlemen."

"To be sure! Men like us don't know what good breeding is--it's for gentlemen to understand that," maintained a third. "We do what men of good breeding hire us to do, and if it isn't proper, it matters nothing to us-- let the gentlemen answer for it."

"Bravo, Stoffel, bravo!" applauded Flachsen. "Yours is the right sort of servility, Stoffel! You are a real human, servile, and genuine reactive kind of a fellow--so you are. I agree with you entirely. The gentlemen do the paying, and it is for them to answer for what happens. We are merely servants, we are hirelings, and what need a hireling care whether that which his master commands is right or not? The master is responsible, not the hireling. What I am telling you belongs to the exact sciences, and the exact sciences are at the pinnacle of modern acquisitions. Hence a hireling who without scruple carries out the orders of his master is up to the highest point of the age--such a fellow has taken his stand on servility. Hallo! the election has commenced. Be off, every man of you, to his post. But mind you don't look too deep into the beer-pots before the election is over. Keep your heads level, be cautious, do your best for the success of the green ticket. Once the election is carried, you may swill beer till you can no longer stand. The gentlemen will foot the bill, and assume all responsibilities."

They dispersed themselves through the various drinking-shops of the neighborhood.

Near the door of the building in which the voting was to take place stood a number of progressionist gentlemen. They all wore heavy beards, smoked cigars, and peered about restlessly. To those of their party who chanced to pass they nodded and smiled knowingly, upon doubtful voters they smiled still more blandly, added some pleasant words, and pressed the acceptance of the green ticket, but for ultramontane voters they had only jeers and coarse witticisms. As Greifmann approached they respectfully raised their hats. The banker drew Gerlach to one side, and stood to make observations.

"What swarms there are around the drinking-shops," remarked Greifmann. "It is there that the tickets are filled under the persuasive influence of beer. The committee provide the tickets which the voters have filled with the names of the candidates by clerks who sit round the tables at the beer-shops. It is quite an ingenious arrangement, for beer will reconcile a voter to the most objectionable kind of a candidate."

A crowd of drunken citizens coming out of the nearest tavern approached. Linked arm-in-arm, they swayed about and staggered along with an unsteady pace. Green tickets bearing the names of the candidates whom progress had chosen to watch over the common weal could be seen protruding from the pockets of their waistcoats. Gerlach, seeing the drunken mob and recollecting the solemn and important nature of the occasion, was seized with loathing and horror at the corruption of social life revealed in the low means to which the party of progress had recourse to secure for its ends the votes of these besotted and ignorant men.

Presently Schwefel stepped up and saluted the young men.

"Do you not belong to the committee in charge of the ballot-box?" inquired Greifmann.

"No, sir, I wished to remain entirely untrammelled this morning," answered the leader with a sly look and tone. "This is going to be an exciting election, the ultramontanes are astir, and it will be necessary for me to step in authoritatively now and then to decide a vote. Moreover, the committee is composed exclusively of men of our party. Not a single ultramontane holds a seat at the polls."

"In that case there can be no question of failure," said the banker. "Your office is closed to-day, no doubt?"

"Of course!" assented the manufacturer of straw hats. "This day is celebrated as a free day by the offices of all respectable houses. Our clerks are dispersed through the taverns and election districts to use their pens in filling up tickets."

"I am forced to return to my old assertion: an election is mere folly, useless jugglery," said the banker, turning to Seraphin. "Holding elections is no longer a rational way of doing, it is no longer a business way of proceeding, it is yielding to stupid timidity. Mr. Schwefel, don't you think elections are mere folly?"

"I confess I have never considered the subject from that point of view," answered the leader cautiously. "But meanwhile--what do you understand by that?"

"Be good enough to attend to my reasoning for a moment. Progress is in a state of complete organization. What progress wills, must be. Another party having authority and power cannot subsist side by side with progress. Just see those men staggering and blundering over the square with green tickets in their hands! To speak without circumlocution, look at the slaves doing the behests of their masters. What need of this silly masquerade of an election? Why squander all this money, waste all this beer and time? Why does not progress settle this business summarily? Why not simply nominate candidates fit for the office, and then send them directly to the legislature? This mode would do away with all this nonsensical ado, and would give the matter a prompt and business cast, conformable to the spirit of the age."

"This idea is a good one, but we have an election law that would stand in the way of carrying it out."

"Bosh--election law!" sneered the banker. "Your election law is a mere scarecrow, an antiquated, meaningless instrument. Do away with the election law, and follow my suggestion."

"That would occasion a charming row on the part of the ultramontanes," observed the leader laughing.

"Was the lion ever known to heed the bleating of a sheep? When did progress ever pay any attention to a row gotten up by the ultramontanes?" rejoined Greifmann. "Was not the fuss made in Bavaria against the progressionist school-law quite a prodigious one? Did not our own last legislature make heavy assaults on the church? Did not the entire episcopate protest against permitting Jews, Neo-pagans, and Freemasons to legislate, on matters of religion? But did progress suffer itself to be disconcerted by episcopal protests and the agonizing screams of the ultramontanes? Not at all. It calmly pursued the even tenor of its way. Be logical, Mr. Schwefel: progress reigns supreme and decrees with absolute authority--why should it not summarily relegate this election law among the things that were, but are no more?"

"You are right, Greifmann!" exclaimed Gerlach, in a feeling of utter disgust. "What need has the knout of Russian despotism of the sanction of constitutional forms? Progress is lord, the rest are slaves!"

"You have again misunderstood me, my good fellow. I am considering the actual state of things. Should ultramontanism at any time gain the ascendency, then it also will be justified in behaving in the same manner."

Upon more mature consideration, Gerlach found himself forced to admit that Greifmann's view, from the standpoint of modern culture, was entirely correct. Progress independently of God and of all positive religion could not logically be expected to recognize any moral obligations, for it had not a moral basis. Everything was determined by the force of circumstances; the autocracy of party rule made anything lawful. Laws proceeded not from the divine source of unalterable justice, but from the whim of a majority-- fashioned and framed to suit peculiar interests and passions.

"We have yet considerable work to do to bring all to thinking as clearly and rationally as you, Mr. Greifmann," said the leader with a winning smile.

Schwefel accompanied the millionaires into a lengthy hall, across the lower end of which stood a table. There sat the commissary of elections surrounded by the committee, animated gentlemen with great beards, who were occupied in distributing tickets to voters or receiving tickets filled up. The extraordinary good-humor prevailing among these gentlemen was owing to the satisfactory course of the election, for rarely was any ultramontane paper seen mingling in the flood that poured in from the ranks of progress. The sides of the hall were hung with portraits of the sovereigns of the land, quite a goodly row. The last one of the series was youthful in appearance, and some audacious hand had scrawled on the broad gilt frame the following ominous words: "May he be the last in the succession of expensive bread-eaters." Down the middle of the hall ran a baize-covered table, on which were numerous inkstands. Scattered over the table lay a profusion of green bills; the yellow color of the ultramontane bills was nowhere to be seen. The table was lined by gentlemen who were writing. They were not writing for themselves, but for others, who merely sighed their names and then handed the tickets to the commissary. Several corpulent gentlemen also occupied seats at the table, but they were not engaged in writing. These gentlemen, apparently unoccupied, wore massive gold watch-chains and sparkling rings, and they had a commanding and stern expression of countenance. They were observing all who entered, to see whether any man would be bold enough to vote the yellow ticket. People of the humbler sort, mechanics and laborers, were constantly coming in and going out. Bowing reverently to the portly gentlemen, they seated themselves and filled out green tickets with the names of the liberal candidates. Most of them did not even trouble themselves to this degree, but simply laid their tickets before the penman appointed for this special service. All went off in the best order. The process of the election resembled the smooth working of an ingenious piece of machinery. And there was no tongue there to denounce the infamous terrorism that had crushed the freedom of the election or had bought the votes of vile and venal men with beer.

Seraphin stood with Greifmann in the recess of a window looking on.

"Who are the fat men at the table?" inquired he.

"The one with the very black beard is house-builder Sand, the second is Eisenhart, machine-builder, the third is Erdfloh, a landowner, the fourth and fifth are tobacco merchants. All those gentlemen are chieftains of the party of progress."

"They show it," observed Gerlach. "Their looks, in a manner, command every man that comes in to take the green ticket, and I imagine I can read on their brows: 'Woe to him who dares vote against us. He shall be under a ban, and shall have neither employment nor bread.' It is unmitigated tyranny! I imagine I see in those fat fellows so many cotton-planters voting their slaves."

"That is a one-sided conclusion, my most esteemed," rejoined the banker. "In country villages, the position here assumed by the magnates of progress is filled by the lords of ultramontanism, clerical gentlemen in cassocks, who keep a sharp eye on the fingers of their parishioners. This, too, is influencing."

"But not constraining," opposed the millionaire promptly. "The clergy exert a legitimate influence by convincing, by advancing solid grounds for their political creed. They never have recourse to compulsory measures, nor dare they do so, because it would be opposed to the Gospel which they preach. The autocrats of progress, on the contrary, do not hesitate about using threats and violence. Should a man refuse to bow to their dictates, they cruelly deprive him of the means of subsistence. This is not only inhuman, but it is also an accursed scheme for making slaves of the people and robbing them of principle."

"Ah! look yonder--there is Holt."

The land cultivator had walked into the hall head erect. He looked along the table and stood undecided. One of the ministering spirits of progress soon fluttered about him, offering him a green ticket. Holt glanced at it, and a contemptuous smile spread over his face. He next tore it to pieces, which he threw on the floor.

"What are you about?" asked the angel of progress reproachfully.

"I have reduced Shund and his colleagues to fragments," answered Holt dryly, then approaching the commissary he demanded a yellow ticket.

"Glorious!" applauded Gerlach. "I have half a mind to present this true German *man* with another thousand as a reward for his spirit."

The fat men had observed with astonishment the action of the land cultivator. Their astonishment turned to rage when Holt, leisurely seating himself at the table, took a pen in his mighty fist and began filling out the ticket with the names of the ultramontane candidates. Whilst he wrote, whisperings could be heard all through the hall, and every eye was directed upon him. After no inconsiderable exertion, the task of filling out the ticket was successfully accomplished, and Holt arose, leaving the ticket lying upon the table. In the twinkling of an eye a hand reached forward to take it up.

"What do you mean, sir?" asked Holt sternly.

"That yellow paper defiles the table," hissed the fellow viciously.

"Hand back that ticket," commanded Holt roughly. "I want it to be here. The yellow ticket has as good a right on this table as the green one--do you hear me?"

"Slave of the priests!" sputtered his antagonist.

"If I am a slave of the priests, then you are a slave of that villain Shund," retorted Holt. "I am not to be browbeaten--by such a fellow as you particularly--least of all by a vile slave of Shund's." He spoke, and then reached his ticket to the commissary.

"That is an impudent dog," growled leader Sand. "Who is he?"

"He is a countryman of the name of Holt," answered he to whom the query was addressed.

"We must spot the boor," said Erdfloh. "His swaggering shall not avail him anything."

Holt was not the only voter that proved refractory. Mr. Schwefel, also, had a disagreeable surprise. He was standing near the entrance, observing with great self-complacency how the workmen in his employ submissively cast their votes for Shund and his associates. Schwefel regarded himself as of signal importance in the commonwealth, for he controlled not less than four hundred votes, and the side which it was his pleasure to favor could not fail of victory. The head of the great leader seemed in a manner encircled with the halo of progress: whilst his retainers passed and saluted him, he experienced something akin to the pride of a field-marshal reviewing a column of his victorious army.

Just then a spare little man appeared in the door. His yellowish, sickly complexion gave evidence that he was employed in the sulphurating of straw. At sight of the commander the sulphur-hued little man shrank back, but his startled look did not escape the restless eye of Mr. Schwefel. He beckoned to the laborer.

"Have you selected your ticket, Leicht?"

"Yes, sir."

"Let me see the ticket."

The man obeyed reluctantly. Scarcely had Schwefel got a glimpse of the paper when his brows gathered darkly.

"What means this? Have you selected the yellow ticket and not the green one?"

Leicht hung his head. He thought of the consequences of this detection, of his four small children, of want of employment, of hunger and bitter need--he was almost beside himself.

"If you vote for the priests, you may get your bread from the priests," said Schwefel. "The moment you hand that ticket to the commissary, you may consider yourself discharged from my employ." With this he angrily turned his back upon the man. Leicht did not reach in his ticket to the commissary. Staggering out of the hall, he stood bewildered hear the railing of the steps, and stared vaguely upon the men who were coming and going. Spitzkopf slipped up to him.

"What were you thinking about, man?" asked he reproachfully. "Mr. Schwefel is furious--you are ruined. Sheer stupidity, nothing but stupidity in you to wish to vote in opposition to the pleasure of the man from whom you get your bread and meat! Not only that, but you have insulted the whole community, for you have chosen to vote against progress when all the town is in favor of progress. You will be put on the spotted list, and the upshot will be that you will not get employment in any factory in town. Do you want to die of hunger, man--do you want your children to die of hunger?"

"You are right--I am ruined," said the laborer listlessly. "I couldn't bring myself to write Shund's name because he reduced my brother-in-law to beggary--this is what made me select the yellow ticket."

"You are a fool. Were Mr. Schwefel to recommend the devil, your duty would be to vote for the devil. What need you care who is on the ticket? You have only to write the names on the ticket--nothing more than that. Do you think progress would nominate men that are unfit--men who would not promote the interests of the state, who would not further the cause of humanity, civilization, and liberty? You are a fool for not voting for what is best for yourself."

"I am sorry now, but it's too late." sighed Leicht. "I wouldn't have thought, either, that Mr. Schwefel would get angry because a man wanted to vote to the best of his judgment."

"There you are prating sillily again. Best of your judgment!--you mustn't have any judgment. Leave it to others to judge; they have more brains, more sense, more knowledge than you. Progress does the thinking: our place is to blindly follow its directions."

"But, Mr. Spitzkopf, mine is only the vote of a poor man; and what matters such a vote?"

"There is your want of sense again. We are living in a state that enjoys liberty. We are living in an age of intelligence, of moral advancement, of civilization and knowledge, in a word, we are living in an age of progress; and in an age of this sort the vote of a poor man is worth as much as that of a rich man."

"If only I had it to do over! I would give my right hand to have it to do over!"

"You can repair the mischief if you want."

"Instruct me how, Mr. Spitzkopf; please tell me how!"

"Very well, I will do my best. As you acted from thoughtlessness and no bad intention, doubtless Mr. Schwefel will suffer himself to be propitiated. Go down into the court, and wait till I come. I shall get you another ticket; you will then vote for progress, and all will be satisfactory."

"I am a thousand times obliged to you, Mr. Spitzkopf--a thousand times obliged!"

The agent went back to the hall. Leicht descended to the courtyard, where he found a ring of timid operators like himself surrounding the sturdy Holt. They were talking in an undertone. As often as a progressionist drew near, their conversation was hushed altogether. Holt's voice alone resounded loudly through the court, and his huge strong hands were cutting the air in animated gesticulations.

"This is not a free election; it is one of compulsion and violence," cried he. "Every factoryman is compelled to vote as his employer dictates, and should he refuse the employer discharges him from the work. Is not this most despicable tyranny! And these very tyrants of progress are perpetually prating about liberty, independence, civilization! That's a precious sort of liberty indeed!"

"A man belonging to the ultramontane party cannot walk the streets to-day without being hooted and insulted," said another. "Even up yonder in the hall, those gentlemen who are considered so cultivated stick their heads together and laugh scornfully when one of us draws near."

"That's so--that's so, I have myself seen it," cried Holt. "Those well-bred gentlemen show their teeth like ferocious dogs whenever they see a yellow ticket or an ultramontane. I say, Leicht, has anything happened you? You look wretched!" Leicht drew near and related what had occurred. The honest Holt's eyes gleamed like coals of fire.

"There's another piece of tyranny for you," cried he. "Leicht, my poor fellow, I fancy I see in you a slave of Schwefel's. From dawn till late you are compelled to toil for the curmudgeon, Sundays not excepted. Your church is the factory, your religion working in straw, and your God is your sovereign master Schwefel. You are ruining your health amid the stench of brimstone, and not so much as the liberty of voting as you think fit is allowed you. It's just as I tell you--you factorymen are slaves. How strangely things go on in the world! In America slavery has been abolished; but lo! here in Europe it is blooming as freshly as trees in the month of May. But mark my word, friends, the fruit is deadly; and when once it will have ripened, the great

God of heaven will shake it from the trees, and the generation that planted the trees will have to eat the bitter fruit."

Leicht shunned the society of the ultramontanes and stole away. Presently Spitzkopf appeared with the ticket.

"Your ticket is filled out. Come and sign your name to it." Schwefel was again standing near the entrance, and he again beckoned the laborer to approach. "I am pacified. You may now continue working for me."

Carl and Seraphin returned to the Palais Greifmann. Louise received them with numerous questions. The banker related what had passed; Gerlach strode restlessly through the apartment.

"The most curious spectacle must have been yourself," said the young lady. "Just fancy you on the rostrum at the 'Key of Heaven'! And very likely the ungrateful ultramontanes would not so much as applaud."

"Beg pardon, they did, miss!" assured Seraphin. "They applauded and cried bravo."

"Really? Then I am proud of a brother whose maiden speech produced such marvellous effects. May be we shall read of it in the daily paper. Everybody will be surprised to hear of the banker Greifmann making a speech at the 'Key of Heaven.'" Carl perceived the irony and stroked his forehead.

"But what can you be pondering over, Mr. Seraphin?" cried she to him. "Since returning from the turmoil of the election, you seem unable to keep quiet." He seated himself at her side, and was soon under the spell of her magical attractions.

"My head is dizzy and my brain confused," said he. "On every hand I see nothing but revolt against moral obligation, sacrilegious disregard of the most sacred rights of man. The hubbub still resounds in my ears, and my imagination still sees those fat men at the table with their slaveholder look-- the white slaves doing their masters' bidding--the completest subjugation in an age of enlightenment--all this presents itself to me in the most repulsive and lamentable guise."

"You must drive those horrible phantoms from your mind," replied Louise.

"They are not phantoms, but the most fearful reality."

"They are phantoms, Mr. Seraphin, so far as your feelings exaggerate the evils. Those factory serfs have no reason to complain. There is nothing to be done but to put up with a situation that has spontaneously developed itself. It is useless to grow impatient because difference of rank between masters and servants is an unavoidable evil upon earth." A servant entered to call them to dinner.

At her side he gradually became more cheerful. The brightness of her eyes dispelled his depression, and her delicate arts put a spell upon his young, inexperienced heart. And when, at the end of the meal, they were sipping delicious wine, and her beautiful lips lisped the customary health, the subdued tenderness he had been feeling suddenly expanded into a strong passion.

"After you will have done justice to your diary," said she at parting, "we shall take a drive, and then go to the opera."

Instead of going to his room, Seraphin went into the garden. He almost forgot the occurrences of the day in musing on the inexplicable behavior of Louise. Again she had not uttered a word of condemnation of the execrable doings of progress, and it grieved him deeply. A suspicion flitted across his mind that perhaps Louise was infected with the frivolous and pernicious spirit of the age, but he immediately stifled the terrible suggestion as he would have hastened to crush a viper that he might have seen on the path of the beautiful lady. He preferred to believe that she suppressed her feelings of disgust out of regard for his presence, that she wisely avoided pouring oil upon the flames of his own indignation. Had she not exerted herself to dispel his sombre reflections? He was thus espousing the side of passion against the appalling truth that was beginning faintly to dawn upon his anxious mind.

But soon the spell was to be broken, and duty was to confront him with the alternative of either giving up Louise, or defying the stern demands of his conscience.

The brother and sister, thinking their guest engaged with his diary, walked into the garden. They directed their steps towards the arbor where Gerlach had seated himself.

He was only roused to consciousness of their proximity by the unusually loud and excited tone in which Louise spoke. He could not be mistaken; it was the young lady's voice--but oh! the import of her words. He looked through an opening in the foliage, and sat thunderstruck.

"You have been attempting to guide Gerlach's overexalted spirit into a more rational way of thinking, but the very opposite seems to be the result. Intercourse with the son of a strait-laced mother is infecting you with sympathy for ultramontanism. Your speech to-day," continued she caustically, "in yon obscure meeting is the subject of the talk of the town. I am afraid you have made yourself ridiculous in the minds of all cultivated people. The respectability of our family has suffered."

"Of our family?" echoed he, perplexed.

"We are compromitted," continued she with excitement. "You have given our enemies occasion to set us down for members of a party who stupidly oppose the onward march of civilization."

"Cease your philippic," broke in the brother angrily. "Bitterness is an unmerited return for my efforts to serve you."

"To serve me?"

"Yes, to serve you. The disturbing of that meeting made a very unfavorable impression on your intended. He scorned the noisy mob, and was roused by what, from his point of view, could not pass for anything better than unpardonable impudence. To me it might have been a matter of indifference whether your intended was pleased or displeased with the fearless conduct of progress. But as I knew both you and the family felt disposed to base the happiness of your life on his couple of millions, as moreover I feared my silence might be interpreted by the shortsighted young gentleman for complicity in progressionist ideas, I was forced to disown the disorderly proceeding. In so doing I have not derogated one iota from the spirit of the times; on the contrary, I have bound a heavy wreath about the brow of glorious humanity."

"But you have pardoned yourself too easily," proceeded she, unappeased. "The very first word uttered by a Greifmann in that benighted assembly was a stain on the fair fame of our family. We shall be an object of contempt in every circle. 'The Greifmanns have turned ultramontanes because Gerlach would have refused the young lady's hand had they not changed their creed,' is what will be prated in society. A flood of derision and sarcasm will be let loose upon us. I an ultramontane?" cried she, growing more fierce; "I caught in the meshes of religious fanaticism? I accept the Syllabus--believe in the Prophet of Nazareth? Oh! I could sink into the earth on account of this disgrace! Did I for an instant doubt that Seraphin may be redeemed from superstition and fanaticism, I would renounce my union with him--I would spurn the tempting enjoyments of wealth, so much do I hate silly credulity."

Seraphin glanced at her through the gap in the foliage. Not six paces from him, with her face turned in his direction, stood the infuriate beauty. How changed her countenance! The features, habitually so delicate and bright, now looked absolutely hideous, the brows were fiercely knit, and hatred poured like streams of fire from her eyes. Sentiments hitherto skilfully concealed had taken visible shape, ugly and repulsive to the view of the innocent youth. His noble spirit revolted at so much hypocrisy and falsehood. What occurred before him was at once so monstrous and so overwhelming that he did not for an instant consider that in case they entered the arbor he would be discovered. He was not discovered, however. Louise and Carl retraced their steps. For a short while the voice of Louise was still audible, then silence reigned in the garden.

Seraphin rose from his seat. There was a sad earnestness in his face, and the vanishing traces of deep pain, which however were soon superseded by a noble indignation.

"I have beheld the genuine Louise, and I thank God for it. It is as I feared, Louise is a progressionist, an infidel that considers it disgraceful to believe in the Redeemer. Out upon such degeneracy! She hates light, and how hideous this hatred makes her. Not a feature was left of the charming, smiling, winning Louise. Good God! how horrible had her real character remained unknown until after we were married! Chained for life to the bitter enemy of everything that I hold dear and venerate as holy--think of it! With eyes bandaged, I was but two paces from an abyss that resembles hell--thank God! the bandage has fallen--I see the abyss, and shudder.

"'The ultramontane Seraphin'--'the fanatical Gerlach'--'the shortsighted Gerlach,' whose fortune the young lady covets that she may pass her life in enjoyment--a heartless girl, in whom there is not a spark of love for her intended husband--how base!

"'Ultramontane'?--'fanatical'?--yes! 'Shortsighted?' by no means. One would need the suspicious eyes of progress to see through the hypocrisy of this lady and her brother--a simple, trusting spirit like mine cannot penetrate such darkness. At any rate, they shall not find me weak. The little flame that was beginning to burn within my heart has been for ever extinguished by her unhallowed lips. She might now present herself in the garb of an angel, and muster up every seductive art of womanhood, 'twould not avail; I have had an insight into her real character, and giving her up costs me not a pang. It is not hollow appearances that determine the worth of woman, but moral excellence, beautiful virtues springing from a heart vivified by faith. No, giving her up shall not cost me one regretful throb."

He hastened from the garden to his room and rang the bell.

"Pack my trunks this very day, John," said he to his servant. "Tomorrow we shall be off."

He then entered in his diary a circumstantial account of the unmasked beauty. He also dwelt at length upon the painful shock his heart experienced when the bright and beautiful creature he had considered Louise to be suddenly vanished before his soul. As he was finishing the last line, John reappeared with a telegraphic despatch. He read it, and was stunned.

"Meet your father at the train this evening." He looked at the concise despatch, and fancied he saw his father's stern and threatening countenance.

The contemplated match had for several years been regarded by the families of Gerlach and Greifmann as a fixed fact. Seraphin was aware how stubbornly his father adhered to a project that he had once set his mind upon. Here now, just as the union had became impossible and as the youth was about to free himself for ever from an engagement that was destructive of his happiness, the uncompromising sire had to appear to enforce unconditional obedience to his will. A fearful contest awaited Seraphin, unequal and painful; for a son, accustomed from childhood to revere and obey his parents, was to maintain this contest against his own father. Seraphin paced the room and wrung his hands in anguish.

CHAPTER VIII
AN ULTRAMONTANE SON

Greifmann and Gerlach had driven to the railway station. The express train thundered along. As the doors of the carriages flew open, Seraphin peered through them with eyes full of eager joy. He thought no more of the fate that threatened him as the sequel of his father's arrival; his youthful heart exulted solely in the anticipation of the meeting. A tall, broad-shouldered gentleman, with severe features and tanned complexion, alighted from a *coupé*. It was Mr. Conrad Gerlach. Seraphin threw his arms around his father's neck and kissed him. The banker made a polite bow to the wealthiest landed proprietor of the country, in return for which Mr. Conrad bestowed on him a cordial shake of the hand.

"Has your father returned?"

"He cannot possibly reach home before September," answered the banker. The traveller stepped for a moment into the luggage-room. The gentlemen then drove away to the Palais Greifmann. During the ride, the conversation was not very animated. Conrad's curt, grave manner and keen look, indicative of a mind always hard at work, imposed reserve, and rapidly dampened his son's ingenuous burst of joy. Seraphin cast a searching glance upon that severe countenance, saw no change from its stern look of authority, and his heart sank before the appalling alternative of either sacrificing the happiness of his life to his father's favorite project, or of opposing his will and braving the consequences of such daring. Yet he wavered but an instant in the resolution to which he had been driven by necessity, and which, it was plain from the lines of his countenance, he had manhood enough to abide by.

Mr. Conrad maintained his reserve, and asked but few questions. Even Carl, habitually profuse, studied brevity in his answers, as he knew from experience that Gerlach, Senior, was singularly averse to the use of many words.

"How is business?"

"Very dull, sir; the times are hard."

"Did you sustain any losses through the failures that have recently taken place in town?"

"Not a farthing. We had several thousands with Wendel, but fortunately drew them out before he failed."

"Very prudent. Has your father entered into any new connections in the course of his travels?"

"Several, that promise fairly."

"Is Louise well?"

"Her health is as good as could be wished."

"General prosperity, then, I see, for you both look cheerful, and Seraphin is as blooming as a clover field.

"How is dear mother?"

"Quite well. She misses her only child. She sends much love."

The carriage drew up at the gate. The young lady was awaiting the millionaire at the bottom of the steps. While greetings were exchanged between them, a faint tinge of warmth could be noticed on the cold features of the land-owner. A smile formed about his mouth, his piercing eyes glanced for an instant at Seraphin, and instantly the smile was eclipsed under the cloud of an unwelcome discovery.

"I am on my way to the industrial exhibition," said he, "and I thought I would pay you a visit in passing. I wish you not to put yourself to any inconvenience, my dear Louise. You will have the goodness to make me a little tea, this evening, which we shall sip together."

"I am overjoyed at your visit, and yet I am sorry, too."

"Sorry! Why so?"

"Because you are in such a hurry."

"It cannot be helped, my child. I am overwhelmed with work. Harvest has commenced; no less than six hundred hands are in the fields, and I am obliged to go to the exhibition. I must see and test some new machinery which is said to be of wonderful power."

"Well, then, you will at least spare us a few days on your return?"

"A few days! You city people place no value on time. We of the country economize seconds. Without a thought you squander in idleness what cannot be recalled."

"You are a greater rigorist than ever," chided she, smiling.

"Because, my child, I am getting older. Seraphin, I wish to speak a word with you before tea."

The two retired to the apartments which for years Mr. Conrad was accustomed to occupy whenever he visited the Palais Greifmann.

"The old man still maintains his characteristic vigor," said Louise. "His face is at all times like a problem in arithmetic, and in place of a heart he carries an accurate estimate of the yield of his farms. His is a cold, repelling nature."

"But strictly honest, and alive to gain," added Carl. "In ten years more he will have completed his third million. I am glad he came; the marriage project is progressing towards a final arrangement. He is now having a talk with Seraphin; tomorrow, as you will see, the bashful young gentleman, in obedience to the command of his father, will present himself to offer you his heart, and ask yours in return."

"A free heart for an enslaved one," said she jestingly. "Were there no hope of ennobling that heart, of freeing it from the absurdities with which it is encrusted, I declare solemnly I would not accept it for three millions. But Seraphin is capable of being improved. His eye will not close itself against modern enlightenment. Servility of conscience and a baneful fear of God cannot have entirely extinguished his sense of liberty."

"I have never set a very high estimate on the pluck and moral force of religious people," declared Greifmann. "They are a craven set, who are pious merely because they are afraid of hell. When a passion gets possession of them, the impotence of their religious frenzy at once becomes manifest. They fall an easy prey to the impulses of nature, and the supernatural fails to come to the rescue. It would be vain for Seraphin to try to give up the unbelieving Louise, whom his strait-laced faith makes it his duty to avoid. He has fallen a victim to your fascinations; all the Gospel of the Jew of Nazareth, together with all the sacraments and unctions of the church, could not loose the coils with which you have encircled him."

In this scornful tone did Carl Greifmann speak of the heroism of virtue and of the energy of faith, like a blind man discoursing about colors. He little suspected that it is just the power of religion that produces characters, and that, on this very account, in an irreligious age, characters of a noble type are so rarely met with; the warmth of faith is not in them.

"Mr. Schwefel desires to speak a word with you," said a servant who appeared at the door.

The banker nodded assent.

"I ask your pardon for troubling you at so unseasonable an hour," began the leader, after bowing lowly several times. "The subject is urgent, and must be settled without delay. But, by the way, I must first give you the good news: Mr. Shund is elected by an overwhelming majority, and Progress is victorious in every ward."

"That is what I looked for," answered the banker, with an air of satisfaction. "I told you whatever Cæsar, Antony, and Lepidus command, must be done."

"I am just from a meeting at which some important resolutions have been offered and adopted," continued the leader. "The strongest prop of ultramontanism is the present system of educating youth. Education must, therefore, be taken out of the hands of the priests. But the change will have to be brought about gradually and with caution. We have decided to make a beginning by introducing common schools. A vote of the people is to be taken on the measure, and, on the last day of voting, a grand barbecue is to be given to celebrate our triumph over the accursed slavery of religious symbols. The ground chosen by the chief-magistrate for the celebration is the common near the Red Tower, but the space is not large enough, and we will need your meadow adjoining it to accommodate the crowd. I am commissioned by the magistrate to request you to throw open the meadow for the occasion."

The banker, believing the request prejudicial to his private interests, looked rather unenthusiastic. Louise, who had been busy with the teapot, had heard every word of the conversation, and the new educational scheme had won her cordial approval. Seeing her brother hesitated, she flew to the rescue:

"We are ready and happy to make any sacrifice in the interest of education and progress."

"I am not sure that it is competent for me in the present instance to grant the desired permission," replied Greifmann. "The grass would be destroyed, and perhaps the sod ruined for years. My father is away from home, and I would not like to take the responsibility of complying with his honor's wish."

"The city will hold itself liable for all damages," said Schwefel.

"Not at all!" interposed the young lady hastily. "Make use of the meadow without paying damages. If my brother refuses to assume the responsibility, I will take it upon my self. By wresting education from the clergy, who only cripple the intellect of youth, progress aims a death-blow at mental degradation. It is a glorious work, and one full of inestimable results that you gentlemen are beginning in the cause of humanity against ignorance and superstition. My father so heartily concurs in every undertaking that responds to the wants of the times, that I not only feel encouraged to make myself responsible for this concession, but am even sure that he would be angry if we refused. Do not hesitate to make use of the meadow, and from its flowers bind garlands about the temples of the goddess of liberty!"

The leader bowed reverently to the beautiful advocate of progress.

"In this case, there remains nothing else for me to do than to confirm my sister's decision," said Greifmann. "When is the celebration to take place?"

"On the 10th of August, the day of the deputy elections. It has been intentionally set for that day to impress on the delegates how genuine and right is the sentiment of our people."

"Very good," approved Greifmann.

"In the name of the chief-magistrate, I thank you for the offering you have so generously laid upon the shrine of humanity, and I shall hasten to inform the gentlemen before they adjourn that you have granted our request." And Schwefel withdrew from the gorgeously furnished apartment.

Meanwhile a fiery struggle was going on between Seraphin and his father. He had briefly related his experience at the Palais Greifmann; had even confessed his preference for Louise, and had, for the first time in his life, incurred his father's displeasure by mentioning the wager. And when he concluded by protesting that he could not marry Louise, Conrad's suppressed anger burst forth.

"Have you lost your senses, foolish boy? This marriage has been in contemplation for years; it has been coolly weighed and calculated. In all the country around, it is the only equal match possible. Louise's dower amounts to one million florins, the exact value of the noble estate of Hatzfurth, adjoining our possessions. You young people can occupy the chateau, I shall add another hundred acres to the land, together with a complete outfit of farming implements, and then you will have such a start as no ten proprietors in Germany can boast of."

Seraphin knew his father. All the old gentleman's thought and effort was concentrated on the management of his extensive possessions. For other subjects there was no room in the head and heart of the landholder. He barely complied with his religious duties. It is true, on Sundays Mr. Conrad attended church, but surrounded invariably by a motley swarm of worldly cares and speculations connected with farming. At Easter, he went to the sacraments, but usually among the last, and after being repeatedly reminded by his wife. He took no interest in progress, humanity, ultramontanism, and such other questions as vex the age, because to trouble himself about them would have interfered with his main purpose. He knew only his fields and woodlands--and God, in so far as his providence blessed him with bountiful harvests.

"What is the good of millions, father, if the very fundamental conditions of matrimonial peace are wanting?"

"What fundamental conditions?"

"Louise believes neither in God nor in revelation. She is an infidel."

"And you are a fanatic--a fanatic because of your one-sided education. Your mother has trained you as priests and monks are trained. During your childhood piety was very useful; it served as the prop to the young tree, causing it to grow up straight and develop itself into a vigorous stem. But you are now full-grown, and life makes other demands on the man than on the boy; therefore, with your fanaticism.

"To my dying hour I shall thank my mother for the care she has bestowed on the child, the boy, and the young man. If her pious spirit has given a right direction to my career, and watched faithfully over my steps, the untarnished record of the son cannot but rejoice the heart of the father--a record which is the undoubted product of religious training."

"You are a good son, and I am proud of you," accorded Mr. Conrad with candor. "Your mother, too, is a woman whose equal is not to be found. All this is very well. But, if Louise's city manners and free way of thinking scandalize you, you are sheerly narrow-minded. I have been noticing her for years, and have learned to value her industry and domestic virtues. She has not a particle of extravagance; on the contrary, she has a decided leaning towards economy and thrift. She will make an unexceptionable wife. Do you imagine, my son, my choice could be a blind one when I fixed upon Louise to share the property which, through years of toil, I have amassed by untiring energy?"

"I do not deny the lady has the qualities you mention, my dear father."

"Moreover, she is a millionaire, and handsome, very handsome, and you are in love with her--what more do you want?"

"The most important thing of all, father. The very soul of conjugal felicity is wanting, which is oneness of faith in supernatural truth. What I adore, Louise denies; what I revere, she hates; what I practise, she scorns.

Louise never prays, never goes to church, never receives the sacraments, in a word, she has not a spark of religion."

"That will all come right," returned Mr. Conrad. "Louise will learn to pray. You must not, simpleton, expect a banker's daughter to be for ever counting her beads like a nun. Take my word for it, the weight of a wife's responsibilities will make her serious enough."

"Serious perhaps, but not religious, for she is totally devoid of faith."

"Enough; you shall marry her nevertheless," broke in the father. "It is my wish that you shall marry her. I will not suffer opposition."

For a moment the young man sat silent, struggling painfully with the violence of his own feelings.

"Father," said he, then, "you command what I cannot fulfil, because it goes against my conscience. I beg you not to do violence to my conscience; violence is opposed to your own and my Christian principles. An atheist or a progressionist who does not recognize a higher moral order, might insist upon his son's marrying an infidel for the sake of a million. But you cannot do so, for it is not millions of money that you and I look upon as the highest good. Do not, therefore, dear father, interfere with my moral freedom; do not force me into a union which my religion prohibits."

"What does this mean?" And a dark frown gathered on the old gentleman's forehead. "Defiance disguised in religious twaddle? Open rebellion? Is this the manner in which my son fulfils the duty of filial obedience?"

"Pardon me, father," said the youth with deferential firmness, "there is no divine law making it obligatory upon a father to select a wife for his son. Consequently, also, the duty of obedience on this point does not rest upon the son. Did I, beguiled by passion or driven by recklessness, wish to marry a creature whose depravity would imperil my temporal and eternal welfare, your duty, as a father, would be to oppose my rashness, and my duty, as a son, would be to obey you. Louise is just such a creature; she is artfully plotting against my religious principles, against my loyalty to God and the church. She has put upon herself as a task to lead me from the darkness of superstition into the light of modern advancement. I overheard her when she said to her brother, 'Did I for an instant doubt that Seraphin may be reclaimed from superstition, I would renounce my union with him, I would forego all the gratifications of wealth, so much do I detest stupid credulity.' Hence I should have to look forward to being constantly annoyed by my wife's fanatical hostility to my religion. There never would be an end of discord and wrangling. And what kind of children would such a mother rear? She would corrupt the little ones, instil into their innocent souls the poison of her own godlessness, and make me the most wretched of fathers. For these reasons Miss Greifmann shall not become my wife---no, never! I implore you, dear father, do not require from me what my conscience will not permit, and what I shall on no condition consent to," concluded the young man with a tone of decision.

Mr. Conrad had observed a solemn silence, like a man who suddenly beholds an unsuspected phenomenon exhibited before him. Seraphin's words produced, as it were, a burst of vivid light upon his mind, dispelling the multitudinous schemes and speculations that nestled in every nook and depth. The effect of this sudden illumination became perceptible at once, for Mr. Gerlach lost the points of view which had invariably brought before his vision the million of the Greifmanns, and he began to feel a growing esteem for the stand taken by his son.

"Your language sounds fabulous," said he.

"Here, father, is my diary. In it you will find a detailed account of what I have briefly stated."

Gerlach took the book and shoved it into the breast-pocket of his coat. In an instant, however, his imagination conjured up to him a picture of the Count of Hatzfurth's splendid estate, and he went on coldly and deliberately: "Hear me, Seraphin! Your marriage with Louise is a favorite project upon which I have based not a few expectations. The observations you have made shall not induce me to renounce this project unconditionally, for you may have been mistaken. I shall take notes myself and test this matter. If your view is confirmed, our project will have been an air castle. You shall be left entirely unmolested in your convictions."

Seraphin embraced his father.

"Let us have no scene; hear me out. Should it turn out, on the other hand, that your judgment is erroneous, should Louise not belong to yon crazy progressionist mob who aim to dethrone God and subvert the order of society, should her hatred against religion be merely a silly conforming to the fashionable impiety of the age, which good influences may correct--then I shall insist upon your marrying her. Meanwhile I want you to maintain a strict neutrality--not a step backward nor a step in advance. Now to tea, and let your countenance betray nothing of what has passed." He drew his son to his bosom and imprinted a kiss on his forehead.

The millionaires were seated around the tea-table. Mr. Conrad playfully commended Louise's talent for cooking. Apparently without design he turned the conversation upon the elections, and, to Seraphin's utter astonishment, eulogized the beneficent power of liberal doctrines.

"Our age," said he, "can no longer bear the hampering notions of the past. In the material world, steam and machinery have brought about changes which call for corresponding changes in the world of intellect. Great revolutions have already commenced. In France, Renan has written a *Life of Christ*, and in our own country Protestant convocations are proclaiming an historical Christ who was not God, but only an extraordinary man. You hardly need to be assured that I too take a deep interest in the intellectual struggles of my countrymen, but an excess of business does not permit me to watch them closely. I am obliged to content myself with such reports as the newspapers furnish. I should like to read Renan's work, which seems to have created a great sensation. They say it suits our times admirably."

The brother and sister were not a little astonished at the old gentleman's unusual communicativeness.

"It is a splendid book," exclaimed Louise--"charming as to style, and remarkably liberal and considerate towards the worshippers of Christ."

"So I have everywhere been told," said Mr. Conrad.

"Have you read the book, Louise?"

"Not less than four times, three times in French and once in German."

"Do you think a farmer whose moments are precious as gold could forgive himself the reading of Renan's book in view of the multitude of his urgent occupations?" asked he, smiling.

"The reading of a book that originates a new intellectual era is also a serious occupation," maintained the beautiful lady.

"Very true; yet I apprehend Renan's attempt to disprove to me the divinity of Christ would remain unsuccessful, and it would only cause me the loss of some hours of valuable time."

"Read it, Mr. Gerlach, do read it. Renan's arguments are unanswerable."

"So you have been convinced, Louise?"

"Yes, indeed, quite."

"Well, now, Renan is a living author, he is the lion of the day, and nothing could be more natural than that the fair sex should grow enthusiastic over him. But, of course, at your next confession you will sorrowfully declare and retract your belief in Renan."

The young lady cast a quick glance at Seraphin, and the brim of her teacup concealed a proud, triumphant smile.

"Our city is about taking a bold step," said Carl, breaking the silence. "We are to have common schools, in order to take education from the control of the clergy." And he went on to relate what Schwefel had reported.

"When is the barbecue to come off?" inquired Mr. Conrad.

"On the 10th of August."

"Perhaps I shall have time to attend this demonstration," said Gerlach. "Hearts reveal themselves at such festivities. One gets a clear insight into the mind of the multitude. You, Louise, have put progress under obligations by so cheerfully advancing to meet it."

After these words the landholder rose and went to his room. The next morning he proceeded on his journey, taking with him Seraphin's diary. The author himself he left at the Palais Greifmann in anxious uncertainty about future events.

CHAPTER IX
FAITH AND SCIENCE OF PROGRESS

Seraphin usually look an early ride with Carl. The banker was overjoyed at the wager, about the winning of which he now felt absolute certainty. He expressed himself confident that before long he would have the pleasure of going over the road on the back of the best racer in the country. "The noble animals," said he, "shall not be brought by the railway; it might injure them. I shall send my groom for them to Chateau Hallberg. He can ride the distance in two days."

Seraphin could not help smiling at his friend's solicitude for the horses.

"Do not sell the bear's skin before killing the bear," answered he. "I may not lose the horses, but may, on the contrary, acquire a pleasant claim to twenty thousand florins."

"That is beyond all possibility," returned the banker. "Hans Shund is now chief-magistrate, has been nominated to the legislature, and in a few days will be elected. Mr. Hans will appear as a shining light to-morrow, when he is to state his political creed in a speech to his constituents. Of course, you and I shall go to hear him. Next will follow his election, then my groom will hasten to Chateau Hallberg to fetch the horses. Are you sorry you made the bet?"

"Not at all! I should regret very much to lose my span of bays. Still, the bet will be of incalculable benefit to me. I will have learned concerning men and manners what otherwise I could never have dreamed of. In any event, the experience gained will be of vast service to me during life."

"I am exceedingly glad to know it, my dear fellow," assured Greifmann. "Your acquaintance with the present has been very superficial. You have learned a great deal in a few days, and it is gratifying to hear you acknowledge the fact."

The banker had not, however, caught Gerlach's meaning.

But for the wager, Seraphin would not have become acquainted with Louise's intellectual standpoint. He would probably have married her for the sake of her beauty, would have discovered his mistake when it could not be corrected, and would have found himself condemned to spend his life with a woman whose principles and character could only annoy and give him pain. As it was, he was tormented by the fear that his father might not coincide in his opinion of the young lady. What if the old gentleman considered her hostility to religion as a mere fashionable mania unsupported by inner conviction, a girlish whim changeable like the wind, which with little effort might be made to veer round to the point or the most unimpeachable orthodoxy? He had not uttered a word condemning Louise's infatuation about Renan. On taking leave he had parted with her in a friendly, almost hearty, manner, proof sufficient that the young lady's doubtful utterances at tea had not deceived him.

Upon reaching home, Gerlach sat in his room with his eyes thoughtfully fixed upon a luminous square cast by the sun upon the floor. Quite naturally his thoughts ran upon the marriage, and to the prospect of having to maintain his liberty by hard contest with his inflexible parent. He was unshaken in his resolution not to accede to the projected alliance, and, when a will morally severe conceives resolutions of this sort, they usually stand the hardest tests. So absorbing were his reflections that he did not hear John announcing a visitor. He nodded mechanically in reply to the words that seemed to come out of the distance, and the servant disappeared.

Soon after a country girl appeared entrance of the room. In both hands she was carrying a small basket made of peeled willows, quite new. A snow-white napkin was spread over the basket. The girl's dress was neat, her figure was slender and graceful. Her hair, which was wound about the head in heavy plaits, was golden and encircled her forehead as with a *nimbus*. Her features were delicate and beautiful, and she looked upon the young gentleman with a pair of deep-blue eyes. Thus stood she for an instant in the door of the apartment. There was a smile about her mouth and a faint flush upon her cheeks.

"Good-morning, Mr. Seraphin!" said a sweet voice.

The youth started at this salutation and looked at the stranger with surprise. She was just then standing on the sunlit square, her hair gleamed like the purest gold, and a flood of light streamed upon her youthful form. He did not return the greeting. He looked at her as if frightened, rose slowly, and bowed in silence.

"My father sends some early grapes which he begs you to have the goodness to accept."

She drew nearer, and he received the basket from her hand.

"I am very thankful!" said he. And, raising the napkin, the delicious fruit smiled in his face. "These are a rarity this season. To whom am I indebted for this friendly attention?"

"The obligation is all on our side, Mr. Seraphin," she replied trustfully to the generous benefactor of her family. "Father is sorry that he cannot offer you something better."

"Ah! you are Holt's daughter?"

"Yes, Mr. Seraphin."

"Your name is Johanna, is it not?"

"Mechtild, Mr. Seraphin."

"Will you be so good as to sit down?" And he pointed her to a sofa.

Mechtild, however, drew a chair and seated herself.

He had noted her deportment, and could not but marvel at the graceful action, the confiding simplicity, and well-bred self-possession of the extraordinary country girl. As she sat opposite to him, she looked so pure, so trusting and sincere, that his astonishment went on increasing. He acknowledged to himself never to have beheld eyes whose expression came so directly from the heart--a heart whose interior must be equally as sunny and pure.

"How are your good parents?"

"They are very well, Mr. Seraphin. Father has gone to work with renewed confidence. The sad--ah! the terrible period is past. You cannot imagine, Mr. Seraphin, how many tears you have dried, how much misery you have relieved!"

The recollection of the ruin that had been hanging over her home affected her painfully; her eyes glistened, and tears began to roll down her cheeks. But she instantly repressed the emotion, and exhibited a beautiful smile on her face. Seraphin's quick eye had observed both the momentary feeling, and that she had resolutely checked it in order not to annoy him by touching sorrowful chords. This trait of delicacy also excited the admiration of the gentleman.

"Your father is not in want of employment?" he inquired with interest.

"No, sir! Father is much sought on account of his knowledge of farming. Persons who have ground, but no team of their own, employ him to put in crops for them."

"No doubt the good man has to toil hard?"

"That is true, sir; but father seems to like working, and we children strive to help him as much as we can."

"And do you like working?"

"I do, indeed, Mr. Seraphin. Life would be worthless if one did not labor. Man's life on earth is so ordered as to show him that he must labor. Doing nothing is abominable, and idleness is the parent of many vices."

Another cause of astonishment for the millionaire. She did not converse like an uneducated girl from the country. Her accurate, almost choice use of words indicated some culture, and her concise observations revealed both mind and reflection. He felt a strong desire to fathom the mystery--to cast a glance into Mechtild's past history.

"Have you always lived at home, or have you ever been away at school?"

She must have detected something ludicrous in the question, for suddenly a degree of archness might be observed in her amiable smile.

"You mean, whether I have received a city education? No, sir! Father used to speak highly of the clearness of my mind, and thought I might even be made a teacher. But he had not the means to give me the necessary amount of schooling. Until I was fourteen years old, I went to school to the nuns here in town. I used to come in of mornings and go back in the evening. I studied hard, and father and mother always had the satisfaction of seeing me rewarded with a prize at the examinations. I am very fond of books, and make good use of the convent library. On Sundays, after vespers, I wait till the door of the book-room is opened. I still spend my leisure time in reading, and on Sundays and holidays I know no greater pleasure than to read nice instructive books. At my work I think over what I have read, and I continue practising composition according to the directions of the good ladies of the convent."

"And were you always head at school?"

"Yes," she admitted, with a blush.

"You have profited immensely by your opportunities," he said approvingly. "And the desire for learning has not yet left you?"

"This inordinate craving still continues to torment me," she acknowledged frankly.

"Inordinate--why inordinate?"

"Because, my station and calling do not require a high degree of culture. But it is so nice to know, and it is so nice to have refined intercourse with each others. For seven years I admired the elegant manners of the convent ladies, and I learned many a lesson from them."

"How old are you now?"

"Seventeen, Mr. Seraphin."

"What a pity you did not enter some higher educational institution!" said he.

A pause followed. He looked with reverence upon the artless girl whom God had so richly endowed, both in body and mind, Mechtild rose.

"Please accept, also, my most heartfelt thanks for your generous aid," she said, with emotion, "All my life long I shall remember you before God, Mr. Seraphin. The Almighty will surely repay you what alas! we cannot."

She made a courtesy, and he accompanied her through all the apartments as far as the front door. Here the girl, turning, bowed to him once more and went away.

Returning to his room, Seraphin stood and contemplated the grapes. Strongly did the delicious fruit tempt him, but he touched not one. He then pulled out a drawer, and hid the gifts as though it were a costly treasure. For the rest of the day, Mechtild's bright form hovered near him, and the sweet charm of her eyes, so full of soul, continually worked on his imagination. When he again went into Louise's company, the grace and innocence of the country girl gained ground in his esteem. Compared with Mechtild's charming naturalness, Louise's manner appeared affected, spoiled; through evil influences. The difference in the expression of their eyes struck him especially. In Louise's eyes there burned a fierce glow at times, which roused passion and stirred the senses. Mechtild's neither glowed nor flashed; but from their limpid depths beamed goodness so genuine and serenity so unclouded, that Seraphin could compare them to nothing but two heralds of peace and innocence. Louise's eyes, thought he, flash like two meteors of the night; Mechtild's beam like two mild suns in a cloudless sky of spring. As often as he entered the room where the grapes lay concealed, he would unlock the drawer, examine the fragrant fruit, and handle the basket which had been carried by her hands. He could not himself help smiling at this childish action, and yet both great delicacy and deep earnestness are manifested in honoring objects that have been touched by pure hands, and in revering places hallowed by the presence of the good.

Next morning the banker asked his guest to accompany him to the church of S. Peter, where Hans Shund was to address a large gathering.

"In a church?" Gerlach exclaimed, with amazement.

"Don't get frightened, my good fellow. The church is no longer in the service of religion. It has been *secularized* by the state, and is customarily used as a hall for dancing. There will be quite a crowd, for several able speakers are to discuss the question of common schools. The church has been chosen for the meeting on account of the crowd."

The millionaires drove to the desecrated church. A tumultuous mass swarmed about the portal. "Let us permit them to push us; we shall get in most easily by letting them do so," said the banker merrily. Two officious progressionists, recognizing the banker, opened a passage for them through the throng. They reached the interior of the church, which was now an empty space, stripped of every ornament proper to a house of God. In the sanctuary could yet be seen, as if in mournful abandonment, a large quadrangular slab, that had been the altar, and attached to one of the side walls was an exquisite Gothic pulpit, which on occasions like the present was used for a rostrum. Everywhere else reigned silence and desolation.

The nave was filled by a motley mass. The chieftains of progress, some elegantly dressed, others exhibiting frivolous miens and huge beards, crowded upon the elevation of the chancel. All the candidates for the legislature were present, not for the purpose of proving their qualifications for the office--progress never troubled itself about those--but to air their views on the subject of education. There were speakers on hand of acknowledged ability in the discussion of the doctrines of progress, who were to lay the result of their investigations before the people.

Seraphia also noted some anxious faces in the crowd. They were citizens, whose sons were alarmed at the thought of yielding up the training of their children into the hands of infidelity. And near the pulpit stood two priests, irreverently crowded against the wall, targets for the scornful pleasantries of the wits of the mob. Leader Schwefel was voted into the chair by acclamation. He thanked the assembly in a short speech for the honor conferred, and then announced that Mr. Till, member of the former assembly, would address the meeting. Amid murmurs of expectation a short, fat gentleman climbed into the pulpit. First a red face with a copper-tipped nose bobbed above the ledge of the pulpit, next came a pair of broad shoulders, upon which a huge head rested without the intermediary of a neck, two puffy hands were laid upon the desk, and the commencement of a well-rounded pauch could just be detected by the eye. Mr. Till, taking two handfuls of his shaggy beard, drew them slowly through his fingers, looked composedly upon the audience, and breathed hotly through mouth and nostrils.

"Gentlemen," he began, with a voice that struggled out from a mass of flesh and fat, "I am not given to many words, you know. What need is there of many words and long speeches? We know what we want, and what we want we will have in spite of the machinations of Jesuits and the whinings of an ultramontane horde. You all know how I acquitted myself at the last legislature, and if you will again favor me with your suffrages, I will endeavor once more to give satisfaction. You know my record, and I shall remain staunch to the last."

Cries of "Good!" from various directions.

"Gentlemen! if you know my record, you must also be aware that I am passionately fond of the chase. I even follow this amusement in the legislative hall. Our country abounds in a sort of black game, and for me it is rare sport to pursue this species of game in the assembly."

A wild tumult of applause burst forth. Jeers and coarse witticisms were bandied about on every side of the two clergymen, who looked meekly upon these orgies of progress.

"Gentlemen!" Till continued, "the *blacks* are a dangerous kind of wild beast. They have heretofore been ranging in a preserve, feeding on the fat of the land. That is an abuse that challenges the wrath of heaven. It must be done away with. The beasts of prey that in the dark ages dwelt in castles have long since been exterminated, and their rocky lairs have been reduced to ruins. Well, now, let us keep up the chase in both houses of the legislature until the last of these *black* beasts is destroyed. Should you entrust to me again your interests, I shall return to the seat of government, to aid with renewed energy in ridding the land of these creatures that are enemies both of education and liberty."

Amid prolonged applause the fat man descended. The chieftains shook him warmly by the hand, assuring him that the cause absolutely demanded his being reelected.

Gerlach was aghast at Till's speech. He hardly knew which deserved most scorn, the vulgarity of the speaker or the abjectness of those who had applauded him. Their wild enthusiasm was still surging through the building, when Hans Shund mounted the pulpit. The chairman rang for order; the tumult ceased. In mute suspense the multitude awaited the great speech of the notorious usurer, thief, and debauchee. And indeed, progress might well entertain great expectations, for Hans Shund had read a pile of progressionist pamphlets, had extracted the strong passages, and out of them had concocted a right racy speech. His speech might with propriety have been designated the Gospel of Progress, for Hans Shund had made capital of whatever freethinkers had lucubrated in behalf of so-called enlightenment, and in opposition to Christianity. The very appearance of the speaker gave great promise. His were not coarse features and goggle eyes like Till's; his piercing feline eyes looked intellectual. His face was rather pale, the result, no doubt, of unusual application, and he had skilfully dyed his sandy hair. His position as mayor of the city seemed also to entitle him to special attention, and these several claims were enhanced by a white necktie, white vest, and black cloth swallowtail coat.

"Gentlemen," began the mayor with solemnity, "my honorable predecessor in this place has told you with admirable sagacity that the kernel of every political question is of a religious character. Indeed, religion is linked with every important question of the day, it is the *ratio ultima* of the intellectual movement of our times. Men of thought and of learning are all agreed as to the condition to which our social life should be and must be brought. The friends of the people are actively and earnestly at work trying to further a healthy development of our social and political status. Nor have their efforts been utterly fruitless. Progress has made great conquests; yet, gentlemen, these conquests are far from being complete. What is it that is most hostile to liberalism in morals, to enlightenment, and to humanity? It is the antiquated faith of departed days. Have we not heard the language of the Holy Father in the Syllabus? But the Holy Father at Rome, gentlemen, is no father of ours--happily he is the father only of stupid and credulous men."

"Bravo! Well said!" resounded from the audience. Flaschen nudged Spitzkopf, who sat next to him. "Shund is no mean speaker. Even that fellow Voelk, of Bavaria, cannot compete with Shund."

"Gentlemen, our good sense teaches us to smile with pity at the infallible declarations of yon Holy Father. We are firmly convinced that papal decrees can no more stop the onward march of civilization than they can arrest the heavenly bodies in their journeys about the sun. 'Tis true, an œcumenical council is lowering like a black storm-cloud. But let the council meet; let it declare the Syllabus an article of faith; it will never succeed in destroying the treasures of independent thought which creative intellects have been hoarding up for centuries among every people. Since men of culture have ceased to yield unquestioning submission, like dumb sheep, to the church, they have begun to discover that nowhere are so many falsehoods uttered as in pulpits."

Tremendous applause, clapping, and swinging of hats, followed this eloquent period. A distinguished gentleman, laying his hand upon Till's shoulder, asked: "What calibre of ammunition do you use in hunting *black* game?"

"Conical balls of two centimetres," replied Till, with no great wit.

"Yon fellow in the pulpit fires shells of a hundredweight, I should say. And if in the legislative assembly his shells all explode, not a man of them will be left alive."

Till thought this witticism so good that he set up a loud roar of laughter, that could be heard above the general uproar.

Stimulated by these marks of appreciation, Shund waxed still more eloquent. "Gentlemen," cried he, "no body of men is more savagely opposed to science and culture than a conventicle of so-called servants of God. Were you to repeat the multiplication table several times over, there would be as much prayer and sense in it as in what is designated the Apostles' Creed."

More cheering and boundless enthusiasm. "Gentlemen!" exclaimed the speaker, with thundering emphasis and a hideous expression of hatred on his face, "the significance of religious dogmas is simply a sort of homœopathic concoction to which every succeeding age contributes some drops of fanaticism. Subjected to the microscope of science, the whole basis of the Christian church evaporates into thin mist. We must shield our children against religious fables. Away with dogmas and saws from the Bible; away with the Trinity; the divinity and humanity of Jesus, and other such stuff! Away with apothegms such as this: *Christ is my life, my death, and my gain.* Such things are opposed to nature. Children's minds are thereby warped to untruthfulness and hyprocrisy. In this manner the child is deprived of the power of thinking; loses all interest in intellectual pursuits, and ceases to feel the need of further culture. The times are favorable for a reformation. Our imperial and royal rulers have at length realized that minds must be set free. For this end it was as unavoidable for them to break with the church and priesthood as it is necessary for us. If we cherish our fatherland and the people, we must take the initiative. We are not striving to effect a revolution; we want intellectual development, profounder knowledge, and healthier morality.

"Shall peace be seen beneath our skies,

The spirit's freedom first must rise,"

concluded the orator poetically, and he came down amidst a very hurricane of applause.

There followed a lull. In the audience, heads protruded and necks were stretched that their possessors might obtain a glimpse of the great Shund. In the chancel, the chiefs and leaders crowded around him, smiling, bowing, and shaking his hand in admiration.

"You have won the laurels," smirked a fellow from amidst a wilderness of beard.

"Your election to the Assembly is a certainty," declared another.

"You carry deadly weapons against Christ," said a professor.

Mr. Hans smiled, and nodded so often that he was seized with a pain in the muscles of the face and neck. At length, the chairman's bell came to the rescue.

"The Rev. Mr. Morgenroth will now address the meeting."

The clergyman mounted the rostrum, but scarcely had he appeared there, when the crowd became possessed by a legion of hissing demons.

"Gentlemen," began the fearless priest, "the duty of my calling as well as personal conviction demands that I should enter a solemn protest against the sundering of school and church."

Further the priest was not allowed to proceed. Loud howling, hissing, and whistling drowned his voice. The president called for order.

"In the name of good-breeding, I beg this most honorable assembly to hear the speaker out in patience," cried Mr. Schwefel.

The mob relaxed into unwilling silence like a growling beast.

"Not all the citizens of this town are affected with infidelity," the reverend gentleman went on to say. "Many honorable gentlemen believe in Jesus Christ, the Son of God, and in his church. These citizens wish their children to receive a religious education; it would, therefore, be unmitigated terrorism, tyrannical constraint of conscience, to force Christian parents to bring up their children in the spirit of unbelief."

This palpable truth progress could not bear to listen to. A mad yell was set up. Clenched fists were shaken at the clergyman, and fierce threats thundered from all sides of the church. "Down with the priest!" "Down with the accursed blackcoat!" "Down with the dog of a Jesuit!" and similar exclamations resounded from all sides. The chairman rang his bell in vain. The mob grew still more furious and noisy. The clergyman was compelled to come down.

"Such is the liberty, the education, the tolerance, the humanity of progress," said he sadly to his colleague.

Once more the bell of the chairman was heard amid the tumult.

"Mr. Seicht, officer of the crown, will now address the meeting," Schwefel announced.

The audience were seized with amazement, and not without a cause. A dignitary of a higher order, a member of the administration, ascended the pulpit for the purpose of making an assault upon Christian education. He was about to make war upon morals and faith, the true supports of every solid government, the sources of the moral sentiment and of the prosperity of human society. A remnant of honesty and a lingering sense of justice may have raised a protest in Seicht's mind against his undertaking; for his bearing was anything but self-possessed, and he had the appearance of a wretch that was being goaded on by an evil spirit. Besides, he had the habit peculiar to bureaucrats of speaking in harsh, snarling tones. Seicht was conscious of these peculiarities of his bureaucratic nature, and labored to overcome them. The effort imparted to his delivery an air of constraint and a sickening sweetness which were climaxed by the fearfully involved style in which his speech was clothed.

"Gentlemen," said Seicht, "in view of present circumstances, and in consideration of the requirements of culture whose spirit is incompatible with antiquated conditions, popular education, which in connection with domestic training is the foundation of the future citizen, must also undergo such changes as will bring it into harmony with modern enlightened sentiment; and this is the more necessary as the provisions of the law, which progress in its enlightenment and clearness of perception cannot refuse to recognize as a fit model for the imitation of a party dangerous to the state--I mean the party of Jesuitism and ultramontranism--allow untrammelled scope for the reformation of the school system, provided the proper clauses of the law and the ordinances relating to this matter are not left out of consideration. Accordingly, it is my duty to refer this honorable meeting especially to the ministerial decree referring to common schools, in accordance with which said common schools may be established, after a vote of the citizens entitled to the elective franchise, as soon as the need of this is felt; which in the present instance cannot be contested, since public opinion has taken a decided stand against denominational schools, in which youth is trained after unbending forms of religion, and in doctrines that evidently conflict with the triumph of the present, and with those exact sciences which make up the only true gospel--the gospel of progress, which scarcely in any respect resembles the narrow gospel of dubious dogmas--dubious for the reason that they lack the spirit of advancement, and are prejudicial to the investigation of the problems of a God, of material nature, and of man."

Here leader Sand thrust his fingers in his ears.

"Thunder and lightning!" exclaimed he wrathfully, "what a shallow babbler! What is he driving at? His periods are a yard long; and when he has done, a man is no wiser than when he began. Gospel--gospel of progress--fool--numskull--down! down!"

"Quite a remarkable instance, this!" said Gerlach to the banker. "Evidently this man is trying might and main to please, yet he only succeeds in torturing his hearers."

"I will explain this man to you," replied the banker. "Heretofore Mr. Seicht has been a most complete exemplar of absolute bureaucracy. The only divinity he knew were the statutes, the only heaven the bureau, and the only safe way of reaching supreme felicity was, in his opinion, to render unquestioning obedience to ministerial rescripts. Suddenly Mr. Seicht heard the card-house of bureaucracy start in all its joints. His divinity lost its worshippers, and his heaven lost all charms for those who were seeking salvation. He felt the ground moving under him, he realized the colossal might of progress, and hastened to commend himself to this party by adopting liberal ideas. He is now aiming to secure a seat in the house of delegates, which is subsequently to serve him as a stepping-stone to a place in the cabinet. Just listen how the man is agonizing! He is wasting his strength, however, and the attitude of the audience is beginning to get alarming."

For some time past, the chieftains in the chancel had been shaking their heads at the efforts of this official advocate of progress. To avoid being tortured by hearing, they had engaged in conversation. The auditors in the nave of the church were also growing restive. The speaker, however, continued blind to every hint and insinuation. At last a tall fellow in the crowd swung his hat and cried, "Three cheers for Mr. Seicht!" The whole nave joined in a deafening cheer. Seicht, imagining the cheering to be a tribute to the excellence of his effort, stopped for a moment to permit the uproar to subside, intending then to go on with his speech; but no sooner had he resumed than the cheering burst forth anew, and was so vigorously sustained that the man, at length perceiving the meaning of the audience, came down amid peals of derisive laughter.

"Serves the gabbler right!" said Sand. "He's a precious kind of a fellow! The booby thinks he can hoist himself into the chamber of deputies by means of the shoulders of progress, and thence to climb up higher. But it happens that we know whom we have to deal with, and we are not going to serve as stirrups for a turn-coat official."

The chairman wound up with a speech in which he announced that the vote on the question of common schools would soon come off, and then adjourned the meeting.

The millionaires drew back to allow the crowd to disperse. Near them stood Mr. Seicht, alone and dejected. The countenances of the chieftains had yielded him no evidence on which to base a hope that his speech had told, and that he might expect to occupy a seat in the assembly. Moreover, Sand had rudely insulted the ambitious official to his face. This he took exceedingly hard. All of a sudden, he spied the banker in the chancel, and went over to greet him. Greifmann introduced Gerlach.

"I am proud," Mr. Seicht asseverated, "of the acquaintance of the wealthiest proprietor of the country."

"Pardon the correction, sir; my father is the proprietor."

"No matter, you are his only son," rejoined Seicht. "Your presence proves that you take an interest in the great questions of the day. This is very laudable."

"My presence, however, by no means proves that I concur in the object of this meeting. Curiosity has led me hither."

The official directed a look of inquiry at the banker.

"Sheer curiosity," repeated this gentleman coldly.

"Can you not, then, become reconciled to the spirit of progress?" asked Seicht, with a smile revealing astonishment.

"The value of my convictions consists in this, that I worship genuine progress," replied the millionaire gravely. "The progress of this community, in particular, looks to me like retrogression."

"I am astonished at what you say," returned the official; "for surely Shund's masterly speech has demonstrated that we are keeping pace with the age."

"I cannot see, sir, how fiendish hatred of religion can be taken for progress. This horrible, bloodthirsty monster existed even in the days of Nero and Tiberius, as we all know. Can the resurrection of it, now that it has been mouldering for centuries, be seriously looked upon as a step in advance? Rather a step backward, I should think, of eighteen hundred years. Especially horrible and revolting is this latest instance of tyranny, forcing parents who entertain religious sentiments to send their children to irreligious schools. Not even Nero and Tiberius went so far. On this point, I agree, there has been progress, but it consists in putting a most unnatural constraint upon conscience."

Gerlach's language aroused the official. He was face to face with an ultramontane. The mere sight of such an one caused a nervous twitching in his person. He resorted at once to bureaucratic weapons in making his onslaught.

"You are mistaken, my dear sir--you are very much mistaken. The spirit of the modern state demands that the schools of the multitude, particularly public institutions, should be accessible to the children of every class of citizens, without distinction of religious profession. Consequently, the schools must be taken from under the authority, direction, and influence of the church, and put entirely under civil and political control. Such, too, is now the mind of our rulers, besides that public sentiment calls for the change."

"But, Mr. Seicht, in making such a change, the state despotically infringes on the province of religion."

"Not despotically, Mr. Gerlach, but legally; for the state is the fountain-head of all right, and consequently possessed of unlimited right."

"You enunciate principles, sir, which differ vastly from what morality and religion teach."

"What signify morals--what signifies religion? Mere antiquated forms, sir, with no living significance," explained Seicht, lavishly displaying the treasures of the storehouse of progressionist wisdom. "The past submitted quietly to the authority of religion, because there existed then a low degree of intellectual culture. At present there is only one authority--it is the preponderance of numbers and of material forces. Consequently, the only real authority is the majority in power. On the other hand, authorities based upon the supposed existence of a supersensible world have lost their cause of being, for the reason that exact science plainly demonstrates the nonexistence of an immaterial world. *Cessante causa, cessat effectus,* the supersensible world, the basis of religious authority, being gone, it logically results that religious authority itself is gone. Hence the only real authority existing in a state is the majority, and to this every citizen is obliged to submit. You marvel, Mr. Gerlach. What I have said is not my own personal view, but the expression of the principles which alone pass current at the present day."

"I agree in what you say," said the banker. "You have spoken from the standpoint of the times. The controlling power is the majority."

"Shund, then, accurately summed up the creed of the present age when he said, 'Progress conquers death, destroys hell, rejects heaven, and finds its god in the sweet enjoyment of life.' It is to be hoped that all-powerful progress will next decree that there are no death and no suffering upon earth, that all the hostile forces of nature have ceased, that want and misery are no more, and that earth is a paradise of sweet enjoyment for all."

Mr. Seicht was rather taken aback by this satire.

"Besides, gentlemen," proceeded Gerlach, "you will please observe that the doctrine of state supremacy is a step backward of nearly two thousand years. In Nero's day, but one source of right, namely, the state, was recognized. In the head of the state, the emperor, were centred all power, all authority, and all right. In his person, the state was exalted into a divinity. Temples and altars were reared to the emperor; sacrifices were offered to him; he was worshipped as a deity. Even human sacrifices were not denied him if the imperial divinity thought proper to demand them. And, now, to what condition did these monstrous errors bring the world of that period? It became one vast theatre of crime, immorality, and despotism. Slavery coiled itself about men and things, and strangled their liberty. Matrimonial life sank into the most loathsome corruption. Infanticide was permitted to pass unpunished. The licentiousness of women was even greater than that of men. Life and property became mere playthings for the whims of the emperor and of his courtiers. Did the divine Cæsar wish to amuse his deeply sunken subjects, he had only to order the gladiators to butcher one another, or some prisoners or slaves or Christians to be thrown to tigers and panthers; this made a Roman holiday. Such, gentlemen, was human society when it recognized no supersensible world, no God above, no moral law. If our own progress proceeds much further in the path on which it is marching, it will soon reach a similar fearful stage. We already see in our midst the commencement of social corruption. We have the only source of right proclaimed to be the divine state. Conscience is being tyrannized over by a majority that rejects God and denies future rewards and punishments. All the rest, even to the divine despot, has already followed, or inevitably will follow. Therefore, Mr. Seicht, the progress you so loudly boast of is mere stupid retrogression, blind superstition, which falls prostrate before the majority of a mob, and worships the omnipotence of the state."

"Don't you think my friend has been uttering some very bitter truths?" asked the banker, with a smile.

"Pretty nearly so," replied the official demurely. "However, one can detect the design, and cannot help getting out of humor."

"What design?" asked Seraphin.

"Of creating alarm against progress."

"Indeed, sir, you are mistaken. I, too, am enthusiastic about progress, but genuine progress. And because I am an advocate of real progress I cannot help detesting the monstrosity which the age would wish to palm off on men instead."

The church was now cleared. Greifmann's carriage was at the door. The millionaires drove off.

"Pity for this Gerlach!" thought the official, as he strode through the street. "He is lost to progress, for he is too solidly rooted in superstition to be reclaimed. War against nature's claims; deny healthy physical nature its rights; re-establish terror of the seven capital sins; permit the priesthood to tyrannize over conscience; restore the worship of an unmathematical triune God--no! no!" cried he fiercely, "I shall all go to the devil!"

A carriage whirled past him. He caste a glance into the vehicle, and raised his hat to Mr. Hans Shund.

The chief magistrate was on his way home from the town-hall. He could not rest under the weight of his laurels; the inebriation of his triumph drove him into the room where sat his lonely and careworn wife.

"My election to the assembly is assured, wife." And he went on with a minute account of the proceedings of the day.

The pale, emaciated lady sat bowed in silence over her work, and did not look up.

"Well, wife, don't you take any interest in the honors won by your husband? I should think you ought to feel pleased."

"All my joys are swallowed up in an abyss of unutterable wretchedness," replied she. "And my husband is daily deepening the gulf. Yesterday you were again at a disreputable house. Your abominable deeds are heaped mountain high--and am I to rejoice?"

"A thousand demons, wife, I'm beginning to believe you have spies on foot!"

"I have not. But you are at the head of this city--your steps cannot possibly remain unobserved."

"Very well!" cried he, "it shall be my effort in the assembly to bring about such a change that there shall no longer be any houses of disrepute. Narrow-minded moralists shall not be allowed to howl any longer. The time is at hand, old lady--so-called disreputable houses are to become places of amusement authorized by law."

He spoke and disappeared.

CHAPTER X
PROGRESS GROWS JOLLY

The agitators of progress were again hurrying through the streets and alleys of the town. They knocked at every door and entered every house to solicit votes in favor of common schools. Thanks to the overwhelming might of the party in power, they again carried their measure. Dependent, utterly enslaved, many yielded up their votes without opposition. It is true conscience tortured many a parent for voting against his convictions, for sacrificing his children to a system with which he could not sympathize; but not a man in a dependent position had the courage to vindicate for his child the religious training which was being so ruthlessly swept away. Even men in high office gave way before the encroaching despotism, for in the very uppermost ranks of society also progress domineered.

One man only, fearless and firm, dared to put himself in the path of the dominant power--the Rev. F. Morgenroth. From the pulpit, he unmasked and scathed the unchristian design of debarring youth from religious instruction, and of rearing a generation ignorant of God and of his commandments. He warned parents against the evil, entreated them to stand up conscientiously for the spiritual welfare of their children, to reject the common schools, and to rescue the little ones for the maternal guardianship of the church.

His sermon roused the entire progressionist camp. The local press fiercely assailed the intrepid clergyman. Lies, calumnies, and scurrility were vomited against him and his profession. Hans Shund seized the pen, and indited newspaper articles of such a character as one would naturally look for from a thief, usurer, and debauchee. Morgenroth paid no attention to their disgraceful clamor, but continued his opposition undismayed. By means of placards, he invited the Catholic citizens to assemble at his own residence, for the purpose of consulting about the best mode of thwarting the designs of the liberals. This unexpected fearlessness put the men of culture, humanity, and freedom beside themselves with rage. They at once decided upon making a public demonstration. The chieftains issued orders to their bands, and these at the hour appointed for the meeting mustered before the residence of the priest. A noisy multitude, uttering threats, took possession of the churchyard. If a citizen attempted to make his way through the mob to the house, he was loaded with vile epithets, at times even with kicks and blows. But a small number had gathered around the priest, and these showed much alarm; for outside the billows of progress were surging and every moment rising higher. Stones were thrown at the house, and the windows were broken. Parteiling, the commissary of police, came to remonstrate with the clergyman.

"Dismiss the meeting," said he. "The excitement is assuming alarming proportions."

"Commissary, we are under the protection of the law and of civil rule," replied Morgenroth. "We are not slaves and helots of progress. Are we to be denied the liberty of discussing subjects of great importance in our own houses?"

A boulder coming through the window crushed the inkstand on the table, and rolled on over the floor. The men pressed to one side in terror.

"Your calling upon the law to protect you is utterly unreasonable under present circumstances," said Parteiling. "Listen to the howling. Do you want your house demolished? Do you wish to be maltreated? Will you have open revolution? This all will surely follow if you persist in refusing to dismiss the meeting. I will not answer for results."

Stones began to rain more densely, and the howling grew louder and more menacing.

"Gentlemen," said Morgenroth to the men assembled, "since we are not permitted to proceed with our deliberations, we will separate, with a protest against this brutal terrorism."

"But, commissary," said a much frightened man, "how are we to get away? These people are infuriated; they will tear us in pieces."

"Fear nothing, gentlemen; follow me," spoke the commissary, leading the way.

The ultramontanes were hailed with a loud burst of scornful laughter. The commissary, advancing to the gate, beckoned silence.

"In the name of the law, clear the place!" cried he.

The mob scoffed and yelled.

"Fetch out the slaves of the priest--make them run the gauntlet--down with the Jesuits!"

At this moment, a man was noticed elbowing his way through the crowd; presently Hans Shund stepped before the embarrassed guardian of public order.

"Three cheers for the magistrate!" vociferated the mob.

Shund made a signal. Profound silence followed.

"Gentlemen," spoke the chief magistrate, in a tone of entreaty, "have goodness to disperse."

Repeated cheers were raised, then the accumulation of corrupt elements began to dissolve and flow off into every direction.

"I deeply regret this commotion of which I but a moment ago received intelligence," said Shund. "The excitement of the people is attributable solely to the imprudent conduct of Morgenroth."

"To be sure--to be sure!" assented Parteiling.

The place was cleared. The Catholics hurried home pursued and hooted by straggling groups of rioters.

The signs of the approaching celebration began to be noticeable on the town-common. Booths were being erected, tables were being disposed in rows which reached further than the eye could see, wagon-loads of chairs and benches were being brought from all parts of town, men were busy sinking holes for climbing-poles and treacherous turnstiles; but the most attractive feature of all the festival was yet invisible--free beer and sausages furnished at public cost. The rumor alone, however, of such cheer gladdened the heart of every thirsty voter, and contributed greatly to the establishment of the system of common schools. Bands of music paraded the town, gathered up voters, and escorted them to the polls. As often as they passed before the residence of a progressionist-chieftain, the bands struck up an air, and the crowd cheered lustily. They halted in front of the priest's residence also. The band played, "Today we'll taste the parson's cheer," the mob roaring the words, and then winding up with whistling and guffaws of laughter. This sort of disorderly work was kept up during three days. Then was announced in the papers in huge type: "An overwhelming majority of the enlightened citizens of this city have decided in favor of common schools. Herewith the existence of these schools is secured and legalized."

On the fourth day, the celebration came off. The same morning Gerlach senior arrived at the Palais Greifmann on his way home from the Exposition.

"I am so glad!" cried Louise. "I was beginning to fear you would not come, and getting provoked at your indifference to the interests of our people. We have been having stirring times, but we have come off victorious. The narrow-minded enemies of enlightenment are defeated. Modern views now prevail, and education is to be remodelled and put in harmony with the wants of our century."

"Times must have been stirring, for you seem almost frenzied, Louise," said Conrad.

"Had you witnessed the struggle and read the newspapers, you, too, would have grown enthusiastic," declared the young lady.

"Even quotations advanced," said the banker. "It astonished me, and I can account for it only by assuming that the triumph of the common-school system is of general significance and an imperative desideratum of the times."

"How can you have any doubt about it?" cried his sister. "Our town has pioneered the way: the rest of Germany will soon adopt the same system."

Seraphin greeted his father.

"Well, my son, you very likely have heard nothing whatever of this hubbub about schools?"

"Indeed, I have, father. Carl and I were in the midst of the commotion at the desecrated church of S. Peter. We saw and heard what it would have been difficult to imagine." He then proceeded to give his father a minute account of the meeting. His powerful memory enabled him to repeat Shund's speech almost verbatim. The father listened attentively, and occasionally directed a glance of observation at the young lady. When Shund's coarse ridicule of Christian morals and dogmas was rehearsed, Mr. Conrad lowered his eyes, and a frown flitted over his brow. For the rest, his countenance was, as usual, cold and stern.

"This Mr. Shund made quite a strong speech," said he, in a nonchalant way.

"He rather intensified the colors of truth, 'tis true," remarked Louise. "The masses, however, like high coloring and vigorous language."

A servant brought the banker a note.

"Good! Shund is elected to the assembly! The span of bays belongs to me," exulted Carl Greifmann.

"Your bays Seraphin?" inquired the father. "How is this?"

Mr. Conrad had twice been informed of the wager; he had learned it first from Seraphin's own lips, then also he had read of it in his diary; still he asked again, and his son detailed the story a third time.

"I should sooner have expected to see the heavens fall than to lose that bet," added Seraphin.

"When a notorious thief and usurer is elected to the chief magistracy and to the legislative assembly, the victory gained is hardly a creditable one to the spirit of progress, my dear Carl. Don't you think so, Louise?" said the landholder.

"You mustn't be too rigorous," replied the lady, with composure. "Rumor whispers many a bit of scandal respecting Shund which does, indeed, offend one's sense of propriety; for all that, however, Shund will play his part brilliantly both in the assembly and in the town council. The greatest of statesmen have had their foibles, as everybody knows."

"Very true," said Gerlach dryly. "Viewed from the standpoint of very humane tolerance, Shund's disgusting habits may be considered justifiable."

Seraphin left the parlor, and retired to his room. Here he wrestled with violent feelings. His father's conduct was a mystery to him. Opinions which conflicted with his own most sacred convictions, and principles which brought an indignant flush to his cheek, were listened to and apparently acquiesced in by his father. Shund's abominable diatribe had not roused the old gentleman's anger; Louise's avowed concurrence with the irreligious principles of the chieftain had not even provoked his disapprobation.

"My God, my God! can it be possible?" cried he in an agony of despair. "Has the love of gain so utterly blinded my father? Can he have sunk so low as to be willing to immolate me, his only child, to a base speculation? Can he be willing for the sake of a million florins to bind me for life to this erring creature, this infidel Louise? Can a paltry million tempt him to be so reckless and cruel? No! no! a thousand times no!" exclaimed he. "I never will be the husband of this woman, never--I swear it by the great God of heaven! Get angry with me, father, banish me from your sight--it would be more tolerable than the consciousness of being the husband of a woman who believes not in the Redeemer of the world. I have sworn--the matter is for ever settled." He threw himself into an arm-chair, and moodily stared at the opposite wall. By degrees, his excitement subsided, and he became quiet.

In fancy, he beheld beside Louise's form another lovely one rise up--that of the girl with the golden hair, the bright eyes, and the winning smile. She had stood before him on this very floor, in her neat and simple country garb, radiant with innocence and purity, adorned with innate grace and uncommon beauty. And the lapse of days, far from weakening, had deepened the impression of her first apparition. The storm that had been raging in his interior was allayed by the recollection of Mechtild, as the fury of the great deep subsides upon the reappearance of the sun. Scarcely an hour had passed during which he had not thought of the girl, rehearsed every word she had uttered, and viewed the basket of grapes she had brought him. Again he pulled out the drawer, and looked upon the gift with a friendly smile; then, locking up the precious treasure, he returned to the parlor.

He found the company on the balcony. The sound of trumpets and drums came from a distance, and presently a motley procession was seen coming up the nearest street.

"You have just arrived in time to see the procession," cried Louise to him. "It is going to defile past here, so we will be able to have a good look at it."

A dusky swarm of boys and half-grown youths came winding round the nearest street-corner, followed immediately by the head of a mock procession. In the lead marched a fellow dressed in a brown cloak, the hood of which was drawn over his head. His waist was encircled with a girdle from which dangled a string of pebbles representing a rosary. To complete the caricature of a Capuchin, his feet were bare, excepting a pair of soles which were strapped to them with thongs of leather. In his hands he bore a tall cross rudely contrived with a couple of sticks. The image of the cross was represented by a broken mineral-water bottle. Behind the cross-bearer followed the procession in a double line, consisting of boys, young men, factory-hands, drunken mechanics, and such other begrimed and besotted beings as progress alone can count in its ranks. The members of the procession were chanting a litany; at the same time they folded their hands, made grimaces, turned their eyes upwards, or played unseemly pranks with genuine rosary beads.

Next in the procession came a low car drawn by a watery-eyed mare which a lad bedizened like a clown was leading by the bridle. In the car sat a fat fellow whose face was painted red, and eyebrows dyed, and who wore a long artificial beard. Over a prodigious paunch, also artificial, he had drawn a long white gown, over which again he wore a many-colored rag shaped like a cope. On his head he wore a high paper cap, brimless; around the cap were three crowns of gilt paper to represent the tiara of the pope. A sorry-looking donkey walked after the car, to which it was attached by a rope. It was the *rôle* of the fellow in the car to address the donkey, make a sign of blessing over it, and occasionally reach it straw drawn from his artificial paunch. As often as he went through this manœuvre, the crowd set up a tremendous roar of laughter. The fat man in the car represented the pope, and the donkey was intended to symbolize the credulity of the faithful.

This mock pope was not a suggestion of Shund's or of any other inventive progressionist. The whole idea was copied from a caricature which had appeared in a widely circulating pictorial whose only aim and pleasure it has been for years to destroy the innate religious nobleness of the German people by means of shallow wit and vulgar caricatures. And this very sheet, leagued with a daily organ equally degraded, can boast of no inconsiderable success. The rude and vulgar applaud its witticisms, the low and infamous regale themselves with its pictures, and its demoralizing influence is infecting the land.

The principal feature of the procession was a wagon, hung with garlands and bestuck with small flags, drawn by six splendid horses. In it sat a youthful woman, plump and bold. Her shoulders were bare, the dress being an exaggerated sample of the style *décolleté*; above her head was a wreath of oak leaves. She was attended by a number of young men in masks. They carried drinking-horns, which they filled from time to time from a barrel, and presented to the *bacchante*, who sipped from them; then these gentlemen in waiting drank themselves, and poured what was left upon the crowd. A band of music, walking in front of this triumphal car, played airs and marches. Not even the mock pope was as great an object of admiration as this shameless woman. Old and young thronged about the wagon, feasting their lascivious eyes on this beastly spectacle which represented that most disgusting of all abominable achievements of progress--the emancipated woman. And perhaps not even progress could have dared, in less excited times, so grossly to insult the chaste spirit of the German people; but the social atmosphere had been made so foul by the abominations of the election, and the spirits of impurity had reigned so absolutely during the canvass in behalf of common schools, that this immoral show was suffered to parade without opposition.

The very commencement of this sacrilegious mockery of religion had roused Seraphin's indignation, and he had retired from the balcony. His father, however, had remained, coolly watching the procession as it passed, and carefully noting Louise's remarks and behavior.

"What does that woman represent?" he asked. "A goddess of liberty, I suppose?"

"Only in one sense, I think," replied the progressionist young lady. "The woman wearing the crown symbolizes, to my mind, the enjoyment of life. She typifies heaven upon earth, now that exact science has done away with the heaven of the next world."

"I should think yon creature rather reminds one of hell," said Mr. Conrad.

"Of hell!" exclaimed Louise, in alarm. "You are jesting, sir, are you not?"

"Never more serious in my life, Louise. Notice the shameless effrontery, the baseness and infamy of the creature, and you will be forced to form conclusions which, far from justifying the expectation of peace and happiness in the family circle, the true sphere of woman, will suggest only wrangling, discord, and hell upon earth."

The young lady did not venture to reply. A gentleman made his way through the crowd, and waved his hat to the company on the balcony. The banker returned the salutation.

"Official Seicht," said he.

"What! an officer of the government in this disreputable crowd!" exclaimed Gerlach, with surprise.

"He is on hand to maintain order," explained Greifmann. "You see some policemen, too. Mr. Seicht sympathizes with progress. At the last meeting, he made a speech in favor of common schools; he sounded the praises of the gospel of progress, gave a toast at the banquet to the gospel of progress, and has won for himself the title of evangelist of progress. He once declared, too, that the very sight of a priest rouses his blood, and they now pleasantly call him the parson-eater. He is very popular."

"I am amazed!" said Gerlach. "Mr. Seicht dishonors his office. He advocates common schools, insults all the believing citizens of his district, and runs with mock processions--a happy state of things, indeed!"

"His conduct is the result of careful calculation," returned Greifmann. "By showing hostility to ultramontanism, he commends himself to progress, which is in power."

"But the government should not tolerate such disgraceful behavior on the part of one of its officials," said Gerlach. "The entire official corps is disgraced so long as this shallow evangelist of progress is permitted to continue wearing the uniform."

"You should not be so exacting," cried Louise. "Why will you not allow officials also to float along with the current of progress until they will have reached the Eldorado of the position to which they are aspiring?"

"The corruption of the state must be fearful indeed, when such deportment in an officer is regarded as a recommendation," rejoined Mr. Conrad curtly.

A servant appeared to call them to table.

"Would you not like to see the celebration?" inquired Louise.

"By all means," answered Gerlach. "The excitement is of so unusual a character that it claims attention. You will have to accompany us, Louise."

"I shall do so with pleasure. When sound popular sentiment thus proclaims itself, I cannot but feel a strong desire to be present."

The procession had turned the corner of a street where stood Holt and two more countrymen looking on. The religious sentiment of these honest men was deeply wounded by the profanation of the cross; and when, besides, they heard the singing of the mock litany, their anger kindled, their eyes gleamed, and they mingled fierce maledictions with the tumult of the mob. Next appeared the mock pope, dispensing blessings with his right hand, reaching straw to the donkey with his left, and distorting his painted face into all sorts of farcical grimaces.

The peasants at once caught the significance of this burlesque. Their countenances glowed with indignation. Avenging spirits took possession of Mechtild's father; his strong, stalwart frame seemed suddenly to have become herculean. His fist of iron doubled itself; there was lightning in his eyes; like an infuriated lion, he burst into the crowd, broke the line of the procession, and, directing a tremendous blow at the head of the mock pope, precipitated him from the car. The paper cap flew far away under the feet of the bystanders, and the false beard got into the donkey's mouth. When the mock pope was down. Holt's comrades immediately set upon him, and tore the many-colored rag from his shoulders. Then commenced a great tumult. A host of furious progressionists surrounded the sturdy countrymen, brandishing their fists and filling the air with mad imprecations.

"Kill the dogs! Down with the accursed ultramontanes!"

Some of the policemen hurried up to prevent bloodshed. Mr. Seicht also hurried to the scene of action, and his shrill voice could be heard high above the noise and confusion.

"Gentlemen, I implore you, let the law have its course, gentlemen!" cried he. "Gentlemen, friends, do not, I beg you, violate the law! Trust me, fellow-citizens--I shall see that the impertinence of these ultramontanes is duly punished."

They understood his meaning. Sticks and fists were immediately lowered.

"Brigadier Forchhaem," cried Mr. Seicht, in a tone of command-- "Forchhaem, hither! Put handcuffs on these ultramontanes, these disturbers of the peace--put irons on these revolutionists."

Handcuffs were forthwith produced by the policemen. The towering, broad-shouldered Holt stood quiet as a lamb, looked with an air of astonishment at the confusion, and suffered himself to be handcuffed. His comrades, however, behaved like anything but lambs. They laid about them with hands and feet, knocking down the policemen, and giving bloody mouths and noses to all who came within their reach.

"Handcuff us!" they screamed, grinding their teeth, bleeding and cursing. "Are we cutthroats?" The bystanders drew back in apprehension. The confusion seemed to be past remedying. A thousand voices were screaming, bawling, and crying at the same time; the circle around the struggling countrymen was getting wider and wider; and when finally they attempted to break through, the crowd took to flight, as if a couple of tigers were after them.

Many of the spectators found a pleasurable excitement in watching the battle between the policemen and the peasants; but they would not move a finger to aid the officers of the law in arresting the culprits. They admired the agility and strength of the countrymen, and the more fierce the struggle became, the greater grew their delight, and the louder their merriment.

Holt had been carried on with the motion of the crowd. When he dealt the blow to the fellow in the car, he was beside himself with rage. The genuine *furor teutonicus* had taken possession of him so irresistibly and so bewilderingly as to leave him utterly without any of the calm judgment necessary to measure the situation. After his first adventure, he had submitted to be handcuffed, and had watched the struggle between Forchhaem and his own comrades in a sort of absence of mind. He had stood perfectly quiet, his face had become pale, and his eyes looked about strangely. The excitement of passion was now beginning to wear off. He felt the cold iron of the manacles around his wrists, his eyes glared, his face became crimson, the sinews of his powerful arm stiffened, and with one great muscular convulsion he wrenched off the handcuffs. Nobody had observed this sudden action, all eyes being directed to the combatants. Shoving the part of the handcuff which still hung to his wrist under the sleeve of his jacket, Holt disappeared through the crowd.

The resistance of the peasants was gradually becoming fainter. At length they succumbed to overpowering force, and were handcuffed.

"Where is the third one?" cried Seicht. "There were three of them."

"Where is the third one? There were three of them," was echoed on every hand, and all eyes sought for the missing one in the crowd.

"The third one has run away, sir," reported Forchhaem.

"What's his name?" asked Seicht.

Nobody knew.

A street boy, looking up at the official, ingenuously cried, "'Twas a Tartar."

Seicht looked down upon the obstreperous little informant.

"A Tartar--do you know him?"

"No; but these here know him," pointing to the captives.

"What is the name of your comrade?"

"We don't know him," was the surly reply.

"Never mind, he will become known in the judicial examination. Off to jail with these rebellious ultramontanes," the official commanded.

Bound in chains, and guarded by a posse of police, these honest men, whose religious sense had been so wantonly outraged as to have occasioned an outburst of noble indignation, were marched through the streets of the town and imprisoned. They were treated as criminals for a crime, however, the guilt of which was justly chargeable to those very rioters who were enjoying official protection.

The procession moved on to the ground selected for the barbecue. A motley mass, especially of factory-men, were hard at work upon the scene. The booths, spread far and wide over the common, were thrown open, and around them moved a swarm of thirsty beings drawing rations of beer and sausages, with which, when they had received them, they staggered away to the tables. Degraded-looking women were also to be seen moving about unsteadily with brimming mugs of beer in their hands. There were several bands of music stationed at different points around the place.

The chieftains of progress, perambulating the ground with an air of triumph, bestowed friendly nods of recognition on all sides, and condescendingly engaged in conversation with some of the rank and file.

Hans Shund approached the awning where the woman with the bare shoulders and indecent costume had taken a seat. She had captivated the gallant chief magistrate, who hovered about her as a raven hovers over a dead carcass. Moving off, he halted within hearing distance, and, casting frequent glances back, addressed immodest jokes to those who occupied the other side of the table, at which they laughed and applauded immoderately.

The men whom Seraphin had met in the subterranean den, on the memorable night before the election, were also present: Flachsen, Graeulich, Koenig, and a host of others. They were regaling themselves with sausages which omitted an unmistakable odor of garlic, and were of a very dubious appearance; interrupting the process of eating with frequent and copious draughts from their beer-mugs.

"Drink, old woman!" cried Graeulich to his wife. "Drink, I tell you! It doesn't cost us anything to-day."

The woman put the jug to her lips and drained it manfully. Other women who were present screamed in chorus, and the men laughed boisterously.

"Your old woman does that handsomely," applauded Koth. "Hell and thunder! But she must be a real spitfire."

Again they laughed uproariously.

"I wish there were an election every day, what a jolly life this would be!" said Koenig. "Nothing to do, eating and drinking gratis--what more would you wish?"

"That's the way the bigbugs live all the year round. They may eat and drink what they like best, and needn't do a hand's turn. Isn't it glorious to be rich?" cried Graeulich.

"So drink, boys, drink till you can't stand! We are all of us big-bugs to-day."

"And if things were regulated as they should be," said Koth, "there would come a day when we poor devils would also see glorious times. We have been torturing ourselves about long enough for the sake of others. I maintain that things will have to be differently regulated."

"What game is that you are wishing to come at? Show your hand, old fellow!" cried several voices.

"Here's what I mean: Coffers which are full will have to pour some of their superfluity into coffers which are empty. You take me, don't you?"

"'Pon my soul, I can't make you out. You are talking conundrums," declared Koenig.

"You blockhead, I mean there will soon have to be a partition. They who have plenty will have to give some to those who have nothing."

"Bravo! Long live Koth!"

"That sort of doctrine is dangerous to the state," said Flachsen. "Such principles bring about revolutions, and corrupt society."

"What of society! You're an ass, Flachsen! Koth is right--partition, partition!" was the cry all round the table.

"As you will! I have nothing against it if only it were practicable," expostulated Flachsen; "for I, too, am a radical."

"It is practicable! All things are practicable," exclaimed Koth. "Our age can do anything, and so can we. Haven't we driven religion out of the schools? Haven't we elected Shund for mayor? It is the majority who rule; and, were we to vote in favor of partition to-morrow, partition would have to take place. Any measure can be carried by a majority, and, since we poor devils are in the majority, as soon as we will have voted for partition it will come without fail."

"That's sensible!" agreed they all. "But then, such a thing has never yet been done. Do you think it possible?"

"Anything is possible," maintained Koth. "Didn't Shund preach that there isn't any God, or hell, or devil? Was that ever taught before? If the God of old has to submit to being deposed, the rich will have to submit to it. I tell you, the majority will settle the business for the rich. And if there's no God, no devil, and no life beyond, well then, you see, I'm capable of laying my hand to anything. If voting won't do, violence will. Do you understand?"

"Bravo! Hurrah for Koth!"

"There must be progress," cried Graeulich, "among us as well as others. We are not going to continue all our lives in wretchedness. We must advance from labor to comfort without labor, from poverty to wealth, from want to abundance. Three cheers for progress--hurrah! hurrah!", And the whole company joined in frantically.

"There comes Evangelist Seicht," cried Koenig. "Though I didn't understand one word of his speech, I believe he meant well. Although he is an officer of the government, he cordially hates priests. A man may say what he pleases against religion, and the church, and the Pope, and the Jesuits, it rather pleases Seicht. He is a free and enlightened man, is he. Up with your glasses, boys; if he comes near, let's give him three rousing cheers."

They did as directed. Men and women cheered lustily. Seicht very condescendingly raised his hat and smiled as he passed the table. The ovation put him in fine humor. Though he had failed in securing a place in the assembly, perhaps the slight would be repaired in the future. Such was the tenor of his thoughts whilst he advanced to the climbing-pole, around which was assembled a crowd of boys. Quite a variety of prizes, especially tobacco-pipes, was hanging from the cross-pieces at the top of the mast. The pole was so smooth that more than ordinary strength and activity were required to get to the top. The greater number of those who attempted the feat gave out and slid back without having gained a prize. There were also grown persons standing around watching the efforts of the boys and young men.

"It's my turn now," cried the fellow who had carried the cross in the procession.

"But, first, let me have one more drink--it'll improve the sliding." He swallowed the drink hastily, then swaying about as he looked and pointed upward, "Do you see that pipe with tassels to it?" he said. "That's the one I'm going after."

Throwing aside his mantle, he began to climb.

"He'll not get up, he's drunk," cried a lad among the bystanders. "Belladonna has given him two pints of double beer for carrying the cross in the procession--that's what ails him."

"Wait till I come down, I'll slap your jaws," cried the climber.

The spectators were watching him with interest. He was obliged to pause frequently to rest himself, which he did by winding his legs tightly round the pole. At last he reached the top. Extending his arm to take the pipe, it was too short. Climbing still higher, he stretched his body to its greatest length, lost his hold, and fell to the ground. The bystanders raised a great cry. The unfortunate youth's head had embedded itself in the earth, streams of blood gushed from his mouth and nostrils--he was lifeless.

"He's dead! It's all over with him," was whispered around.

"Carry him off," commanded Seicht, and then walked on.

One of the bystanders loosed the cross-piece of the mock crucifix; the corpse was then stretched across the two pieces of wood and carried off the scene. As the body was carried past, the noise and revelry everywhere ceased.

"Wasn't that the one who carried the cross?" was asked. "Is he dead? Did he fall from the pole? How terrible!"

Even the progressionist revellers were struck thoughtful, so deeply is the sense of religion rooted in the heart of man. Many a one among them, seeing the pale, rigid face of the dead man, understood his fate to be a solemn warning, and fled from the scene in terror.

The progressionist element of the town was much flattered by the presence at its orgies of the wealthiest property owner of the country.

The women had already made the discovery that the millionaire's only son, Mr. Seraphin Gerlach, was on the eve of marrying a member of the highly respectable house of Greifmann, bankers. But it occasioned them no small amount of surprise that the young gentleman was not in attendance on the beautiful lady at the celebration. Louise's radiant countenance gave no indication, however, that any untoward occurrence had caused the absence of her prospective husband. The wives and daughters of the chieftains were sitting under an awning sipping coffee and eating cake. When Louise approached leaning on her brother's arm, they welcomed her to a place in the circle of loveliness with many courtesies and marks of respect.

Mr. Conrad strolled about the place, studying the spirit which animated the gathering.

CHAPTER XI
PROGRESS GROWS JOLLY

In passing near the tables Gerlach overheard conversations which revealed to him unmistakably the communistic aspirations and tendencies prevailing among the lower orders, their fiendish hatred of religion and the clergy, their corruption and appalling ignorance. On every hand he perceived symptoms of an alarmingly unhealthy condition of society. He heard blasphemies uttered against the Divinity which almost caused his blood to run cold; sacred things were scoffed at in terms so coarse and with an animus so plainly satanical that his hair rose on his head. It was clear to him that the firmest supports, the only true foundations of the social order, were tottering--rotted away by an incurable corruption.

In Gerlach's life, also, as in that of many other men, there had been a period of mental struggle and of doubt. He, too, had at one time himself face to face with questions the solution of which involved the whole aim of his existence. During this period of mental unrest, he had thought and studied much about faith and science, but not with a silly parade of superficial scepticism. He had resolutely engaged in the soul struggle, and had tried to end it for once and all. Supported by a good early training and a disposition naturally noble, instructed and guided by books of solid learning, he had come out from that crisis stronger in faith and more correct in his views of human science. The scenes which he was witnessing reminded him vividly of that turning-point in his life; they were to him an additional proof that man's dignity disappears as soon as he refuses to follow the divine guidance of religion. Grave in mood, he returned to the table around which were gathered the chieftains. The marks of respect shown to the millionaire were numerous and flattering. Even the bluff Sand exerted himself unusually in paying his respects to the wealthy landholder, and Erdblatt, whose embarrassed financial condition enabled him beyond them all to appreciate the worth of money, filled a glass with his own hand, and reached it to Mr. Conrad with the deference of an accomplished butler, Gerlach was pleased to speak in terms of praise of the nut-brown beverage, which greatly tickled Belladonna, the fat brewer. Naturally enough, the conversation turned upon the subject of the celebration.

"I confess I am not quite clear respecting the purpose of your city in the matter of schools," said Mr. Conrad. "How do you intend to arrange the school system?"

"In such a way as to make it accord with the requirements of the times and the progressive spirit of civilization," answered Hans Shund. "An end must be put to priest rule in the schools. The establishment of common schools will be a decided step towards this object. For a while, of course, the priests will be allowed to visit the schools at specified times, but their influence and control in school matters will be greatly restricted. Education will be withdrawn from the church's supervision, and after a few years we hope to reach the point when the school-rooms will be closed altogether against the priests. There is not a man of culture but will agree that children should not be required to learn things which are out of date, and the import of which must only excite smiles of compassion."

"Whom do you intend to put in the place of the clergy?" inquired Mr. Conrad.

"We intend to impart useful information and a moral sense in harmony with the spirit of the age," replied Hans Shund.

"It seems to me the elementary branches have been very competently taught heretofore in our schools, consequently I do not see the need of a change on this head," said Gerlach. "But you have not understood my question, I mean, who are to fill the office of instructors in morals and in religion?"

The chieftains looked puzzled, for such a question they had not expected to hear from the wealthiest man of the country.

"You see, Mr. Gerlach," said Sand bluntly, "religion must be done away with entirely. We haven't any use for such trash. Children ought to spend their time in learning something more sensible than the catechism."

"I am not disposed to believe that what you have just uttered is a correct expression of the general opinion of this community on the subject of the school question," returned the millionaire with some warmth. "It is impossible to bring up youth morally without religion. You are a housebuilder, Mr. Sand. What would you think of the man who would expect you to build him a house without a foundation--a castle in the air?"

"Why, I would regard him as nothing less than a fool," cried Sand.

"The case is identically the same with moral education. Morality is an edifice which a man must spend his life in laboring at. Religion is the groundwork of this edifice. Moral training without religion is an impossibility. It would be just as possible to build a house in the air, as to train up a child morally without a religious belief, without being convinced of the existence of a holy and just God."

"Facts prove the contrary," maintained Hans Shund. "Millions of persons are moral who have no religious belief."

"That's an egregious mistake, sir," opposed the landholder. "The repudiation of a Supreme Being and the violent extinction of the idea of the Divinity in the breast are of themselves grave offences against moral conscience. I grant you that, in the eyes of the public, thousands of men pass for moral who have no faith in religion. But public opinion is anything but a criterion of certainty when the moral worth of a man is to be determined. A man's interior is a region which cannot be viewed by the eye of the public. You know yourselves that there are men who pass for honorable, moral, pure men, whose private habits are exceedingly filthy and corrupt."

Hans Shund's color turned a palish yellow; the eyes of the chieftains sank.

"Besides, gentleman, it would be labor lost to try to educate youth independently of religion. Man is by his very nature a religious being. It is useless to attempt to educate the young without a knowledge of God and of revealed religion; to be able to do so you would previously have to pluck out of their own breasts the sense of right and wrong, and out of their souls the idea of God, which are innate in both. Were the attempt made, however, believe me, gentlemen, the yearning after God, alive in the human breast, would soon impel the generation brought up independently of religion to seek after false gods. For this very reason we know of no people in history that did not recognize and worship some divinity, were it but a tree or a stone, that served them for an object of adoration. In my opinion, it would be far more indicative of genuine progress to adhere to the God of Christians, who is incontestably holy, just, omnipotent, and kind, whilst to return to the sacred oaks of ancient Germany or to adopt the fetichism of uncivilized tribes would be a most monstrous reaction, the most degrading barbarism."

The chieftains looked nonplussed. Earnest thinking and investigation upon subjects pertaining to religion were not customary among the disciples of progress. They looked upon religion as something so common and trivial that anybody was free to argue upon and condemn it with a few flippant or smart sayings; But the millionaire was now disclosing views so new and vast, that their weak vision was completely dazzled, and their steps upon the unknown domain became unsteady.

Mr. Seicht, observing the embarrassment of the leaders, felt it his duty to hasten to their relief. His polemical weapons were drawn from the armory of bureaucracy.

"The progressive development of humanity," said Mr. Seicht, "has revealed an admirable substitute for all religious ideas. A state well organized can exist splendidly without any religion. Nay, I do not hesitate to maintain that religion is a drawback to the development of the modern state, and that, therefore, the state should have nothing whatever to do with religion. An invisible world should not exert an influence upon a state--the wants of the times are the only rule to be consulted."

"What do you understand by a state, sir?" asked the millionaire.

"A state," replied the official, "is a union of men whose public life is regulated by laws which every individual is bound to observe."

"You speak of laws; upon what basis are these laws founded?"

"Upon the basis of humanity, morality, liberty, and right," answered the official glibly.

"And what do you consider moral and just?"

"Whatever accords with the civilization of the age."

A faint smile passed over the severe features of Mr. Conrad.

"I was watching the procession," spoke he. "I have seen the religious feelings of a large number of citizens publicly ridiculed and grossly insulted. Was that moral? Was it just? You are determined to oust God and religion from the schools; yet there are thousands in the country who desire and endeavor to secure a religious education for their children. Is it moral and just to utterly disregard the wishes of these thousands? Does it accord with a profession of humanity and freedom to put constraint on the consciences of fellow-citizens?"

"The persons of whom you speak are a minority in the state, and the minority is obliged to yield to the will of the majority," answered Seicht.

"It follows, then, that the basis of morality and justice is superior numbers?"

"Yes, it is! In a state, it appertains to the majority to determine and regulate everything."

"Gentlemen," spoke Gerlach with great seriousness, "as I was a moment ago strolling over this place, I overheard language at several tables, which was unmistakably communistic. Laborers and factory men were maintaining that wealth is unequally distributed; that, whilst a small number are immensely rich, a much greater number are poor and destitute; that progress will have to advance to a point when an equal division of property must be made. Now, the poor and the laboring population are in the majority. Should they vote for a partition, should they demand from us what hitherto we have regarded as exclusively our own, we, gentlemen, will in consistency be forced to accept the decree of the majority as perfectly moral and just--will we not?"

There was profound silence.

"I, for my part, should most emphatically protest against such a ruling of the majority," declared Greifmann.

"Your protest would be contrary to morals and equity; for, according to Mr. Seicht, only what the majority wills is moral and just," returned the landowner. "And, in mentioning partition of property, I hinted at a red monster which is not any longer a mere goblin, but a thing of real flesh and bone. We are on the verge of a fearful social revolution which threatens to break up society. If there is no holy and just God; if he has not revealed himself, and man is not obliged to submit to his will; if the only basis of right and of morals is the wish of the majority, this terrible social revolution must be moral and just, for the majority wills it and carries it out."

"Of course, there must be a limit," said the official feebly.

"The demands of the majority must be reasonable."

"What do you understand by reasonable, sir?"

"I call reasonable whatever accords with the sense of right, with sound thinking, with moral ideas."

"Sense of right--moral ideas? I beg you to observe that these notions differ vastly from the sole authority of numbers. You have trespassed upon God's kingdom in giving your explanation, for ideas are supersensible; they are the thought of God himself. And the sense of right was not implanted in the human breast by the word of a majority; it was placed there by the Creator of man."

The official was driven to the wall. The chieftains thoughtfully stared at their beer-pots.

"It is clear that the will of the majority alone cannot be accepted as the basis of a state," said Schwefel. "The life of society cannot be put at the mercy of the rude and fickle masses. There must be a moral order, willed and regulated by a supreme ruler, and binding upon every man. This is plain."

"I agree with you, sir," said the millionaire. "Let us continue building on Christian principles. As everybody knows, our civilization has sprung from Christianity. If we tear down the altars and destroy the seats from which lessons of Christian morality are taught, confusion must inevitably follow. And I, gentlemen, have too exalted an opinion of the German nation, of its earnest and religious spirit, to believe that it can be ever induced to fall away completely from God and his holy law. Infidelity is an unhealthy tendency of our times; it is a pernicious superstition which sound sense and noble feeling will ultimately triumph over. We will do well to continue advancing in science, art, refinement, and industry, in true liberty and the right understanding of truth; we will thus be making real progress, such progress as I am proud to call myself a partisan of."

The chieftains maintained silence. Some nodded assent. Hans Shund gave an angry bite to his pipe-stem, and puffed a heavy cloud of smoke across the table.

"I have confidence in the enlightenment and good sense of our people," said he. "You have called modern progress 'a pernicious superstition and an unhealthy tendency of the times,' Mr. Gerlach," turning towards the millionaire with a bow. "I regret this view of yours."

"Which I have substantiated and proved," interrupted Gerlach.

"True, sir! Your proofs have been striking, and I do not feel myself competent to refute them. But I can point you to something more powerful than argument. Look at this scene; see these happy people meeting and enjoying one another's society in most admirable harmony and order. Is not this spectacle a beautiful illustration and vindication of the moral spirit of progress?"

"These people are jubilant from the effect of beer, why shouldn't they be? But, sir, a profound observer does not 'suffer himself to be deceived by mere appearances.'"

An uproar and commotion at a distance interrupted the millionaire. At the same instant a policeman approached out of breath.

"Your honor, the factorymen and the laborers are attacking one another!"

"What are you raising such alarm for," said Hans Shund gruffly. "It is only a small squabble, such as will occur everywhere in a crowd."

"I ask your honor's pardon: it is not a small squabble, it is a bloody battle."

"Well, part the wranglers."

"We cannot manage them; there are too many of them. Shall I apply for military?"

"Hell and thunder--military!" cried Hans Shund, getting on his feet. "Are you in your senses?"

"Several men have already been carried off badly wounded," reported the policeman further. "You have no idea how serious the affray is, and it is getting more and more so; the friends of both sides are rushing in to aid their own party. The police force is not a match for them."

Women, screaming and in tears, were rushing in every direction. The bands had ceased playing, and noise and confusion resounded from the scene of action. Louise ran to take her brother's arm in consternation. The wives and daughters of the chieftains huddled round their natural protectors.

"Hurry away and report this at the military post," was Seicht's order to the policeman. "The feud is getting alarming. One moment!"

Tearing a leaf from a memorandum book, he wrote a short note, which he sent by the messenger.

"Off to the post--be expeditious!"

Louise hastened with her brother and Gerlach senior to their carriage, and her feeling of security returned only when the noise of the combat had died away in the distance.

The next day the town papers contained the following notice: "The beautiful celebration of yesterday, which, on account of its object, will be long remembered by the citizens of this community, was unfortunately interrupted by a serious conflict between the laborers and factorymen. A great many were wounded during the *mêlée*, of whom five have since died, and it required the interference of an armed force to separate the combatants."

CHAPTER XII
BROWN BREAD AND BONNYCLABBER

Seraphin had not gone to the celebration. He remained at home on the plea of not feeling well. He was stretched upon a sofa, and his soul was engaged in a desperate conflict. What it was impossible for himself to look upon, had been viewed by his father with composure: the burlesque procession, the public derision of holy practices, the mockery of the Redeemer of the world, in whose place had been put a broken bottle on the symbol of salvation. He himself had been stunned by the spectacle; and his father? Was it his father? Again, his father had accompanied the brother and sister to the infamous celebration. Was not this a direct confirmation of his own suspicions? His father had become a fearful enigma to his soul! And what if, upon his return from the festival, the father were to come and insist upon the marriage with Louise, declaring her advanced notions to be an insufficient ground for renouncing a pet project? A wild storm was convulsing his interior. He could not bear it longer, he was driven forth. Snatching his straw hat, he rushed from the house, ran through the alleys and streets, out of the town, onward and still onward. The August sun was burning, and its heat, reflected from the road, was doubly intense. The perspiration was rolling in large drops down the glowing face of the young man, whom torturing thoughts still kept goading on. Holt's whitewashed dwelling became visible on the summit of a knoll, and gleamed a friendly welcome as he came near it--a welcome which seemed opportune for one who hardly knew whither he was hastening. The walnut-tree which could be seen from afar was casting an inviting shade over the table and bench that seemed to be confidingly leaning against its stem. A flock of chickens were taking a sand-bath under the table, flapping their wings, ruffling their feathers, and wallowing in the dust. Seated on the sunny hillock, the cottage appeared quiet, almost lonesome but for a ringing sound which came from the adjoining field and was made by the sickle passing through the corn. A broad-brimmed straw hat with a blue band could be noticed from the road moving on over the fallen grain, and presently Mechtild's slender form rose into view as she pushed actively onward over the harvest field. Hasty steps resounded from the road. She raised her head, and her countenance first indicated surprise, then embarrassment. Whom did her eyes behold rushing wildly by, like a fugitive, but the generous rescuer of her family from the clutches of the usurer Shund. His hat was in his hand, his auburn locks were hanging down over his forehead, his face aglow, his whole being seemed to be absorbed in a mad pursuit. To her quick eye his features revealed deep trouble and violent excitement She was frightened, and the sickle fell from her hand. Not a day passed on which she would not think of this benefactor. Perhaps there was not a being on earth whom she admired and revered as much as she did him. All the pure and elevated sentiments of an innocent and blooming girl, united to form a halo of affection round the head of Seraphin. At evening prayer when her father said, "Let us pray for our benefactor Seraphin," her soul sent up a fervent petition to God, and she declared with joy that she was willing to sacrifice all for him. But behold this noble object of her admiration and affection suddenly presented before her in a state that excited the greatest uneasiness. With his head sunk and his eyes directed straight before him, he would have rushed past without noticing the sympathizing girl, when a greeting clear and sweet as the tone of a bell caused him to look up. He beheld Mechtild with her beautiful eyes fixed upon him in an expression of anxiety.

"Good-morning, Mr. Seraphin," she said again.

"Good-morning," he returned mechanically, and staring about vaguely. His bewilderment soon passed, however, and his gaze was riveted by the apparition.

She was standing on the other side of the ditch. The fear of some unknown calamity had given to her beautiful face an expression of tender solicitude, and whilst a smile struggled for possession of her lips her look indicated painful anxiety. Mechtild's appearance soon directed the young man's attention to his own excited manner. The dark shadow disappeared from his brow, he wiped the perspiration from his face, and began to feel the effect of his walk under the glowing heat of midsummer.

"Ah! here is the neat little white house, your pretty country home, Mechtild," he said pleasantly. "If you had not been so kind as to wish me good-morning, I should actually have passed by in an unpardonable fit of distraction."

"I was almost afraid to say good-morning, Mr. Seraphin, but--" She faltered and looked confused.

"But--what? You didn't think anything was wrong?"

"No! But you were in such a hurry and looked so troubled, I got frightened," she confessed with amiable uprightness. "I was afraid something had happened you."

"I am thankful for your sympathy. Nothing has happened me, nor, I trust, will," he replied, with a scarcely perceptible degree of defiance in his tone. "This is a charming situation. Corn-fields on all sides, trees laden with fruit, the skirt of the woods in the background--and then this magnificent view! With your permission, I will take a moment's rest in the shade of yon splendid walnut-tree planted by your great-grandfather."

She joyfully nodded assent and stepped over the ditch. She shoved back the bolt of the gate. Together they entered the yard, which a hedge separated from the road. The cock crew a welcome to the stranger, and led his household from the sand-bath into the sunshine near the barn.

"This is a cool, inviting little spot," said the millionaire, as he pointed to the shade of the walnut-tree. "No doubt you often sit here and read?"

"Yes, Mr. Seraphin; but the dirty chickens have scattered dust all over the bench and table. Wait a minute, you'll get your clothes dusty."

She hurried into the house. His eyes followed her receding form, his ears kept listening for her departing steps, he heard the opening and closing of doors: presently she reappeared, dusted the bench and table with a brush, and spread a white cloth over the table. Seraphin looked on with a smile.

"I do not wish to be troublesome, Mechtild!"

"It is no trouble, Mr. Seraphin! Sit down, now, and rest yourself. I am so sorry father and mother are not at home. They will be ever so glad to hear that you have honored us with a visit."

"Is nobody at home?"

"Father is in town, and mother is at work with the children in the harvest field."

"Are you not afraid to stay here by yourself?"

"What should I be afraid of? There are no ghosts in daytime," she said with a bewitching archness; "and as for thieves, they never expect to find anything worth having at our house."

She was standing on the other side of the table, looking at him with a beautiful smile.

"Won't you have a seat on this bench?" said he, making room for her. "You need rest more than I do. You have been working, and I am merely an idle stroller. Do take a seat, Mechtild."

"Thank you, Mr. Seraphin--I could not think of doing so! It would not be becoming," she answered with some confusion.

"Why not becoming?"

"Because you are a gentleman, and I am only a poor girl."

"Your objection on the score of propriety is not worth anything. Oblige me by doing what I ask of you."

"I will do so, Mr. Seraphin, since you insist upon it, but after a while. I would like to offer you some refreshments beforehand, if you will allow me."

"With pleasure," he said, nodding assent.

A second time she hurried away to the house, whilst he kept listening to her footsteps. The extraordinary neatness and cleanliness which could be seen everywhere about the little homestead did not escape his observation. On all sides he fancied he saw the work of Mechtild. The purity of her spirit, which beamed so mildly from her eyes and was revealed in the beauty of her countenance and the grace of her person, seemed embodied in the very odor of roses wafted over from the neighboring flower garden. He was unconscious of the rapid growth within his bosom of a deep and tender feeling. This feeling was casting a warm glow, like softest sunshine, over all that he beheld. Not even the chickens looked to him like other fowls of their kind; they were ennobled by the reflection that they were objects of Mechtild's care, that she fed them, that when they were still piping little pullets she had held them in her lap and caressed them. He abandoned himself completely to this sentiment; it carried him on like a smooth current; and he could not tell, did not suspect even, why so wonderful a reaction had in so short a time taken place in his interior. Beholding himself seated under the walnut-tree surrounded only by evidences of honorable poverty and rural thrift, and yet feeling a degree of happiness and peace he had never known before, he fancied he was performing a part in some fairy tale which he was dreaming with his eyes open. And now the fairy appeared at the door having on a snowy-white apron, and carrying a shallow basket from which could be seen, protruding above the rest of its contents, a milk jar. She set before him a pewter plate, bright as silver. Then she took out the jar and a cup, next she laid a knife and spoon for him, and finished her hospitable service with a huge loaf of bread.

"Don't get dismayed at the bread, Mr. Seraphin! I am sorry I cannot set something better before you. But it is well baked and will not hurt you!"

"You baked it yourself, did you not?"

"Yes, Mr. Seraphin!"

He attacked the loaf resolutely. From the dimensions of the slice which he cut off, it was plain that appetite and his confidence in her skill were satisfactory. She raised the jar of bonnyclabber, which lurched out in jerks upon his plate, whilst he kept gayly stirring it with the spoon. Then she dipped a spoonful of rich cream out of the cup and poured it into the refreshing contents of the plate.

"Let me know when you want me to stop, Mr. Seraphin." Mechtild poured spoonful after spoonful; he sat immovable, seemingly observing the spoon, but in reality watching her soft plump fingers, then her well-shaped hand, next her exquisitely arm, and, when finally he raised his eyes to her face, they were met by a mischievous smile. The cup was empty, and all the cream was in his plate.

"May I go and fetch some more?" she asked.

"No, Mechtild, no! Why, this is a regular yellow sea!"

"You wouldn't cry 'enough!'"

"I forgot about it," he replied, somewhat confused. "To atone for my forgetfulness, I will eat it all."

"I hope you will relish it, Mr. Seraphin!"

"Thank you! Where is your plate?"

"I had my dinner before you came."

"Well, then, at any rate you must not continue standing. Won't you share this seat with me?"

She seated herself upon the bench, took off her hat, smoothed down her apron, and appeared happy at seeing him eating heartily.

"Don't you find that dish refreshing, Mr. Seraphin?"

"You have done me a real act of charity," he replied. "This bread, is excellent. Who taught you how to make bread?"

"I learned from mother; but there isn't much art in making that sort of bread, Mr. Seraphin. The food which people in the country eat does not require artistic preparation. It only needs good, pure material, so that it may give strength to labor."

"I suppose you attend to the kitchen altogether, do you not?"

"Yes, Mr. Seraphin. That's not very difficult, our meals are of the plainest kind. We have meat once a week, on Sundays. When the work is unusually hard, as in harvest time, we have meat oftener. We raise our own meat and cure it."

"You have assumed household cares at quite an early age, Mechtild."

"Early? I am seventeen now, and am the oldest. Mother has a great deal of trouble with the small ones, so the housework falls chiefly to my share.

It does not require any great exertion, however, to do it. Plain and saving is our motto. Mother specially recommends four things: industry, cleanliness, order, and economy. She advises me not to neglect any one of these points when once I will have a household of my own."

"Do you think you will soon set up a separate household?" asked he with some hesitation.

"Not for some time to come, Mr. Seraphin, yet it must be done one day. If my own inclination were consulted, I would prefer never to leave home. I should like things to continue as they are. But a separation must come. Death will pay us a visit as it has done to others, father and mother will pass away, and the course of events will sever us from one another."

Her head sank, the brightness of her face became obscured beneath the shadow of these sombre thoughts, and, when she again looked up, there appeared in her eyes so touching and childlike a sadness that he felt pained to the soul. And yet this revelation of tenderness pleased him, for it made known to him a new phase of her amiable nature.

For a long time he continued conversing with the artless girl. Every word she uttered, no matter how trifling, had an interest for him. Besides her charming artlessness, he had frequent occasions to admire the wisdom of her language and her admirable delicacy. The setting sun had already cast a subdued crimson over the hilltops, hours had sped away, the chickens had gone to roost, still he remained riveted to the spot by Mechtild's grace and loveliness.

"Father is just coming," she said, pointing down the road. "How glad he will be to find you here!"

His head bent forward. Holt came wearily plodding up the road. His right hand was hidden in the pocket of his pantaloons, and his head was bowed, as if beneath a heavy weight. As Mechtild's clear voice rang out, he raised his head, caught sight of his high-hearted benefactor, and smiled in joyful surprise.

"Welcome, Mr. Seraphin; a thousand times welcome!" he cried from the other side of the road. "Why, this is an honor that I had not expected!"

He stood uncovered, holding his cap in the left hand, his right hand was still concealed. Mechtild at once noticed her father's singular behavior, and her eye watched anxiously for the hidden hand.

"Your daughter has been so kind as to offer refreshments to a weary wanderer," said Gerlach, "and it has been a great pleasure for me to sit awhile. We have been chatting for several hours under this glorious tree, and may be I am to blame for keeping her from her work."

Holt's honest face beamed with satisfaction. He entirely forgot about his secret, he drew his hand out of his pocket, Mechtild turned pale, and a sharp cry escaped her lips.

"For mercy's sake, father!" And she pointed to the broken chain.

"What are you screaming for, foolish girl? Don't be alarmed, Mr. Seraphin! this chain has got on my arm in an honorable cause. I will tell you the whole story; I know you will not inform on me."

Seating himself on the bench, he related the adventures of the day.

The mock procession passed before Mechtild's imagination with the vividness of reality. The narration transformed her. Her mildness was changed to noble anger. She had heard of the vicar of Christ being insulted, of holy things being scoffed at, of the Redeemer being derided by a horde of wretches. With her arms akimbo, she drew up her lithe and graceful form to its full height, and with flashing eyes looked at her father while he related what had befallen him. Seraphin could not help wondering at the transformation. Such a display of spirit he had not been prepared to witness in a girl so gentle and beautiful. When her father had ended his account, she seized his hand passionately, pressed it warmly between her own hands, and kissed the chain.

"Father, dear father," she exclaimed in a burst of feeling, "I thank you from my heart for acting as you did! Those wretches were scoffing at our holy religion, but you behaved bravely in defence of the faith. For this they put chains on you, as the heathen did to S. Peter and S. Paul."

Once more she kissed the chain, then, turning quickly, hastened across the yard to the house.

"Mechtild isn't like the rest of us," said Holt, smiling. "There's a great deal of spirit in her. I have often noticed it. But I am not astonished at her being roused at the mock procession--I was roused myself. I declare, Mr. Seraphin, it is a shame, a crying shame, that persons are permitted to rail at doctrines and things which we revere as holy. One would almost believe Satan himself was in some people, they take so fanatical a delight in scoffing at a religion which is holy and enjoins nothing but what is good."

"It is incontestable that infidelity hates and opposes God and religion," replied Gerlach. "The boasted culture of those who find a pleasure in grossly wounding the most sacred feelings of their neighbors, is wicked and stupid."

Mechtild returned with a file in her hand.

"Right, my child! I was just thinking of the file myself. Here, cut the catches of the lock."

He laid his arm across the table. A few strokes of the file caused the lock and remnant of chain to fall from his wrist.

"We will keep this as a precious memento," said she. "Only think, father, that wicked official ordered you to be manacled, and he is the representative of authority. How can one respect or even pray for authorities when they allow religion to be ridiculed?"

"Pray for your enemies," answered the countryman gravely.

"I will do so because God commands me; but I shall never again be able to respect the official!"

Her anger had fled; she appeared again all light and loveliness. He did not fail to observe a searching look which she directed upon him, but its meaning became clear to him only when, as he was taking leave, she said in a tone of humility: "Pardon my vehemence, Mr. Seraphin! Don't think me a bad girl."

"There is nothing to be forgiven, Mechtild. You were indignant against godless wretches, and they who are not indignant against evil cannot themselves be good."

"We are most heartily thankful for this visit," spoke Holt. "I need not say that we will consider it a great happiness as often as you will be pleased to come."

"Good-night!" returned the young man, and he walked away.

Deeply immersed in his thoughts, Seraphin went back to town. What he was thinking about, his diary does not record. But the excitement under which he had rushed forth was gone--dispelled by the magic of a rural sorceress. He walked on quietly like a man who seems filled with confidence in his own future. The recent painful impressions seemed to his mind to lie far back in the past; their place was taken up by beautiful anticipations which, like the aurora, shed soft and pleasing light upon his path. He halted frequently in a dream-like reverie to indulge the happiness with which his soul was flooded. The full moon, just peering over the hills, shed around him a mystic brightness that harmonized perfectly with the indefinable contentment of his heart, and seemed to be gazing quizzingly into the countenance of the young man, who almost feared to confess to himself that he had found an invaluable treasure.

As he stopped before the Palais Greifmann, all the bright spirits that had hovered round about him on the way back from the little whitewashed cottage, fled. He awoke from his dream, and, ascending the stairs with a feeling of discomfort, he entered his apartment, where his father sat awaiting him.

"At last," spoke Mr. Conrad, looking up from a book. "You have kept me waiting a long time, my son."

"I was in need of a good long walk, father, to get over what I witnessed this morning. The country air has dispelled all those horrible impressions. There is only one thing more required to make me feel perfectly well, dear father, which is that you will not insist on my allying myself to people who are utterly opposed to my way of thinking and feeling."

"I understand and approve of your request, Seraphin. The impressions made on me, too, are exceedingly disagreeable. The advancement of which this town boasts is stupid, immoral, detestable. How this state of society has come about, is inexplicable to me who live secluded in the country. Society is diseased, fatally diseased. Many of the new views professed are sheer superstition, and their morality is a mere cloak for their corruption and wickedness. All the powers of progress so-called are actively at work to subvert all the safeguards of society. And what your diary reports of Louise, I have found fully confirmed. Though it cost the sacrifice of a long cherished plan, a son of mine shall never become the husband of a progressionist woman."

"O father! how deeply do I thank you!" cried the youth, carried away by his feelings.

"I must decline being thanked, for I have not merited it," spoke Mr. Conrad earnestly. "A father's duty determines very clearly what my decision upon the matter of your marriage with Louise, ought to be. But I am under obligations to you, my son, which justice compels me to acknowledge. Your discernment and moral sense have prevented a great deal of discord and unhappiness in our family. Continue good and true, my Seraphin!"

He pressed his son to his bosom and imprinted a kiss on his forehead.

"To-morrow we shall start for home by the first train. Fortunately your prudent behavior makes it easy for us to get away, and the final breaking off of this engagement I will myself arrange with Louise's father."

SERAPHIN GERLACH TO THE AUTHOR

Dear Sir: Two years ago, I took the liberty of sending you my diary, with the request that you would be pleased to publish such portions of its contents as might be useful, in the form of a tale illustrative of the times. I made the request because I consider it the duty of a writer who delineates the condition of society, to transmit to posterity a faithful picture of the present social status, and I am vain enough to believe that my jottings will be a modest contribution towards such a tableau.

The meagre account given by the diary of my intercourse with Mechtild, will probably have enabled you to perceive the germ of a pure and true relation likely to develop itself further. I shall add but a few items to complete the account of the diary, knowing that poets, painters, and artists have rigorously determined bounds, and that a twilight cannot be represented when the sun is at the zenith. I am emboldened to use this illustration because your unbounded admiration of pure womanhood is well known to me, and because the brightness of Mechtild's character, were it further described, would no more be compatible with the sombre colorings in which a true picture of modern progress would have to be exhibited, than the noonday sun with the shadows of evening.

My memoranda concerning Mechtild, which, despite studied soberness, betrayed a considerable degree of admiration, made known to my parents, naturally enough, the secret of my heart. Hence it came that a quiet smile passed over my father's face every time I commenced to speak of Mechtild. Holt's manly deed at the mock procession had already gained for him my father's esteem, and, as I spoke a great deal about Holt's thoroughness as a cultivator, my father began to look upon him as a very desirable man to employ.

"We want an experienced man on the 'green farm,'" said father, one day. "Offer the situation to Holt, and tell him to come to see me about it. I want to talk with him."

"Give the good man my compliments," said mother; "tell him I would be much pleased to become acquainted with Mechtild, who sympathized with you so kindly on that memorable day!"

I wrote without delay. Holt came, and so did Mechtild. But few moments were necessary to enable mother to detect the girl's fine qualities. Father, too, was delightfully surprised at her modesty, the beauty of her form, and grace of her manner. He visited the farm accompanied by Holt. The cultivator's extraordinary knowledge, his practical manner of viewing things, and the shrewdness of his counsels in regard to the improvement of worn-out land and the cultivation of poor soil, completely charmed my father. A contract containing very favorable conditions for Holt was entered into, and three weeks later the family took charge of the "green farm."

Upon mother's suggestion, Mechtild was sent to an educational institution, where she acquired in ten months' time the learning and culture necessary for associating with cultivated people.

Father and mother had received her on her return like a daughter. This reception was given her not only in consideration of Holt's skilful and faithful management of business, but also on account of Mechtild's own splendid womanly character--perhaps, too, partly on account of my unbounded admiration for the rare girl.

"The girl is an ornament to her sex," lauded my father. "Her polished manner and ease in company do not suffer one to suspect ever so remotely that she at any time plied the reaping-hook, and came out of a stubblefield to regale a weary wanderer with brown bread and bonnyclabber. I am quite in harmony with, your secret wishes, my dear Seraphin! At the same time, I am of opinion that a step promising so much happiness ought not to be longer deferred. I think, then, you should ask the father for his daughter without delay, so that I may soon have the pleasure of giving you my blessing."

From my father's arms, into which. I had thrown myself in thankfulness, I hastened away to the "green farm," where Mechtild with maidenly blushes, and Holt in speechless astonishment, heard and granted my petition.

I am now four months married. I am the blest husband of a wife whose lovely qualities are daily showing themselves to greater advantage. Mechtild presides over Chateau Hallberg like an angel of peace. Towards my father and mother she conducts herself with filial reverence and never-ceasing delicate attentions. Mother loves her unspeakably, and no access of ill humor in father can withstand her charming smile and prudent mirth. Concerning the banking-house of Greifmann, I have only sad things to tell. Carl's father had entered into very considerable speculations which failed and drove him into bankruptcy. Carl saw the blow coming, and saved himself in a disgraceful manner. There was a savings institution connected with the bank in which poor people and servants deposited the savings of their hard labor. Carl appropriated this fund and made off a short time before the failure of the house. Thousands of poor persons were robbed of the little sums which they were saving for old age, by denying themselves many even of the necessaries of life.

The maledictions and curses of these unfortunate people followed across the ocean the thief whose modern culture and progressive humanity did not hinder him from committing a crime which no Christian can be guilty of without losing his claim to the title. Carl, however, still continues to pass for a man of culture and humanity notwithstanding his deed. And why should he not, since without faith in the Deity moral obligations do not exist, and consequently every species of crime is allowable? The old gentleman Greifmann died shortly after his ruin; Louise lost her mind.

My father felt the misfortune of the Greifmanns deeply, without, however, regretting in the smallest degree the wise determination which their godless principles and actions had driven him to. Formerly he could never find time to take part in the elections. But now he is constantly speaking about the duty of every respectable man to oppose the infernal machinations and plans of would-be progress. He intends at the next election to use all his influence for the election of conscientious deputies, so that the evil may be put an end to which consists in trying to undermine the foundations of society.

Accept, dear sir, the assurance of the esteem with which I have the honor to be

Your most obedient servant,

Seraphin Gerlach.

Chateau Hallberg, Jan. 4, 1872.

FOOTNOTE TO THE PROGRESSIONISTS

Footnote 1: Proverbs vi., vii.

ANGELA

CHAPTER I
CRINOLINE

An express train was just on the eve of leaving the railway station in Munich. Two fashionably dressed gentlemen stood at the open door of a railway carriage, in conversation with a third, who sat within. These two young men bore on their features the marks of youthful dissipation, indicating that they had not been sparing of pleasures. The one in the carriage had a handsome, florid countenance, two clear, expressive eyes, and thick locks of hair, which he now and then stroked back from his fine forehead. He scarcely observed the conversation of the two friends, who spoke of balls, dogs, horses, theatres, and ballet-girls.

In the same carriage sat another traveller, evidently the father of the young man. He was reading the newspaper--that is the report of the money market--while his fleshy left hand dallied with the heavy gold rings of his watch-chain. He had paid no attention to the conversation till an observation of his son brought him to serious reflection.

"By the bye," said one of the young men quickly, "I was nearly forgetting to tell you the news, Richard! Do you know that Baron Linden is engaged?"

"Engaged? To whom?" said Richard carelessly.

"To Bertha von Harburg. I received a card this morning, and immediately wrote a famous letter of congratulation."

Richard looked down earnestly, and shook his head.

"I commiserate the genial baron," said he. "What could he be thinking of, to rush headlong into this misfortune?"

The father looked in surprise at his son; the hand holding the paper sank on his knee.

"Permit me, gentlemen," said the conductor; the doors were closed, the friends nodded good-by, and the train moved off.

"Your observation about Linden's marriage astonishes me, Richard. But perhaps you were only jesting."

"By no means," said Richard. "Never more earnest in my life. I expressed my conviction, and my conviction is the result of careful observation and mature reflection."

The father's astonishment increased.

"Observation--reflection--fudge!" said the father impatiently, as he folded the paper and shoved it into his pocket. "How can a young man of twenty-two talk of experience and observation! Enthusiastic nonsense! Marriage is a necessity of human life. And you will yet submit to this necessity."

"True, if marriage be a necessity, then I suppose I must bow to the yoke of destiny. But, father, this necessity does not exist. There are intelligent men enough who do not bind themselves to woman's caprices."

"Oh! certainly, there are some strange screech-owls in the world---some enthusiasts. But certainly you do not wish to be one of them. You, who have such great expectations. You, the only son of a wealthy house. You, who have a yearly income of thousands to spend."

"The income can be enjoyed more pleasantly, free and single, father."

"Free and single--and enjoyed! Zounds! you almost tempt me to think ill of you. Happily, I know you well. I know your strict morality, your solidity, your moderate pretensions. All these amiable qualities please me. But this view of marriage I did not expect; you must put away this sickly notion."

The young man made no answer, but leaned back in his seat with a disdainful smile.

Herr Frank gazed thoughtfully through the window. He reflected on the determined character of his son, whose disposition, even when a child, shut him out from the world, and who led an interior, meditative life. Strict regularity and exact employment of time were natural to him. At school, he held the first place in all branches. His ambition and effort were to excel all others in knowledge. His singular questions, which indicated a keen observation and capacity, had often excited the surprise of his father. And while the companions of the youth hailed with delight the time which released them from the benches of the school and from their studies, Richard cheerfully bound himself to his accustomed task, to appease his longing for knowledge. Approaching manhood had not changed him in this regard. He was punctual to the hours of business, and labored with zeal and interest, to the great joy of his father. He recreated himself with music and, painting, or by a walk in the open country, for whose beauties he had a keen appreciation. The few shades of his character were, a proud haughtiness, an unyielding perseverance in his determinations, and a strength of conviction difficult to overcome. But perhaps these shades were, after all, great qualities, which were to brighten up and polish his maturity. This obstinacy the father was now considering, and, in reference to his singular view of marriage, it filled him with great anxiety.

"But, Richard," began Herr Frank again, "how did you come to this singular conclusion?"

"By observation, and reflection--and also by experience, although you deny my years this right."

"What have you experienced and observed?"

"I have observed woman as she is, and found that such a creature would only make me miserable. What occupies their minds? Fineries, pleasures; and trifles. The pivot of their existence turns on dress, ornaments, balls, and the like. We live in an age of crinoline, and you know how I abominate that dress; I admit my aversion is abnormal, perhaps exaggerated, but I cannot overcome it. When I see a woman going through the streets with swelling hoops, the most whimsical fancies come into my mind. It reminds me of an inflated balloon, whose clumsy swell disfigures the most beautiful form. It reminds me of a drunken gawk, who swaggers along and carries the foolish gewgaw for a show. The costume is indeed expressive. It reveals the interior disposition. Crinoline is to me the type of the woman of our day--an empty, vain, inflated something. And this type repels me."

"Then you believe our women to be vain, pleasure-seeking, and destitute of true womanhood, because they wear crinoline?"

"No, the reverse. An overweening propensity to show and frivolity characterizes our women, and therefore they wear crinoline in spite of the protestations of the men."

"Bah! Nonsense; you lay too much stress on fashion. I know many women myself who complain of this fashion."

"And afterward follow it. This precisely confirms my opinion. Women have no longer sufficient moral force to disregard a disagreeable restraint. Their vanity is still stronger than their inclinations to a natural enjoyment of life."

"Do you want a wife who would be sparing and saving; who, by her frugality, would increase your wealth; who, by her social seclusion, would not molest your cash-box?"

"No; I want no wife," answered the young man, somewhat pettishly. "And I am not alone in this. The young men are beginning to awaken. A sound, natural feeling revolts against the vitiated taste of the women. Alliances are forming everywhere. The last paper announced that, at Marseilles, six thousand young men have, with joined hands, vowed never to marry until the women renounce their ruinous costumes and costly idleness, and return to a plain style of dress and frugal habits. I object to this propensity to ease and pleasure--this desire of our women for finery and the gratification of vanity. Not because this inclination is expensive, but because it is objectionable. Every creature has an object. But, if we consider the women of our day, we might well ask, for what are they here?

"For what are women here, foolish man?" interrupted Herr Frank. "Are they to go about without any costume, like Eve before the fall? Are they to know the trials of life, and not its joys? Are they to exist like the women of the sultan, shut up in a harem? For what are they here? I will tell you. They are here to make life cheerful. Does not Schiller say,

"'Honor to woman! she scatters rife

Heavenly roses, 'mid earthly life;

Love she weaves in gladdening bands;

Chastity's veil her charm attires;

Beautiful thoughts' eternal fires,

Watchful, she feeds with holy hands.'"

Richard smiled.

"Poetical fancy!" said he. "My unhappy friend Emil Schlagbein often declaimed and sang with passion that same poem of Schiller's. Love had even made a poet of him. He wrote verses to his Ida. And now, scarcely three years married, he is the most miserable man in the world--miserable through his wife. Ida has still the same finely carved head as formerly; but that head, to the grief of Emil, is full of stubbornness--full of whimsical nonsense. Her eyes have still the same deep blue; but the charming expression has changed, and the blue not unfrequently indicates a storm. How often has Emil poured out his sorrows to me! How often complained of the coldness of his wife! A ball missed--missed from necessity--makes her stupid and sulky for days. In vain he seeks a cheerful look. When he returns home worried by the cares of business, he finds no consolation in Ida's sympathy, but is vexed by her stubbornness and offended by her coldness. Emil sprang headlong into misery. I will beware of such a step."

"You are unjust and prejudiced. Must all women, then, be Ida Schlagbeins?"

"Perhaps my Ida might be still worse," retorted Richard sharply.

Herr Frank drummed on his knees, always a sign of displeasure.

"I tell you, Richard," said he emphatically. "Your time will come yet. You will follow the universal law, and this law will give the lie to your one-sided view--to your contempt of woman."

"That impulse, father, can be overcome, and habit becomes a second nature. Besides--"

"Besides--well, what besides?"

"I would say that the time of which you speak is, in my case, happily passed," answered Richard, still gazing through the window. "For me the time of sentimental delusion has been short and decisive," he concluded with a bitter smile.

"Can I, your father, ask a clearer explanation?"

The young man leaned back in his seat and looked at the opposite side while he spoke.

"Last summer I visited Baden-Baden. On old Mount Eberstein, which is so picturesquely enthroned above the village, I fell in with a party. Among the number was a young lady of rare beauty and great modesty. An acquaintance gave me an opportunity of being introduced to her. We sat in pleasant conversation under the black oaks until the approaching twilight compelled us to return to the town. Isabella--such was the name of the beauty--had made a deep impression on me. So deep that even the detested crinoline that encircled her person in large hoops found favor in my sight. Her manner was in no wise coquettish. She spoke with deliberation and spirit. Her countenance had always the same expression. Only when the young people, into whose heads the fiery wine had risen, gave expression to sharp words, did Isabella look up and a displeased expression, as of injured delicacy, passed over her countenance. My presence seemed agreeable to her. My conversation may have pleased her. As we descended the mountain, we came to a difficult pass. I offered her my arm, which she took in the same unchanging, quiet manner which made her so charming in my sight. I soon discovered my affection for the stranger, and wondered how it could arise so suddenly and become so impetuous. I was ashamed at abandoning so quickly my opinion of women. But this feeling was not strong enough to stifle the incipient passion. My mind lay captive in the fetters of infatuation."

He paused for a moment. The proud young man seemed to reproach himself for his conduct, which he considered wanting in manly independence and clear penetration.

"On the following day," he continued, "there was to be a horse-race in the neighborhood. Before we parted, it was arranged that we would be present at it. I returned to my room in the hotel, and dreamed waking dreams of Isabella. My friend had told me that she was the daughter of a wealthy merchant, and that she had accompanied her invalid mother here. This mark of love and filial affection was not calculated to cool my ardor. Isabella appeared more beautiful and more charming still. We went to the race. I had the unspeakable happiness of being in the same car and sitting opposite her. After a short journey--to me, at least, it seemed short--we arrived at the grounds where the race was to take place. We ascended the platform. I sat at Isabella's side. She did not for a moment lose her quiet equanimity. The race began. I saw little of it, for Isabella was constantly before my eyes, look where I would. Suddenly a noise--a loud cry--roused me from my dream. Not twenty paces from where we sat, a horse had fallen. The rider was under him. The floundering animal had crushed both legs of the unfortunate man. Even now I can see his frightfully distorted features before me. I feared that Isabella's delicate sensibility might be wounded by the horrible sight. And when I looked at her, what did I see? A smiling face! She had lost her quiet, weary manner, and a hard, unfeeling soul lighted up her features!

"'Do you not think this change in the monotony of the race quite magnificent?' said she.

"I made no answer. With an apology, I left the party and returned alone to Baden."

"Very well," said the father, "your Isabella was an unfeeling creature--granted. But now for your application of this experience."

"We will let another make the application, father. Listen a moment. In Baden a bottle of Rhine wine, whose spirit is so congenial to sad and melancholy feelings, served to obliterate the desolate remembrance. I sat in the almost deserted dining-room. The guests were at the theatre, on excursions in the neighborhood, or dining about the park. An old man sat opposite me. I remarked that his eyes, when he thought himself unobserved, were turned inquiringly on me. The sudden cooling of my passion had perhaps left some marks upon me. The stranger believed, perhaps, that I was an unlucky and desperate player. A player I had indeed been. I had been about to stake my happiness on a beautiful form. But I had won the game.

"The wine soon cheered me up and I entered into conversation with the stranger. We spoke of various things, and finally of the race. As there was a friendly, confiding expression in the old man's countenance, I related to him the unhappy fall of the rider, and dwelt sharply on the impression the hideous spectacle made on Isabella. I told him that such a degree of callousness and insensibility was new to me, and that this sad experience had shocked me greatly.

"'This comes,' said he, 'from permitting yourself to be deceived by appearances, and because you do not know certain classes of society. If you consider the beautiful Isabella with sensual eyes, you will run great danger of taking appearances for truth--the false for the real. Even the plainest exterior is often only sham. Painted cheeks, colored eyebrows, false hair, false teeth; and even if these forms were not false, but true--if you penetrate these forms, if, under the constraint of graceful repose, we see modesty, purity, and even humility--there is then still greater danger of deception. A wearied, enervated nature, nerves blunted by the enjoyment of all kinds of pleasures, are frequently all that remains of womanly nature.

"'Do you wish to see striking examples of this? Go into the gaming saloons--into, those horrible places where fearful and consuming passions seethe; where desperation and suicide lurk. Go into the corrupt, poisonous atmosphere of those gambling hells, and there you will find women every day and every hour. Whence this disgusting sight? The violent excitement of gambling alone can afford sufficient attraction for those who have been sated with all kinds of pleasures. Is a criminal to be executed? I give you my word of honor that women give thousands of francs to obtain the best place, where they can contemplate more conveniently the shocking spectacle and read every expression in the distorted features of the struggling malefactor.

"'Isabella was one of these exhausted, enervated creatures, and hence her pleasure at the sight of the mangled rider.'

"Thus spoke the stranger, and I admitted that he was right. At the same time I tried to penetrate deeper into this want of sensibility. Like a venturesome miner, I descended into the psychological depth. I shuddered at what I there discovered, and at the inferences which Isabella's conduct forced upon my mind. No, father, no," said he impetuously, "I will have no such nuptials--I will never rush into the miseries of matrimony!"

"Thunder and lightning! are you a man?" cried Herr Frank. "Because Emil's wife and Isabella are good-for-nothings, must the whole sex be repudiated? Both cases are exceptions. These exceptions give you no right to judge unfavorably of all women. This prejudice does no honor to your good sense, Richard. It is only eccentricity can judge thus."

The train stopped. The travellers went out, where a carriage awaited them.

"Is everything right?" said Herr Frank to the driver.

"All is fixed, sir, as you required,"

"Is the box of books taken out?"

"Yes, sir."

The coach moved up the street. The dark mountain-side rose into view, and narrow, deep valleys yawned beneath the travellers. Fresh currents of air rushed down the mountain and Herr Frank inhaled refreshing draughts.

Richard gazed thoughtfully over the magnificent vineyards and luxuriant orchards.

The road grew steeper and the wooded summit of the mountain approached. A light which Frank beheld with satisfaction glared out from it. Its rays shot out upon the town that, amid rich vineyards, topped the neighboring hill.

"Our residence is beautifully located," said Herr Frank. "How cheerful it looks up there! It is a home fit for princes."

"You have indeed chosen a magnificent spot, father. Everything unites to make Frankenhöhe a delightful place. The vineyards on the slopes of the hills, the smiling hamlet of Salingen to the right. In the background the stern mountain with its proud ruins on the summit of Salburg, the deep valleys and the dark ravines, all unite in the landscape: to the east that beautiful plain."

These words pleased the father. His eyes rested long on the beautiful property.

"You have forgotten a reason for my happy choice," said he, while a smile played on his features. "I mean the habit of my friend and deliverer, who, for the last eight years, spends the month of May at Frankenhöhe. You know the singular character of the doctor. Nothing in the world can tear him from his books. He has renounced all pleasure and enjoyment, to devote his whole time to his books. When Frankenhöhe entices and captivates the man of science, so strict, so dead to the world, it is, as I think, the highest compliment to our place."

Richard did not question his father's opinion. He knew his unbounded esteem for the learned doctor.

The road grew steeper and steeper. The horses labored slowly along. The pleasant hamlet of Salingen lay a short distance to the left. A single house, separated from the village, and standing near the road in the midst of vineyards, came into view. The features of Herr Frank darkened as he turned his gaze from Frankenhöhe to this house. It was as though some unpleasant recollection was associated with it. Richard looked at the stately mansion, the large out-houses, the walled courts, and saw that everything about it was neat and clean.

"This must be a wealthy proprietor or influential landlord who lives here," said Richard. "I have indeed seen this place in former years, but it did not interest me. How inviting and pleasant it looks. The property must have undergone considerable change; at least, I remember nothing that indicated the place to be other than an ordinary farmhouse."

Herr Frank did not hear these observations. He muttered some bitter imprecation. The coach gained the summit, left the road, and passed through vineyards and chestnut groves to the house.

Frankenhöhe was a handsome two-story house whose arrangements corresponded to Frank's taste and means. Near it stood another, occupied by the steward. A short distance from it were stables and out-houses for purposes of agriculture.

Herr Frank went directly to the house, and passed from room to room to see if his instructions had been carried out.

Richard went into the garden and walked on paths covered with yellow sand. He strolled about among flower-beds that loaded the air with agreeable odors. He examined the blooming dwarf fruit-trees and ornamental plants. He observed the neatness and exact order of everything. Lastly, he stood near the vineyard whence he could behold an extensive view. He admired the beautiful, fragrant landscape. He stood thoughtfully reflecting. His conversation made it evident to him that his feelings and will did not agree with his father's wishes. He saw that between his inclinations and his love for his father he must undergo a severe struggle--a struggle that must decide his happiness for life. The strangeness of his opinion of women did not escape him. He tested his experience. He tried to justify his convictions, and yet his father's claims and filial duty prevailed.

CHAPTER II
THE WEATHER-CROSS

The next morning Richard was out with the early larks, and returned after a few hours in a peculiar frame of mind. As he was entering his room, he saw through the open door his father standing in the saloon. Herr Frank was carefully examining the arrangements, as the servants were carrying books into the adjoining room and placing them in a bookcase. Richard, as he passed, greeted his father briefly, contrary to his usual custom. At other times he used to exchange a few words with his father when he bid him good-morning, and he let no occasion pass of giving his opinion on any matter in which he knew his father took an interest.

The young man walked to the open window of his room, and gazed into the distance. He remained motionless for a time. He ran his fingers through his hair, and with a jerk of the head threw the brown locks back from his forehead. He walked restlessly back and forth, and acted like a man who tries in vain to escape from thoughts that force themselves upon him. At length he went to the piano, and beat an impetuous impromptu on the keys.

"Ei, Richard!" cried Herr Frank, whom the wild music had brought to his side. "Why, you rave! How possessed! One would think you had discovered a roaring cataract in the mountains, and wished to imitate its violence."

Richard glanced quickly at his father, and finished with a tender, plaintive melody.

"Come over here and look at the rooms."

Richard followed his father and examined carelessly the elegant rooms, and spoke a few cold words of commendation.

"And what do you say to this flora?" said Herr Frank pointing to a stepped framework on which bloomed the most beautiful and rare flowers.

"All very beautiful, father. The doctor will be much pleased, as he always is here."

"I wish and hope so. I have had the peacocks and turkeys sent away, because Klingenberg cannot endure their noise. The library here will always be his favorite object, and care has been taken with it. Here are the best books on all subjects, even theology and astronomy."

"Frankenhöhe is indeed cheerful as the heart of youth and quiet as a cloister," said Richard "Your friend would indeed be ungrateful if this attention did not gratify him."

"I have also provided that excellent wine which he loves and enjoys as a healthful medicine. But, Richard, you know Klingenberg's peculiarities. You must not play as you did just now; you would drive the doctor from the house."

"Make yourself easy about that, father; I will play while he is on the mountain."

Richard took a book from the shelf, and glanced over it. Herr Frank left him, and he immediately replaced the book and returned to his own room. There he wrote in his diary:

> "12th of May.--Man is too apt to be led by his inclination. And what is inclination? A feeling caused by external impressions, or superinduced by a disposition of the body. Inclination, therefore, is something inimical to intellectual life. A vine that threatens to overgrow and smother clear conviction. Never act from inclination, if you do not wish to be unfaithful to conviction and guilty o a weakness."

He went into the garden, where he talked to the gardener about trees and flowers.

"Are you acquainted in Salingen, John?"

"Certainly, sir. I was born there."

"Do strangers sometimes come there to stop and enjoy the beautiful neighborhood?"

"Oh! no, sir; there is no suitable hotel there--only plain taverns; and people of quality would not stop at them."

"Are there people of rank in Salingen?"

"Only farmers, sir. But--stay. The rich Siegwart appears to be such, and his children are brought up in that manner."

"Has Siegwart many children?"

"Four--two boys and two girls. One son is at college. The other takes care of the estate, and is at home. The oldest daughter has been at the convent for three years. She is now nineteen years old. The second is still a child."

Richard went further into the garden; he looked over at Salingen, and then at the mountains. His eye followed a path that went winding up the mountain like a golden thread and led to the top. Then his eye rested for a time on a particular spot in that yellow path. Richard remained taciturn and reserved the rest of the day. He sat in his room and tried to read, but the subject did not interest him. He often looked dreamily from the book. He finally arose, took his hat and cane, and was soon lost in the mountain. The next morning Richard went to the borders of the forest, and looked frequently over at Salingen as it lay in rural serenity before him. The pleasant hamlet excited his interest. He then turned to the right and pursued the yellow path which he had examined the day before, up the mountain. The birds sang in the bushes, and on the branches of the tallest oak perched the black-bird whose morning hymn echoed far and wide. The sweet notes of the nightingale joined in the general concert, and the shrill piping of the hawk struck in discordantly with the varied and beautiful song. Even unconscious nature displayed her beauties. The dew hung in great drops on the grass-blades and glittered like so many brilliants, and wild flowers loaded the air with sweet perfumes. Richard saw little of these beauties of spring. He ascended still higher. His mind seemed agitated and burdened. He had just turned a bend in the road when he saw a female figure approaching. His cheeks grew darker as his eyes rested on the approaching figure. He gazed in the distance, and a disdainful flush overspread his face. He approached her as he would approach an enemy whose power he had felt, and whom he wished to conciliate.

She was within fifty paces of him. Her blue dress fell in heavy folds about her person. The ribbons of her straw bonnet, that hung on her arm, fluttered in the breeze. In her left hand she held a bunch of flowers. On her right arm hung a silk mantle, which the mild air had rendered unnecessary. Her full, glossy hair was partly in a silk net and partly plaited over the forehead and around the head, as is sometimes seen with children. Her countenance was exquisitely beautiful, and her light eyes now rested full and clear on the stranger who approached her. She looked at him with the easy, natural inquisitiveness of a child, surprised to meet such an elegant gentleman in this place.

Frank looked furtively at her, as though he feared the fascinating power of the vision that so lightly and gracefully passed him. He raised his hat stiffly and formally. This was necessary to meet the requirement of etiquette. Were it not, he would perhaps have passed her by without a salutation. She did not return his greeting with a stiff bow, but with a friendly "good-morning;" and this too in a voice whose sweetness, purity, and melody harmonized with the beautiful echoes of the morning.

Frank moved on hastily for some distance. He was about to look back, but did not do so; and continued on his way, with contracted brows, till a turn in the road hid her from his view. Here he stopped and wiped the sweat from his forehead. His heart beat quickly, and he was agitated by strong, emotions. He stood leaning on his cane and gazing into the shadows of the forest. He then continued thoughtfully, and ascended some hundred feet higher till he gained the top of the mountain. The tall trees ceased; a variegated copsewood crowned the summit, which formed a kind of platform. Human hands had levelled the ground, and on the moss that covered it grew modest little violets. Near the border of the platform stood a stone cross of rough material. Near this cross lay the fragments of another large rock, that might have been shattered by lightning years before. A few steps back of this, on two square blocks of stone, stood a statue of the Virgin and Child, of white stone very carefully wrought, but without much art. The Virgin had a crown of roses on her head. The Child held a little bunch of forget-me-nots in its hand, and as it held them out seemed to say, "Forget me not." Two heavy vases that could not be easily overturned by the wind, standing on the upper block, also contained flowers. All these flowers were quite fresh, as if they had just been placed there.

Richard examined these things, and wondered what they, meant in this solitude of the mountain. The fresh flowers and the cleanliness of the statue, on which no dust or moss could be seen, indicated a careful keeper. He thought of the young woman whom he met. He had seen the same kind of flowers in her hand, and doubtless she was the devotee of the place.

Scarcely had his thoughts taken this direction when he turned away and walked to the border of the plot; and gazed at the country before him. He looked down toward Frankenhöhe, whose white chimneys appeared above the chestnut grove. He contemplated the plains with their luxuriant fields reflecting every shade of green--the strips of forests that lay like shadows in the sunny plain--numberless hamlets with church towers whose gilded crosses gleamed in the sun. He gazed in the distance where the mountain ranges vanished in the mist, and long he enjoyed the magnificence of the view. He was aroused from his dreamy contemplation by the sound of footsteps behind him.

An old man with a load of wood on his shoulders came up to the place. Breathing heavily, he threw down the wood and wiped the sweat from his face. He saw the stranger, and respectfully touched his cap as he sat down on the wood.

Frank went to him.

"You are from Salingen, I suppose," he began.

"Yes, sir."

"It is very hard for an old man like you to carry such a load so far."

"It is indeed, but I am poor and must do it."

Frank looked at the patched clothes of the old man, his coarse shoes, his stockingless feet, and meagre body, and felt compassion for him.

"For us poor people the earth bears but thistles and thorns." After a pause, the old man continued, "We have to undergo many tribulations and difficulties, and sometimes we even suffer from hunger. But thus it is in the world. The good God will reward us in the next world for our sufferings in this."

These words sounded strangely to Richard. Raised as he was in the midst of wealth, and without contact with poverty, he had never found occasion to consider the lot of the poor; and now the resignation of the old man, and his hope in the future, seemed strange to him. He was astonished that religion could have such power--so great and strong--to comfort the poor in the miseries of a hopeless, comfortless life.

"But what if your hope in another world deceive you?"

The old man looked at him with astonishment.

"How can I be deceived? God is faithful. He keeps his promises."

"And what has he promised you?"

"Eternal happiness if I persevere, patient and just, to the end."

"I wonder at your strong faith!"

"It is my sole possession on earth. What would support us poor people, what would keep us from despair, if religion did not?"

Frank put his hand into his pocket,

"Here," said he, "perhaps this money will relieve your wants."

The old man looked at the bright thalers in his hand, and the tears trickled down his cheeks.

"This is too much, sir; I cannot receive six thalers from you."

"That is but a trifle for me; put it in your pocket, and say no more about it."

"May God reward and bless you a thousand times for it!"

"What does that cross indicate?"

"That is a weather cross, sir. We have a great deal of bad weather to fear. We have frequent storms here, in summer; they hang over the mountain and rage terribly. Every ravine becomes a torrent that dashes over the fields, hurling rocks and sand from the mountain. Our fields are desolated and destroyed. The people of Salingen placed that cross there against the weather. In spring the whole community come here in procession and pray God to protect them from the storms."

Richard reflected on this phenomenon; the confidence of these simple people in the protection of God, whose omnipotence must intervene between the remorseless elements and their victims, appeared to him as the highest degree of simplicity. But he kept his thoughts to himself, for he respected the religious sentiments of the old man, and would not hurt his feelings.

"And the Virgin, why is she there?"

"Ah! that is a wonderful story, sir," he answered, apparently wishing to evade an explanation.

"Which every one ought not to know?"

"Well--but perhaps the gentleman would laugh, and I would not like that!"

"Why do you think I would laugh at the story?"

"Because you are a gentleman of quality, and from the city, and such people do not believe any more in miracles."

This observation of rustic sincerity was not pleasing to Frank. It expressed the opinion that the higher classes ignore faith in the supernatural.

"If I promise you not to laugh, will you tell me the story?"

"I will; you were kind to me, and you can ask the story of me. About thirty years ago," began the old man after a pause, "there lived a wealthy farmer at Salingen whose name was Schenck. Schenck was young. He married a rich maiden and thereby increased his property. But Schenck had many great faults. He did not like to work and look after his fields. He let his servants do as they pleased, and his fields were, of course, badly worked and yielded no more than half a crop. Schenck sat always in the tavern, where he drank and played cards and dice. Almost every night he came home drunk. Then he would quarrel with his wife, who reproached him. He abused her, swore wickedly, and knocked everything about the room, and behaved very badly altogether. Schenck sank lower and lower, and became at last a great sot. His property was soon squandered. He sold one piece after another, and when he had no more property to sell, he took it into his head to sell himself to the devil for money. He went one night to a cross-road, and called the devil, but the devil would not come; perhaps because Schenck belonged to him already, for the Scripture says, 'A drunkard cannot enter the kingdom of heaven.' At last a suit was brought against him, and the last of his property was sold, and he was driven from his home. This hurt Schenck very much, for he always had a certain kind of pride. He thought of the past times when he was rich and respected, and now he had lost all respect with his neighbors. He thought of his wife and his four children, whom he had made poor and miserable. All this drove him to despair. He determined to put an end to himself. He bought a rope and came up here one morning to hang himself. He tied the rope to an arm of the cross, and had his head in the noose, when all at once he remembered that he had not yet said his three 'Hail! Marys.' His mother who was dead had accustomed him, when a child, to say every day three 'Hail! Marys.' Schenck had never neglected this practice for a single day. Then he took his head out of the noose and said, 'Well, as I have said the "Hail! Marys" every day, I will say them also to-day, for the last time.' He knelt down before the cross and prayed. When he was done, he stood up to hang himself. But he had scarcely stood on his feet when he was snatched up by a whirlwind and carried through the air till he was over a vineyard, where he fell without hurting himself. As he stood up, an ugly man stood before him and said, 'This time you have escaped me, but the next time I will get you.' The ugly man had horses' hoofs in place of feet, and wore green clothes. He disappeared before Schenck's eyes. Schenck swears that this ugly man was the devil. He declares also that he has to thank the Mother of God, through whose intercession he escaped the claws of the devil. Schenck had that statue placed there in memory of his wonderful escape--that is why the Mother of God is there."

"A wonderful story indeed!" said Richard. "Although I do not laugh as you see, yet I must assure that I do not believe the story."

"I thought so," answered the old man. "But you can ask Schenck himself. He is still living, and is now seventy. Since that day he has changed entirely. He drinks nothing but water. He never enters a tavern, but goes every day to church. From that time to this Schenck has very industrious, and has saved a nice property."

"That the drunkard reformed is most remarkable and best part of the story," said Frank. "Drunkards very seldom reform. But," continued he smiling, "the devil acted very stupidly in the affair. He should have known that his appearance would have made a deep impression on the man, and that he would not let himself be caught a second time."

"That is true," said the old man. "I believe the devil was forced to appear and speak so."

"Forced? By whom?"

"By Him before whom the devils believe and tremble. Schenck was to understand that God delivered on account of his pious custom, and the devil had to tell him his would not happen a second time."

"How prudent you are in your superstition!" said Frank.

"As the gentleman has been kind, it hurts me to hear him speak so."

"Now," said Richard quickly, "I would not hurt your feelings. One may be a good Christian without believing fables. And the flowers near the statue. Has Schenck placed them there too?"

"Oh! no--the Angel did that."

"The Angel. Who is that?" said Frank, surprised.

"The Angel of Salingen--Siegwart's angel."

"Ah! angel is Angela, is it not?"

"So she may be called. In Salingen they call her only Angel. And she is indeed as lovely, good, and beautiful as an angel. She has a heart for the poor, and she gives with an open hand and a smiling face that does one good. She is like her father, who gives me as many potatoes as I want, and seed for my little patch of ground."

"Why does Angela decorate this statue?"

"I do not know; perhaps she does it through devotion."

"The flowers are quite fresh; does she come here every day?"

"Every day during the month of May, and no longer."

"Why no longer?"

"I do not know the reason; she has done so for the last two years, since she came home from the convent, and she will do so this year."

"As Siegwart is so good to the poor, he must be rich."

"Very rich--you can see from his house. Do you see that fine building there next to the road? That is the residence of Herr Siegwart."

It was the same building that had arrested Richard's attention as he passed it some days before, and the sight of which had excited the ill-humor of his father. Richard returned by a shorter way to Frankenhöhe. He was serious and meditative. Arrived at home, he wrote in his diary:

"May 13th.--Well, I have seen her. She exhibits herself as the 'Angel of Salingen.' She is extremely beautiful. She is full of amiability and purity of character. And to-day she did not wear that detestable crinoline. But she will have other foibles in place of it. She will, in some things at least, yield to the superficial tendencies of her sex. Isabella was an ideal, until she descended from the height where my imagination, deceived by her charms, had placed her. The impression which Angela's appearance produced has rests on the same foundation--deception. A better acquaintance will soon discover this. Curious! I long to become better acquainted!

"Religion is not a disease or hallucination, as many think. It is a power. Religion teaches the poor to bear their hard lot with patience. It comforts and keeps them from despair. It directs their attention to an eternal reward, and this hope compensates them for all the afflictions and miseries of this life. Without religion, human society would fall to pieces."

A servant entered, and announced dinner.

"Ah Richard!" said Herr Frank good-humoredly. "Half an hour late for dinner, and had to be called! That is strange; I do not remember such a thing to have happened before. You are always as punctual as a repeater."

"I was in the mountain and had just returned."

"No excuse, my son. I am glad the neighborhood diverts you, and that you depart a little from your regularity. Now everything is in good order, as I desired, for my friend and deliverer. I have just received a letter from him. He will be here in two days. I shall be glad to see the good man again. If Frankenhöhe will only please him for a long time!"

"I have no doubt of that," said Richard. "The doctor will be received like a friend, treated like a king, and will live here like Adam and Eve in paradise."

"Everything will go on as formerly. I will be coming and going on account of business. You will, of course, remain uninterruptedly at Frankenhöhe. You are high in the doctor's esteem. You interest him very much. It is true you annoy him sometimes with your unlearned objections and bold assertions. But I have observed that even vexation, when it comes from you, is not disagreeable to him."

"But the poor should not annoy him with their sick," said Richard. "He never denies his services to the poor, as he never grants them to the rich. Indeed, I have sometimes observed that he tears himself from his books with the greatest reluctance, and it is not without an effort that he does it."

"But we cannot change it," said Herr Frank; "we cannot send the poor away without deeply offending Klingenberg. But I esteem him the more for his generosity."

After dinner the father and son went into the garden and talked of various matters; suddenly Richard stopped and pointing over to Salingen, said,

"I passed to-day that neat building that stands near the road. Who lives there?"

"There lives the noble and lordly Herr Siegwart," said Herr Frank derisively.

His tone surprised Richard. He was not accustomed to hear his father speak thus.

"Is Siegwart a noble?"

"Not in the strict sense. But he is the ruler of Salingen. He rules in that town, as absolutely as princes formerly did in their kingdoms."

"What is the cause of his influence?"

"His wealth, in the first place; secondly, his charity; and lastly, his cunning."

"You are not favorable to him?"

"No, indeed! The Siegwart family is excessively ultramontane and clerical. You know I cannot endure these narrow prejudices and this obstinate adherence to any form of religion. Besides, I have a particular reason for disagreement with Siegwart, of which I need not now speak."

"Excessively ultramontane and clerical!" thought Richard, as he went to his room. "Angela is undoubtedly educated in this spirit. Stultifying confessionalism and religious narrow-mindedness have no doubt cast a deep shadow over the 'angel.' Now--patience; the deception will soon banish."

He took up Schlosser's History, and read a long time. But his eyes wandered from the page, and his thoughts soon followed.

The next morning at the same hour Richard went to the weather cross. He took the same road and again he met Angela; she had the same blue dress, the same straw hat on her arm, and flowers in her hand. She beheld him with the same clear eyes, with the same unconstrained manner--only, as he thought, more charming--as on the first day. He greeted her coolly and formally, as before. She thanked him with the same affability. Again the temptation came over him to look back at her; again he overcame it. When he came to the statue, he found fresh flowers in the vases. The child Jesus had fresh forget-me-nots in his hand, and the Mother had a crown of fresh roses on her head. On the upper stone lay a book, bound in blue satin and clasped with a silver clasp. When he took it up, he found beneath it a rosary made of an unknown material, and having a gold cross fastened at the end. He opened the book. The passage that had been last read was marked with a silk ribbon. It was as follows:

> "My son, trust not thy present affection; it will be quickly changed into another. As long as thou livest thou art subject to change, even against thy will; so as to be sometimes joyful, at other times sad; now easy, now troubled; at one time devout, at another dry; sometimes fervent, at other times sluggish; one day heavy, another day lighter. But he that is wise and well instructed in spirit stands above all these changes, not minding what he feels in himself, nor on what side the wind of instability blows; but that the whole bent of his soul may advance toward its due and wished-for end; for thus he may continue one and the self-same without being shaken, by directing without ceasing, through all this variety of events, the single eye of his intention toward me. And by how much more pure the eye of the intention is, with so much greater constancy mayest thou pass through these divers storms.
>
> "But in many the eye of pure intention is dark; for men quickly look toward something delightful that comes in their way. And it is rare to find one who is wholly free from all blemish of self-seeking."

Frank remembered having written about the same thoughts in his diary. But here they were conceived in another and deeper sense.

He read the title of the book. It was *The Following of Christ*.

He copied the title in his pocketbook. He then with a smile examined the rosary, for he was not without prejudice against this kind of prayer.

He had no doubt Angela had left these things here, and he thought it would be proper to return them to the owner. He came slowly down the mountain reading the book. It was clear to him that *The Following of Christ* was a book full of very earnest and profound reflections. And he wondered how so young a woman could take any interest in such serious reading. He was convinced that all the ladies he knew would throw such a book aside with a sneer, because its contents condemned their lives and habits. Angela, then, must be of a different character from all the ladies he knew, and he was very desirous of knowing better this character of Angela.

In a short time he entered the gate and passed through the yard to the stately building where Herr Siegwart dwelt. He glanced hastily at the long out-buildings--the large barns; at the polished cleanliness of the paved court, the perfect order of every thing, and finally at the ornamented mansion. Then he looked at the old lindens that stood near the house, whose trunks were protected from injury by iron railings. In the tops of these trees lodged a lively family of sparrows, who were at present in hot contention, for they quarrelled and cried as loud and as long as did formerly the lords in the parliament of Frankfort. The beautiful garden, separated from the yard by a low wall covered with white boards, did not escape him. Frank entered, upon a broad and very clean path; as his feet touched the stone slabs, he heard, through the open door, a low growl, and then a man's voice saying, "Quiet, Hector."

Frank walked through the open door into a large room handsomely furnished, and odoriferous with a multitude of flowers in vases. A man in the prime of life sat on the sofa reading and smoking. He wore a light brown overcoat, brown trousers, and low, thick boots. He had a fresh, florid complexion, red beard, blue eyes, and an expressive, agreeable countenance. When Frank entered he arose, laid aside the paper and cigar, and approached the visitor.

"I found these things on the mountain near the weather-cross." said Frank, after a more formal than affable bow. "As your daughter met me, I presume they belong to her. I thought it my duty to return them."

"These things certainly belong to my daughter," answered Herr Siegwart. "You are very kind, sir. You have placed us under obligations to you."

"I was passing this way," said Frank briefly.

"And whom have we the honor to thank?"

"I am Richard Frank."

Herr Siegwart bowed. Frank noticed a slight embarrassment in his countenance. He remembered the expressions his father had used in reference to the Siegwart family, and it was clear to him that a reciprocal ill feeling existed here. Siegwart soon resumed his friendly manner, and invited him with much formality to the sofa. Richard felt that he must accept the invitation at least for a few moments. Siegwart sat on a chair in front of him, and they talked of various unimportant matters. Frank admired the skill which enabled him to conduct, without interruption, so pleasant a conversation with a stranger.

While they were speaking, some house-swallows flew into the room. They fluttered about without fear, sat on the open door, and joined their cheerful twittering with the conversation of the men. Richard expressed his admiration, and said he had never seen anything like it.

"Our constant guests in summer," answered Siegwart. "They build their nests in the hall, and as they rise earlier than we do, an opening is left for them above the hall door, where they can go in and out undisturbed when the doors are closed. Angela is in their confidence, and on the best of terms with them. When rainy or cold days come during breeding time they suffer from want of food. Angela is then their procurator. I have often admired Angela's friendly intercourse with the swallows, who perch upon her shoulders and hands."

Richard looked indeed at the twittering swallows, but their friend Angela passed before his eyes, so beautiful indeed that he no longer heard what Siegwart was saying.

He arose; Siegwart accompanied him. As they passed through the yard, Frank observed the long row of stalls, and said,

"You must have considerable stock?"

"Yes, somewhat. If you would like to see the property, I will show you around with pleasure."

"I regret that I cannot now avail myself of your kindness; I shall do so in a few days," answered Frank.

"Herr Frank," said Siegwart, "may the accident which has given us the pleasure of your agreeable visit, be the occasion of many visits in future. I know that as usual you will spend the month of May at Frankenhöhe. We are neighbors--this title, in my opinion, should indicate a friendly intercourse."

"Let it be understood, Herr Siegwart; I accept with pleasure your invitation."

On the way to Frankenhöhe Richard walked very slowly, and gazed into the distance before him. He thought of the swallows that perched on Angela's shoulders and hands. Their sweet notes still echoed in his soul.

The country-like quiet of Siegwart's house and the sweet peace that pervaded it were something new to him. He thought of the simple character of Siegwart, who, as his father said, was "ultramontane and clerical," and whom he had represented to himself as a dark, reserved man. He found nothing in the open, natural manner of the man to correspond with his preconceived opinion of him. Richard concluded that either Herr Siegwart was not an ultramontane, or the characteristics of the ultramontanes, as portrayed in the free-thinking newspapers of the day, were erroneous and false.

Buried in such thoughts, he reached Frankenhöhe. As he passed through the yard, he did not observe the carriage that stood there. But as he passed under the window, he heard a loud voice, and some books were thrown from the window and fell at his feet. He looked down in surprise at the books, whose beautiful binding was covered with sand. He now observed the coach, and smiled.

"Ah! the doctor is here," said he. "He has thrown these unwelcome guests out of the window. Just like him."

He took up the books and read the titles, *Vogt's Pictures from Animal Life, Vogt's Physiological Letters, Czolbe's Sensualism.*

He took the books to his room and began to read them. Herr Frank, with his joyful countenance, soon appeared.

"Klingenberg is here!" said he.

"I suspected as much already," said Richard. "I passed by just as he threw the books out of the window with his usual impetuosity."

"Do not let him see the books; the sight of them sets him wild."

"Klingenberg walks only in his own room. I wish to read these books; what enrages him with innocent paper?"

"I scarcely know, myself. He examined the library and was much pleased with some of the works. But suddenly he tore these books from their place and hurled them through the window."

"'I tolerate no bad company among these noble geniuses,' said he, pointing to the learned works.

"'Pardon me, honored friend,' said I, 'if, without my knowledge, some bad books were included. What kind of writings are these, doctor?"

"'Stupid materialistic trash,' said he. 'If I had Vogt, Moleschott, Colbe, and Büchner here, I would throw them body and bones out of the window.'

"I was very much surprised at this declaration, so contrary to the doctor's kind disposition. 'What kind of people are those you have named?' said I.

"'No people, my dear Frank,' said he. 'They are animals. This Vogt and his fellows have excluded themselves from the pale of humanity, inasmuch as they have declared apes, oxen, and asses to be their equals.'"

"I am now very desirous to know these books," said Richard.

"Well, do not let our friend know your intention," urged Frank.

Richard dressed and went to greet the singular guest. He was sitting before a large folio. He arose at Richard's entrance and paternally reached him both hands.

Doctor Klingenberg was of a compact, strong build. He had unusually long arms, which he swung back and forth in walking. His features were sharp, but indicated a modest character. From beneath his bushy eyebrows there glistened two small eyes that did not give an agreeable expression to his countenance. This unfavorable expression was, however, only the shell of a warm heart.

The doctor was good-natured--hard on himself, but mild in his judgments of others. He had an insatiable desire for knowledge, and it impelled him to severe studies that robbed him of his hair and made him prematurely bald.

"How healthy you look, Richard!" said he, contemplating the young man. "I am glad to see you have not been spoiled by the seething atmosphere of modern city life."

"You know, doctor, I have a natural antipathy to all swamps and morasses.

"That is right, Richard; preserve a healthy naturalness."

"We expected you this morning."

"And would go to the station to bring me. Why this ceremony? I am here, and I will enjoy for a few weeks the pure, bracing mountain air. Our arrangements will be as formerly--not so, my dear friend?"

"I am at your service."

"You have, of course, discovered some new points that afford fine views?"

"If not many, at least one--the weather cross," answered Frank. "A beautiful position. The hill stands out somewhat from the range. The whole plain lies before the ravished eyes. At the same time, there are things connected with *that* place that are not without their influence on me. They refer to a custom of the ultramontanists that clashes with modern ideas; I will have an opportunity of seeing whether your opinion coincides with mine."

"Very well; since we have already an object for our next walk--and this is according to our old plan--tomorrow after dinner at three o'clock," and saying this he glanced wistfully at the old folio. Frank, smiling, observed the delicate hint and retired.

CHAPTER III
QUOD ERAT DEMONSTRANDUM

On the following day, Richard went to the weather-cross. He did not meet Angela. She must have been unusually early; for the flowers had evidently just been placed before the statue.

He returned, gloomy, to the house, and wrote in his diary:

"May 14th.

"She did not meet me to-day, and probably will not meet me again. I should have left the book where it was; it might have awakened her gratitude; for I think she left it purposely, to give me an opportunity to make her acquaintance.

"How many young women would give more than a book to get acquainted with a wealthy party! The 'Angel' is very sensitive; but this sensibility pleases me, because it is true womanly delicacy.

"She will now avoid meeting me in this lonely road. But I will study her character in her father's house. I will see if she does not confirm my opinion of the women of our times. It was for this purpose alone that I accepted Siegwart's invitation. Angela must not play Isabella; no woman ever shall. Single, and free from woman's yoke, I will go through the world."

He put aside the diary, and began reading Vogt's *Physiological Letters*.

At three o'clock precisely, Richard with the punctual doctor left Frankenhöhe. They passed through the chestnut grove and through the vineyard toward Salingen. The doctor pushed on with long steps, his arms swinging back and forth. He was evidently pleased with the subject he had been reading. He had, on leaving the house, shaken Richard by the hand, and spoken a few friendly words, but not a syllable since. Richard knew his ways; and knew that it would take some time for him to thaw.

They were passing between Siegwart's house and Salingen, when they beheld Angela, at a distance, coming toward them. She carried a little basket on her arm, and on her head she wore a straw hat with broad fluttering ribbons. Richard fixed his eyes attentively on her. This time, also, she did not wear hoops, but a dress of modest colors. He admired her light, graceful movement and charming figure. The blustering doctor moderated his steps and went slower the nearer he came to Angela, and considered her with surprise. Frank greeted her, touching his hat. She did not thank him, as before, with a friendly greeting, but by a scarcely perceptible inclination of the head; nor did she smile as before, but on this account seemed to him more charming and ethereal than ever. She only glanced at him, and he thought he observed a slight blush on her cheeks.

These particulars were engrossing the young man's attention when he heard the doctor say,

"Evidently the Angel of Salingen."

"Who?" said Richard in surprise.

"The Angel of Salingen," returned Klingenberg. "You are surprised at this appellation; is it not well-merited?"

"My surprise increases, doctor; for exaggeration is not your fashion."

"But she deserves acknowledgment. Let me explain. The maiden is the daughter of the proprietor Siegwart, and her name is Angela. She is a model of every virtue. She is, in the female world, what an image of the Virgin, by one of the old masters, would be among the hooped gentry of the present. As you are aware, I have been often called to the cabins of the sick poor, and there the quiet, unostentatious labors of this maiden have become known to me. Angela prepares suitable food for the sick, and generally takes it to them herself. The basket on her arm does service in this way. There are many poor persons who would not recover unless they had proper, nourishing food. To these Angela is a great benefactor. For this reason, she has a great influence over the minds of the sick, and the state of the mind greatly facilitates or impedes their recovery.

"I have often entered just after she had departed, and the beneficial influence of her presence could be still seen in the countenances of the poor. Her presence diffused resignation, peace, contentment, and a peculiar cheerfulness in the meanest and most wretched hovels of poverty, where she enters without hesitation. This is certainly a rare quality in so young a creature. She rejoices the hearts of the children by giving them clothes, sometimes made by herself, or pictures and the like. Her whole object appears to be to reconcile and make all happy. I have just seen her for the first time; her beauty is remarkable, and might well adorn an angel.

The common people wish only to Germanize 'Angela' when they call her 'Angel.' But she is indeed an angel of heaven to the poor and needy."

Frank said nothing. He moved on in silence toward the weather-cross.

"I have accidentally discovered a singular custom of your 'angel,' doctor. There is at the weather-cross a Madonna of stone. Angela has imposed upon herself the singular task of adorning this Madonna, daily, with fresh flowers."

"You are a profane fellow, Richard. You should not speak in such a derisive tone of actions which are the out-flowings of pious sentiment."

"Every one has his hobby. What will not people do through ambition? I know ladies who torture a piano for half the night, in order to catch the tone of the prima-donna at the opera. I know women who undergo all possible privations to be able to wear as fine clothes, as costly furs, as others with whom they are in rivalry. This exhaustive night-singing, these deprivations, are submitted to through foolish vanity. Perhaps Angela is not less ambitious and vain than others of her sex. As she cannot dazzle these country folk with furs or toilette, she dazzles their religious sentiment by ostentatious piety."

"Radically false!" said the doctor. "Charity and virtue are recognized and honored not only in the country, but also in the cities. Why do not your coquettes strive for this approval? Because they want Angela's nobility of soul. And again, why should Angela wish to gain the admiration of the peasants? She is the daughter of the wealthiest man in the neighborhood. If such was her object, she could gratify her ambition in a very different way."

"Then Angela is a riddle to me," returned Richard. "I cannot conceive the motives of her actions."

"Which are so natural! The maiden follows the impulses of her own noble nature, and these impulses are developed and directed by Christian culture, and convent education. Angela was a long time with the nuns, and only returned home two years ago. Here you have the very natural solution of the riddle."

"Are you acquainted with the Siegwart family?"

"No; what I know of Angela I learned from the people of Salingen."

They arrived at the platform. Klingenberg stood silent for some time admiring the landscape. The view did not seem to interest Richard. His eyes rested on Angela's home, whose white walls, surrounded by vineyards and corn-fields, glistened in the sun.

"It is worth while to come up here oftener," said Klingenberg.

"Angela's work," said Richard as he drew near the statue. The doctor paused a moment and examined the flowers.

"Do you observe Angela's fine taste in the arrangement of the colors?" said he. "And the forget-me-nots! What a deep religious meaning they have."

They returned by another way to Frankenhöhe.

"Angela's pious work," began Richard after a long pause, "reminds me of a religious custom against which modern civilization has thus far warred in vain. I mean the veneration of saints. You, as a Protestant, will smile at this custom, and I, as a Catholic, must deplore the tenacity with which my church clings to this obsolete remnant of heathen idolatry."

"Ah! this is the subject you alluded to yesterday," said the doctor. "I must, in fact, smile, my dear Richard! But I by no means smile at 'the tenacity with which your church clings to the obsolete remnants of heathen idolatry.' I smile at your queer idea of the veneration of the saints. I, as a reasonable man, esteem this veneration, and recognize its admirable and beneficial influence on human society."

This declaration increased Frank's surprise to the highest degree. He knew the clear mind of the doctor, and could not understand how it happened that he wished to defend a custom so antagonistic to modern thought.

"You find fault," continued Klingenberg, "with the custom of erecting statues to these holy men in the churches, the forest, the fields, the houses, and in the market?"

"Yes, I do object to that."

"If you had objected to the lazy Schiller at Mayence, or the robber's poet Schiller, as he raves at the theatre in Mannheim, or to the conqueror and destroyer of Germany, Gustavus Adolphus, whose statue is erected as an insult in a German city, then you would be right."

"Schiller-worship has its justification," retorted Frank. "They erect public monuments to the genial spirit of that man, to remind us of his services to poetry, his aspirations, and his German patriotism."

"It is praiseworthy to erect monuments to the poet. But do not talk of Schiller's patriotism, for he had none. But let that pass; it is not to the point.

The question is, whether you consider it praiseworthy to erect monuments to deserving and exalted genius?"

"Without the least hesitation, I say yes. But I see what you are driving at, doctor. I know the remorseless logic of your inferences. But you will not catch me in your vise this time. You wish to infer that the saints far surpassed Schiller in nobility and greatness of soul, and that honoring them, therefore, is more reasonable, and more justifiable, than honoring Schiller. I dispute the greatness of the so-called saints. They were men full of narrowness and rigorism. They despised the world and their friends. They carried this contempt to a wonderful extent--to a renunciation of all the enjoyments of life, to voluntary poverty and unconditional obedience. But all these are fruits that have grown on a stunted, morbid tree, and are in opposition to progress, to industry, and to the enlightened civilization of modern times. The dark ages might well honor such men, but our times cannot. Schiller, on the contrary, that genial man, taught us to love the pleasures of life. By his fine genius and his odes to pleasure, he frightened away all the spectres of these enthusiastic views of life. He preached a sound taste and a free, unconstrained enjoyment of the things of this beautiful earth. And for this reason precisely, because he inaugurated this new doctrine, does he deserve monuments in his honor."

"How does it happen then, my friend," said the doctor, in a cutting tone that was sometimes peculiar to him, "that you do not take advantage of the modern doctrine of unconstrained enjoyment? Why have you preserved fresh your youthful vigor, and not dissipated it at the market of sensual pleasures? Why is your mode of life so often a reproach to your dissolute friends? Why do you avoid the resorts of refined pleasures? Why are the coquettish, vitiated, hollow inclinations of a great part of the female sex so distasteful to you? Answer me!"

"These are peculiarities of my nature; individual opinions that have no claim to any weight."

"Peculiarities of your nature--very right; your noble nature, your pure feelings rebel against these moral acquisitions of progress. I begin with your noble nature. If I did not find this good, true self in you, I would waste no more words. But because you are what you are, I must convince you of the error of your views. Schiller, you say, and, with him, the modern spirit, raised the banner of unrestrained enjoyment, and this enjoyment rests on sensual pleasures, does it not?"

"Well--yes."

"I knew and know many who followed this banner--and you also know many. Of those whom I knew professionally, some ended their days in the hospital, of the most loathsome diseases. Some, unsatiated with the whole round of pleasures, drag on a miserable life, dead to all energy, and spiritless. They drank the full cup of pleasure, and with it unspeakable bitterness and disgust. Some ended in ignominy and shame--bankruptcy, despair, suicide. Such are the consequences of this modern dogma of unrestrained enjoyments."

"All these overstepped the proper bounds of pleasure," said Richard.

"The proper bounds? Stop!" cried the doctor, "No leaps, Richard! Think clearly and logically. Christianity also allows enjoyment, but--and here is the point--in certain limits. Your progress, on the contrary, proclaims freedom in moral principles, a disregard of all moral obligations, unrestricted enjoyment--and herein consists the danger and delusion. I ask, Are you in favor of restricted or unrestricted enjoyment?"

Frank hesitated. He felt already the thumbscrew of the irrepressible doctor, and feared the inferences he would draw from his admissions.

"Come!" urged Klingenberg, "decide."

"Sound reason declares for restricted enjoyment," said Frank decidedly.

"Good; there you leave the unlimited sphere which godless progress has given to the thoughts and inclinations of men. You admit the obligation of self-control, and the restraint of the grosser emotions. But let us proceed; you speak of industry. The modern spirit of industry has invoked a demon--or, rather, the demoniac spirit of the times has taken possession of industry. The great capitalists have built thrones on their money-bags and tyrannize over those who have no money. They crush out the work-shop of the industrious and well-to-do tradesman, and compel him to be their slave. Go into the factories of Elfeld, or England; you can there see the slaves of this demon industry--miserable creatures, mentally and morally stunted, socially perishing; not only slaves, but mere wheels of the machines. This is what modern industry has made of those poor wretches, for whom, according to modern enlightenment, there is no higher destiny than to drag through life in slavery, to increase the money-bags of their tyrants. But the capitalists have perfect right, according to modern ideas; they only use the means at their command. The table of the ten commandments has been broken; the yoke of Christianity broken. Man is morally and religiously free; and from this false liberalism the tyranny of plutocracy and the slavery of the poor has been developed. Are you satisfied with the development, and the principles that made it possible?"

"No," said Frank decidedly. "I despise that miserable industrialism that values the product more than the man. My admissions are, however, far from justifying the exaggerated notions of the saints."

"Wait a bit!" cried Klingenberg hastily. "I have just indicated the cause of this wretched egotism, and also a consequence--namely, the power of great capitalists and manufacturers over an army of white slaves. But this is by no means all. This demon of industry has consequences that will ruin a great portion of mankind. Now mark what I say, Richard! The richness of the subject allows me only to indicate. The progressive development of industry brings forth products of which past ages were ignorant, because they were not necessary for life. The existence of these products creates a demand. The increased wants increase the outlay, which in most cases does not square with the income, and therefore the accounts of many close with a deficit The consequences of this deficit for the happiness, and even for the morals of the family, I leave untouched. The increased products beget luxury and the desire for enjoyment; the ultimate consequences of which enervate the individual and society. Hence the phenomenon, in England, that the greater portion of the people in the manufacturing towns die before the age of fifteen, and that many are old men at thirty. Enervated and demoralized peoples make their existence impossible. They go to the wall. This is a historical fact. Ergo, modern industry separated from Christian civilization hastens the downfall of nations."

"I cannot dispute the truth of your observations. But you have touched only the dark side of modern industry, without mentioning its benefits. If industry is a source of fictitious wants, it affords, on the other hand, cheap prices to the poor for the most necessary wants of life; for example, cheap materials for clothing."

"Very cheap, but also very poor material," answered Klingenberg. "In former times, clothing was dearer, but also better. They knew nothing of the rags of the present fabrication. And it may be asked whether that dearer material was not cheaper in the end for the poor. When this is taken into consideration, the new material has no advantage over the old. I will freely admit that the inventions of modern times do honor to human genius. I acknowledge the achievements of industry, as such. I admire the improvements of machinery, the great revolution caused by the use of steam, and thousands of other wonders of art. No sensible man will question the relative worth of all these. But all these are driven and commanded by a bad influence, and herein lies the injury. We must consider industrialism from this higher standpoint. What advantage is it to a people to be clothed in costly stuffs when they are enervated, demoralized, and perishing? Clothe a corpse as you will, a corpse it will be still. And besides, the greatest material good does not compensate the white factory-slaves for the loss of their liberty. The Lucullan age fell into decay, although they feasted on young nightingales, drank liquified pearls, and squandered millions for delicacies and luxuries. The life of nations does not consist in the external splendor of wealth, in easy comfort, or in unrestrained passions. Morality is the life of nations, and virtue their internal strength. But virtue, morality, and Christian sentiment are under the ban of modern civilization. If Christianity does not succeed in overcoming this demon spirit of the times, or at least confining it within narrow limits, it will and must drive the people to certain destruction. We find decayed peoples in the Christian era, but the church has always rescued and regenerated them. While the acquisitions of modern times-- industrialism, enlightenment, humanitarianism, and whatever they may be called--are, on the one hand, of little advantage or of doubtful worth, they are, on the other hand, the graves of true prosperity, liberty, and morality. They are the cause of shameful terrorism and of degrading slavery, in the bonds of the passions and in the claws of plutocracy."

Frank made no reply.

For a while they walked on in silence.

"Let us," continued Klingenberg, "consider personally those men whose molten images stand before us. Schiller's was a noble nature, but Schiller wrote:

> "'No more this fight of duty, hence no longer
> This giant strife will I!
> Canst quench these passions evermore the stronger?
> Then ask not virtue, what I must deny.

> "'Albeit I have sworn, yea, sworn that never
> Shall yield my master will;
> Yet take thy wreath; to me 'tis lost for ever!
> Take back thy wreath, and let me sin my fill.'

"Is this a noble and exalted way of thinking? Certainly not. Schiller would be virtuous if he could clothe himself in the lustre of virtue without sacrifice. The passionate impulses of the heart are stronger in him than the sense of duty. He gives way to his passions. He renounces virtue because he is too weak, too languid, too listless to encounter this giant strife bravely like a strong man. Such is the noble Schiller. In later years, when the fiery impulses of his heart had subsided, he roused himself to better efforts and nobler aims.

"Consider the prince of poets, Goethe. How morally naked and poor he stands before us! Goethe's coarse insults to morality are well known. His better friend, Schiller, wrote of him to Koerner, 'His mind is not calm enough, because his domestic relations, which he is too weak to change, cause him great vexation.' Koerner answered, 'Men cannot violate morality with impunity.' Six years later, the 'noble' Goethe was married to his 'mistress' at Weimar. Goethe's detestable political principles are well known. He did not possess a spark of patriotism. He composed hymns of victory to Napoleon, the tyrant, the destroyer and desolator of Germany. These are the heroes of modern sentiment, the advance guard of liberty, morality, and true manhood! And these heroes so far succeeded that the noble Arndt wrote of his time, 'We are base, cowardly, and stupid; too poor for love, too listless for anger, too imbecile for hate. Undertaking everything, accomplishing nothing; willing every thing, without the power of doing any thing.' So far has this boasted freethinking created disrespect for revealed truth. So far this modern civilization, which idealizes the passions, leads to mockery of religion and lets loose the baser passions of man. If they cast these representatives of the times in bronze, they should stamp on the foreheads of their statues the words of Arndt:

"'We are base, cowardly, and stupid; too poor for love, too listless for anger, too imbecile for hate. Undertaking every thing, accomplishing nothing; willing every thing, without the power of doing any thing.'"

"You are severe, doctor."

"I am not severe. It is the truth."

"How does it happen that a people so weak, feeble, and base could overthrow the power of the French in the world?"

"That was because the German people were not yet corrupted by that shallow, unreal, hollow twaddle of the educated classes about humanity. It was not the princes, not the nobility, who overthrew Napoleon. It was the German people who did it. When, in 1813, the Germans rose, in hamlet and city, they staked their property and lives for fatherland. But it was not the enlightened poets and professors, not modern sentimentality, that raised their hearts to this great sacrifice; not these who enkindled this enthusiasm for fatherland. It was the religious element that did it. The German warriors did not sing Goethe's hymns to Napoleon, nor the insipid model song of 'Luetzows wilder Jagd,' as they rushed into battle. They sang religious hymns, they prayed before the altars. They recognized, in the terrible judgment on Russia's ice-fields, the avenging hand of God. Trusting in God, and nerved by religious exaltation, they took up the sword that had been sharpened by the previous calamities of war. So the feeble philanthropists could effect nothing. It was only a religious, healthy, strong people could do that."

"But the saints, doctor! We have wandered from them."

"Not at all! We have thrown some light on inimical shadows; the light can now shine. The lives of the saints exhibit something wonderful and remarkable. I have studied them carefully. I have sought to know their aims and efforts. I discovered that they imitated the example of Christ, that they realized the exalted teachings of the Redeemer. You find fault with their contempt for the things of this world. But it is precisely in this that these men are great. Their object was not the ephemeral, but the enduring. They considered life but as the entrance to the eternal destiny of man--in direct opposition to the spirit of the times, that dances about the golden calf. The saints did not value earthly goods for more than they were worth. They placed them after self-control and victory over our baser nature. Exact and punctual in all their duties, they were animated by an admirable spirit of charity for their fellow-men. And in this spirit they have frequently revived society. Consider the great founders of orders--St. Benedict, St. Dominic, St. Vincent de Paul! Party spirit, malice, and stupidity have done their worst to blacken, defame, and calumniate them. And yet, in a spirit of self-sacrifice, the sons of St. Benedict came among the German barbarians, to bring to them the ennobling doctrines of Christianity. It was the Benedictines who cleared the primeval forests, educated their wild denizens, and founded schools; who taught the barbarians handiwork and agriculture. Science and knowledge flourished in the cloisters. And to the monks alone we are indebted for the preservation of classic literature. What the monks did then they are doing now. They forsake home, break all ties, and enter the wilderness, there to be miserably cut off in the service of their exalted mission, or to die of poisonous fevers. Name me one of your modern heroes, whose mouths are full of civilization, humanity, enlightenment--name me one who is capable of such sacrifice. These prudent gentlemen remain at home with their gold-bags and their pleasures, and leave the stupid monk to die in the service of exalted charity. It is the hypocrisy and the falsehood of the modern spirit to exalt itself, and belittle true worth. And what did St.

Vincent de Paul do? More than all the gold-bags together. St. Vincent, alone, solved the social problem of his time. He was, in his time, the preserver of society, or rather, Christianity through him. And to-day our gold-bags tremble before the apparition of the same social problem. Here high-sounding phrases and empty declamation do not avail. Deeds only are of value. But the inflated spirit of the times is not capable of noble action. It is not the modern state--not enlightened society, sunk in egotism and gold--that can save us. Christianity alone can do it. Social development will prove this."

"I do not dispute the services of the saints to humanity," said Frank. "But the question is, Whether society would be benefited if the fanatical, dark spirit of the middle ages prevailed, instead of the spirit of modern times?"

"The fanatical, dark spirit of the middle ages!" cried the doctor indignantly. "This is one of those fallacious phrases. The saints were not fanatical or dark. They were open, cheerful, natural, humble men. They did not go about with bowed necks and downcast eyes; but affable, free from hypocrisy, and dark, sullen demeanor, they passed through life. Many saints were poets. St. Francis sang his spiritual hymns to the accompaniment of the harp. St. Charles played billiards. The holy apostle, St. John, resting from his labors, amused himself in childish play with a bird. Such were these men; severe toward themselves, mild to others, uncompromising with the base and mean. They were all abstinent and simple, allowing themselves only the necessary enjoyments. They concealed from observation their severe mode of life, and smiled while their shoulders bled from the discipline. Pride, avarice, envy, voluptuousness, and all the bad passions, were strangers to them; not because they had not the inclinations to these passions, but because they restrained and overcame their lower nature.

"I ask you, now, which men deserve our admiration--those who are governed by unbounded selfishness, who are slaves to their passions, who deny themselves no enjoyment, and who boast of their degrading licentiousness; or those who, by reason of a pure life, are strong in the government of their passions, and self-sacrificing in their charity for their fellowmen?"

"The preference cannot be doubtful," said Frank. "For the saints have accomplished the greatest, they have obtained the highest thing, self-control. But, doctor, I must condemn that saint-worship as it is practised now. Human greatness always remains human, and can make no claims to divine honor."

The doctor swung his arms violently. "What does this reproach amount to? Where are men deified? In the Catholic Church? I am a Protestant, but I know that your church condemns the deification of men."

"Doctor," said Frank, "my religious ignorance deserves this rebuke."

"I meant no rebuke. I would only give conclusions. Catholicism is precisely that power that combats with success against the deifying of men. You have in the course of your studies read the Roman classics. You know that divine worship was offered to the Roman emperors. So far did heathen flattery go, that the emperors were honored as the sons of the highest divinity--Jupiter. Apotheosis is a fruit of heathen growth; of old heathenism and of new heathenism. When Voltaire, that idol of modern heathen worship, was returning to Paris in 1778, he was in all earnestness promoted to the position of a deity. This remarkable play took place in the theatre. Voltaire himself went there. Modern fanaticism so far lost all shame that the people kissed the horse on which the philosopher rode to the theatre. Voltaire was scarcely able to press through the crowd of his worshippers. They touched his clothes--touched handkerchiefs to them-- plucked hairs from his fur coat to preserve as relics. In the theatre they fell on their knees before him and kissed his feet. Thus that tendency that calls itself free and enlightened deified a man--Voltaire, the most trifling scoffer, the most unprincipled, basest man of Christendom.

"Let us consider an example of our times. Look at Garibaldi in London. That man permitted himself to be set up and worshipped. The saints would have turned away from this stupidity with loathing indignation. But this boundless, veneration flattered the old pirate Garibaldi. He received 267,000 requests for locks of his hair, to be cased in gold and preserved as relics. Happily he had not much hair. He should have graciously given them his moustaches and whiskers."

Frank smiled. Klingenberg's pace increased, and his arms swung more briskly.

"Such is the man-worship of modern heathenism. This humanitarianism is ashamed of no absurdity, when it sinks to the worship of licentiousness and baseness personified."

"The senseless aberrations of modern culture do not excuse saint-worship. And you certainly do not wish to excuse it in that way. There is, however, a reasonable veneration of human greatness. Monuments are erected to great men. We behold them and are reminded of their genius, their services; and there it stops. It occurs to no reasonable man to venerate these men on his knees, as is done with the saints."

"The bending of the knee, according to the teaching of your church, does not signify adoration, but only veneration," replied Klingenberg. "Before no Protestant in the world would I bend the knee; before St. Benedict and St. Vincent de Paul I would willingly, out of mere admiration and esteem for their greatness of soul and their purity of morals. If a Catholic kneels before a saint to ask his prayers, what is there offensive in that? It is an act of religious conviction. But I will not enter into the religious question. This you can learn better from your Catholic brethren--say from the Angel of Salingen, for example, who appears to have such veneration for the saints."

"You will not enter into the religious question; yet you defend saint-worship, which is something religious."

"I do not defend it on religious grounds, but from history, reason, and justice. History teaches that this veneration had, and still has, the greatest moral influence on human society. The spirit of veneration consists in imitating the example of the person venerated. Without this spirit, saint-worship is an idle ceremony. But that true veneration of the saints elevates and ennobles, you cannot deny. Let us take the queen of saints, Mary. What makes her worthy of veneration? Her obedience to the Most High, her humility, her strength of soul, her chastity. All these virtues shine out before the spiritual eyes of her worshippers as models and patterns of life. I know a lady, very beautiful, very wealthy; but she is also very humble, very pure, for she is a true worshipper of Mary. Would that our women would venerate Mary and choose her for a model! There would then be no coquettes, no immodest women, no enlightened viragoes. Now, as saint-worship is but taking the virtues of the saints as models for imitation, you must admit that veneration in this sense has the happiest consequences to human society."

"I admit it--to my great astonishment, I must admit it," said Richard.

"Let us take a near example," continued Klingenberg. "I told you of the singular qualities of Angela. As she passed, I beheld her with wonder. I must confess her beauty astonished me. But this astonishing beauty, it appears to me, is less in her charming features than in the purity, the maidenly dignity of her character. Perhaps she has to thank, for her excellence, that same correct taste which leads her to venerate Mary. Would not Angela make an amiable, modest, dutiful wife and devoted mother? Can you expect to find this wife, this mother among those given to fashions--among women filled with modern notions?"

While Klingenberg said this, a deep emotion passed over Richard's face. He did not answer the question, but let his head sink on his breast.

"Here is Frankenhöhe," said the doctor. "As you make no more objections, I suppose you agree with me. The saints are great, admirable men; therefore they deserve monuments. They are models of virtue and the greatest benefactors of mankind; therefore they deserve honor. '*Quod erat demonstrandum.*'"

"I only wonder, doctor, that you, a Protestant, can defend such views."

"You will allow Protestants to judge reasonably," replied Klingenberg. "My views are the result of careful study and impartial reflection."

"I am also astonished--pardon my candor--that with such views you can remain a Protestant."

"There is a great difference between knowing and willing, my young friend. I consider conversion an act of great heroism, and also as a gift of the highest grace."

Richard wrote in his diary:

"If Angela should be what the doctor considers her! According to my notions, such a being exists only in the realm of the ideal. But if Angela yet realizes this ideal? I must be certain. I will visit Siegwart to-morrow."

CHAPTER IV
THE BUREAUCRAT AND THE SWALLOWS

Herr Frank returned to the city. Before he went he took advantage of the absence of Richard, who had gone out about nine o'clock, to converse with Klingenberg about matters of importance. They sat in the doctor's studio, the window of which was open. Frank closed it before he began the conversation.

"Dear friend, I must speak to you about a very distressing peculiarity of my son. I do so because I know your influence over him, and I hope much from it."

Klingenberg listened with surprise, for Herr Frank had begun in great earnestness and seemed greatly depressed.

"On our journey from the city, I discovered in Richard, to my great surprise, a deep-seated antipathy, almost an abhorrence of women. He is determined never to marry. He considers marriage a misfortune, inasmuch as it binds a man to the whims and caprices of a wife. If I had many sons, Richard's idiosyncrasy would be of little consequence; but as he is my only son and very stubborn in his preconceived opinions, you will see how very distressing it must be to me."

"What is the cause of this antipathy of your son to women?"

Herr Frank related Richard's account of his meeting with Isabella and his knowledge of the unhappy marriage of his friend Emil.

"Do you not think that experiences of this kind must repel a noble-minded young man?" said the doctor.

"Admitted! But Isabella and Laura are exceptions, and exceptions by no means justify my son's perverted judgment of women. I told him this. But he still declared that Isabella and Laura were the rule and not the exception; that the women of the present day follow a perverted taste; and that the wearing of crinoline, a costume he detests, proves this."

"I know," said the doctor, "that Richard abominates crinoline. Last year he expressed his opinion about it, and I had to agree with him."

"My God!" said the father, astonished, "you certainly would not encourage my son in his perverted opinion?"

"No," returned the doctor quietly; "but you must not expect me to condemn sound opinions. His judgment of woman is prejudiced--granted. But observe well, my dear Frank. This judgment is at the same time a protest of a noble nature against the age of crinoline. Your son expects much of women. Superficiality, vanity, passion for dress, fickleness, and so forth, do not satisfy his sense of propriety. Marriage, to him, is an earnest, holy union. He would unite himself to a well-disposed woman, to a noble soul who would love her husband and her duties, but not to a degenerate specimen of womankind. Such I conceive to have been the reasons which have produced in your son this antipathy."

"I believe you judge rightly," answered Frank. "But it must appear clear to Richard that his views are unjust, and that there are always women who would realize his expectations."

The doctor thought for a moment, and a significant smile played over his features.

"This must become clear to him--yes, and it will become clear to him sooner, perhaps, than you expect," said the doctor.

"I do not understand you, doctor."

"Yesterday we met Angela," said Klingenberg. "This Angela is an extraordinary being of dazzling beauty; almost the incarnation of Richard's ideal. I told him of her fine qualities, which he was inclined to question. But happily! was able to establish these qualities by facts. Now, as Angela lives but a mile from here and as the simple customs of the country render access to the family easy, I have not understood the character of your son if he does not take advantage of this opportunity to become more intimately acquainted with Angela, even if his object were only to confirm his former opinions of women. If he knew Angela more intimately, it is my firm conviction that his aversion would soon change into the most ardent affection."

"Who is this Angela?"

"The daughter of your neighbor, Siegwart."

Frank looked at the doctor with open mouth and staring eyes.

"Siegwart's daughter!" he gasped. "No, I will never consent to such a connection."

"Why not?"

"Well--because the Siegwart family are not agreeable to me."

"That is no reason. Siegwart is an excellent man, rich, upright, and respected by the whole neighborhood. Why does he happen to appear so unfavorably in your eyes?"

Frank was perplexed. He might have reasons and yet be ashamed to give them.

"Ah!" said the doctor, smiling, "it is now for you to lay aside prejudice."

"An explanation is not possible," said Frank. "But my son will rather die a bachelor than marry Siegwart's daughter."

Klingenberg shrugged his shoulders. There was a long pause.

"I renew my request, my friend," urged Frank. "Convince my son of his errors."

"I will try to meet your wishes," returned Klingenberg. "Perhaps this daughter of Siegwart will afford efficient aid."

"My son's liberty will not be restricted. He may visit the Siegwart family when he wishes. But in matters where the mature mind of the father has to decide, I shall always act according to my better judgment."

The doctor again shrugged his shoulders. They shook hands, and in ten minutes after Herr Frank was off for the train. Richard had left Frankenhöhe two hours before. He passed quickly through the vineyard. A secret power seemed to impel the young man. He glanced often at Siegwart's handsome dwelling, and hopeful suspense agitated his countenance. When he reached the lawn, he slackened his pace. He would reflect, and understand clearly the object of his visit. He came to observe Angela, whose character had made such a strong impression on him and who threatened to compel him to throw his present opinions of women to the winds. He would at the same time reflect on the consequences of this possible change to his peace and liberty.

"Angela is beautiful, very beautiful, far more so than a hundred others who are beautiful but wear crinoline." He had written in his diary:

> "Of what value is corporal beauty that fades when it is disfigured by bad customs and caprices? I admit that I have never yet met any woman so graceful and charming as Angela; but this very circumstance warns me to be careful that my judgment may not be dazzled. If it turns out that Angela sets herself up as a religious coquette or a Pharisee, her fine figure is only a deceitful mask of falsehood, and my opinion would again be verified. I must make observations with great care."

Frank reviewed these resolutions as he passed slowly over the lawn, where some servants were employed, who greeted him respectfully as he passed. In the hall he heard a man's voice that came from the same room he had entered on his first visit. The door was open, and the voice spoke briskly and warmly.

Frank stopped for a moment and heard the voice say,

"Miss Angela is as lovely as ever."

These words vibrated disagreeably in Richard's soul, and urged him to know the man from whom they came.

Herr Siegwart went to meet the visitor and offered him his hand. The other gentleman remained sitting, and looked at Frank with stately indifference.

"Herr Frank, my esteemed neighbor of Frankenhöhe," said Siegwart, introducing Frank.

The gentleman rose and made a stiff bow.

"The Assessor von Hamm," continued the proprietor.

Frank made an equally stiff and somewhat colder bow.

The three sat down.

While Siegwart rang the bell, Richard cast a searching glance at the assessor who had said, "Angela is as lovely as ever."

The assessor had a pale, studious color, regular features in which there was an expression of official importance. Frank, who was a fine observer, thought he had never seen such a perfect and sharply defined specimen of the bureaucratic type. Every wrinkle in the assessor's forehead told of arrogance and absolutism. The red ribbon in the buttonhole of Herr von Hamm excited Frank's astonishment. He thought it remarkable that a young man of four or five and twenty could have merited the ribbon of an order. He might infer from this that decorations and merit do not necessarily go together.

"How glad I am that you have kept your word!" said Siegwart to Frank complacently. "How is your father?"

"Very well; he goes this morning to the city, where business calls him."

"I have often admired your father's attentions to Dr. Klingenberg," said Siegwart after a short pause. "He has for years had Frankenhöhe prepared for the accommodation of the doctor. You are Klingenberg's constant companion, and I do not doubt but such is the wish of your father. And your father tears himself from his business and comes frequently from the city to see that the doctor's least wish is realized. I have observed this these last eight years, and I have often thought that the doctor is to be envied, on account of this noble friendship."

"You know, I suppose, that the doctor saved my father when his life was despaired of?"

"I know; but there are many physicians who have saved lives and who do not find such a noble return."

These words of acknowledgment had something in them very offensive to the assessor. He opened and shut his eyes and mouth, and cast a grudging, envious look at Richard.

The servant brought a glass.

"Try this wine," said Siegwart; "my own growth," he added with some pride.

They touched glasses. Hamm put his glass to his lips, without drinking; Frank tasted the noble liquor with the air of a connoisseur; while Siegwart's smiling gaze rested on him.

"Excellent! I do not remember to have drank better Burgundy."

"Real Burgundy, neighbor--real Burgundy. I brought the vines from France."

"Do you not think the vines degenerate with us?" said Frank.

"They have not degenerated yet. Besides, proper care and attention make up for the unsuitableness of our soil and climate.

"You would oblige me, Herr Siegwart, if you would preserve me some shoots when you next trim them."

"With pleasure. I had them set last year; they shot forth fine roots, and I can let you have any number of shoots."

"Is it not too late to plant them?"

"Just the right time. Our vine-growers generally set them too early. It should be done in May, and not in April. Shall I send them over?"

"You are too kind, Herr Siegwart. My request must certainly destroy your plan in regard to those shoots."

"Not at all; I have all I can use. It gives me great pleasure to be able to accommodate a neighbor. It's settled; I'll send over the Burgundies this evening."

It was clear to Hamm that Siegwart desired to be agreeable to the wealthy Frank. The assessor opened and shut his eyes and mouth, and fidgeted about in his chair. While he inwardly boiled and fretted, he very properly concluded that he must consider himself offended. From the moment of Frank's arrival, the proprietor had entirely forgotten him. He was about to leave, in order not to expose his nerves to further excitement, when chance afforded him an opportunity to give vent to his ill-humor.

Two boys came running into the room. They directed their bright eyes to Siegwart, and their childish, joyful faces, seemed to say,

"Here we are again; you know very well what we want."

One of them carried a tin box in his hand; there was a lock on the box, and a small opening in the top--evidently a money-box.

"Gelobt sei Jesus Christus," said the children, and remained standing near the door.

"In Ewigkeit," returned Siegwart. "Are you there again, my little ones? That's right; come here, Edward." And Siegwart took out his purse and dropped a few pennies into the box.

"A savings-box? Who gave the permission?" said the assessor in a tone that frightened the children, astonished Richard, and caused Siegwart to look with embarrassment at the questioner.

"For the pope, Herr von Hamm," said Siegwart.

The official air of the assessor became more severe.

"The ordinances make no exceptions," retorted Hamm. "The ordinances forbid all collections that are not officially permitted." And he eyed the box as if he had a notion to confiscate it.

Perhaps the lads noticed this, for they moved backward to the door and suddenly disappeared from the room.

"I beg pardon, Herr Assessor," said Siegwart. "The Peter-pence is collected in the whole Catholic world, and the Catholics of Salingen thought they ought to assist the head of their church, who is so sorely pressed, and who has been robbed of his possessions."

"I answer--the ordinances make no exceptions; the Peter-pence comes under the ordinances. I find myself compelled to interpose against this trespass."

"But the Peter-pence is collected in the whole country, Herr von Hamm! Why, even in the public journals we read the results of this collection, and I have never heard that the government forbade the Peter-pence."

"Leave the government out of the question. I stand on my instructions. The government forbids all collections unless permission is granted. You must not expect an official to connive at an open breach of the ordinances. I will do my duty and remind the burgomaster of Salingen that he has not done his."

The occurrence was very annoying to Siegwart; this could be seen in his troubled countenance. He thought of the reproof of the timid burgomaster, and feared that the collection might in future be stopped.

"You have the authority, Herr Assessor, to permit it; I beg you will do so."

"The request must be made in written official form," said Hamm. "You know, Herr Siegwart, that I am disposed to comply with your wishes, but I regret I cannot do so in the present case; and I must openly confess I oppose the Peter-pence on principle. The temporal power of the pope has become unnecessary. Why support an untenable dominion?"

"I consider the temporal power of the pope to be a necessity," said Siegwart emphatically. "If the pope were not an independent prince, but the subject of another ruler, he would in many things have to govern the church according to the mind and at the command of his superior. Sound common sense tells us that the pope must be free."

"Certainly, as far as I am concerned," returned Hamm. "But why drain the money out of the country for an object that cannot be accomplished? I tell you that the political standing of the bankrupt papal government will not be saved by the Peter-pence."

"Permit me to observe, Herr Assessor, that I differ with you entirely. The papal government is by no means bankrupt--quite the contrary. Until the breaking out of the Franco-Sardinian revolution, its finances were as well managed and flourishing as those of any state in Europe. I will convince you of this in a moment." He went to the bookcase and handed the assessor a newspaper. "These statistics will convince you of the correctness of my assertion."

"As the documents to prove these statements are wanting, I have great reason to doubt their correctness," said Hamm. "Paper will not refuse ink, and in the present case the pen was evidently driven by a friendly hand."

"Why do you draw this conclusion?"

"From the contradictions between this account of the papal finances and that given by all independent editors."

"Permit me to call that editor not 'an independent,' but a 'friend of the church.' The enemies of the church will not praise a church which they hate. The papal government is the most calumniated government on earth; and calumny and falsehood perform wonders in our times. The Italian situation furnishes at present a most striking illustration. The king of Piedmont has been raised to the rulership of Italy by the unanimous voice of the people--so say the papers. But the revolution in the greater part of Italy at the present time proves that the unanimous voice of the people was a sham, and that the Piedmontese government is hated and despised by the majority of the Italians. It is the same in many other things. If falsehood and calumny were not the order of the day, falsehood and calumny would not sit crowned on the throne."

"Right!" said Richard. "It is indisputable. It is nothing but the depravity of the times that enables the emperor to domineer over the world."

Siegwart heard Frank's observation with pleasure. Hamm read this in the open countenance of the proprietor, and he made a movement as though he would like to tramp on Frank's toes.

"I admit the flourishing condition of the former Papal States," said Hamm, with a mock smile. "I will also admit that the former subjects of the pope, who have been impoverished by the hungry Piedmontese, desire the milder papal government. 'There is good living under the crozier,' says an old proverb. But what does all this amount to? Does the beautiful past overthrow the accomplished facts of the present? The powers have determined to put an end to papal dominion. The powers have partly accomplished this. Can the Peter-pence change the programme of the powers? Certainly not. The papal government must go the way of all flesh, and if the Catholics are taxed for an unattainable object, it is, in my opinion, unjust, to say the least."

The proprietor shook his head thoughtfully. "We consider the question from very different stand-points," said he. "Pius IX. is the head of the church--the spiritual father of all Catholics. The revolution has robbed him of his revenues. Why should not Catholics give their father assistance?"

"And I ask," said Hamm, "why give the pope alms when the powers are ready to give him millions?"

"On what conditions, Herr Assessor?"

"Well--on the very natural condition that he will acknowledge accomplished facts."

"You find this condition so natural!" said Siegwart, somewhat excited. "Do you forget the position of the pope? Remember that on those very principles of which the pope is the highest representative, was built the civilization of the present. The pope condemns robbery, injustice, violence, and all the principles of modern revolution. How can the pope acknowledge as accomplished facts, results which have sprung from injustice, robbery, and violence? The moment the pope does that, he ceases to be the first teacher of the people and the vicar of Christ on earth."

"You take a strong religious position, my dear friend," said Hamm, smiling compassionately.

"I do, most assuredly," said the proprietor with emphasis. "And I am convinced that my position is the right one."

Hamm smiled more complacently still. Frank observed this smile; and the contemptuous manner of the official toward the open, kind-hearted proprietor annoyed him.

"Pius IX. is at any rate a noble man," said he, looking sharply at the assessor, "There exists a critical state of uncertainty in all governments. All the courts and principalities look to Paris, and the greatest want of principle seems to be in the state taxation. The pope alone does not shrink; he fears neither the anger nor the threats of the powers. While thrones are tumbling, and Pius IX. is not master in his own house, that remarkable man does not make the least concession to the man in power. The powers have broken treaties, trampled on justice, and there is no longer any right but the right of revolution--of force. There is nothing any longer certain; all is confusion. The pope alone holds aloft the banner of right and justice. In his manifestoes to the world, he condemns error, falsehood, and injustice. The pope alone is the shield of those moral forces which have for centuries given stability and safety to governments. This firmness, this confidence in the genius of Christianity, this unsurpassed struggle of Pius, deserves the highest admiration even of those who look upon the contest with indifference."

Siegwart listened and nodded assent. Hamm ate sardines, without paying the least attention to the speaker.

"The Roman love of power is well known, and Rome has at all times made the greatest sacrifices for it," said he.

The proprietor drummed with his fingers on the table. Frank thought he observed him suppressing his anger, before he answered,

"Rome does not contend for love of dominion. She contends for the authority of religion, for the maintenance of those eternal principles without which there is no civilization. This even Herder, who is far from being a friend of Rome, admits when he says, 'Without the church, Europe would, perhaps, be a prey to despots, a scene of eternal discord, and a Mogul wilderness.' Rome's battle is, therefore, very important, and honorable. Had it not been for her, you would not have escaped the bloody terrorisms of the power-seeking revolution. Think of French liberty at present, think of the large population of Cayenne, of the Neapolitan prisons, where thousands of innocent men hopelessly languish."

"You have not understood me, my dear Siegwart. Take an example for illustration. The press informs us almost daily of difficulties between the government and the clergy. The cause of this trouble is that the latter are separated from and wish to oppose the former. To speak plainly, the Catholic clergy are non-conforming. They will not give up that abnormal position which the moral force of past times conceded to them. But in organized states, the clergy, the bishops, and the pastors should be nothing more than state officials, whose rule of conduct is the command of the sovereign."

"That is to make the church the servant of the state," said Siegwart. "Religion, stripped of her divine title, would be nothing more than the tool of the minister to restrain the people."

"Well, yes," said the official very coolly. "Religion is always a strong curb on the rough, uneducated masses; and if religion restrains the ignorant, supports the moral order and the government, she has fulfilled her mission."

The proprietor opened wide his eyes.

"Religion, according to my belief, educates men not for the state but for their eternal destiny."

"Perfectly right, Herr Siegwart, according to your view of the question. I admire the elevation of your religious convictions, which all men cannot rise up to."

A mock smile played on the assessor's pale countenance as he said this. Siegwart did not observe it; but Frank did.

"If I understand you rightly, Herr Assessor, the clergy are only state officials in clerical dress."

The assessor nodded his head condescendingly, and continued to soak a sardine in olive-oil and take it between his knife and fork as Frank began to speak. The fine-feeling Frank felt nettled at this contempt, and immediately chastised Hamm for his want of politeness.

"I take your nod for an affirmative answer to my question," said he. "You will allow me to observe that your view of the position and purpose of the clergy must lead to the most absurd consequences."

The assessor turned an ashy color. He threw himself back on the sofa and looked at the speaker with scornful severity.

"My view is that of every enlightened statesman of the nineteenth century," said he proudly. "How can you, a mere novice in state matters, come to such a conclusion."

"I come to it by sound thinking," said Frank haughtily. "If the clergy are only the servants of the state, they are bound in the exercise of their functions to follow the instructions of the state."

"Very natural," said the official.

"If the government think a change in the church necessary, say the separation of the school from the church, the abolition of festivals, the appointing of infidel professors to theological chairs, the compiling of an enlightened catechism--and all these relate to the spirit of the times or the supposed welfare of the state--then the clergy must obey."

"That is self-evident," said the assessor.

"You see I comprehend your idea of the supreme power of the state," continued Frank. "The state is supreme. The church must be deprived of all independence. She must not constitute a state within a state. If it seems good to a minister to abolish marriage as a sacrament, or the confessional, or to subject the teaching of the clergy to a revision by the civil authority, because a majority of the chambers wish it, or because the spirit of the age demands it, then the opposition of the clergy would be illegal and their resistance disobedience."

"Naturally--naturally," said the official impatiently. "Come, now, let us have the proof of your assertion."

"Draw the conclusions from what I have said, Herr Assessor, and you have the most striking proof of the absurdity and ridiculousness of your gagged state church," said Frank haughtily.

"How so, how so?" cried Hamm inquiringly.

"Simply thus: If the priest must preach according to the august instructions of the state and not according to the principles of religious dogma, he would then preach Badish in Baden, Hessish in Hesse, Bavarian in Bavaria, Mecklenburgish in Mecklenburg; in short, there would be as many sects as there are states and principalities. And these sects would be constantly changing, as the chambers or ministerial instructions would command or allow. All religion would cease; for it would be no longer the expression of the divine will and revelation, but the work of the chambers and the princes. Such a religion would be contemptible in the eyes of every thinking man. I would not give a brass button for such a religion."

"You go too far, Herr Frank," said Hamm. "Religion has a divine title, and this glory must be retained."

"Then the clergy must be free."

"Certainly, that is clear," said the assessor as he arose, and, with a smiling face, bowed lowly. Angela had entered the hall, and in consequence of Hamm's greeting was obliged to come into the room. She might have returned from a walk, for she wore a straw hat and a light shawl was thrown over her shoulders. She led by the hand her little sister Eliza, a charming child of four years.

The sisters remained standing near the door. Eliza looked with wondering eyes at the stranger, whose movements were very wonderful to the mind of the little one, and whose pale face excited her interest.

Angela's glance seemed to have blown away all the official dust that remained in the soul of Hamm. The assessor was unusually agreeable. His face lost its obstinate expression, and became light and animated. Even its color changed to one of life and nature.

To Richard, who liked to take notes, and whose visit to Siegwart's had no other object, the change that could be produced in a bureaucrat by such rare womanly beauty was very amusing. He had arisen and stepped back a little. He observed the assessor carefully till a smile between astonishment and pity lit up his countenance. He then looked at Angela, who stood motionless on the same spot. It seemed to require great resignation on her part to notice the flattering speech and obsequious attentions of the assessor. Richard observed that her countenance was tranquil, but her manner more grave than usual. She still held the little one by the hand, who pressed yet closer to her the nearer the wonderful man came. Hamm's voice rose to a tone of enthusiasm, and he took a step or two toward the object of his reverence, when a strange enemy confronted him. Some swallows had come in with Angela. Till now they were quiet and seemed to be observing the assessor; but when he approached Angela, briskly gesticulating, the swallows raised their well-known shrill cry of anxiety, left their perches and fluttered around the official. Interrupted in the full flow of his eloquence, he struck about with his hands to frighten them. The swallows only became the noisier, and their fluttering about Hamm assumed a decidedly warlike character. They seemed to consider him as a dangerous enemy of Angela whom they wished to keep off. Richard looked on in wonder, Siegwart shook his head and stroked his beard, and Angela smiled at the swallows.

"These are abominable creatures," cried Hamm warding them off. "Why, such a thing never happened to me before. Off with you! you troublesome wretches."

The birds flew out of the room, still screaming; and their shrill cries could be heard high up in the air.

"The swallows have a grudge against you," said Siegwart. "They generally treat only the cats and hawks in this way."

"Perhaps they have been frightened at this red ribbon," returned Hamm. "I regret, my dear young lady, to have frightened your little pets. When I come again, I will leave the object of their terror at home."

"You should not deprive yourself of an ornament which has an honorable significance on account of the swallows, particularly as we do not know whether it was really the red color that displeased them," said she.

"You think, then, Miss Angela, that there is something else about me they dislike?"

"I do not know, Herr Assessor."

"Oh! if I only knew the cause of their displeasure," said Hamm enthusiastically. "You have an affection for the swallows, and I would not displease any thing that you love."

She answered by an inclination, and was about to leave the room.

"Angela," said her father, "here is Herr Frank, to whom you are under obligations."

She moved a step or two toward Richard.

"Sir," said she gently, "you returned some things that were valuable to me; were it not for your kindness, they would probably have been lost. I thank you."

A formal bow was Frank's answer. Hamm stood smiling, his searching glance alternating between the stately young man and Angela. But in the manner of both he observed nothing more than reserve and cold formality.

Angela left the room. The assessor sat down on the sofa and poured out a glass of wine.

Eliza sat on her father's knee. Richard observed the beautiful child with her fine features and golden silken locks that hung about her tender face. The winning expression of innocence and gentleness in her mild, childish eyes particularly struck him.

"A beautiful, lovely child," said he involuntarily, and as he looked in Siegwart's face he read there a deep love and a quiet, fatherly fondness for the child.

"Eliza is not always as lovely and good as she is now," he returned. "She has still some little faults which she must get rid of."

"Yes, that's what Angela said," chattered the little one. "Angela said I must be very good; I must love to pray; I must obey my father and mother; then the angels who are in heaven will love me."

"Can you pray yet, my child," said Richard.

"Yes, I can say the 'Our Father' and the 'Hail Mary.' Angela is teaching me many nice prayers."

She looked at the stranger a moment and said with childish simplicity,

"Can you pray too?"

"Certainly, my child," answered Frank, smiling; "but I doubt whether my prayers are as pleasing to God as yours."

"Angela also said we should not lie," continued Eliza. "The good God does not love children who lie."

"That is true," said Frank. "Obey your sister Angela."

Here the young man was affected by a peculiar emotion. He thought of Angela as the first instructor of the child; placed near this little innocent, she appeared like its guardian angel. He saw clearly at this moment the great importance of first impressions on the young, and thought that in after life they would not be obliterated. He expressed his thoughts, and Siegwart confirmed them.

"I am of your opinion, Herr Frank. The most enduring impressions are made in early childhood. The germ of good must be implanted in the tender and susceptible heart of the child and there developed. Many, indeed most parents overlook this important principle of education. This is a great and pernicious error. Man is born with bad propensities; they grow with his growth and increase with his strength. In early childhood, they manifest themselves in obstinacy, wilfulness, excessive love of play, disobedience, and a disposition to lie. If these outgrowths are plucked up and removed in childhood by careful, religious training, it will be much easier to form the heart to habits of virtue than in after years. Many parents begin to instruct their children after they have spoiled them. Is this not your opinion, Herr Assessor?"

Hamm was aroused by this sudden question. He had not paid any attention to the conversation, but had been uninterruptedly stroking his moustache and gazing abstractedly into vacancy.

"What did you ask, my dear Siegwart? Whether I am of your opinion? Certainly, certainly, entirely of your opinion. Your views are always sound, practical, and matured by great experience, as in this case."

"Well, I can't say you were always of my opinion," said Siegwart smiling; "have we not just been sharply disputing about the Peter-pence?"

"O my dear friend! as a private I agree with you entirely on these questions; but an official must frequently defend in a system of government that which he privately condemns."

Frank perceived Hamm's object. We wished to do away with the unfavorable impressions his former expressions might have made on the proprietor. The reason of this was clear to him since he had discovered the assessor's passion for Angela.

"I am rejoiced," said Siegwart, "that we agree at least in that most important matter, religion."

Frank remembered his father's remark, "The Siegwart family is intensely clerical and ultramontane." It was new and striking to him to see the question of religion considered the most important. He concluded from this, and was confirmed in his conclusions by the leading spirit of the Siegwart family, that, in direct contradiction to modern ideas, religion is the highest good.

"Nevertheless," said Siegwart, "I object to a system of government that is inimical to the church."

"And so do I," sighed the assessor.

Richard took his departure. At home, he wrote a few hasty lines in his diary and then went into the most retired part of the garden. Here he sat in deep thought till the servant called him to dinner.

"Has Klingenberg not gone out yet to-day?"

"No, but he has been walking up and down his room for the last two hours."

Frank smiled. He guessed the meaning of this walk, and as they both entered the dining-room together his conjecture was confirmed.

The doctor entered somewhat abruptly and did not seem to observe Richard's presence. His eyes had a penetrating, almost fierce expression and his brows were knit. He sat down to the table mechanically, and ate what was placed before him. It is questionable whether he knew what he was eating, or even that he was eating. He did not speak a word, and Frank, who knew his peculiarities, did not disturb him by a single syllable. This was not difficult, as he was busily occupied with his own thoughts.

After the meal was over, Klingenberg came to himself. "My dear Richard, I beg your pardon," said he in a tone of voice which was almost tender. "Excuse my weakness. I have read this morning a scientific article that upsets all my previous theories on the subject treated of. In the whole field of human investigation there is nothing whatever certain, nothing firmly established. What one to-day proves by strict logic to be true, to-morrow another by still stronger logic proves to be false. From the time of Aristotle to the present, philosophers have disagreed, and the infallible philosopher will certainly never be born. It is the same in all branches. I would not be the least astonished if Galileo's system would be proved to be false. If the instruments, the means of acquiring astronomical knowledge, continue to improve, we may live to learn that the earth stands still and that the sun goes waltzing around our little planet. This uncertainty is very discouraging to the human mind. We might say with Faust,

"'It will my heart consume

That we can nothing know.'"

"In my humble opinion," said Frank, "every investigator moves in a limited circle. The most profound thinker does not go beyond these set limits; and if he would boldly overstep them, he would be thrown back by evident contradiction into that circle which Omnipotence has drawn around the human intellect."

"Very reasonable, Richard; very reasonable. But the desire of knowledge must sometimes be satiated," continued the doctor after a short pause. "If the human mind were free from the narrow limits of the deceptive world of sense, and could see and know with pure spiritual eyes, the barriers of which you speak would fall. Even the Bible assures us of this. St. Paul, writing to the Corinthians, says, 'We see now through a glass in an obscure manner, but then face to face; now I know in part, but then I shall know as I am known.' I would admire St. Paul on account of this passage alone if he never had written another. How awful is the moral quality of the human soul taken in connection with its future capacity for knowledge. And how natural, how evident, is the connection. The human mind will receive knowledge from the source of all knowledge--God, in proportion as it has been just and good. For this reason our Redeemer calls the world of the damned 'outer darkness,' and the world of the blessed, the 'kingdom of light.'"

"We sometimes see in that way even now," said Frank after a pause. "The wicked have ideas very different from those of the good. A frivolous spirit mocks at and derides that which fills the good with happiness and contentment. We might, then, say that even in this life man knows as he is known."

The doctor cast an admiring glance at the young man. "We entirely agree, my young friend; wickedness is to the sciences what a poisonous miasma and the burning rays of the sun are to the young plants. Yes, vice begets atheism, materialism, and every other abortion of thought."

Klingenberg arose.

"We will meet again at three," said he with a friendly nod.

Richard took from his room *Vogt's Physiological Letters*, went into the garden, and buried himself in its contents.

CHAPTER V
THE PROGRESSIVE PROFESSOR

When Frank returned from the walk, he found a visitor at Frankenhöhe.

The visitor was an elegantly dressed young man, with a free, self-important air about him.

He spoke fluently, and his words sounded as decisive as though they came from the lips of infallibility. At times this self-importance was of such a boastful and arrogant character as to affect the observer disagreeably.

"It is now vacation, and I do not know how to enjoy it better than by a visit to you," said he.

"Very flattering to me," answered Frank. "I hope you will be pleased with Frankenhöhe."

"Pleased?" returned the visitor, as he looked through the open window at the beautiful landscape. "I would like to dream away here the whole of May and June. How charming it is! An empire of flowers and vernal delights."

"I am surprised, Carl, that you have preserved such a love for nature. I thought you considered the professor's chair the culminating point of attraction."

Carl bowed his head proudly, and stood with folded arms before the smiling Frank.

"That is evidently intended for flattery," said he. "The professor's chair is my vocation. He who does not hold his vocation as the acme of all attraction is indeed a perfect man. Besides, it will appear to you, who consider everything in the world, not excepting even the fair sex, with blank stoicism--it will appear even to you that the rostrum is destined to accomplish great things. Ripe knowledge in mighty pulsations goes forth from the rostrum, and permeates society. The rostrum governs and educates the rising young men who are destined to assume leading positions in the state. The rostrum overthrows antiquated forms of religious delusion, ennobles rational thought, exact science, and deep investigation. The rostrum governs even the throne; for we have princes in Germany who esteem liberty of thought and progress of knowledge more than the art of governing their people in a spirit of stupidity."

Frank smiled.

"The glory of the rostrum I leave undisputed," said he. "But I beg of you to conceal from the doctor your scientific rule of faith. You may get into trouble with the doctor."

"I am very desirous of becoming acquainted with this paragon of learning--you have told me so much about him; and I confess it was partly to see him that I made this visit. Get into trouble? I do not fear the old syllogism-chopper in the least. A good disputation with him is even desirable."

"Well, you are forewarned. If you go home with a lacerated back, it will not be my fault."

"A lacerated back?" said the professor quietly. "Does the doctor like to use *striking* arguments?"

"Oh! no; but his sarcasm is as cutting as the slash of a sword, and his logical vehemence is like the stroke of a club."

"We will fight him with the same weapons," answered Carl, throwing back his head. "Shall I pay him my respects immediately?"

"The doctor admits no one. In his studio he is as inaccessible as a Turkish sultan in his harem. I will introduce you in the dining-room, as it is now just dinner-time."

They betook themselves to the dining-room, and soon after they heard the sound of a bell.

"He is just now called to table," said Richard. "He does not allow the servant to enter his room, and for that reason a bell has been hung there."

"How particular he is!" said the professor.

A door of the ante-room was opened, quick steps were heard, and Klingenberg hastily entered and placed himself at the table, as at a work that must be done quickly, and then observed the stranger.

"Doctor Lutz, professor of history in our university," said Frank, introducing him.

"Doctor Lutz--professor of history," said Klingenberg musingly. "Your name is familiar to me, if I am not mistaken; are you not a collaborator on Sybel's historical publication?"

"I have that honor," answered the professor, with much dignity.

They began to eat.

"You read Sybel's periodical?" asked the professor.

"We must not remain entirely ignorant of literary productions, particularly the more excellent."

Lutz felt much flattered by this declaration.

"Sybel's periodical is an unavoidable necessity at present," said the professor. "Historical research was in a bad way; it threatened to succumb entirely to the ultramontane cause and the clerical party."

"Now Sybel and his co-laborers will avert that danger," said the doctor. "These men will do honor to historical research. The ultramontanists have a great respect for Sybel. When he taught in Munich, they did not rest till he turned his back on Isar-Athen. In my opinion, Sybel should not have gone to Munich. The stupid Bavarians will not allow themselves to be enlightened. So let them sit in darkness, the stupid barbarians who have no appreciation for the progress of science."

The professor looked astonished. He could not understand how an admirer of Sybel's could be so prejudiced. Frank was alarmed lest the professor might perceive the doctor's keen sarcasm--which he delivered with a serious countenance--and feel offended. He changed the conversation to another subject, in which Klingenberg did not take part.

"You have represented the doctor incorrectly," said the professor, after the meal. "He understands Sybel and praises his efforts--the best sign of a clear mind."

"Klingenberg is always just," returned Frank.

On the following afternoon, Lutz joined in the accustomed walk. As they were passing through the chestnut grove, a servant of Siegwart's came up breathless, with a letter in his hand, which he gave to Frank.

"Gentlemen," said Frank after reading the letter, "I am urgently requested to visit Herr Siegwart immediately. With your permission I will go."

"Of course, go," said Klingenberg. "I know," he added with a roguish expression, "that you would as lief visit that excellent man as walk with us."

Richard went off in such haste that the question occurred to him why he fulfilled with such zeal the wishes of a man with whom he had been so short a time acquainted; but with the question Angela came before his mind as an answer. He rejected this answer, even against his feelings, and declared to himself that Siegwart's honorable character and neighborly feeling made his haste natural and even obligatory. The proprietor may have been waiting his arrival, for he came out to meet him. Frank observed a dark cloud over the countenance of the man and great anxiety in his features.

"I beg your forgiveness a thousand times, Herr Frank. I know you go walking with Herr Klingenberg at this hour, and I have deprived you of that pleasure."

"No excuse, neighbor. It is a question which would give me greater pleasure, to serve you or to walk with Klingenberg."

Richard smiled while saying these words; but the smile died away, for he saw how pale and suddenly anxious Siegwart had become. They had entered a room, and he desired to know the cause of Siegwart's changed manner.

"A great and afflicting misfortune threatens us," began the proprietor. "My Eliza has been suddenly taken ill, and I have great fears for her young life. Oh! if you knew how that child has grown into my heart." He paused for a moment and suppressed his grief, but he could not hide from Frank the tears that filled his eyes. Richard saw these tears, and this paternal grief increased his respect for Siegwart.

"The delicate life of a young child does not allow of protracted medical treatment, of consultation or investigation into the disease or the best remedies. The disease must be known immediately and efficient remedies applied. There are physicians at my command, but I do not dare to trust Eliza to them."

"I presume, Herr Siegwart, that you wish for Klingenberg."

"Yes--and through your mediation. You know that he only treats the sick poor; but resolutely refuses his services to the wealthy."

"Do not be uneasy about that. I hope to be able to induce Klingenberg to correspond with your wishes. But is Eliza really so sick, or does your apprehension increase your anxiety?"

"I will show you the child, and then you can judge for yourself." They went up-stairs and quietly entered the sick-room. Angela sat on the little bed of the child, reading. The child was asleep, but the noise of their entrance awoke her. She reached out her little round arms to her father, and said in a scarcely audible whisper,

"Papa--papa!"

This whispered "papa" seemed to pierce the soul of Siegwart like a knife. He drew near and leant over the child.

"You will be well to-morrow, my sweet pet. Do you see, Herr Frank has come to see you?"

"Mamma!" whispered the child.

"Your mother will come to-morrow, my Eliza. She will bring you something pretty. My wife has been for the last two weeks at her sister's, who lives a few miles from here," said Siegwart, turning to Frank. "I sent a messenger for her early this morning."

While the father sat on the bed and held Eliza's hand in his, Frank observed Angela, who scarcely turned her eyes from the sick child. Her whole soul seemed taken up with her suffering sister. Only once had she looked inquiringly at Frank, to read in his face his opinion of the condition of Eliza. She stood immovable at the foot of the bed, as mild, as pure, and as beautiful as the guardian angel of the child.

Both men left the room.

"I will immediately seek the doctor, who is now on his walk," said Frank.

"Shall I send my servant for him?"

"That is unnecessary," returned Frank. "And even if your servant should find the doctor, he would probably not be inclined to shorten his walk. Our gardener, who works in the chestnut grove, will show me the way the doctor took. In an hour and a half at furthest I will be back."

The young man pressed the outstretched hand of Siegwart, and hastened away.

In the mean time the doctor and the professor had reached a narrow, wooded ravine, on both sides of which the rocks rose almost perpendicularly. The path on which they talked passed near a little brook, that flowed rippling over the pebbles in its bed. The branches of the young beeches formed a green roof over the path, and only here and there were a few openings through which the sun shot its sloping beams across the cool, dusky way, and in the sunbeams floated and danced dust-colored insects and buzzing flies.

The learned saunterers continued their amusement without altercation until the professor's presumption offended the doctor and led to a vehement dispute.

Klingenberg did not appear on the stage of publicity. He left boasting and self-praise to others, far inferior to him in knowledge. He despised that tendency which pursues knowledge only to command, which cries down any inquiry that clashes with their theories. The doctor published no learned work, nor did he write for the periodicals, to defend his views. But if he happened to meet a scientific opponent, he fought him with sharp, cutting weapons.

"I do not doubt of the final victory of true science over the falsifying party spirit of the ultramontanes," said the professor. "Sybel's periodical destroys, year by year, more and more the crumbling edifice which the clerical zealots build on the untenable foundation of falsified facts."

Klingenberg tore his cap from his head and swung it about vehemently, and made such long strides that the other with difficulty kept up with him. Suddenly he stopped, turned about, and looked the professor sharply in the eyes.

"You praise Sybel's publication unjustly," said he excitedly. "It is true Sybel has founded a historical school, and has won many imitators; but his is a school destructive of morality and of history--a school of scientific radicalism, a school of falsehood and deceitfulness. Sybel and his followers undertake to mould and distort history to their purposes. They slur over every thing that contradicts their theories. To them the ultramontanes are partial, prejudiced men--or perhaps asses and dunces; you are unfortunately right when you say Sybel's school wins ground; for Sybel and his fellows have brought lying and falsification to perfection. They have in Germany perplexed minds, and have brought their historical falsifications to market as true ware."

The professor could scarcely believe his own ears.

"I have given you freely and openly my judgment, which need not offend you, as it refers to principles, not persons."

"Not in the least," answered Lutz derisively. "I admit with pleasure that Sybel's school is anti-church, and even anti-Christian, if you will. There is no honor in denying this. The denial would be of no use; for this spirit speaks too loudly and clearly in that school. Sybel and his associates keep up with the enlightenment and liberalism of our times. But I must contradict you when you say this free tendency is injurious to society; the seed of free inquiry and human enlightenment can bring forth only good fruits."

"Oh! we know this fruit of the new heathenism," cried the doctor. "There is no deed so dark, no crime so great, that it may not be defended according to the anti-Christian principles of vicious enlightenment and corrupt civilization. Sybel's school proves this with striking clearness. Tyrants are praised and honored. Noble men are defamed and covered with dirt."

"This you assert, doctor; it is impossible to prove such a declaration."

"Impossible! Not at all. Sybel's periodical exalts to the seventh heaven the tyrant Henry VIII. of England. You extol him as a conscientious man who was compelled by scruples of conscience to separate from his wife. You commend him for having but one mistress. You say that the sensualities of princes are only of 'anecdotal interest.' Naturally," added the doctor contemptuously, "a school that cuts loose from Christian principles cannot consistently condemn adultery. Fie! fie! Debauchees and men of gross sensuality might sit in Sybel's enlightened school. Progress overthrows the cross, and erects the crescent. We may yet live to see every wealthy man of the new enlightenment have his harem. Whether society can withstand the detestable consequences of this teaching of licentiousness and contempt for Christian morality, is a consideration on which these progressive gentlemen do not reflect."

"I admit, doctor," said Lutz, "that the clear light of free, impartial science must needs hurt the eyes of a pious believer. According to the opinions of the ultramontanes, Henry VIII. was a terrible tyrant and bloodhound. Sybel's periodical deserves the credit of having done justice to that great king."

"Do you say so?" cried the doctor, with flaming eyes. "You, a professor of history in the university! You, who are appointed to teach our young men the truth! Shame on you! What you say is nothing but stark hypocrisy. I appeal to the heathen. You may consider religion from the stand-point of an ape, for what I care; your cynicism, which is not ashamed to equalize itself with the brute, may also pass. But this hypocrisy, this fallacious representation of historical facts and persons, this hypocrisy before my eyes--this I cannot stand; this must be corrected."

The doctor actually doubled up his fists. Lutz saw it and saw also the wild fire in the eyes of his opponent, and was filled with apprehension and anxiety.

Erect and silent, fiery indignation in his flushed countenance, stood Klingenberg before the frightened professor. As Lutz still held his tongue, the doctor continued,

"You call Henry VIII. a 'great king,' you extol and defend this 'great king' in Sybel's periodical. I say Henry VIII. was a great scoundrel, a blackguard without a conscience, and a bloodthirsty tyrant. I prove my assertion. Henry VIII. caused to be executed two queens who were his wives--two cardinals, twelve dukes and marquises, eighteen barons and knights, seventy-seven abbots and priors, and over sixty thousand Catholics. Why did he have them executed? Because they were criminals? No; because they remained true to their consciences and to the religion of their fathers. All these fell victims to the cruelty of Henry VIII., whom you style a 'great king.' You glorify a man who for blood-thirstiness and cruelty can be placed by the side of Nero and Diocletian. That is my retort to your hypocrisy and historical mendacity."

The stern doctor having emptied his vials of wrath, now walked on quietly; Lutz with drooping head followed in silence.

"Sybel does not even stop with Henry VIII.," again began the doctor. "These enlightened gentlemen undertake to glorify even Tiberius, that inhuman monster. They might as well have the impudence to glorify cruelty itself. On the other hand, truly great men, such as Tilly, are abandoned to the hatred of the ignorant."

"This is unjust," said the professor hastily. "Sybel's periodical in the second volume says that Tilly was often calumniated by party spirit; that the destruction of Magdeburg belongs to the class of unproved and improbable events. The periodical proves that Tilly's conduct in North Germany was mild and humane, that he signalized himself by his simplicity, unselfishness, and conscientiousness.

"Does Sybel's periodical say all this?"

"Word for word, and much more in praise of that magnanimous man," said Lutz. "From this you may know that science is just even to pious heroes."

Klingenberg smiled characteristically, and in his smile was an expression of ineffable contempt.

He stopped before the professor.

"You have just quoted what impartial historical research informs us of Tilly, in the second and third volumes. It is so. I remember perfectly having read that favorable account. Now let me quote what the same periodical says of the same Tilly in the seventeenth volume. There we read that Tilly was a hypocrite and a blood-hound, whose name cannot be mentioned without a shudder; furthermore, we are told that Tilly burned Magdeburg, that he waged a ravaging war against men, women, children, and property. You see, then, in the second and third volumes that Tilly was a conscientious, mild man and pious hero; in the seventeenth volume, that he was a tyrant and blood-hound. It appears from this with striking clearness that the enlightened progressionists do not stick at contradiction, mendacity, and defamation."

The professor lowered his eyes and stood embarrassed.

"I leave you, 'Herr Professor,' to give a name to such a procedure. Besides, I must also observe that the strictly scientific method, as it labels itself at present, does not stop at personal defamation. As every holy delusion and religious superstition must be destroyed in the hearts of the students, this lying and defamation extends to the historical truths of faith. It is taught from the professors' chairs, and confirmed by the journals, that confession is an invention of the middle ages; while you must know from thorough research that confession has existed up to the time of the apostles. You teach and write that Innocent III. introduced the doctrine of transubstantiation in the thirteenth century; while every one having the least knowledge of history knows that at the council of 1215 it was only made a duty to receive the holy communion at Easter, that the fathers of the first ages speak of transubstantiation--that it has its foundation in Scripture. You know as well as I do that indulgences were imparted even in the first century; but this does not prevent you from teaching that the popes of the middle ages invented indulgences from love of money, and sold them from avarice. Thus the progressive science lies and defames, yet is not ashamed to raise high the banner of enlightenment; thus you lead people into error, and destroy youth! Fie! fie!"

The doctor turned and was about to proceed when he heard his name called. Frank hastened to him, the perspiration running from his forehead, and his breast heaving from rapid breathing. In a few words he made known Eliza's illness, and Siegwart's request.

"You know," said Klingenberg, "that I treat only the poor, who cannot easily get a physician."

"Make an exception in this case, doctor, I beg of you most earnestly! You respect Siegwart yourself for his integrity, and I also of late have learned to esteem the excellent man, whose heart at present is rent with anxiety and distress. Save this child, doctor; I beg of you save it."

Klingenberg saw the young man's anxiety and goodness, and benevolence beamed on his still angry face.

"I see," said he, "that no refusal is to be thought of. Well, we will go." And he immediately set off with long strides on his way back. Richard cast a glance at the professor, who followed, gloomy and spiteful. He saw the angry look he now and then turned on the hastening doctor, and knew that a sharp contest must have taken place. But his solicitude for Siegwart's child excluded all other sympathy. On the way he exchanged only a few words with Lutz, who moved on morosely, and was glad when Klingenberg and Richard separated from him in the vicinity of Frankenhöhe.

Ten minutes later they entered the house of Siegwart. The doctor stood for a moment observing the child without touching it. The little one opened her eyes, and appeared to be frightened at the strange man with the sharp features. Siegwart and Angela read anxiously in the doctor's immovable countenance. As Eliza said "Papa," in a peculiar, feverish tone, Klingenberg moved away from the bed. He cast a quick glance at the father, went to the window and drummed with his fingers on the glass. Frank read in that quick glance that Eliza must die. Angela must also have guessed the doctor's opinion, for she was very much affected; her head sank on her breast and tears burst from her eyes.

Klingenberg took out his notebook, wrote something on a small slip of paper, and ordered the recipe to be taken immediately to the apothecary. He then took his departure.

"What do you think of the child?" said Siegwart, as they passed over the yard.

"The child is very sick; send for me in the morning if it be necessary."

Frank and the doctor went some distance in silence. The young man thought of the misery the death of Eliza would bring on that happy family, and the pale, suffering Angela in particular stood before him.

"Is recovery not possible?"

"No. The child will surely die to-night. I prescribed only a soothing remedy. I am sorry for Siegwart; he is one of the few fathers who hang with boundless love on their children--particularly when they are young. The man must call forth all his strength to bear up against it."

When Frank entered his room, he found Lutz in a very bad humor.

"You have judged that old bear much too leniently," began the professor. "The man is a model of coarseness and intolerable bigotry."

"I thought so," said Frank. "I know you and I know the doctor; and I knew two such rugged antitheses must affect each other unpleasantly. What occasioned your dispute?"

"What! A thousand things," answered his friend ill-humoredly. "The old rhinoceros has not the least appreciation of true knowledge. He carries haughtily the long wig of antiquated stupidity, and does not see the shallowness of the swamp in which he wallows. The genius of Christianity is to him the sublime. Where this stops, pernicious enlightenment--which corrupts the people, turns churches into ball-rooms, and the Bible into a book of fables--begins."

"The doctor is not wrong there," said Frank earnestly. "Are they not endeavoring with all their strength to deprive the Bible of its divine character? Does not one Schenkel in Heidelberg deny the divinity of Christ? Is not this Schenkel the director of a theological faculty? Do not some

Catholic professors even begin to dogmatize and dispute the authority of the holy see?"

"We rejoice at the consoling fact that Catholic *savants* themselves break the fetters with which Rome's infallibility has bound in adamantine chains the human mind!" cried Lutz with enthusiasm.

"It appears strange to me when young men--scarcely escaped from the school, and boasting of all modern knowledge--cast aside as old, worthless rubbish what great minds of past ages have deeply pondered. The see of Rome and its dogmas have ruled the world for eighteen hundred years. Rome's dogmas overthrew the old world and created a new one. They have withstood and survived storms that have engulfed all else besides. Such strength excites wonder and admiration, but not contempt."

"I let your eulogy on Rome pass," said the professor. "But as Rome and her dogmas have overthrown heathenism, so will the irresistible progress of science overthrow Christianity. Coming generations will smile as complacently at the God of Christendom as we consider with astonishment the great and small gods of the heathen."

"I do not desire the realization of your prophecy," said Frank gloomily; "for it must be accompanied by convulsions that will transform the whole world, and therefore I do not like to see an anti-Christian tendency pervading science."

"Tendency, tendency!" said Lutz, hesitating. "In science there is no tendency; there is but truth."

"Easy, friend, easy! Be candid and just. You will not deny that the tendency of Sybel's school is to war against the church?"

"Certainly, in so far as the church contends against truth and thorough investigation."

"Good; and the friends of the church will contend against you in so far as you are inimical to the spirit of the church. And so, tendency on one side, tendency on the other. But it is you who make the more noise. As soon as a book opposed to you appears,--'Partial!' you say with contemptuous mien; 'Odious!' 'Ecclesiastical!' 'Unreadable!' and it is forthwith condemned. But it appears to me natural that a man should labor and write in a cause which is to him the noblest cause."

"I am astonished, Richard! You did not think formerly as you now do. But I should not be surprised if your intercourse with the doctor is not without its effects." This the professor said in a cutting tone. Frank turned about and walked the room. The observation of his friend annoyed him, and he reflected whether his views had actually undergone any change.

"You deceive yourself. I am still the same," said he. "You cannot mistrust me because I do not take part with you against the doctor."

Carl sat for a time thinking.

"Is my presence at the table necessary?" said he. "I do not wish to meet the doctor again."

"That would be little in you. You must not avoid the doctor. You must convince yourself that he does not bear any ill-will on account of that scientific dispute. With all his rough bluntness, Klingenberg is a noble man. Your non-appearance at table must offend him, and at the same time betray your annoyance."

"I obey," answered Lutz. "Tomorrow I will go for a few days to the mountains. On my return I will remain another day with you."

Frank's assurance was confirmed. The doctor met the guest as if nothing unpleasant had happened. In the cool of the evening he went with the young men into the garden, and spoke with such familiarity of Tacitus, Livy, and other historians of antiquity that the professor admired his erudition.

Frank wrote in his diary:

> "May 20th.--After mature reflection, I find that the views which I believed to be strongly founded begin to totter. What would the professor say if he knew that not the doctor, but a country family, and that, too, ultramontane, begin to shake the foundation of my views? Would he not call me weak?"

He laid down the pen and sat sullenly reflecting.

> "All my impressions of the ultramontane family be herewith effaced," he wrote further. "The only fact I admit is, that even ultramontanes also can be good people. But this fact shall in no wise destroy my former convictions."

CHAPTER VI
THE ULTRAMONTANE WAY OF THINKING

On the following morning, no message was sent for the doctor. The child had died, as Klingenberg foretold. Frank thought of the great affliction of the Siegwart family--Angela in tears, and the father broken down with grief. It drove him from Frankenhöhe. In a quarter of an hour he was at the house of the proprietor.

A servant came weeping to meet him.

"You cannot speak to my master," said she. "We had a bad night. My master is almost out of his mind; he has only just now lain down. Poor Eliza! the dear, good child." And the tears burst forth again.

"When did the child die?"

"At four o'clock this morning; and how beautiful she still looks in death! You would think she is only sleeping. If you wish to see her, just go up to the same room in which you were yesterday."

After some hesitation, Frank ascended the stairs and entered the room. As he passed the threshold, he paused, greatly surprised at the sight that met his view. The room was darkened, the shutters closed, and across the room streamed the broken rays of the morning sun. On a white-covered table burned wax candles, in the midst of which stood a large crucifix; there was also a holy-water vase, and in it a green branch. On the white cushions of the bed reposed Eliza, a crown of evergreens about her forehead, and a little crucifix in her folded hands. Her countenance was not the least disfigured; only about her softly closed eyes there was a dark shade, and the lifelike freshness of the lips had vanished. Angela sat near the bed on a low stool; she had laid her head near that of her sister, and in consequence of a wakeful night was fast asleep. Eliza's little head lay in her arms, and in her hand she held the same rosary that he had found near the statue. Frank stood immovable before the interesting group.

The most beautiful form he had ever beheld he now saw in close contact with the dead. Earnest thoughts passed through his mind. The fleetingness of all earthly things vividly occurred to him. Eliza's corpse reminded him impressively that her sister, the charming Angela, must meet the same inevitable fate. His eyes rested on the beautiful features of the sufferer, which were not in the least disfigured by bitter or gloomy dreams, and which expressed in sleep the sweetest peace. She slept as gently and confidingly near Eliza as if she did not know the abyss which death had placed between them. The only disorder in Angela's external appearance was the glistening curls of hair that hung loose over her shoulders on her breast.

At length Frank departed, with the determination of returning to make his visit of condolence. After the accustomed walk with Klingenberg, he went immediately back to Siegwart's.

When he returned home, he wrote in his diary:

"May 21st.--Surprising and wonderful!

"When my uncle's little Agnes died, my aunt took ill, and my uncle's condition bordered on insanity; tortured by excruciating anguish, he murmured against Providence. He accused God of cruelty and injustice, because he took from him a child he loved so much, he lost all self-control, and had not strength to bear the misfortune with resignation. And now the Siegwart family are in the same circumstances; the father is much broken down, much afflicted, but very resigned; his trembling lips betray the affliction that presses on his heart, but they make no complaints against Providence.

"'I thank you for your sympathy,' said he to me. 'The trial is painful; but God knows what he does. The Lord gave me the dear child; the Lord has taken her away. His holy will be done.' So spoke Siegwart. While he said this, a perceptible pain changed his manly countenance, and he lay like a quivering victim on the altar of the Lord. Siegwart's wife, a beautiful woman, with calm, mild eyes, wept inwardly. Her mother's heart bled from a thousand wounds; but she showed the same self-control and resignation as Siegwart did to the will of the Most High.

"And Angela? I do not understand her at all. She speaks of Eliza as of one sleeping, or of one who has gone to a place where she is happy. But sometimes a spasm twitches her features; then her eyes rest on the crucifix that stands amid the lighted candles. The contemplation of the crucifix seems to afford her strength and vigor. This is a mystery to me. I cannot conceive the mysterious power of that carved figure.

"Misery does not depress these people: it ennobles them. I have never seen the like. When I compare their conduct with that of those I have known, I confess that the Siegwart family puts my acquaintance as well as myself to shame.

"What gives these people this strength, this calm, this resignation? Religion, perhaps. Then religion is infinitely more than a mere conception, a mere external rule of faith.

"I am beginning to suspect that between heaven and earth there exists, for those who live for heaven, a warm, living union. It appears to me that Providence does not, indeed, exempt the faithful from the common lot of earthly affliction; but he gives them strength which transcends the power of human nature.

"I have undertaken the task of putting Angela to the test, and what do I find? Admiration for her--shame for myself; and also the certainty that my views of women must be restricted."

He had scarcely written down these thoughts, when he bit impatiently the pen between his teeth.

"We must not be hasty in our judgments," he wrote further. "Perhaps it is my ignorance of the depth of the human heart that causes me to consider in so favorable a light the occurrences in the Siegwart family.

"Perhaps it is a kind of stupidity of mind, an unrefined feeling, a frivolous perception of fatality, that gives these people this quiet and resignation. My judgment shall not be made up. Angela may conceal beneath the loveliness of her nature characteristics and failings which may justify my opinion of the sex, notwithstanding."

With a peculiar stubbornness which struggles to maintain a favorite conviction, he closed the diary.

On the second day after Eliza's death, the body was consigned to the earth. Frank followed the diminutive coffin, which was carried by four little girls dressed in white. The youthful bearers had wreaths of flowers on their heads and blue silk ribbons about their waists, the ends of which hung down.

After these followed a band of girls, also dressed in white and blue. They had flowers fixed in their hair, and in their hands they carried a large wreath of evergreens and roses. The whole community followed the procession- -a proof of the great respect the proprietor enjoyed among his neighbors. Siegwart's manner was quiet, but his eyes were inflamed. As the coffin was lowered into the ground, the larks sang in the air, and the birds in the bushes around joined their sweet cadences with the not plaintive but joyful melodies which were sung by a choir of little girls. The church ceremonies, like nature, breathed joy and triumph, much to Richard's astonishment. He did not understand how these songs of gladness and festive costumes could be reconciled with the open grave. He believed that the feelings of the mourners must be hurt by all this. He remained with the family at the grave till the little mound was smoothed and finished above it. The people scattered over the graveyard, and knelt praying before the different graves. The cross was planted on Eliza's resting-place, and the girls placed the large wreath on the little mound. Siegwart spoke words of consolation to his wife as he conducted her to the carriage. Angela, sunk in sadness, still remained weeping at the grave. Richard approached and offered her his arm. The carriage proceeded toward Salingen and stopped before the church, whose bells were tolling. The service began. Again was Richard surprised at the joyful melody of the church hymns. The organ pealed forth joyfully as on a festival. Even the priest at the altar did not wear black, but white vestments. Frank, unfamiliar with the deep spirit of the Catholic liturgy, could not understand this singular funeral service.

After service the family returned. Frank sat opposite to Angela, who was very sad, but in no way depressed. He even thought he saw now and then the light of a peculiar joy in her countenance. Madame Siegwart could not succeed in overcoming her maternal sorrow. Her tears burst forth anew, and her husband consoled her with tender words.

Frank strove to divert Angela from her sad thoughts. As he thought it would not be in good taste to speak of ordinary matters, he expressed his surprise at the manner of the burial.

"Your sister," said he, "was interred with a solemnity which excited my surprise, and, I confess, my disapprobation. Not a single hymn of sorrow was sung, either at the grave or in the church. One would not believe that those white-clad girls with wreaths of flowers on their heads were carrying the soulless body of a beloved being to the grave. The whole character of the funeral was that of rejoicing. How is this, Fräulein Angela; is that the custom here?"

She looked at him somewhat astonished.

"That is the custom in the whole Catholic Church," she replied. "At the burial of children she excludes all sadness; and for that reason masses of requiem in black vestments are never said for them; but masses of the angels in white."

"Do you not think the custom is in contradiction to the sentiments of nature--to the sorrowful feelings of those who remain?"

"Yes, I believe so," she answered tranquilly. "Human nature grieves about many things over which the spirit should rejoice."

These words sounded enigmatically to Richard.

"I do not comprehend the meaning of your words, Fräulein Angela."

"Grief at the death of a relative is proper for us, because a beloved person has been taken from our midst. But the church, on the contrary, rejoices because an innocent, pure soul has reached the goal after which we all strive--eternal happiness. You see, Herr Frank, that the church considers the departure of a child from this world from a more exalted point of view, and comprehends it in a more spiritual sense, than the natural affection. While the heart grows weak from sadness, the church teaches us that Eliza is happy; that she has gone before us, and that we will be separated from her but for a short time; that between us there is a spiritual union which is based on the communion of saints. Faith teaches me that Eliza, rescued from all afflictions and disappointments, is happy in the kingdom of the blessed. If I could call her back, I would not do it; for this desire springs from egotism, which can make no sacrifices to love."

Her eyes were full of tears as she said these last words. But that peculiar joy which Richard had before observed, and the meaning of which he now understood, again lighted up her countenance. He leaned back in the carriage, and was forced to admit that the religious conception of death was very consoling, even grand, when compared with that conception which modern enlightenment has of it.

The carriage moved slowly through the silent court-yard, which lay as gloomy under the clouds as though it had put on mourning for the dead. The chickens sat huddled together in a corner, their heads sadly drooping. Even the garrulous sparrows were silent, and through the linden tops came a low, rustling sound like greetings from another world.

Assisted by Richard's hand, Angela descended from the carriage. Her father thanked him for his sympathy, and expressed a wish to see him soon again in the family circle. As Richard glanced at Angela, he thought he read in her look a confirmation of all her father said. Siegwart's invitation was unnecessary. The young man was attracted more strongly to the proprietor's house as Angela's qualities revealed themselves to his astonished view more clearly. But Frank would not believe in the spotlessness and sublime dignity of a Christian maiden. He did not change his former judgment against the sex. His stubbornness still persisted in the opinion that Angela had her failings, which, if manifested, would obscure the external brilliancy of her appearance, but which remained hidden from view. Continued observation alone would, in Frank's opinion, succeed in disclosing the repulsive shadows.

Perhaps a proud determination to justify his former opinions lay less at the bottom of this obstinate tenacity than an unconscious stratagem. The young man anticipated that his respect for Angela would end in passionate affection as soon as she stood before him in the full, serene power of her beauty. He feared this power, and therefore combated her claims.

The professor had returned from his excursion into the mountains, and related what he had seen and heard. "Such excursions on historic grounds," said he, "are interesting and instructive to the historical inquirer. What historical sources hint at darkly become distinct, and many incredible things become clear and intelligible. Thus, I once read in an old chronicle that the monks during choral service sung with such enchanting sweetness that the empress and her ladies and knights who were present burst into tears. I smiled at this passage from the garrulous old chronicler, and thought that the fabulous spirit of the middle ages had descended into the pen of the good man. How often have I heard Mozart's divine music, how often have I been entranced by the stormy, thrilling fantasies of Beethoven! But I was never moved to tears, and I never saw even delicate ladies weep. Two days ago, I wandered alone among the ruins of the abbey of Hagenroth. I stood in the ruined church; above was the unclouded sky, and high round about me the naked walls. Here and there upon the walls hung patches of plaster, and these were painted. I examined the paintings and found them of remarkable purity and depth of sentiment. I examined the painted columns in the nave and choir, and found a beautiful harmony. I admired the excellence of the colors, on which it has snowed, rained, and frozen for three hundred and twenty years. I then examined the fallen columns, the heavy capitals, the beauty of the ornaments, and from these significant remnants my imagination built up the whole structure, and the church loomed up before me in all its simple grandeur and charming finish. I was forced to recognize and admire those artists who knew how to produce such wonderful and charming effects by such simple combinations. I thought on that passage of the chronicle, and I believe if, at that moment, the simple, pure chant of the monks had echoed through the basilica, I also would have been moved to tears. If the monks knew, thought I, how to captivate and charm by their architecture, why could they not do the same with music?"

"The stupid monks!" said Richard.

"If you had spoken those words at my side in that tone as I stood amid those ruins, they would have sounded like malicious envy from the mouth of the spirit of darkness."

"Your admiration for the monks is indeed a great curiosity," said Frank, smiling. "Sybel's congenial friend a eulogist of the monks! That indeed is as strange as a square circle."

"If I admire the splendor of heathenism, must I not also admire the fascinating, still depth of Christian childhood? In heathenism as well as in Christianity human genius accomplishes great and sublime things."

"That, in its whole extent, I must dispute," said Frank. "Where is the splendor and greatness of heathenism? The heathen built palaces of great magnificence, but crime stalked naked about in them. When the lord of the palace killed his slaves for his amusement, there was no law to condemn him. When lords and ladies at their epicurean feasts would step aside into small apartments, there by artificial means to empty their gorged stomachs, they did not offend either against heathen decency or its law of moderation. The marble columns proudly supported gilded arches; but when beneath those arches a human victim bled under the knife of the priests, this was in harmony with the genius of heathenism. The amphitheatres were immense halls, full of art and magnificence, in which a hundred thousand spectators could sit and behold with delight the lions and tigers devour slaves, or the gladiators slaughtering each other for their amusement. No. True greatness and real splendor I do not find in heathenism. Where heathen greatness is, there terrible darkness, profound error, and horrible customs abound. Christianity had to contend for three hundred years to destroy the abominations of heathenism."

"I will not dispute about it now," said Lutz. "You shall not destroy by your criticism the beautiful impressions of my excursion. I also met the Swedes on my tour. About thirty miles from here there is, among the hills, a valley. The peasants call the place the 'murder-chamber.' I suspected that the name might be associated with some historical event, and, on inquiry, I found such to be the case. In the Thirty Years' War, when Gustavus Adolphus, the pious hero, passed through the German provinces murdering and robbing, the inhabitants of the neighborhood fled with their wives, children, and property to this remote valley. They imagined themselves hid in these woods and defiles from the wandering Swedes, but they deceived themselves. Their hiding-place was discovered, and every living thing-- Cows, calves, and oxen excepted--was put to the sword. 'The blood of the massacred,' said my informer, 'flowed down the valley like a brook; and for fifty years the neighborhood was desolate, because the Swedes had destroyed every thing.' Such masterpieces of Swedish blood-thirstiness are found in many places in Germany; and as the people celebrate them in song and story, it is certain that the pious hero has won for himself imperishable fame in the art of slaughter."

"Do you not wish to have the 'murder-chamber' appear in Sybel's periodical?"

"No; fable must be carefully separated from history; and in this case I want the inclination for the subject."

"Fabulous! I find in the 'murder-chamber' nothing but the true Swedish nature of that time."

The professor shrugged his shoulders.

"Gustavus Adolphus may wander for ever about Germany as the 'pious hero,' if for no other purpose than to annoy the ultramontanes."

Frank thought of the Siegwart family.

"I believe we are unjust in our judgments of the ultramontanes," said he. "I visit every day a family which my father declares not only to be ultramontane, but even clerical, and on account of it will not associate with them. But I saw there only the noble, good, and beautiful." And he reported circumstantially what he knew of the Siegwart family.

"You have observed carefully; and in particular no feature of Angela has escaped you. This Angela," he continued jocosely, "must be an incarnate ideal of the other world, since she has excited the interest of my friend, even though she wears crinoline."

"But she does not wear crinoline," said Frank.

"Not!" returned the professor, smiling. "Then it is just right. The Angel of Salingen belongs to the nine choirs of angels, and was sent to the earth in woman's form to win my proud, woman-hating friend to the fair sex."

"My conversion to the highest admiration of women is by no means impossible; at least in one case," answered Richard, in the same earnest tone.

"I am astonished!" said the professor. "My interest is boundless. Could I not see this wonderful lady?"

"Why not? It is eight o'clock. At this hour I am accustomed to make my visit."

"Let us go, by all means," urged Lutz.

On the way Frank spoke of Angela's charitable practices, of her love for the poor, her pious customs, and of her deep religious sentiment, which manifested itself in every thing; of her activity in household matters, of her modesty and humility. All this he said in a tone of enthusiasm. The professor listened with attention and smiled.

As they went through the gate into the large court-yard, they saw Angela standing under the lindens. She held a large dish in her hand. About her pressed and crowded the representatives of all races and nations of that multitude which material progress has raised from slavish degradation.

From Angela's hand rained golden corn among the chattering brood, who, pressed by a ravenous appetite, hungrily shoved, pushed, and upset each other. Even the chivalrous cocks had forgotten their propriety, and greedily snatched up the yellow fruit without gallantly cooing and offering the treasure to the females. Nimble ducks glided between the legs of the turkeys and snatched up, quick as lightning, the grains from their open bills. This did not please the turkeys, who gobbled and struck their sharp bills into the bobbing heads of the ducks. A solitary turkey cock alone scorned to participate in the hungry pleasures of the common herd. He spread his wings stiffly like a crinoline around his body, strutted about the yard, uttered a gallant guttural gobble, and played the fine lady in style.

Near the gate stood the stalls. They all had double doors, so that the upper part could be opened while the lower half remained closed. As the two friends passed, they saw a massive head protruding through the open half of one of those doors. The head was red, and was set upon the powerful shoulders of a steer who had broken loose from his fastening to take a walk about the yard. When he saw the strangers, he began to snort, cock his ears, and shake his head, while his fiery eyes rolled wildly in his head.

"A handsome beast," said Frank, as he stopped. "How wide his forehead, how strong his horns, how powerful his chest!"

"His head," said Lutz, "would be an expressive symbol for the evangelist Luke."

The steer was not pleased with these compliments. Bellowing angrily he rushed against the door, which gave way. Slowly and powerfully came forth from the darkness of the stall the colossal limbs of the dangerous beast. The friends, unexpectedly placed in the power of this terrible enemy, stood paralyzed. They beheld the colossus lashing his sides with his tail, lowering his head threateningly, and maliciously stealing toward them like a cat stealing to a mouse till she gets within a sure spring of it. The steer had evidently the same design on strangers. He thought to crush them with his iron forehead and amuse himself with tossing up their lifeless bodies. They saw this, clearly enough, but there was no time for flight. The red steer in his mad onset would certainly overtake and run them down. Luckily, the professor remembered from the Spanish bull-fights how they must meet these beasts, and he quickly warned his friend.

"If he charges, slip quickly to one side."

Scarcely had the words escaped his trembling lips, when the steer gave a short bellow, lowered his head, and, quick as an arrow, rushed upon Frank. He jumped to one side, but slipped and fell to the ground. The steer dashed against a wagon that was standing near, and broke several of the spokes.

Maddened at the failure of his charge, he turned quickly about and saw Frank lying on the ground, and rejoiced over his helpless victim. Richard commended his soul to God, but had enough presence of mind not to move a limb; he even kept his eyes closed. The steer snuffed about, and Frank felt his warm breath. The steer evidently did not know how to begin with the lifeless thing, until he took it into his head to stick his horns into the yielding mass. The young man was lost--now the steer lowered his horns--now came the rescue.

Angela had only observed the visitor as the bellowing steer rushed at him. All this took but a minute. The servants were not then in the yard; and before they could be called, Richard would be gored a dozen times by the sharp weapons of the steer. The professor trembled in every limb; he neither dared to cry for help, lest he might remind the steer of his presence, nor to move from the place. He seemed destined to be compelled to see his friend breathe out his life under the torturing stabs.

Before this happened, however, Angela's voice rang imperatively through the yard. The astonished steer raised his head, and when he saw the frail form coming toward him with the dish in her hand, he gave forth a friendly low, and had even the good grace to go a few steps to meet her.

"Falk, what are you about?" said she reproachfully. "You are a terrible beast to treat visitors so."

Falk lowed his apology, and, as he perceived the contents of the dish, he awkwardly sank his mouth into it. Angela scratched his jaws, at which he was so delighted that he even forgot the dish and held still like a child. The professor looked on this scene with amazement--the airy form before the murderous head of the steer. As Master Falk began even to lick Angela's hand, the professor was very near believing in miracles.

"So now, be right good, Falk!" said she coaxingly; "now go back where you belong. Keep perfectly quiet, Herr Frank; do not move, and it will be soon over."

She patted the steer on the broad neck, and holding the dish before him, led him to the stall, into which he quickly disappeared.

Frank arose.

"You are not hurt?" asked Lutz with concern.

"Not in the least," answered Frank, taking out his pocket handkerchief and brushing the dust from his clothes. The professor brought him his hat, which had bounced away when he fell, and placed it on the head of his trembling friend.

Angela returned after housing the steer. Frank went some steps toward her, as if to thank her on his knees for his life; but he concluded to stand, and a sad smile passed over his countenance.

"Fräulein Angela," said he, "I have the honor of introducing to you my friend, Herr Lutz, professor at our university."

"It gives me pleasure to know the gentleman," said she. "But I regret that, through the negligence of Louis, you have been in great danger. Great God! if I had not been in the yard." And her beautiful face became as pale as marble.

Richard observed this expression of fright, and it shot through his melancholy smile like rays of the highest delight; but for his preserver he had not a single word of thanks. Lutz, not understanding this conduct, was displeased at his friend, and undertook himself to return her thanks.

"You have placed yourself in the greatest danger, Fräulein Angela," said he. "Had I been able when you went to meet the steer, I would have held you back with both hands; but I must acknowledge that I was palsied by fear."

"I placed myself in no danger," she replied. "Falk knows me well, and has to thank me for many dainties. When father is away, I have to go into the stalls to see if the servants have done their work. So all the animals know me, and I can call them all by name."

They went into the house.

"It is well that my parents are absent to-day, and that the accident was observed by no one; for my father would discharge the Swiss who has charge of the animals, for his negligence. I would be sorry for the poor man. I beg of you, therefore, to say nothing of it to my father. I will correct him for it, and I am sure he will be more careful in future."

While she spoke, the eyes of the professor rested upon her, and it is scarcely doubtful that in his present judgment the splendor of the rostrum was eclipsed. Frank sat silent, observing. He scarcely joined in the conversation, which his friend conducted with great warmth.

"This occurrence," said Lutz, on his way home, "appears to me like an episode from the land of fables and wonders. First, the steer fight; then the overcoming of the beast by a maiden; lastly, a maid of such beauty that all the fair ones of romance are thrown in the shade. By heaven, I must call all my learning to my aid in order to be able to forget her and not fall in love up to the ears!"

Frank said nothing.

"And you did not even thank her!" said Lutz vehemently. "Your conduct was more than ungallant. I do not understand you."

"Nothing without reason," said Frank.

"No matter! Your conduct cannot be justified," growled the professor. "I would like to know the reason that prevented you from thanking your preserver for your life?"

Richard stopped, looked quietly into the glowing countenance of his friend, and proceeded doubtingly,

"You shall know all, and then judge if my offensive conduct is not pardonable."

He began to relate how he met Angela for the first time on the lonely road in the forest, how she then made a deep impression on him, what he learned of her from the poor man and from Klingenberg, and how his opinion of womankind had been shaken by Angela; then he spoke of his object in visiting the Siegwart family, of his observations and experience.

"I had about come to the conclusion, and the occurrence of to-day realizes that conclusion, that Angela possesses that admirable virtue which, until now, I believed only to exist in the ideal world. If there is a spark of vanity in her, I must have offended her. She must have looked resentfully at me, the ungrateful man, and treated me sulkily. But such was not the case; her eyes rested on me with the same clearness and kindness as ever. My coarse unthankfulness did not offend her, because she does not think much of herself, because she makes no pretensions, because she does not know her great excellence, but considers her little human weaknesses in the light of religious perfection--in short, because she is truly humble. She will bury this dauntless deed in forgetfulness. She does not wish the little and great journals to bring her courage into publicity. Tell me a woman, or even a man, who could be capable of such modesty? Who would risk life to rescue a stranger from the horns of a ferocious steer without hesitation, and not desire an acknowledgment of the heroic deed? How great is Angela, how admirable in every act! I was unthankful; yes, in the highest degree unthankful. But I placed myself willingly in this odious light, in order to see Angela in full splendor. As I said," he concluded quietly, "I must soon confess myself besieged--vanquished on the whole line of observation."

"And what then?" said the professor.

"Then I am convinced," said Richard, "that female worth exists, shining and brilliant, and that in the camp of the ultramontanes."

"A shaming experience for us," replied the professor. "You make your studies practical, you destroy all the results of learned investigation by living facts. To be just, it must be admitted that a woman like what you have described Angela to be only grows and ripens on the ground of religious influences and convictions."

"And did you observe," said Richard, "how modestly she veiled the splendor of her brave action? She denied that there was any danger in the presence of the steer, although it is well known that those beasts in moments of rage forget all friendship. Angela must certainly have felt this as she went to meet the horns of the infuriated animal to rescue me."

Frank visited daily, and sometimes twice a day, the Siegwart family; he was always received with welcome, and might be considered an intimate friend. The family spirit unfolded itself clearer and clearer to his view. He found that every thing in that house was pervaded by a religious influence, and this without any design or haughty piety. The assessor was destined to receive a striking proof of this.

One afternoon a coach rolled into the court-yard. The family were at tea. The Assessor von Hamm entered, dressed entirely in black; even the red ribbon was wanting in the button-hole.

"I have learned with grief of the misfortune that has overtaken you," said he after a very formal reception. "I obey the impulse of my heart when I express my sincere sympathy in the great affliction you have suffered in the death of the dear little Eliza."

The tears came into the eyes of Madame Siegwart. Angela looked straight before her, as if to avoid the glance of the assessor.

"We thank you, Herr von Hamm," returned the proprietor. "We were severely tried, but we are reasonable enough to know that our family cannot be exempted from the afflictions of human life."

Hamm sat down, a cup was set before him, and Angela poured him out a cup of fragrant tea. The assessor acknowledged this service with his sweetest smile, and the most obliged expression of thanks.

"You are right," he then said. "No one is exempt from the stroke of fate. Man must submit to the unavoidable. To the ancients, blind fate was terrific and frightful. The present enlightenment submits with resignation."

If a bomb had plunged into the room and exploded upon the table, it could not have produced greater confusion than these words of the assessor. Madame Siegwart looked at him with astonishment and shook her head. The proprietor, embarrassed, sipped his tea. Angela's blooming cheeks lost their color. Hamm did not even perceive the effect of his fatal words, and Frank was scarcely able to hide his secret pleasure at Hamm's sad mishap.

"We know no fate, no blind, unavoidable destiny," said Siegwart, who could not forgive the assessor his unchristian sentiment. "But we know a divine providence, an all-powerful will, without whose consent the sparrow does not fall from the house-top. We believe in a Father in heaven who, counts the hairs of our heads, and whose counsels rule our destiny."

Hamm smiled.

"You believe then, Herr Siegwart, that divine providence, or rather God, has aimed that blow at you?"

"Yes; so I believe."

"Pardon me. I think you judge too hard of God. It is inconsistent with his paternal goodness to afflict your beloved child with such misfortune."

"Misfortune? It is to be doubted whether Eliza's death is a misfortune. Perhaps her early departure from this world is precisely her happiness; and then we must reflect that God is master of life and death. It is not for us to call the Almighty to account, even if his divine ordinances should be counter to our wishes."

"I respect your religious convictions, Herr Siegwart. Permit me, however, to observe that God is much too exalted to have an eye to all human trifles. He simply created the natural law; this he leaves to its course. All the elements must obey these laws. Every creature is subject to them; and when Eliza died, she died in consequence of the course of these laws, but not through God's express will. Do you not think that this view of our misfortunes reconciles us with the conceptions we have of God's goodness?"

"No; I do not believe it, because such a view contradicts the Christian faith," replied Siegwart earnestly. "What kind of a God, what kind of a Father would he be who would let every thing go as it might? He would be less a father than the poorest laborer who supports his family in the sweat of his brow."

"And the whole army of misfortunes that daily overtake the human family? Does this army await the command of God?"

"Do not forget, Herr Assessor, that the most of these misfortunes are deserved; brought on by our sins and passions. If excesses would cease, how many sources of nameless calamities would disappear! For the rest, it is my firm conviction that nothing happens or can happen in the whole universe without the express will of God, or at least by his permission."

The official shook his head.

"This question is evidently of great importance to every man," said Frank. "Man is often not master of the course of his life; for it is developed by a chain of circumstances, accidents, and providential interferences that are not in man's power. I understand very well that to be subject to blind chance, to an irrevocable fate, is something disquieting and discouraging to man. Equally consoling, on the other hand, is the Christian faith in the loving care of an all-powerful Father, without whose permission a hair of our head cannot be touched. But things of such great injustice, of such irresistible power, and of such painful consequences happen on earth, that I cannot reconcile them with divine love."

While Frank spoke, Angela's eyes rested on him with the greatest attention; and when he concluded, she lowered her glance, and an earnest, thoughtful expression passed over her countenance.

"There are accidents that apparently are not the result of man's fault," said Siegwart. "Torrents sweep over the land and destroy all the fruit of man's industry. Perhaps these torrents are only the scourges which the justice of God waves over a lawless land. But I admit that among the victims there are many good men. Storms wreck ships at sea, and many human lives are lost. Avalanches plunge from the Alps and bury whole towns in their resistless fall. It is such accidents as these you have in view."

"Precisely--exactly so. How will you reconcile all these with the fatherly goodness of God?" cried Hamm triumphantly.

The proprietor smiled.

"Permit me to ask a question, Herr Assessor. Why does the state make laws?"

"To preserve order."

"I anticipated this natural reply," continued the proprietor. "If malefactors were not punished, thieves and desperadoes, their bad practices being permitted, would have full play. Then all order would vanish; human society would dissolve into a chaos of disorder. God also created laws which are necessary for the preservation of the natural order. Storms destroy ships. If there were no storms, all growth in the vegetable kingdom would cease. Poisonous vapors would fill the air, and every living thing must miserably die. Avalanches destroy villages. But if it did not snow, the torrents would no longer run, the streams would dry up and the wells would disappear, and man and beast would die of thirst. You see, gentlemen, God cannot abolish that law of nature without endangering the whole creation."

"That explains some, but not all," replied Hamm. "God is all-powerful; it would be but a trifle for him to protect us by his almighty power from the destructive forces of the elements. Why does he not do so?"

"The reason is clear," answered Angela's father: "God would have constantly to work miracles. Miracles are exceptions to the workings of the laws of nature. Now, if God would constantly suppress the power, and unceasingly interrupt the laws of nature, then there would be no longer a law of nature. The supernatural would have devoured the natural. The Almighty would have destroyed the present creation."

"No matter," said the official. "God might destroy the natural forces that are inimical to man; for all that exists is only of value because of its use to man."

"Then nothing whatever would remain. All would be lost," said Siegwart. "We speak and write much about earthly happiness that soon passes away. We glorify the beauty of creation; but we forget that God's curse rests on this earth, and it does not require great penetration to see this curse in all things."

"You believe, then, in the future destruction of the earth?" asked Hamm.

"Divine revelation teaches it," said Siegwart. "The Holy Scriptures expressly say there will be a new earth and a new heaven; and the Lord himself assures us that the foundations of the earth will be overturned and the stars shall fall from the heavens."

"The stars fall from the heavens!" cried Hamm, laughing. "If you could only hear what the astronomers say about that."

"What the astronomers say is of no consequence. They did not create the heavenly bodies, and cannot give them boundaries; besides, we need not take the falling of the stars literally. This expression may signify their disappearance from the earth, perhaps the abolition of the laws by which they have heretofore been moved, and the reconstruction of those relations which existed between heaven and earth prior to the fall. God will then do what you now demand of him, Herr von Hamm," concluded Siegwart, smiling. "He will destroy the inimical power of nature, so that the new earth will be free from thorns, tears, and lamentations."

Thus they continued to dispute, and the debate became so animated that even Angela entered the list in favor of providence.

"I believe," said she with charming blushes, "that the miseries of this earthly life can only be explained and understood in view of man's eternal destiny. God spares the sinner through forbearance and mercy; he sends trials and misfortunes to the good for their purification. God demanded of Abraham the sacrifice of his only son; but when Abraham showed obedience to the command, and consented to make that boundless sacrifice, he was provided with another victim to offer sacrifice to God."

"Fräulein Angela," exclaimed Hamm enthusiastically, "you have solved the problem. Your comprehensive remark reconciles even the innocent sufferers with repulsive decrees. O Fräulein!"--and the assessor fell into a tone of reverie--"were it permitted me to go through life by the side of a partner who possesses your spirit and your conciliatory mildness!"

Angela looked down blushing. She was embarrassed, and dared not raise her eyes. Her first glance, after a few moments, was at Richard.

Frank wrote in his diary:

"Even the preaching tone becomes her admirably. Morality and religion flow from her lips as from a pure fountain that vivifies her soul."

As yet he had not surrendered to Angela.

Frank sprang from an obstinate Westphalian stock; and that the Westphalians have not exchanged their stiff necks for those of shepherds, is sufficiently proved by their stubborn fight with the powers who menaced their liberties. Had Frank been a good-natured South-German or even Municher, he would long since have bowed head and knees to the "Angel of Salingen." But he now maintained the last position of his antipathy to women against Angela's superior powers.

He visited the Siegwart family not twice, but thrice, even four times a day. He appeared suddenly and unexpectedly before Angela like a spy who wished to detect faults.

Just as he was going over the court, on one occasion, a tall lad came up to him. The boy came from the same fatal door through which Master Falk had rushed out upon Richard with such bad intentions. The servant held his hat in his right hand, and with his left fumbled the bright buttons on his red vest.

"Herr Frank, excuse me; I have something to say to you. I have wanted to speak to you for the last three days, but could not because my master was always in the way. But now, as my master is in the fields, I can state my trouble, if you will allow me."

"What trouble have you?"

"I am the Swiss through whose fault the steer came near doing you a great injury. It is inexplicable to me, even now, how the animal got loose. But Falk is very cunning. I cannot be too watchful of him. His head is full of schemes; and before you can turn around, he has played one of his tricks. The chain has a clasp with a latch, and how he broke it, he only knows."

"It is all right," replied Frank. "I believe you are not to blame."

"I am not to blame about the chain. But I am for the door being open, Miss Angela said; and she is perfectly right. Therefore, I beg your pardon and promise you that nothing of the kind shall happen in future."

"The pardon is granted, on condition that you guard the steer better."

"Miss Angela said that too; and she required me to ask your pardon, which I have done."

Angela stood in the garden, hidden behind the rose-bushes, and heard, smiling, the conversation.

As Frank passed over the yard, she came from the garden carrying a basketful of vegetables. At the same time a harvest-wagon, loaded with rapes and drawn by four horses, came into the yard.

"Your industry extends to the garden also, Miss Angela," said Frank, "Now I know no branch of housekeeping that you cannot take a part in."

"My work is, however, insignificant," she returned. "In a large house there is always a great deal to do, and every one must try to be useful."

"Your garden deserves all praise," continued Richard, eyeing the contents of the baskets. "What magnificent peas and beans!"

For the first time Frank observed in her face something like flattered vanity, and he almost rejoiced at this small shadow on the celestial form before him. But the supposed shadow was quickly changed into light before his eyes. "Father brought these early beans into the neighborhood; they are very tender and palatable. Father likes them, and I am glad to be able to make him a salad this evening. He will be astonished to see his young favorites of this year, eight days earlier than formerly. There he comes; he must not see them now." She covered them with some lettuce.

And this was the shadow of flattered vanity! Childish joy, to be able to astonish her father with an agreeable dish.

The loaded wagon stopped in the yard; the horses snorted and pawed the ground impatiently. The servants opened the barn-doors, and Frank saw on all sides activity and haste to house the valuable crop.

Siegwart shook hands with the visitor.

"The first blessing of the year," said the proprietor. "The rapes have turned out well. We had a fine blooming season, and the flies could not do much damage."

"I have often observed those little flies in the rape-fields," said Frank. "You can count millions of them; but I did not know that they injured the crop."

They both went into the house, where a bottle of Munich beer awaited them. Soon after, the servants went through the hall, and Frank heard Angela's voice from the kitchen, where she was busily occupied. The servants brought bread, plates, cheese, and jugs of light wine to the servants' room.

"Neighbor," said Siegwart, "I invite you to-morrow afternoon at four o'clock to a family entertainment--providing it will be agreeable to you."

The invitation was accepted.

"You must not expect much from the entertainment. It will, at least, be new to you."

Frank was much interested in the character of this ultramontane entertainment. He thought of a May party, a coronation party; but rejected this idea, for Siegwart promised a family entertainment, and this could not be a May party. He thought of all kinds of plays, and what part Angela would take in them. But the play also seemed improbable, and at last the subject of the invitation remained an interesting mystery to him, the solution of which he awaited with impatience.

An hour before the appointed time Richard left Frankenhöhe, after Klingenberg had excused him from the daily walk. He took a roundabout way along the edge of the forest; for he knew that the Siegwart family would be at divine service, and he did not wish to arrive at the house a moment before the time. Sunday stillness rested on all. The mountains rose up a deep blue; the vari-colored fields were partly yellow; the vineyards alone were of a deep green, and when the wind blew through them it wafted with it the pleasant odors of the vine-blossoms.

Madame Siegwart was just returning home from Salingen between her two children. Henry, a youth of seventeen and the future proprietor of the property, had the same manners as his father. He walked leisurely on the road-side, examining the blooming wheat and ripening corn. When he discovered nests of vine weevils, he plucked them off and crushed the eggs of the hated enemies of all wine-growers. Angela remained constantly at her mother's side, and as she accidentally raised her eyes to where Richard stood, he made a movement as though he was caught disadvantageously.

A short distance behind them came Siegwart, surrounded by some men. They often stopped and talked in a lively manner. Frank thought that these men were also invited, and hoped to become acquainted with the *élite* of Salingen. He was, however, disappointed; for a short distance from Siegwart's house the men turned back to Salingen. They had only accompanied the proprietor part of the way. The servants of Siegwart also came hastening along the road, first the men-servants, and some distance behind them the maid-servants. Frank had observed this separation before, and thought it must be in consequence of the strict orders of the master. Frank considered this narrow-minded, and thought of finding fault with it, in true modern spirit. But then he considered the results of his observations, which had extended to the servants. He often admired the industry and regular conduct of these people. He never heard any oath or rough expressions of passion; every one knew his work, and performed it with care and attention. He observed this regular order with admiration, particularly when he thought of the disobedience, dissatisfaction, and untrustworthiness of the generality of servants. Siegwart must possess a great secret to keep these people in agreement and order; therefore he rejected his former opinion of narrow-mindedness, and believed the proprietor must have good reason for this separation of the sexes.

Frank remained for a time under the shadow of an oak, looked at his watch, and finally descended the shortest way. He was expected by Siegwart, and immediately conducted to the large room. The arrangement of the room showed at a glance its use. There was a small altar at one side, and religious pictures hung on the walls. There was also a harmonium, and on the windows hung curtains on which were painted scenes from sacred history. In the middle of the room there was a desk, on which lay a book. To the right of the desk sat the men-servants, to the left the maids, the Siegwart family in the centre. A smile passed over Frank's countenance at the present religious entertainment--for him, at least, a new sort of recreation. At his entrance the whole assembly rose. He greeted Angela and her mother, pressed warmly the hand of Henry, and took the seat allotted to him.

Angela ascended the pulpit, sat down and opened the book. She read the life of the servant St. Zitta, whom the church numbers among the saints. Angela read in a masterly manner. The narrative tone of her soft, melodious voice ran like a quickening stream through the soul. Some passages she pronounced with plastic force, and into the delivery of others she breathed warm life. All listened with great attention. Zitta's childhood passed in quick review, then her hard lot with a master difficult to please. The servants listened with astonishment. They heard with pious attention of Zitta's pure conduct, of her fidelity and humility, of her industry and self-denial. They all felt personally their own deficiency in comparison with this shining model. When Angela closed the book, Frank saw that the servants were deeply impressed. Meditatively they left the room, as though they had heard a striking sermon.

"Ah!" thought Frank. "Now I know one of the means by which Siegwart influences his people."

"Now comes the second part of the entertainment," said the proprietor, taking Richard's arm. "We will now go into the garden."

On the way thither Frank saw under the lindens a long table set with food and wine, and at it sat the servants. Richard heard their conversation in passing. They talked of St. Zitta and recounted the striking facts of her life.

Near the garden wall grew a vine-arbor, which caught the cool air as it passed and loaded it with pleasant odors. Thousands of the flowers of the blooming vine appeared between the indented leaves. Each of these diminutive flowers breathed forth a fragrance which for sweetness of odor could not be surpassed.

A young brood of goldfinches, who had taken possession of the arbor, now cleared off. They flew up on the dwarf trees, or hid among the roses, which of all colors and kinds grew in the garden. The hungry young ones cried incessantly, and tested severely the parental duty of support. But the old ones were not ashamed of this duty. Here and there they caught flies and other insects, and carried them to the young ones, who stood with outstretched wings and flabby bills wide open. Then the old ones would fly away again, light on the branches--mostly on bean-stalks--make quick dodges, wave their tails, smack their tongues, and seize as quick as lightning a harmless passing fly. The sparrows did not behave so harmlessly. They pecked at the bright shining cherries that hung in full clusters on the swaying branches. Others of this sharp-billed gentry hopped about on the strawberry-beds, and disfigured the large berries as they tore off great pieces of the soft meat. One of them had even the boldness to hop about on the decorated table that stood at the upper end of the arbor, to strike his sharp bill into the buttered bread, make an examination of the preserves, ogle the slices of ham, and admire the black bottles that stood on the ground. He also took to flight as the company arrived. The vine-blossoms seemed to send forth a sweeter fragrance as Angela, bright and beaming, approached, leaning on the arm of her mother.

"Do you have this edifying reading every Sunday?" asked Richard.

"Regularly," answered the proprietor. "It is an old custom of our family, and I find it has such good results that I will not have it abolished. The servants are not obliged to be present. They are free after vespers, each one to employ himself as best suits him. But it seldom happens that a servant or a maid is absent. They like to hear the legends, and you may have remarked that they listen with great attention to the reading."

"I have observed it," said Frank. "Miss Angela is also such an excellent reader that only deaf people would not attend."

She smiled and blushed a little at this praise.

"I consider it a strict obligation of employers to have a supervision over the conduct of the servants," said Madame Siegwart. "Many, perhaps most, servants are treated like the slaves in old heathen times. They work for their masters, are paid for it, and there the relation between master and servant ends. This is why they neglect divine service on Sundays and feast-days; their moral wants are not satisfied, their natural inclinations are not purified by restraints of a higher order. The servants sit in the taverns, where they squander their wages, and the maids rove about and gossip. This is a great injustice to the servants, and full of bad consequences. It cannot be questioned that masters should shield their servants from error and keep them under moral discipline."

"Precisely my opinion," returned Frank. "If servants are frequently spoiled and general complaint is made of it, the masters are greatly in fault. I have long since admired the conduct of your servants. I looked upon Herr Siegwart as a kind of sorcerer, who conjured every thing under his charge according to his will. Now a part of the sorcery is clear to me."

"Well, you were favorable in your judgment," said the proprietor, laughing. "So you considered me a magician; others consider me an ultramontanist, and that is something still worse."

Richard smiled and blushed slightly.

"You no doubt have heard this honorable title applied to me, Herr Frank?"

"Yes, I have heard of it."

"And I scarcely deceive myself in supposing," continued Siegwart good-humoredly, "that your father has spoken to you of his neighbor, the ultramontane."

"You do not deceive yourself at all," answered Frank. "I consider it a great honor to have become better acquainted with the ultramontane."

"I have often wished to speak to you," continued the proprietor, "of the reason which called forth your father's displeasure with me. I suppose, however, that you have heard it."

"My father never spoke of it, and I am eager to know the unfortunate cause."

"It is as follows. About ten years ago your father, with some other gentlemen, wished to establish a great factory in this neighborhood. The land on which it was to stand is a marsh lying near a pond, the water of which was to be made of use to the factory. I tried with all my power to prevent this design, and even for social and religious reasons. Our neighborhood needed no factory. There are but few very poor people, and these support themselves sufficiently well among the farmers. Experience proves that factories have a bad effect on the people in their neighborhood. Our people are firm believers. The peasants keep conscientiously the Sundays and festivals. In all their cares for the earthly they do not forget the eternal life. This religious sentiment spreads happiness and peace over our quiet neighborhood. The factory, which knows no Sunday, and the operatives, who are sometimes very bad men, would have brought a harsh discordance into the quiet harmony of the neighborhood. I considered these and other injurious influences, and offered a higher price for the swamp than your father and his friends. As there was no other convenient place about, the enterprise had to be given up. Since that time your father is offended with me because I made his favorite project impossible. This is the way it stands. That it is painful to me, I need not assure you. But according to my principles and views I could not do otherwise. Now judge how far I am to be condemned."

"I speak freely," said Frank. "You have acted from principles that one must respect, and which my father would have respected if he had known them."

The proprietor could have observed that he had, in a long letter, justified himself to Herr Frank. But he suppressed the observation, as he felt it would be painful to his son.

"Father," said Henry, "hunger and thirst are appeased. Can I ride out for an hour?"

"Yes, my son; but not longer. Be back by supper-time."

The young man promised, and, after a friendly bow to Frank, hastened from the garden. The little circle continued some time in friendly chat. The servants under the lindens became noisy and sang merry songs. The maids sat around the tea-table in the kitchen and praised St. Zitta.

The cook appeared in the arbor and announced that Herr von Hamm was in the house, and wished to speak on important business to Herr and Madame Siegwart.

"What can he want?" said the proprietor in surprise. "Excuse me, Herr Frank; the business will soon be over. I beg you to remain till we return. Angela, prevent him from going."

Angela, smiling, looked after her retiring parents and then at Richard.

"I must keep you, Herr Frank. How shall I begin?"

"That is very easy, Fräulein. Your presence is sufficient to realize your father's wish. A weak child of human nature cannot resist one who can conquer steers."

"Now you make a steer-catcher of me. Such a thing never happened in Spain; for there the steers are not so cultivated and docile as they are with us."

She took out her knitting.

"This is Sunday, Miss Angela!"

"Do you consider knitting unlawful after one has fulfilled one's religious duties?"

"The case is not clear to me," said Frank, smiling secretly at the earnestness of the questioner. "My casuistic knowledge is not sufficient to solve such a question reasonably."

"The church only forbids servile work," said she. "I consider knitting and sewing as something better than doing nothing."

"I am rejoiced that you are not narrow-minded, Fräulein. But this little stocking does not fit your feet?"

"It is for little bare feet in Salingen," she replied, laying the finished stocking on the table and stroking it with both hands as a work of love.

"I have heard of your beneficence," said Frank. "You knit, sew, and cook for the poor people. You are a refuge for all the needy and distressed. How good in you!"

"You exaggerate, Herr Frank. I do a little sometimes, but not more than I can do with the house-work, which is scarcely worth mentioning. I make no sacrifice in doing it; on the contrary, the poor give me more than I give them; for giving is to every one more pleasant than receiving."

"To every one, Fräulein?"

"To every one who can give without denying herself."

"But you are accustomed also to visit the sick, and the hovels of poverty are certainly not attractive."

"Indeed, Herr Frank, very attractive," she answered quickly. "The thanks of the poor sick are so affecting and elevating that one is paid a thousand times for a little trouble."

Frank let the subject drop. Angela did not give charities from pride or the gratification of vanity, as he had been prepared to assume, but from natural goodness and inclination of the heart. He looked at the beautiful girl who sat before him industriously sewing, and was almost angry at his failure to detect a fault in her pure nature.

"Do you always adorn the statue of the Virgin on the mountain?" said he after a pause.

"No; not now. The month of our dear Lady is over. I always think with pleasure of the happy hours when in the convent we adorned her altar with beautiful flowers."

"You must have a great reverence for Mary, or you would not ascend the mountain daily."

"I admire the exalted virtues of Mary, and think with sorrow of her painful life on earth; and then, a weak creature needs much her powerful protection."

"Do you expect, Miss Angela, by such attention as you show the statue to obtain protection of the saint?"

"No, I do not believe that. The adorning of the pictures of saints would be idle trifling if the heart wandered far from the spirit of the saints. Our church teaches, as you know, that the real, true veneration of the saints consists in imitating their virtues."

Frank sat reflecting. The examination and probation were thoroughly disgusting to him. Siegwart appeared in the garden, and came with quick steps to the arbor. His countenance was agitated and his eyes glowed with indignation. Without speaking a word, he drank off a glass of wine. Frank saw how he endeavored not to exhibit his anger.

"Has Herr von Hamm departed?" asked Richard.

"Yes, he is off again," said the proprietor. "Angela, your mother has something to say to you."

"Now guess what the assessor wanted?" said Siegwart, after his daughter had left the arbor.

"Perhaps he wanted the Peter-pence collection," said Frank, smiling.

"No. Herr von Hamm wanted nothing more or less than to marry my daughter!"

Frank was astonished. Although he long since saw through Hamm's designs, he did not expect so sudden and hasty a step.

"And in what manner did he demand her?"

"It is revolting," said the proprietor, much offended. "Herr von Hamm graciously condescends to us peasants. He showed that it would be a great good fortune for us to give our daughter to the noble, the official with brilliant prospects."

"Herr von Hamm does not think little of himself," said Richard drily.

"How did the man ever come to ask my daughter? He and Angela! What opposites!"

"Which, of course, you made clear to him."

"I reminded the gentleman that identity of moral and religious principles alone could render matrimonial happiness possible. I reminded him that Angela was an ultramontane, whose opinions would daily annoy him, while his modern opinions must deeply offend Angela. This I set before him briefly. Then I told him frankly and freely that I did not wish to make either him or Angela unhappy, and at this he went away angrily."

"You have done your duty," said Frank. "I am also of opinion that similar convictions in the great principles of life alone insure the happiness of married life."

When Richard came home, he wrote in his diary:

> "June 4.--Unconditional surrender. What I supposed only to exist in the ideal world is realized in the daughter of an ultramontane. Angela, compared to our crinolines, our flirts, our insipid coquettes--how brilliant the light, how deep the shadow!

> "My visits to that family have no longer a purpose. I feel they must be discontinued for the sake of my peace. I dare not dream of a happiness of which I am unworthy. But my future life will feel painfully the want of a happiness the possibility of which I did not dream. This is a punishment for presuming to penetrate the pure, glorious character of the Angel of Salingen."

He buried his face in his hands, and leaned on the table. He remained thus a long time; when he raised his head, his face was pale, and his eyes were moist with tears.

CHAPTER VII
POISONOUS FOOD

"Herr Frank has not been here for four days," said Siegwart as he returned one day from the field. "He will not come to-day, for it is already nine o'clock, I hope the young man is not ill."

Angela started.

"Ill? May God forbid!"

"At least, I know no other reason that could prevent him from coming. He has become a necessity to me; I seem to miss something."

Angela concealed her uneasiness in true womanly fashion. She busied herself about the room, dusted the furniture, arranged the vases, and trimmed the flowers; but one could see that her mind was not in the work.

"Would it not be well, father, to send and inquire after his health?"

"It would if we were certain that he was ill. I only made a conjecture. However, if he does not come to-morrow, I will send Henry over.

"We owe him this attention; he is sensible, modest, and very intelligent. We find at present in the cities and first families few young men of so little assumption and so much goodness and manliness."

Angela pricked her finger. She had incautiously wandered into the thicket, as if she did not know that roses have thorns.

"Many things tell of his kind-heartedness," she replied, with averted face. "He sends five dollars every week to the old blind woman in Salingen; he often takes the money himself, and comforts the unfortunate creature. The blind woman is full of enthusiasm about him. He bought the cooper a full set of tools, that he might be able to support his mother and seven little sisters."

"Very praiseworthy," said the father.

As Siegwart came home in the evening, Angela met him in the yard. She carried a basket and was about to go into the garden.

"Herr Frank is not unwell," said he; "I saw him in the field and went through the vineyard to meet him; but when he discovered my intention, he turned about and hastened toward the house. That surprises me."

Angela went into the garden. She stood on the bed and gazed at the lettuce. The empty basket awaited its contents, and in it lay the knife whose bright blade glistened before the idle dreamer. She stood thus meditating, lost in thought for a long time, which was certainly not her custom.

Herr Frank had returned from the city, and was roughly received by the doctor.

"Have you spoken to your son?" said he sharply.

"No! I have just alighted from the carriage," answered Frank in astonishment.

The doctor walked up and down the room, and Frank saw his face growing darker.

"You disturb me, good friend. How is Richard?"

"Bad, very bad! And it is all your fault. You gave Richard those materialistic books which I threw out of the window. He has read the trash--not read, but studied it; and now we have the consequences."

"Pardon me, doctor. I did not give my son those books. He was passing the window when you threw them out, and took them to his room."

"You knew that! Why did you leave him the miserable trash?"

"I had no idea of the danger of these writings. Explain yourself further, I entreat."

"You must first see your son. But I bind it on your conscience to use the greatest precaution. Do not show the least surprise. We have to deal with a dangerous disorder. Do not say a word about his changed appearance. Then come back to me again."

Greatly disturbed, the father passed to the room of his son. Richard sat on the sofa gazing at the floor. His cheeks had lost their bloom, his face was emaciated, and his eyes deeply sunken. Vogt's *Physiological Letters* lay open near him. He did not rise quickly and joyfully to kiss his father, as was his custom. He remained sitting, and smiled languidly at him. Herr Frank, grieved and perplexed, sat down near him, and took occasion to pick up the book:

"How are you, Richard?"

"Very well, as you see."

"You are industrious. What book is this?"

"A rare book, father--a remarkable book. One learns there to know what man is and what he is not. Until now, I did not know that cats, dogs, monkeys, and all animals were of our race. Now I know; for it is clearly demonstrated in that book."

"You certainly do not believe such absurdities?"

"Believe? I believe nothing at all. Faith ends where proof begins."

Herr Frank read the open page.

"All this sounds very silly," said he. "Vogt asserts that man has no soul, and proves it from the fact that men become idiotic. If the functions of the brain are disturbed, the soul ceases, says Vogt. He therefore concludes that the spirit consists in the brain. The man must have been crazy when he wrote that. I am no scholar; but I see at the first glance how false and groundless are Vogt's inferences. Every reasonable man knows that the brain is the instrument of the mind, which enables it to participate in the world of sense; now, when the instrument is destroyed, the participation of the mind with the outward world must cease. Although a man may be an expert on the violin, he cannot play if the strings are broken or out of tune. But the player, his ideas, the art, still remain. In like manner the spirit remains, although it can no longer play on the injured or discordant fibres of the brain."

"You must read the whole book, father, and then those others there."

"But, Richard, you must not read books that rob man of all dignity."

"Of course not. I should do as the ostrich. When he is in danger, he sticks his head into the bushes not to see the danger. A prudent plan. But I cannot close my eyes to the light, even if that light should destroy my human respect."

Greatly afflicted, Herr Frank returned to the doctor.

"Great God! in what a condition is my poor Richard!" said the oppressed father.

"He will, I hope, be rescued. My stay at Frankenhöhe was to end with the month of May; but I cannot forsake a young man whom I love, in this helpless state of mental delirium."

"I do not understand the condition of my son; and your words give me great anxiety. Have the goodness to tell me what is the matter with Richard, and how it came about."

"It would be very difficult to make your son's condition clear to you. In you there is only business, lucrative undertakings, speculative combinations. The bustle of the money market is your world. You have no idea of the power of an intellectual struggle. You know the thoughtful, intellectual nature of your son; and here I begin. In the first place, I will remind you that Richard wishes to be governed by the power of deduction. With him fantasies and passions retreat before this force, although usually in men of his years, and even in men with gray hair, clearness of mind and keen penetration are often swept away by the current of stormy passions. Richard's aversion to women is the result of cool reflection and inevitable inference, and therefore on this question I do not dispute his views. I know it would be useless, and I know that the study of a pure feminine nature would overcome this prejudice. The same force of logical inferences places Richard in this unhappy condition. He read the writings of the materialist. There he found the physiological proofs that man is a beast. From these proofs Richard drew all the terrible consequences contained in those destructive doctrines. As the intellectual life predominates in him, and as he has a strong repugnance to materialistic madness, his nature must be stirred in its profoundest depths. If Richard succumbs, he will act in his habitual consistent manner. All moral basis lost, morality would be foolishness to him, since it is useless for beasts to curb the passions by moral laws. As with immortality disappears man's eternal destiny, it would be foolish to 'fight the giant fight of duty.' If he is convinced that man is a beast, he will live like a beast--although he might cloak his conduct with the varnish of decency--and thus suddenly would the sensible Richard stand before his astonished father a ruined man. This is one view; there is still another," said the doctor hesitatingly. "I remember in the course of my practice a suicide who wrote on a slip of paper, 'What do I here? Eat, drink, sleep, worry, and fret; much suffering, little joy; therefore--' and the man sent a bullet through his head. This suicide thought logically. This earthly life is insupportable; it is foolishness to a man who thinks and is at the same time a materialist."

"What prospects--horrible!" cried Herr Frank, wringing his hands. "Accursed be those books; and I am the cause of this misfortune!"

"The involuntary cause," said Klingenberg consolingly. "You now have a firm conviction of the devastating effects of those bad books. But how many are there who consider every warning in this connection an exhibition of prejudice or narrow-mindedness! How few readers are so modest as to admit that they want the scientific culture to refute a bad book, to separate the poison from the honey of sweet phrases and winning style! How few can see that they cannot read those bad books without detriment! No one would sit on a cask of powder and touch it off for amusement; and yet those hellish books are more dangerous than a cask full of powder. To me this is incomprehensible. Poisonous food is always injurious; yet thousands and millions drink greedily from this poisonous stream of bad reading which deluges all grades of society."

"I will do immediately what must be done," said Herr Frank as he hastily rose.

"What will you do?"

"Take from my son those execrable books."

"By no means," said Klingenberg. "This would be a psychological mistake. Richard would buy the same books again at the book-shop, and read them secretly. A man who has the resolution of your son must be won by honorable combat. Authority would here be badly applied. Therefore I forbid you to interfere. You know nothing of the matter. Treat him kindly, and have forbearance with his sensitiveness. That is what I must require of you."

Greatly afflicted, Herr Frank left the doctor. Overwhelming himself with reproaches, he wandered restlessly about the house and garden. He saw Richard standing at the open window with folded arms, dreamy and pale, his hair in disorder like a storm-beaten wheat-field--truly a painful sight for the father. He went up to his room, where the small library stood in its beautiful binding. A servant stood near him with a basket. The works of Eugene Sue, Gutzkow, and like spirits fell into the basket.

"All to the fire!" commanded Herr Frank.

The doctor had compared bad literature to poisonous food. The comparison was not inapt; at least, it gave Richard the appearance of a man in whose body destructive poison was working. He was listless and exhausted; in walking, his hands hung heavily by his side. His eyes were directed to the ground, as if he were seeking something. If he saw a snail, he stopped to examine the crawling creature. He sought to know why the snail crawls about, and, to his astonishment, found that the snail always followed an object; which is not always the case with man, animal of the moment, who goes about without an object. If a caterpillar accidentally got under his foot, he pushed it carefully aside and examined if it had been hurt. It seemed to him logical that creeping and flying things had the same claims to forbearance and proper treatment as man, since according to Vogt and Büchner's striking proofs, all creeping and flying things are not essentially different from man.

He paid particular attention to the spiders. If he came to a place where their web was stretched, he examined attentively the artistic texture; he saw the firmly fastened knot on the twig which held the web apart, the circular meshes, the cunning arrangement to catch the wandering fly.

He was convinced that such a spider would be a thousand times more intelligent than Herr Vogt and Herr Büchner, with half as big a head as those wise naturalists. The enterprising spirit of the ants excited not less his admiration. He always found them busy and in a bustle, to which a market-day could not be compared. Even London and Paris were solitary in comparison to the throng in an ant-hill. They dragged about large pieces of wood, as also leaves and fibres, to construct their house, which was laid out with design and finished with much care. If he pushed his cane into the hill, there forthwith arose a great revolution. The inhabitants rushed out upon him, nipped him with their pincers, and showed the greatest rage against the invader of their kingdom, while others with great celerity placed the eggs in safety. He observed that the ants gave no quarter, and considered every one a mortal enemy who disturbed their state.

The young man sat on a stone and examined a snail that crawled slowly from the wet grass. It carried a gray house on its back, and beslimed the way as it went, and stretched out its horns to discover the best direction. Its delicate touch astonished Frank. When obstacles came in its way which it did not see nor touch, it would perceive them by means of a wonderful sensibility.

How stupid did Richard appear to himself, beside a horned, blind snail. How many men only discover obstacles in their way when they have run their heads against them, and how many wish to run their heads through walls without any reason! He arose and looked toward Angela's home. He was dejected, and heaved a sigh.

"All is of no avail. The activity of the animal world affords no diversion, the benumbing strokes of materialism lose their effect. The rare becomes common, and does not attract attention. There walks an angel in the splendor of superior excellence, and I endeavor in vain to distract my mind from her by studying the animals. I follow willingly the professors' exact investigations, into the labyrinth of their studied arguments to make it appear that I am only an animal, that all our sentiment is only imagination and fallacy. It is all in vain. Can these gentlemen teach me how we can cease to have admiration for the noble and exalted? Here man forcibly breaks through. Here self, irresistible and disgusted with error, brings the nobility of human nature to consciousness, and all the wisdom of boasted materialism becomes idle nonsense."

"Thank God! I see you again, my dear neighbor," said Siegwart cordially. "Where have you kept yourself this last week? Why do you no longer visit us? My whole house is excited about you. Henry is angry because he cannot show you the horses he bought lately. My wife bothers her head with all kinds of forebodings, and Angela urged me to send and see if you were ill."

A new life permeated Frank's whole being at these last words; his cheeks flushed and his languid eyes brightened up.

"I know no good reason as an apology, dear friend. Be assured, however, that the apparent neglect does not arise from any coolness toward you and your esteemed family." And he drew marks in the sand with his cane.

"Perhaps your father took offence at your visits to us?"

"Oh! no. No; I alone am to blame."

Siegwart gave a searching glance at the pale face of the young man who, broken-spirited, stood before him, and whose mental condition he did not understand, although he had a vague idea of it.

"I will not press you further," said he cheerfully. "But, as a punishment, you must now come with me. I received yesterday a fresh supply of genuine Havanas, and you must try them."

He took Richard by the arm, and the latter yielded to the friendly compulsion. They went through the vineyard. Frank broke from a twig a folded leaf.

"Do you know the cause of this?"

"Oh! yes; it is the work of the vine-weevil," answered Siegwart. "These mischief-makers sometimes cause great damage to the vineyards. Some years I have their nests gathered and the eggs destroyed to prevent their doing damage."

"You consider every thing with the eyes of an economist. But I admire the art, the foresight, and the intelligence of these insects."

"Intelligence--foresight of an insect!" repeated Siegwart, astonished. "I see in the whole affair neither intelligence nor foresight."

"But just look here," said Richard, carefully unfolding the leaf. "What a degree of considerate management is necessary to fix the leaf in such order. The ribs of this leaf are stronger than the force of the beetle. Yet he wished to fold the eggs in it. What does he do? He first pierces the stem with his pincers; in consequence of this, the leaf curls up and becomes soft and pliable to the frail feet of the insect. This is the first act of reflection. The piercing of the stem had evidently as its object to cause the leaf to roll up. Then he begins to work with a perfection that would do honor to human skill. The leaf is rolled up in order to put the eggs in the folds. Here is the first egg; he rolls further--here is the second egg, some distance from the first, in order to have sufficient food for the young worm--again an act of reflection; lastly, he finishes the roll with a carefully worked point, to prevent the leaf from unfolding--again an act of reflection."

Siegwart heard all this with indifference. What Richard told him he had known for years. His employment in the fields revealed to his observing mind wonderful facts in nature and in the animal world. The wisdom of the vine-weevil gave him ho difficulty. He looked again in Frank's deep-sunken eyes and noticed a peculiar expression, and in his countenance great anxiety.

He concluded that the work of the vine-weevil must have some connection with the young man's condition.

"You see actions of reflection and design where I see only unconscious instinct."

Frank became nervous.

"The common evasion of superficial examination!" cried he. "Man must be just even to the animals. Their works are artistic, intelligent, and considerate. Why then deny to animals those powers which operate with intelligence and reflection?"

"I do not for a moment dispute this power of the animals," replied the proprietor quickly. "You find mind in the animals?" interrupted Frank hastily. "This conviction once reached, have you considered the consequences that follow?"--and he became more excited. "Have you considered that with this admission the whole world becomes a fabulous structure, without any higher object? If the spider is equal to man, then its torn web that flutters in the wind is worth as much as the crumbling fragments of art which remain from classic antiquity. Virtue, the careful restraining of the passions, is stark madness. The disgusting ape, lustful and brutish, is as good as the purest virgin who performs severe penances for her idle dreams. It is with justice that the criminal scoffs at the good as bedlamites who, with fanatical delusion, strive for castles in the air. Every outcast from society, sunk and saturated in the basest vices, is precisely as good as the purest soul and the noblest heart; for all distinction between right and wrong, good and evil, is destroyed."

Angela's father gazed with solicitude into the perplexed look and distorted countenance of the young man.

"You deduce consequences, Herr Frank, that could not be drawn from my admissions," said he mildly. "There is no conscious power in animals--no reflecting soul. The animal works with the power that is in it, as light and heat in the fire, as in the lightning the destructive force, as the exciting and purifying effects in the storm. The animal does not act freely, like man; but from necessity--according to instinct and laws which the Almighty has imposed, upon it."

"A gratuitous assumption! A shallow artifice," exclaimed Frank. "The animal shows understanding, design, and will; we must not deny him these faculties."

"If the lightning strikes my house and discovers with infallible certainty all the metal in the walls, even where the sharpest eye could not detect it, must you recognize mental faculties in the lightning in discovering the metal?"

Frank hemmed and was silent.

"What a botcher is the most learned chemist compared with the root-fibres of the smallest plant," continued Siegwart. "Every plant has its own peculiar life; this I observe every day. All plants do not flourish alike in the same soil. They only flourish where they find the necessary conditions for their peculiar life; where they find in the air and earth the conditions necessary for their existence. Set ten different kinds of plants together in a small plat of ground. The different fibres will always seek and absorb only that material in the earth which is proper to their kind; they will pass by the useless and injurious substances. Now, where is the chemist who with such certainty, such power of discrimination, and knowledge of substances, can select from the inert clod the proper material? A chemist with such knowledge does not exist. Now, must you admit that the fibres possess as keen an understanding and as deep a knowledge of chemistry as the man who is versed in chemistry?"

"That would be manifest folly."

"Well," concluded Siegwart quietly, "if the vine-weevil weaves its wrapper, the spider its web, the bird builds its nest, and the beaver his house, they all do it in their way, as the root-fibres in theirs."

Richard remained silent, and they passed into the house.

Angela and her mother looked with astonishment and sympathy on their friend.

Soon in the mild countenance of Madam Siegwart there appeared nearly the same expression as in the first days after the death of Eliza--so much did the painful appearance of the young man afflict her. Angela turned pale, her eyes filled, and she strove to hide her emotion. Frank only looked at her furtively. Whatever he had to say to her, he said with averted eyes. Siegwart expended all his powers of amusement; but he did not succeed in cheering the young man. He continued depressed, embarrassed, and sad, and constantly avoided looking at Angela. When she spoke he listened to the sound of her voice, but avoided her look. Presently a low barking was heard in the room and Hector, who had growlingly received Frank at his first visit, but who in time had become an acquaintance of his, lay stretched at full length dreaming. Scarcely did Richard notice the dreaming animal when he exclaimed,

"The dog dreams! See how his feet move in the chase, how he opens his nostrils, how he barks, how his limbs reach for the game! The dog dreams he is in the chase."

"I have often observed Hector's dreams," said Siegwart coolly.

Frank continued,

"Have you considered the consequences that follow from the dreams of the dog? Dreams show a thinking faculty," said he hastily. "Animals, then, think like men; thoughts are the children of the mind; therefore, animals have minds. Animals and men are alike."

Angela started at these words. Her mother shook her head.

"You conclude too hastily, my dear friend," said Siegwart coolly. "You must first know that animals dream like men. Men think, reflect, and speak in dreams. The dreams of animals are very different from those mental acts."

"How will you explain it?" said Richard excitedly.

"Very easily. Hector is now in the chase. The dog's sense of smell is remarkable. By means of the fragrant wind Hector smells the partridges miles away. He acts then just as in the dream; feet, nose, and limbs come into activity. Suppose that in the surrounding fields there is a covey of partridges. The air would indicate them to Hector's smelling organs; these organs act, as in the waking state, on the brain of the animal; the brain acts on the other organs. Where is there thought? Have we not a purely material effect? The cough, the appetite, the sneezing, the aversion--what have all these to do with mind or thought? Nothing at all. The dream of the dog is an entirely muscular process, the mere co-working of the muscular organs; as with us, digestion, the flowing of the blood, the twitching of the muscles--facts with which the mind has nothing to do."

"Your assertion is based on the assumption that partridges are near," said Richard; "and I will be obliged to you if, with Hector's assistance, you convince me of this fact."

"That is unnecessary, my dear friend. Suppose there are no partridges in the neighborhood. The same affection of the brain which would be produced by the smell of the partridges could be produced by accident. If it is accidental, it will have the same effect in the sleeping condition of the dog.[2] Affections accidentally arise in man the causes of which are not known. We are uneasy, we know not why; we are discouraged without any knowledge of the cause. We are joyful without being able to give any reason for it. The mind can rise above all these dispositions, affections, and humors; can govern, cast out, and disperse them. Proof enough that a king lives in man--the breath of God, which is not taken from the earth, and to which all matter must yield if that power so wills."

The dog stretched his strong legs without any idea of the important question to which he had given occasion.

"Herr Frank," began Madam Siegwart earnestly, "I have learned to respect you, and have often wished that my son, at your years, would be like you. I see now with painful astonishment that you defend opinions which contradict your former expressions, and the sentiments we must expect from a Christian. Will you not be so good as to tell me how you have so suddenly changed your views?"

"Esteemed madam," answered Frank, with emotion, "I thank you for this undeserved motherly sympathy; but I beg of you not to believe that the opinions I expressed are my firm convictions. No, I have not yet fallen so deep that for me there is no difference between man and beast. I can yet continue to believe that materialism is a crime against mankind. On the other hand, I freely acknowledge that my mind is in great trouble; that every firm position beneath my feet totters; that I have been tempted to hold doctrines degrading to the individual and destructive to society. I have been brought into this difficulty by reading books whose seductive proofs I am not able to refute. Oh! I am miserable, very miserable; my appearance must have shown you that already."

He looked involuntarily at Angela; he saw tears in her eyes; he bowed his head and was silent.

"I see your difficulties," said the proprietor. "They enter early or late into the mind of every man. It is good, in such uncertainties and doubts, to lean on the authority of truth. This authority can only be God, who is truth itself, who came down from heaven and brought light into the darkness. We can prove, inquire, and speculate; but the keenest human intellect is not always free from delusion. As there is in man a spiritual tendency which raises him far above the visible and material, God has been pleased to lead and direct that tendency by revelation, that man may not err. I consider divine revelation a necessity which God willed when he created the mind. As the mind has an instinctive thirst after truth, God must, by the revelation of truth, satisfy this thirst Therefore is revelation as old as the human race. It reached its completion and perfection by the coming of the Lord, who said, 'I am the truth;' and this knowledge of the truth remains in the church through the guidance of the Spirit of truth, till the latest generation. This is only my ultramontane conviction," said Siegwart, smiling; "but it affords peace and certainty."

Angela had gone out, and now returned with a basket, in which lay a little dog, of a few days old, asleep. She set the basket carefully down before Frank, so as not to awaken the sleeper.

"As you appreciate the full worth of striking proofs, I am glad to be able to place one before you, in the shape of this little dog," said she, appearing desirous of cheering her dejected friend. But Frank did not receive from her cheerful countenance either strength or encouragement, for he did not look up.

"This little dog is only eight days old," she continued; "its eyes are not yet open; it can neither walk nor bark; it can only growl a little; and it does nothing but sleep and dream. I have noticed its dreams since the first day of its birth. You can convince yourself of its dreaming." She stooped over the basket and her soft hair disturbed the sleeper.

For a moment Frank saw and heard nothing.

"See," she continued, "how its little feet move, and how its body jerks. Hear the low growl, and see the hairs round the mouth how they twitch, how the nose shrinks and expands--all the same as in Hector. The little thing knows nothing at all of the world--no more than a child eight days old. We certainly, therefore, will not deceive ourselves in assuming that all these movements are only muscular twitchings; that neither the pup nor Hector dreams like a man."

Frank first looked at the dog in great surprise, and then gazed admiringly on Angela.

"O fraulein! how I thank you."

She appeared most lovely in his eyes. He suddenly turned toward her father.

"Your house is a great blessing to me. It appears that the pure atmosphere of religious conviction which you breathe victoriously combats all dark doubts, as light dissipates darkness."

Angela stood in her room. She knew that the spirit of unbelief pervaded the world, taking possession of thousands and destroying all life and effort. She saw Richard threatened by this spirit, and feared for his soul. She became very anxious, and sank on her knees before the crucifix and cried to heaven for succor.

Night was upon all things. The black clouds, lowering deep and heavy, shut out all light from heaven. The wind swept the mountains, the forest moaned, and thunder muttered in the distance. Klingenberg sat before his folios. A fitful light glimmered from the room of Richard's father. Richard himself came home late, took his supper, and retired to his chamber; there he walked back and forth, thinking, contending with himself, and speaking aloud. Before his door stood a dark figure--immovable and listening.

It knocked at the door of the elder Frank. Jacob, a servant who had grown gray in the service of the house, entered. Frank received him with surprise, and awaited expectantly what he had to say.

"We are all wrong," said Jacob. "My poor young master has now spoken out clearly. He is not sick because of the foolish trash in the books. He is in love, terribly in love."

"Ah! in love?" said Herr Frank.

"You should just have heard how he complains and laments that he is not worthy of her. 'O Angela, Angela!' he cried at least a hundred times, 'could I only raise myself to your level, and make myself worthy! But your soul, so pure, your character, so immaculate and good, thrusts me away. I look up to you with admiration and longing, as the troubled pilgrim on earth looks up to the peace and grandeur of heaven.' This is the way he talked. He is to be pitied, sir."

"So--so--in love, and with Siegwart's daughter," said Frank sadly. "The tragedy will change into comedy. Even if they were not so unapproachably high, but like other people on earth, my son should never take an ultramontane wife."

"But if he loves her so deeply, sir?"

"Be still; you know nothing about it. Has he lain down?"

"Yes; or, at least, he is quiet."

"Continue to watch him. I must immediately make known to the doctor this love affair. He will be surprised to find the philosopher changed into a love-sick visionary."

CHAPTER VIII
AVOWALS

In the same deep valley where the brook rippled over the pebbles in its bed, where the mountain sides rose up abruptly, where the moss hung from the old oaks, where Klingenberg plucked the tender beard of the young professor of history, took place the meditated attack of the doctor on the poison of materialism which was destroying the body and soul of Richard.

Slowly and carefully the doctor advanced, as against an enemy who will defend his position to the last. But how was he astonished, when, being attacked, Frank showed no disposition to defend that most highly vaunted doctrine of modern science--materialism! This was almost as puzzling to the doctor as the eternity of matter. Tired of skirmishing, the doctor set to work to close with the enemy, and strike him down.

"I have looked only cursorily at the writings of the materialists: you have studied them carefully; and you will oblige me much if you would give me the foundation on which the whole structure of materialism rests."

"The materialistic system is very simple," answered Frank. "Materialists reject all existence that is not sensibly perceptible. They deny the existence of invisible and supersensible things. There is no spirit in man or anywhere else. Matter alone exists, because matter alone manifests its existence."

"I understand. The materialist will only be convinced by seeing and feeling. As a spirit is neither spiritual nor tangible, then there is none. Is it not so, friend Richard?"

"You have included in one sentence the whole of materialism," said Frank coolly.

"I cannot understand," said Klingenberg hesitatingly, "how the materialists can make assertions which are untenable to the commonest understandings. Why, thought can neither be seen nor felt; yet it is an existence."

"Thought is a function of the brain."

"Then, it is incomprehensible how the sensible can beget the supersensible. How matter--the brain--can produce the immaterial, the spiritual."

Richard was silent.

"At every step in materialism I meet insurmountable difficulties," continued the doctor. "I know perfectly the organization of the human body, as well as the function and purpose of each part. The physician knows the purpose of the lungs, heart, kidneys, and stomach, and all the noble and ignoble parts of the body. But no physician knows the origin of the activity of the organism. The blood stops, the pulse no longer beats, the lungs, kidneys, nerves, and all the rest cease their functions. The man is dead. Why? Because the activity, the movement, the force is gone. What, then, is this vivifying force? In what does it consist? What color, what taste, what form has it? No physician knows. The vivifying principle is invisible, intangible perfectly immaterial. Yet it exists. Therefore the fundamental dogma of materialism is false. There are existences which can neither be felt, tasted, nor seen."

"The vivifying principle is also in animals," said Richard.

"Certainly; and in them also intangible and mysterious. Materialism cannot even stand before animal life; for even there the vivifying principle is an immaterial existence."

"The materialist stumbles at the existence of human spirit, because he cannot get a conception of it."

"How could this be possible?" cried the doctor. "The conception is a picture in the mind, an apprehension of the senses. Spiritual being is as unapproachable by the senses as the vivifying principle, of which also man can form no conception. To deny existence because you cannot have a conception of it, is foolish. The blind would have the same right to deny the existence of colors, or the deaf that of music. And who can have a conception of good, of eternity, of justice, of virtue? No one. These are existences that do not fall under the senses. To be logical, the materialist must conclude that there is nothing good, nothing noble, no justice; for we have not yet seen nor felt nor smelt these things. Virtuous actions we can, of course, see; but these actions are not the cause but the consequence, not the thing working but the thing wrought. As these actions will convince every thinking man of the existence of virtue and justice, so must the workings of the spirit prove its existence."

"Precisely," replied Frank. "Materialism only surprises and captivates one like a dream of the night. It vanishes the moment it is seen. I read the works of Vogt and Büchner only for diversion; my object was perfectly gained."

"You read for diversion! What did you wish to forget?"

"Dark clouds that lowered over my mind."

"Have you secrets that I, your old friend and well-meaning adviser, should not know?"

Frank was confused; but his great respect for the doctor forced him to be candid.

"You know my views of women. When I tell you that Angela, the well-known Angel of Salingen, has torn these opinions up by the roots, you will not need further explanation."

"You found Angela what I told you? I am glad," said Klingenberg. And his disputative countenance changed to a pleasant expression. "I suspected that the Angel of Salingen made a deep impression on you. I did not guess; I read it in large characters on your cheeks. Have you made an avowal?"

"No; it will never come to that."

"Why not? Are you ashamed to confess that you love a beautiful young lady? That is childish and simple. There is no place here for shame. You want a noble, virtuous wife. You have Angela in view. Woo her; do not be a bashful boy."

"Bashfulness might be overcome, but not the conviction that I am unworthy of her."

"Unworthy! Why, then? Shall I praise you? Shall I exhibit your noble qualities, and convince, you why you are worth more than any young man that I know? You have not Angela's religious tone; but the strong influence of the wife on the husband is well known. In two or three years I shall not recognize in the ultramontane Richard Frank the former materialist." And the doctor laughed heartily.

"It is questionable," said the young man, "whether Angela's inclination corresponds to mine."

"The talk of every true lover," said the doctor pleasantly. "Pluck the stars of Bethlehem, like Faust's Grethe, with the refrain, 'She loves, she loves not--she loves.' But you are no bashful maiden; you are a man. Propose to her. Angela's answer will show you clearly how she feels."

The doctor was scarcely in his room when Richard's father entered.

"All as you foretold," said Klingenberg. "Your son is cured of his hatred of women by Angela. The materialistic studies were not in earnest; they were only a shield held up against the coming passion. The love question is so absorbing, and the sentiment so strong, that Richard left me near

Frankenhöhe to hasten over there. I expect from your sound sense that you will place no obstacles in the way of your son's happiness."

"I regret," said Frank coldly, "that I cannot be of the same opinion with you and Richard in this affair."

"Make your son unhappy?" said Klingenberg. "Do you consider the possible consequences of your opposition?"

"What do you understand by possible consequences?"

"Melancholy, madness, suicide, frequently come from this. I leave tomorrow, and I hope to take with me the assurance that you will sacrifice your prejudice to the happiness of Richard."

Among the numerous inhabitants of Siegwart's yard was a hen with a hopeful progeny. The little chicks were very lively. They ran about after insects till the call of the happy mother brought them to her. Escaped from the shell some few days before, they had instead of feathers delicate white down, so that the pretty little creatures looked as though they had been rolled in cotton. They had black, quick eyes, and yellow feet and bills. If a hawk flew in the air and the mother gave a cry, the little ones knew exactly what it meant, and ran under the protecting wings of the mother from the hawk, although they had never seen one--had never studied in natural history the danger of the enemy. If danger were near, she called, and immediately they were under her wings. The whole brood now stopped under the lindens. The little ones rested comfortably near the warm body of the mother. Now here, now there, their little heads would pop out between the feathers. One smart little chirper, whose ambition indicated that he would be the future cock of the walk, undertook to stand on the back of the hen and pick the heads of the others as they appeared through the feathers.

Angela came under the lindens, carrying a vessel of water and some crumbs in her apron for the little ones. She strewed the crumbs on the ground, and the old hen announced dinner. The little ones set to work very awkwardly. The old hen had to break the crumbs smaller between her bill. Angela took one of the chickens in her hand and fondled it, and carried it into the house. The hen went to the vessel to drink and the whole brood followed. It happened that the one that stood on her back fell into the water, and cried loudly; for it found that it had got into a strange element of which it had no more idea than Vogt and Büchner of the form of a spirit. At this critical moment Frank came through the yard. He saw it fluttering about in the water, and stopped. The old hen went clucking anxiously about the vessel. And although she could without difficulty have taken the chicken out with her bill, yet she did not do it. Richard observed this with great interest; but showed no desire to save the little creature, which at the last gasp floated like a bunch of cotton on the water.

Angela may have heard the noise of the hen, for she appeared at the door. She saw Frank standing near the lindens looking into the vessel. At the same time she noticed the danger of one of her little darlings, and hastened out. She took the body from the water and held it sadly in her hands.

"It is dead, the little dear," said she sadly. "You could have saved it, Herr Frank, and you did not do it." She looked at Frank, and forgot immediately, on seeing him, the object of her regrets. The young man stood before her so dejected, so depressed and sad, that it touched her heart. She knew what darkened his soul. She knew his painful struggle, his great danger, and she could have given her life to save him. She was moved, tears came into her eyes, and she hastened into the house.

Siegwart was reading the paper when his daughter hastened in such an unusual way through the room and disappeared.

This astonished him.

"What is the matter, Angela?" he exclaimed.

There was no answer. He was about to go after her when Frank entered.

"I can give you some curious news of the assessor," said the proprietor after some careless conversation. "The man is terribly enraged against me and full of bad designs. The reason of this anger is known to you." And he added, "Angela is in the next room, and she must know nothing of his proposal."

Frank nodded assent.

"About ten paces from the last house in Salingen," continued Siegwart, "I have had a pile of dirt thrown up. It was now and then sprinkled with slops, to make manure of it. Herr Hamm has made the discovery that the slops smell bad; that it annoys the inhabitants of the next house; and he has ordered it to be removed."

Richard shook his head disapprovingly.

"Perhaps Herr Hamm will come to the conclusion that, in the interest of the noses, all like piles must be removed from Salingen."

"But that is not all," said Siegwart. "It has been discovered that the common good forbids my keeping fowls, because my residence is surrounded by fields and vineyards, where the fowls do great damage. The Herr Assessor has had the goodness, accompanied by the guards, to examine personally the amount of destruction. So I have got instructions either to keep my fowls confined or to make away with them."

"Mean and contemptible!" said Frank.

Angela came into the room. Her countenance was smiling and clear as ever; but her swollen eyes did not escape Richard's observation. She greeted the guest, and sat down in her accustomed place near the window. Scarcely had she done this, when Frank stood up, went toward her, and knelt down before the astonished girl.

"Miss, I have greatly offended you, and beg your pardon."

Siegwart looked on in surprise--now at his daughter, who was perplexed; now at the kneeling young man.

"For God's sake! Herr Frank, arise," said the confused Angela. She was about to leave the seat, but he caught her hand and gently replaced her.

"If I may approach so near to you, my present position is the proper one. Hear me! I have deeply offended you. I could with ease have saved a creature that was dear to you, and I did not do it. My conduct has brought tears to your eyes--hurt your feelings. When you went away to regain your composure, and to show your offender a serene, reconciled countenance, it made my fault more distressing. Forgive me; do not consider me hard and heartless, but see in me an unfortunate who forgets himself in musing."

She looked into Frank's handsome face as he knelt before her, in such sadness, lowering his eyes like a guilty boy, and smiled sweetly.

"I will forgive yon, Herr Frank, on one condition."

"Only speak. I am prepared for any penance."

"The condition is, that you burn those godless books that make you doubt about the noblest things in man, and that you buy no more."

"I vow fulfilment, and assure you that the design of those books, which you rightly call godless, is recognized by me as a crime against the dignity of man--and condemned."

"This rejoices no one more than me," said she with a tremulous voice.

He stood up, bowed, and returned to his former place.

"But, my dear neighbor, how did this singular affair happen?" said the proprietor.

Frank told him about the death of the chicken.

"The love of the hen for her chickens is remarkable. She protects them with her wings and warns them of danger, which she knows by instinct.

How easy would it have been for the hen to have taken the young one from the water with her bill--the same bill with which she broke their food and gave it to them. But she did not do it, because it is strange to her nature. This case is another striking proof that animals act neither with understanding nor reflection. Acts beyond their instinct are impossible to them. This would not be the case, if they had souls."

The old servant stood with an empty basket before the library of the son, as he had stood before that of the father. Büchner, Vogt, and Czolbe fell into the fire. Jacob shook his head and regretted the beautiful binding; but the evil spirits between the covers he willingly consigned to the flames.

Again the cars stopped at the station; again the two gentlemen stood at the open window of the car to receive their returning friends. The travellers took a carriage and drove through the street.

"Baron Linden has indeed gone headlong into misery," said Lutz humorously. "Eight days ago the young pair swore eternal fidelity. It was signed and sealed. Until to-day no could one know that they were on the brink of misery."

Richard remembered his remark on the former occasion, and wondered at his sudden change of opinion.

"I wish them all happiness," said he.

"Amen!" answered Lutz. "Richard, however, considers happiness in matrimony possible. So we may hope that he will not always remain a bachelor. How is the Angel of Salingen? Have you seen her since that encounter with the steer?"

"The angel is well," said Richard, avoiding the glance of his friend.

"What do you mean by the 'Angel of Salingen'?" said the father.

"Thereby I understand the unmarried daughter of Herr Siegwart, of Salingen, named Angela, who richly deserves to be called the 'Angel of Salingen.'"

Frank knit his brows darkly and drummed on his knees.

"And the encounter with the steer?" continued he.

The professor related the occurrence.

"Ah! you did not tell me any thing of that," said the father, turning to Frank. "An act of such great courage deserves to be mentioned."

The carriage passed into the court of a stately mansion. The servant sprang from his seat and opened the carriage-door. The professor looked at his watch.

"Herr Frank, will you allow your coachman to drive me to the university? I must be at my post in ten minutes. I cannot go on foot in that time."

"With pleasure, Herr Professor."

"Richard," said the other friend, "shall we meet at the opera tonight?"

"Scarcely. I must to-day enter upon my usual business."

"Come, if possible. The evening promises great amusement, for the celebrated Santinilli dances."

The accustomed routine of business began for Richard. He sat in the counting-room and worked with his habitual punctuality. Nevertheless invidious spirits lured him toward Salingen, so that the figures danced before his eyes, words had no meaning, and he was often lost in day-dreams. The watchful father had observed this, and was perplexed.

Richard's plan of studies also underwent a change. He left the house regularly at half-past five and returned at half-past six. The father, desiring to know what this meant, set the faithful Jacob on the watch.

"Herr Richard," reported the spy, "hears mass at the Capuchins."

Frank drummed a march on his knees.

"So, so!" he hummed. "The ultramontanes understand proselytizing. They have turned the head of my son. If I live long enough, I may yet see him turn Capuchin, build a cloister, and go about begging."

When Herr Frank entered the counting-room, he found his son busy at work. He stood up and greeted his father.

"I have observed, Richard," he began after a time, "that you go out early every morning. What does it mean?"

"I have imposed upon myself the obligation of hearing mass every morning."

"How did you come to take that singular obligation upon yourself?"

"From the conviction that religion is no empty idea, but a power that can give peace and consolation in all conditions of life."

"It is evident that you have breathed ultramontane air. This churchgoing is not forbidden--but no trifling or fanatical nonsense."

"It is my constant care, father, to give you no cause of uneasiness."

"I am rejoiced at this, my son; but I must observe that a certain gloomy, reserved manner of yours disturbs me. Your conduct is exemplary, your industry praiseworthy, your habits regular; but you keep yourself too much shut up; you do not give evening parties any more. You do not visit the concert-hall or theatre. This is wrong; we should enjoy life, and not move about like dreamers."

"I have no taste for amusements," answered Richard. "However, if you think a change would be good, I beg you to permit me to take a run out to Frankenhöhe for a couple of days."

"And why to Frankenhöhe? I do not know any amusement there for you."

"I have planted a small vineyard, as you know, and I would like to see how the Burgundies thrive."

Herr Frank was not in a hurry to give the permission. He thought and drummed.

"You can go," he said resignedly. "I hope the mountain air will cheer you up."

Herr Siegwart had remarked the same symptoms in his daughter that Herr Frank had in his son; but Angela did not give way to discontent. She was always the same obedient daughter. The poor and sick of Salingen could not complain of neglect. But she was frequently absent-minded, gave wrong answers to questions, and sought solitude. If Frank was mentioned, she revived; the least circumstance connected with him was interesting to her. Her sharp-sighted father soon discovered the inmost thoughts and feelings of his daughter. He thought of Herr Frank's ill-humor toward him, and was disposed to regret the hour that Richard entered his house.

The Burgundies at Frankenhöhe were scarcely looked at. The young man hastened to Salingen. He found the landscape changed in a few weeks. The fields had clothed themselves in yellow. The wheat-stalks bent gracefully under their load. Everywhere industrious crowds were in the fields. The stalks fell beneath the reapers. Men bound the sheaves. Wagons stood here and there. The sheaves were raised into picturesque stacks. The sun beamed down hot, and the sweltering weather wrote on the foreheads of the men, "Adam, in the sweat of thy brow thou shalt eat thy bread."

In the proprietor's house all was still, the old cook sat beneath the lindens, and with spectacles on her nose tried to mend a stocking which she held in her hand. She arose and smiled on Richard's approach.

"They are all in the fields. We have much work, Herr Frank. The grain is ripe, and we have already gathered fifty wagon-loads. I am glad to see you looking so much better. The family will also be glad. They think a great deal of you--particularly Herr Siegwart."

"Give them many kind greetings from me. I will come back in the evening."

"Off so soon? Will you not say good-day to Miss Angela? She is in the garden. Shall I call her?"

"No," said he after a moment's reflection; "I will go into the garden myself."

After unlatching the gate, he would have turned back, for he became nervous and embarrassed.

Angela sat in the arbor; her embroidery-frame leaned against the table, and she was busily working. As she heard the creaking of footsteps on the walk, she looked up and blushed. Frank raised his hat, and when the young woman stood up before him in beauty and loveliness, his nervousness increased, and he would gladly have escaped; but his spirit was in the fetters of a strange power, and necessity supplied him with a few appropriate remarks.

"I heard that the family were absent; but I did not wish to go away without saluting you. Miss Angela."

She observed the bashful manner of the young man, and said kindly, "I am glad to see you again, Herr Frank," and invited him to sit down. He looked about for a seat; but as there was none, he had to sit on the same bench with her.

"Do you remain long at Frankenhöhe?"

"Only to-day and to-morrow. Work requires dispatch, and old custom has so bound me to my occupation that the knowledge of work to be done makes me feel uneasy."

"Do you work every day regularly in the counting-room?"

"I am punctual to the hours, for the work demands regularity and order. There are every day some hours for recreation."

"And what is the most pleasant recreation for you?"

"Music and painting. I like them the best. But of late," he added hesitatingly, "unavoidable thoughts press on me, and many hours of recreation pass in useless dreaming."

Angela thought of his former mental troubles and looked anxiously in his eyes.

"Now, you have promised me," she said softly, "to forget all those things in those bad books that disturbed your mind."

"The fulfilment of no duty was lighter or more pleasant to me than to keep my promise to you, Angela."

His voice trembled. She leaned over her work and her cheeks glowed. The delicate fingers went astray; but Frank did not notice that the colors in the embroidery were getting into confusion. There was a long pause. Then Frank remembered the doctor's final admonition, "Be not like a bashful boy; put aside all false shame and speak your mind;" and he took courage.

"I have no right to ask what disturbs and depresses you," said she, in a scarcely audible voice and without moving her head.

"It is you who have the best right, Angela! You have not only saved my life, but also my better convictions. You have purified my views, and influenced my course of life. I was deeply in error, and you have shown me the only way that leads to peace. This I see more clearly every day. The church is no longer a strange, but an attractive place to me. All this you have done without design. I tell you this because I think you sympathize with me."

He paused; but the declaration of his love hovered on his lips.

"You have not deceived yourself as to my sympathy," she answered. "The discovery that one so insignificant as myself has any influence with you makes me glad."

"O Angela! you are not insignificant in my eyes. You are more than all else on earth to me!" he cried. "You are the object of my love, of my waking dreams. If you could give me your hand before the altar in fidelity and love, my dearest wishes would be realized."

She slowly raised her head, her modest countenance glowed in a virginal blush, and her eyes, which met Richard's anxious look, were filled with tears. She lowered her head, and laid her hand in that of the young man. He folded her in his arms, pressed her to his heart, and kissed her forehead. The swallows flew about the arbor, twittered noisily, and threatened the robber who was trying to take away their friend. The sparrows, through the leaves of the vines, looked with wonder at the table where Angela's head rested on the breast of her affianced.

They arose.

"We cannot keep this from our parents, Richard. My parents esteem you. Their blessing will not be wanting to our union."

Suddenly she paused, and stood silent and pale, as though filled with a sudden fear. Richard anxiously inquired the cause.

"You know your father's opinion of us," she said, disturbed.

"Do not be troubled about that. Father will not object to my arrangements. But even if he does, I am of age, and no power shall separate me from you."

"No, Richard; no! I love you as my life; but without your father's consent, our union wants a great blessing. Speak to him in love; beg him, beseech him, but do not annoy him on account of your selfishness."

"So it shall be. Your advice is good and noble. As long as this difficulty exists, I am uneasy. I will therefore go back. Speak to your parents; give them my kind greeting, and tell them how proud I shall feel to be acknowledged as their son." He again folded her in his arms and hastened away.

The old cook still sat under the lindens, and the stocking lost many a stitch as Frank, with a joyous countenance, passed her without speaking, without having noticed her. She shook wonderingly her old gray head.

Angela sat in the arbor. Her work lay idly on the table. With a countenance full of sweetness she went to her room, and knelt and prayed.

Herr Frank looked up astonished, as Richard, late in the evening, entered his chamber.

"Excuse me, father," said he joyfully and earnestly; "something has happened of great importance to me, and of great interest to you. I could not delay an explanation, even at the risk of depriving you of an hour's sleep."

"Well, well! I am really interested," said Herr Frank, as he threw himself back on the sofa. "Your explanation must be something extraordinary, for I have never seen you thus before. What is it, then?"

"For a right understanding of my position, it is necessary to go back to that May-day on which we went to Frankenhöhe. Your displeasure at my well-grounded aversion to women you will remember."

With childish simplicity he related the whole course of his inner life and trials at Frankenhöhe. He described the deep impression Angela had made upon him. He took out his diary and read his observations, his stubborn adherence to his prejudices, and the victory of a virtuous maiden over them. The father listened with the greatest attention. He admired the depth of his son's mind and the noble struggle of conviction against the powerful influence of error. But when Richard made known what had passed between himself and Angela, Herr Frank's countenance changed.

"I have told you all," said Richard, "with that openness which a son owes to his father. From the disposition and character of Angela, as you have heard them, you must have learned to respect her, and have been convinced that she and I will be happy. Therefore, father, I beg your consent and blessing on our union."

He arose and was about to kneel, when Herr Frank stopped him.

"Slowly, my son. With the exception of what happened to-day, I am pleased with your conduct. You have convinced yourself of the injustice of your opinion of women. You have found a noble woman. I am willing to believe that Angela is a magnificent and faultless creature, although she have an ultramontane father. But my consent to your union with Siegwart's daughter you will never receive. Now, Richard, you can without trouble find a woman that will suit you, and who is as beautiful and as noble-minded as the Angel of Salingen."

"May I ask the reason of your refusal, father?"

"There are many reasons. First, I do not like the ultramontane spirit of the Siegwart family. Angela it educated in this spirit. You would be bound to a wife whose narrow views would be an intolerable burden."

"Pardon, father! The extracts from my diary informed you that I have examined this ultramontane spirit very carefully, and that I was forced at last to correct my opinions of the ultramontanes--to reject an unjust prejudice."

"The stained glass of passion has beguiled you into ultramontane sentiments; and further, remember that Siegwart is personally objectionable to me." And he spoke of the failure of the factory through Angela's father.

"Herr Siegwart has told me of that enterprise, and, at the same time, gave me the reasons that induced him to prevent its realization. He showed the demoralizing effects of factories. He showed that the inhabitants of that neighborhood support themselves by farming; that the religious sentiment of the country people is endangered by Sunday labor and other evil influences that accompany manufacturing."

"And you approved of this narrow-mindedness of the ultramontane?" cried Frank.

"Siegwart's conduct is free from narrow-mindedness. You yourself have often said that faith and religion had much to fear from modern manufactories. If Siegwart has made great sacrifices, if he has interfered against his own interest in favor of faith and morality, he deserves great respect for it."

"Has it gone so far? Do you openly take part with the ultramontane against your father?"

"I take no part; I express frankly my views," answered Richard tranquilly.

"The views of father and son are very different, and we may thank your intercourse with the ultramontanes for it."

"Your acquaintance, father, with that excellent family is very desirable. You would soon be convinced that you ought to respect them."

"I do not desire their acquaintance. It is near midnight; go to rest, and forget the hasty step of to-day."

"I will never regret what has taken place with forethought and reflection," answered Richard firmly. "I again ask your consent to the happiness of your son."

"No, no! Once for all--never!" cried Frank hastily.

The son became excited. He was about to fly into a passion, and to show his father that he was not going to follow blind authority like an inexperienced child, when he thought of what Angela said, "Speak to your father in love;" and his rising anger subsided.

"You know, father," he said hesitatingly, "that my age permits me to choose a wife without reference to your will. As the consent is withheld without valid reasons, I might do without it. But Angela has urgently requested me not to act against your will, and I have promised to comply with her wishes."

"Angela appears to have more sense than you. So she requested this promise from you? I esteem the young lady for this sentiment, although she be a child of Siegwart, who shall never have my son for a son-in-law."

The young man arose.

"It only remains for me to declare," said he calmly, "that to Angela, and to her alone, shall I ever belong in love and fidelity. If you persevere in your refusal, I here tell you, on my honor, I shall never choose another wife."

He made a bow and left the room. It was long past midnight, and Herr Frank was still sitting on the sofa, drumming on his knees and shaking his head.

"An accursed piece of business!" said he. "I know he will not break his word of honor under any circumstances. I know his stubborn head. But this Siegwart, this clerical ultramontane fellow--it is incompatible; mental progress and middle-age darkness, spiritual enlightenment and stark confessionalism--it won't do. Angela certainly is not her father. She is an innocent country creature; does not wear crinoline, dresses in blue like a bluebell, has not a dainty stomach, and has no toilette nonsense. The nuns, together with perverted views of the world, may, perhaps, have taught her many principles that adorn an honorable woman; but--but--" And Herr Frank threw himself back grumbling on the sofa.

On the following day Richard wrote Angela a warm, impassioned letter. The vow of eternal love and fidelity was repeated. In conclusion, he spoke of his father's refusal, but assured her that his consent would yet be given.

Many weeks passed. The letters of the lovers came and went regularly and without interruption. She wrote that her parents had not hesitated a moment to give their consent. In her letters Richard admired her tender feeling, her dove-like innocence and pure love. He was firm in his conviction that she would make him happy, would be his loadstar through life. He read her letters hundreds of times, and these readings were his only recreation. He spoke not another word about the matter to his father. He kept away from all society. He devoted himself to his calling, and endeavored to purify his heart in the spirit of religion, that he might approach nearer to an equality with Angela. The father observed him carefully, and was daily more and more convinced that a spiritual change was coming over his son. Murmuringly he endured the church-going, and vexedly he shook his head at Richard's composure and perseverance, which he knew time would not change. The more quietly the son endured, the more disquieted Herr Frank became. "Sacrifice your prejudices to your son's happiness," he heard the doctor saying; and he felt ashamed when he thought of this advice.

"What cannot be cured must be endured," he was accustomed to say for some days, as often as he went into his room. "The queer fellow makes it uncomfortable for me; this cannot continue; days and years pass away. I am growing old, and the house of Frank must not die out."

One morning he gave Richard charge of the establishment. "I have important business," said he. "I will be back to-morrow."

The father smiled significantly as he said this. Richard heard from the coachman that Herr Frank took a ticket for the station near Frankenhöhe. He knew the great importance to him of this visit, and prayed God earnestly to move his father's heart favorably. His uneasiness increased hourly, and rendered all work impossible. He walked up and down the counting-room like a man who feared bankruptcy, and expected every moment the decision on which depended his happiness for life. He went into the hall where the desks of the clerks stood in long rows. He went to the desks, looked at the writing of the clerks, and knew not what he did, where he went, or where he stood.

The next day Herr Frank returned. Richard was called to the library, where his father received him with a face never more happy or contented.

"I have visited your bride," he began, "because I had a curiosity to know personally the one who has converted my son to sound views of womankind. I am perfectly satisfied with your taste, and also with myself;

for I have become reconciled with Siegwart, and find that he is as willing to live with his neighbors in harmony as in discord. You now have my blessing on your union. The marriage can take place when you please; only it would please me if it came off as soon as possible."

Richard stood speechless with emotion, which so overcame him that tears burst from his eyes. He embraced his father, kissed him tenderly, and murmured his thanks.

"That will do, Richard," said Herr Frank, much affected. "Your happiness moves me. May it last long. And I do not doubt it will; for Angela is truly a woman the like of whom I have never met. Her character is as clear and transparent as crystal; and her eyes possess such power, and her smile such loveliness, that I fear for my freedom when she is once in the house."

Crisp, cold weather. The December winds sweep gustily through the streets of the city, driving the well-clad wanderer before them and sporting with the weather-vanes. A carriage stops before the door of the Director Schlagbein. Professor Lutz steps out and directs the driver to await him.

Emil Schlagbein, Richard's unhappy married friend, had moved his easy-chair near the stove and leaned his head against its back. He looked as though despair had seized him and thrown him into it. Hasty steps were heard in the ante-room, and Lutz stood before him.

"Still in your working-clothes, Emil? Up! the tea-table of the Angel of Salingen awaits us."

"Pardon me; my head is confused, my heart is sad; grief wastes my life away."

"War--always war; never peace!" said Lutz. "I fear, Emil, that all the fault is not with your wife. You are too sensitive, too particular about principles. Man must tolerate, and not be niggardly in compliance. Take old Frank as a model. With Angela entered ultramontanism into his house. Frank lives in peace with this spirit--even on friendly terms. Angela reads him pious stories from the legends of the saints. He goes with her to church, where he listens with attention to the word of God. He hears mass as devoutly as a Capuchin; not to say any thing of Richard, who runs a race with Angela for the prize of piety. Could you not also make some sacrifice to the whims of your wife?"

"Angela and Ida--day and night!" said the director bitterly. "The two Franks make no sacrifice to female whims. They appreciate her exalted views, they admire her purity, her unspeakable modesty, her shining virtues. The two Franks acted reasonably when they adopted the principles that produced such a woman. Angela never speaks to her husband in defiance and bad temper. If clouds gather in the matrimonial heaven, she dissipates them with the breath of love. Is the sacrifice of a wish wanted? Angela makes it. Is her pure feeling offended by Richard's faults? She kisses them away and raises him to her level. My wife--is she not just the opposite in every thing? Is she not quick-tempered, bitter, loveless, extravagant, and stiff-necked? Has she a look--I will not say of love--but even of respect for me? Do not all her thoughts and acts look to the pleasures of the toilette, the opera, balls, and concerts? O my poor children! who grow up without a mother, in the hands of domestics. How is any concession possible here? Must not my position, my self-respect, the last remnant of manly dignity go to the wall?"

"Your case is lamentable, friend! Your principles and those of your wife do not agree. Concession to the utmost point of duty, joined with prudent reform in many things, may, perhaps, bring back, harmony and a good understanding between you. You praise Angela: follow her example. She abominates the air of the theatre. The opera-glasses of the young men levelled at her offend her deeply, and bring to her angelic countenance the blush of shame. Her fine religious feeling is offended at many words, gestures, and dances which a pious Christian woman should not hear and see. Yet she goes to the opera because Richard wishes it. Her husband will at last observe this heroism of love, and sacrifice the opera to it. What Angela cannot obtain by prayers and representations, she gains by the all-conquering weapons of love. In like manner and for a like object yield to your wife. She is, at least, not a firebrand. Love must overcome her stubbornness."

Schlagbein shook his head sadly.

"A father cannot do what is inconsistent with paternal duty," said he. "Shall I join in the course of my wife? Whither does this course lead? To the destruction of all family ties, to financial bankruptcy--to dishonor. For home my wife has no mind, no understanding. My means she throws carelessly into the bottomless pit of pleasure-seeking and love of dress. She does not think of the future of her children. Every day brings to her new desires for prodigality. If her wishes are fulfilled, ruin is unavoidable. If they are not fulfilled, she sits ill-humored and obstinate in her room, and leaves the care of the house to her domestics, and the children to the nurses. How often have I consented to her vain desire for show, only to see her extravagant wishes thereby increased. She is without reason."

The unfortunate man's head sunk upon his breast. Lutz stood still without uttering a word.

"Yes, Angela is a noble woman," continued Emil, "she is the spirit of order, the angel of peace and love. Just hear Richard's father. He revels in enthusiasm about her. 'My Richard is the happiest man in the world,' said he to me lately. 'I myself must be thankful to him for his prudent choice. Abounding in every thing, my house was empty and desolate before Angela came; but now every thing shines in the sun of her orderly housekeeping, of her tender care. Although served with fidelity, I have been until the present almost neglected. But now that the angel hovers over me, observes my every want, and with her smile lights my old age, I am perfectly happy.' Has my wife a single characteristic of this noble woman?"

"Angela is unapproachable in the little arts that win the heart and drive away melancholy," said Lutz. "A few weeks ago, Herr Frank came home one day from the counting-room all out of sorts. He sat silently in his easy-chair drumming on his knee. Angela noticed his ill-humor. She sought to dissipate it--to cheer him; but she did not succeed. She then arose, and, going to him, said with unspeakable affection, 'Father, may I play and sing for you the "Lied der Kapelle?"' Herr Frank looked in her face, and smiled as he replied, 'Yes, my angel' When her sweet voice resounded in the next room in beautiful accord with the accompaniment, which she played most feelingly, the old man revived and joined in her song with his trembling bass."

"How often we have twitted Richard with his views of modern women," said Emil. "It was his cool judgment, perhaps, that saved him from a misfortune like mine."

Just then a carriage stopped before the house. Emil went uneasily to the window, and Lutz followed him. Bandboxes and trunks were taken from the house. The professor looked inquiringly at his friend, whose hand appeared to tremble as it rested on the window-glass.

"What does this mean, Emil?"

"My wife is going to her aunt's for an indefinite time. She leaves me to enjoy the pleasures of Christmas alone. The children also remain here; they might be in her way."

The professor pitied his unhappy friend.

"Emil," said he, almost angrily, "it is for you to determine how a man should act in regard to the freaks and caprices of his wife. But you should not steep yourself in gall, even though your wife turn into a river of bitterness. Drive away sadness and be happy. Do not let your present humor rob you of every thing. Forget what you cannot change."

A beautiful woman approached the carriage. Schlagbein turned away from the sight. Lutz observed the departing wife and mother. She did not look up at the window where her husband was. She got into the carriage without even saying farewell. She sat in the midst of bandboxes, surrounded by finery and tinsel; and as the wheels rolled over the pavement, the director groaned in his chair.

"A happy journey to you, Xantippe!" cried the angry professor. "Emil, be a man. Dress yourself; forget at the Angel of Salingen's your domestic devil."

Schlagbein moved his head disconsolately.

"What have the wretched to do in the home of the happy? There I shall only see more clearly that I suffer and am miserable."

Lutz, out of humor, threw himself into the carriage. With knitted brows he buried himself in one of its corners. That professional head was perplexed with a question which ordinary men would have quickly seen through and settled. Frank's happiness and Schlagbein's misery stood as two irrefutable facts before the mind of the professor. Now came the question. Why this happiness, why this misery? The dashing Ida he had known for years; also her enlightened views of life, and her flexible principles, perfectly conformable to the spirit of progress. Whence, then, the dissoluteness of her desires, the bitterness of her humor, the heartlessness of the wife, the callousness of the mother?

The professor continued his musing. He gave a scrutinizing glance at the marriages of all his acquaintances. Everywhere he found a clouded sky, and, in the semi-darkness, lightning and thunder. Only one marriage stood before him bright and clear in the sunlight of happiness, in the raiment of peace, and that was ultramontane. That ultramontane principles had produced this happiness and peace, the professor's industrious mind saw with clearness. He raised his head and said solemnly, "Marriage is an image of religion. It proceeds from the lips of God, and is perfected at the altar. The marriage duties are children of the religious sentiment, fetters of the divine law. Ida was faithful and true so long as it agreed with the longings of her heart. But with the cooling of affection died love and fidelity. She recognizes no religious duty, because she has progressed to liberty and independence. From this follows with striking clearness the incompatibility of Christian marriage with the spirit of the age. Marriage will be a thing of the past as soon as intellectual maturity conquers in the contest with religion. Sound sense, liberty of emotion and inclination will supplant the terrible marriage yoke."

The professor paused and examined his conclusion. It smiled upon him like a true child of nature. It clothed itself in motley flesh, and passed through green meadows and shady forests. It pointed encouragingly to the beasts of the field and the birds of the air, long in possession of intellectual maturity. Sensual marriages, intended to last only for weeks or months, danced around the professor. Cannibal hordes, who extended to him their brotherly paws and claws, pressed about him. In astonishment, he contemplated his conclusion; it made beastly grimaces, knavish and jeering, and he dashed into fragments the provoking mockery.

In strong contrast to the animal kingdom, stood before him again the Christian marriage. He cunningly tried to give his new conclusion human shape; but here the carriage stopped, and the speculation vanished before the clear light in the house of the "Angel of Salingen."

FOOTNOTE TO ANGELA

Footnote 2: This argument is not conclusive, nor is it at all necessary. Animals have memory; and there is no more reason why their waking sensations, emotions, and acts should not repeat themselves in dreams than there is in the case of men. The difference between the soul of man and the soul of the brute is constituted by the presence of the gift of reason, or the faculty of knowing necessary and universal truths in the former, and its absence in the latter.--Ed. Catholic World.